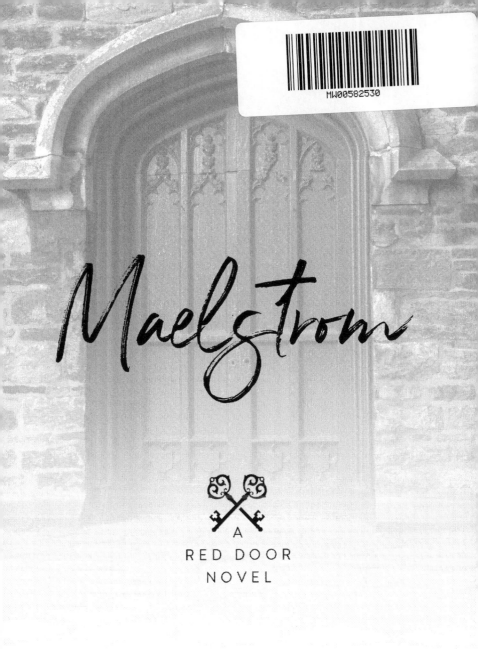

Maelstrom

A
RED DOOR
NOVEL

DYAN LAYNE

ISBN: 978-1-7364765-0-5

ASIN: B08SJHQS3M

Cover photography: Cover Photography:
Michelle Lancaster, Lanefotograf, @lanefotograf

Cover model: David Tomasic

Cover designer: Lori Jackson, Lori Jackson Design

Editing: Michelle Morgan, FictionEdit.com

Formatting: Stacey Blake, Champagne Book Design

This book contains subject matter which may be sensitive or triggering to some and is intended for mature audiences.

A storm is coming...

Plagued by tragedy. Used to the darkness.

Brendan Murray never dared to dream of a happily ever after.

Not until she came crashing into his life.

Until he kissed an angel in the park.

Pure and sweet and untouched.

Dare he love her?

She was the only light in his dark, twisted world. His ticket straight to hell.

He took the risk and loved her anyway.

Now the storm is here and hell was coming for him.

He had to keep her safe. At any cost.

But a storm can't last forever, can it?

And sometimes it takes darkness to see the light.

Playlist

Tommee Profitt (feat. Liv Ash) | *A Storm is Comin*
Buckethead | *The Fairy and the Devil*
AC/DC | *Thunderstruck*
Des Rocs | *Used to the Darkness*
The Shutters | *Paint It Black*
The Pretty Reckless | *Sweet Things*
Two Feet | *BBY*
Matt Maeson | *Tribulation*
Dennis Lloyd | *Nevermind*
Rag'n'Bone Man | *Human*
Two Feet | *Back Of My Mind*
Guns N' Roses | *Welcome To The Jungle*
JVLA | *Such a Whore*
Kerli | *Where the Dark Things Are*
CORPSE ft. Savage Ga$p | *E-GIRLS ARE RUINING MY LIFE!*
CORPSE REVENGE | *SPOOKY GIRLS ARE RUINING MY LIFE*
Fever Ray | *If I Had a Heart*
VioDance | *If I Had a Heart (Instrumental)*
Alice In Chains | *Bleed The Freak*
Everybody Loves an Outlaw | *I See Red*
Avenged Sevenfold | *Scream*
Type O Negative | *Love You to Death*
Landon Tewers | *Need to Change*
Amber Run | *I Found*
Dua Lipa | *Pretty Please*
Lana Del Rey | *Let Me Love You Like A Woman*
Red Devil Vortex | *Viper*
Billie Eilish | *bad guy*

Nine Inch Nails | *Closer*

NoMBe | *Sex*

The Score | *Hunger*

MISSIO | *Bottom of the Deep Blue Sea*

Black Atlass | *Kinda Like It*

Pearl Jam | *Garden*

Bishop Briggs | *Dark Side*

Lana Del Rey | *Freak*

Hucci | *Desire (Slowed)*

Disturbed | *Inside the Fire*

STANE | *Vampire*

Soundgarden | *Fell On Black Days*

Alice In Chains | *Sea of Sorrow*

Jerry Cantrell | *Angel Eyes*

Highly Suspect | *Chicago*

Evanescence | *Cloud Nine*

Lana Del Rey | *Happiness is a butterfly*

Bishop Briggs | *Dream*

CORPSE | *Miss YOU!*

The Weeknd | *Blinding Lights*

Dio | *Rainbow in the Dark*

Thrice | *Hurricane*

Oshins feat. Hael | *Darkside*

Disturbed | *The Light*

Alice In Chains | *Sunshine*

Metallica | *Loverman*

Ruelle | *War of Hearts*

Andrew Belle | *Dive Deep*

Sully Erna | *My Light*

Ed Sheeran | *Afterglow*

Metallica | *Nothing Else Matters*

Author's Note

This book contains subject matter which may be sensitive or triggering to some and is intended for mature audiences.

While you don't need to read the previous books in the series, as this is a standalone novel featuring a unique romance, it is *highly* recommended. *Red Door* is a series of interconnected standalone novels. All of the main characters reappear and some storylines connect throughout each book. For the best experience, read the series in order.

If you are following the series, while there is a brief overlap, **Maelstrom** begins immediately after the events in **Affinity**.

For my grandmother, Mary Manno Imbraguglio, who taught me just about everything I needed to know in life before the age of twelve.

Baci e abbracci in paradiso, Nonna. Ti amo.

Life is a storm, my young friend. You will bask in the sunlight one moment, be shattered on the rocks the next. What makes you a man is what you do when that storm comes.

—Alexandre Dumas, *The Count of Monte Cristo*

Maelstrom

Prologue

Fuck this.

His head was pounding. One hundred and twenty decibels pumping out of the amplifiers wasn't helping. Brendan gulped his whiskey down in one easy swallow and tossed the plastic cup into the trash. That probably wasn't helping either. Maybe he just needed to get away from the concert for a bit. Take a walk.

He glanced at his cousin who sat at the VIP table with him near the stage, then he got up from his seat. "I'll be back."

"Where you going?" Dillon shouted over the music, looking up at him with a perplexed tilt of his head. "You okay?"

"Yeah, man." He patted Dillon on the shoulder. "Just need some air to clear my head."

"Bren, we're sitting outside." He gestured around the table. "There's plenty of air," and he chuckled.

Brendan pointed toward the path that meandered through Coventry Park behind them. "I won't be too long."

"Whatever, man." Dillon shrugged with a smirk on his face, then his voice took on an Irish brogue. "Be mindful, the fair folk are about tonight."

Litha. Midsummer.

When they were young boys, their parents, aunts, and uncles often recounted Celtic folklore that had been passed down from one generation to the next. He smiled at the reminder of their fond childhood memories. Tonight was the eve of the summer solstice. A night for faeries, magic, and dreams of your true love—not that he actually believed any of that.

"Sure, Dill." Shaking his head, he left the blaring music behind him, walked past the commissary tent and Venery's bus, in the direction of the old oak trees along the path.

He just needed to let it all go for a few minutes. The tension. The worries. The load he carried. It was a weight Brendan took upon himself gladly. No one asked him to, but he felt responsible for them all. His family. And the shit coming down on them was his fault anyway. He should have listened to Taylor and Jesse the night they met that fucking viper. Why hadn't he?

'Did you love her or something?'

Brendan told Taylor he didn't, and that was true. Hell, most of the time he didn't even like her. He tried to once. He'd tried to love her or like her—to feel something for her. To feel anything at all. He felt nothing. He did like fucking her, though. And as it turned out, that was his first mistake.

He'd made a lot of fucking mistakes.

He'd think of a way to fix them.

His head was down, both hands stuffed in his pockets, as he walked the paved trail that wound through the century-old oaks at the back of the park. He inhaled a deep breath of city air, the first breaths of summer, and thought he should turn around and go back before Venery finished their set or Dillon came looking for him.

She ran smack dab into him the instant he turned around.

Hands clutched onto his shirt and his arms instinctively wrapped themselves around her so she wouldn't fall. She was probably average height—maybe five and a half feet. But next to him she was a little wisp of a thing. Her long hair gently fluttered in the breeze. The beautiful face of an angel looked up at him. Full lips. Flushed cheeks. Eyes a shade of blue he couldn't quite make out in the dark.

Her breathing was uncontrolled, ragged pants that passed

through parted lips. Why was she running? Brendan gazed out along the path but he didn't see anything. They were alone. She wasn't in danger of falling anymore. He should let her go. But she wasn't letting go of him either. She still held onto his shirt, looking up at him with those enchanting eyes of hers.

A pink tongue peeked past her lips to wet them. Brendan didn't even stop to think about it. He lowered his head and brushed those lips with his. Her hands unclenched to rest flat on his pecs. He pressed her closer against him and softly took her mouth. Sweet spun sugar. Her hands slid up to his shoulders and he deepened the kiss, tracing her lips with his tongue.

Open up for me, sweet girl.

And she did.

His hands reached around her thighs as his tongue slipped inside and he lifted her up. She wrapped her legs around his waist, her arms around his neck. He inhaled deeply through his nose. Sunshine. White chocolate. Jasmine. She kissed him back with those full soft lips. His cock throbbed beneath his jeans in time to her sweet tongue dancing with his.

Her tits pressed into his chest. He could feel her nipples harden and wondered how they'd fit in his hands. How they'd feel between his teeth. He held her with one hand splayed between her shoulders and slid the other up her thigh, past her belly, to cup her breast over the cotton sundress she wore. He squeezed. She fit perfectly in his palm.

What the fuck was he doing, kissing some random girl in the middle of the park? And who the fuck was she letting him? But he kept on. She smelled so good, and she tasted so good, and she felt so good. He hadn't felt anything in a long, long time.

He should let her go.

Slowly, he lifted his lips from hers and lowered her back down. She smiled up at him, but never spoke a word. He kissed the crown of her head and watched her walk away from him for a moment before he turned to walk in the opposite direction. His dick ached. He rubbed it over the denim. He could hear the faint strains of

Venery up ahead in the distance. He didn't even know her name. He should've asked her. Why didn't he ask her?

He turned around, but she was gone.

That night in his bed, he dreamt of a girl with long hair streaked in gold by the sun. It gently fluttered in the breeze. The beautiful face of an angel. Lips swollen from his kisses. Cheeks flushed pink. Her eyes were neither blue nor green, but the color of a stormy tropical sea. He asked her for her name, but she just smiled and turned away. She took the light with her.

Brendan sat up in the dark, alone in the middle of his big bed. For a moment he could have sworn he smelled the sweet scent of jasmine. He shook the cobwebs of the dream from his mind, laid back down, and closed his eyes.

Take the light with you, sweet girl.

I'm used to the darkness anyway.

One

"Come on, baby."

Dillon was balls deep inside of Gillian, who clutched at his shoulders as she straddled his thighs. Brendan knew it couldn't be easy taking two men their size inside you, no matter how much you wanted it. How much you begged for it. And Gillian, one of their weekend bartenders, had been begging for weeks. Dillon needed the distraction and he was tired of her incessant pleading, so here he was in a private alcove slowly pushing his dick in her ass.

He wasn't getting very far.

"Relax, Gillie," he crooned.

Brendan soothingly rubbed her back in an attempt to get her to relax, so she could open up and take him. She was so fucking tense, her asshole clamped shut so tight on the head of his dick, that he feared it might get stuck in there and never come back out.

"Rub her clit, Dill."

Something.

Admittedly, he wasn't at all into this scene. And if Gillian were to be honest with herself, she wasn't either. Sometimes, a fantasy is best left as just that. An imaginary vision in your head to get yourself off with—or whatever. It was his cousin she really wanted to fuck anyway, not him. Sadly, she was about to find out that reality almost never lived up to the expectations you built in your mind.

Dillon would never be into her like she dreamed of.

Brendan and Dillon were the only remaining bachelors of the four cousins. Jesse was married with a two-month-old baby at home and Kyan was as good as married—his wedding to Linnea only a little more than a month away. They rarely came to the club anymore, unless it was for business, so he and Dillon were left to their vices on their own.

Well, that wasn't exactly true. The Venery boys were here quite often. He could use one of them to take his place here right about now, because no matter what he and Dillon did, his big dick wasn't getting in.

Brendan patted Gillian on the back and tweaked her nipples. "Hold on."

If this is going to work she needs a smaller dick.

Not that Matt had a pencil dick or anything like that, but most chicks looked at his dick as if they were about to be skewered like a pig on a spit. That was one of the reasons Brendan pretty much only fucked at the club. The female membership here knew very well that not only could he bring them pleasure—or pain, their choice—but that he knew their limits. And Gillian was at her limit so he tapped out a quick message on his cell.

When Matt slipped past the velvet drape into the alcove, Gillian was writhing on top of Dillon, and begging him—no surprise there—to fuck her harder. Brendan lay beside them with his dick in his hand and nodded at Venery's rhythm guitarist to take his place and satisfy Gillian's greatest desire.

Brendan rolled over. "Gillian, this will be better for you with someone else. Matt's here. Is that okay, sweetheart?"

"Yes. Hurry."

Matt stripped out of his clothes, grabbed a condom and lube, then positioned himself behind Gillian. Brendan was impressed at just how patient and how gentle he was with her. "Hey, Gillie girl." He stroked the skin on her back and kissed her nape as he lubed them both up. Brendan heard her whimper and Matt soothed her. "Shh. Relax now."

Dillon kissed her lips and her nipples. "That's it, baby. Let him in."

Brendan knew Matt made his way inside her when she starting singing "Fuck!" on repeat like it was a new hit song. He got off the bed and zipped up his pants to the sounds of three people coming, and grinned.

"I love you, Linnea. Always gonna love you, sweet girl."

Oh, shit.

Dead silence.

"What did you say?"

And then Gillian began to cry while Matt held her.

Dillon reached over to touch her, but she shrugged him off. "I'm so sorry," he whispered. Then he hurriedly dressed and bolted out of the alcove.

Brendan followed.

He grabbed him by the arm and stopped him. "What the fuck, Dillon?"

"I know, Bren." He ran his fingers through the blond hair on top of his head, making a mess of it. "I'm a dick—an asshole. I feel like shit. I didn't mean to say that."

Not out loud anyway.

"You've got to get over it and get your shit together, brother."

"My shit's together, man." And he stalked off.

Brendan made his way over to their booth by the bar. Bo and Kit lounged against the back of it, sipping on their drinks as they watched the erotic theatrical troupe on the raised stage perform a daisy chain. He glanced up at the big-screen and felt the blood rush to his dick. All that pussy.

Beautiful.

Where the fuck is Dillon?

He reclaimed his seat in the booth and poured himself a finger of whiskey. "You see my cousin?"

"Saw him leave," Kit lazily drawled, absently staring at the girls on the stage.

"He looked pissed, man," Bo added. "What's up with him?"

Brendan shrugged. "Might've been something I said." It wasn't for him to say. Dillon had said enough already.

Bo nodded. "Yeah, you can be a real asshole."

Truth.

"I know." He winked and took a sip of his whiskey.

"You look tired, B."

He was. Most nights, by the time Brendan finished up at the club it was four or five in the morning. Then he'd drag his ass out of bed to help his cousins in the office, or Taylor and the guys with the studio. They were in the process of converting the last three-flat building on Park Place into offices for their business, a recording studio for Venery, a gym, and a guest apartment.

"You saying I look like shit, Bo?"

"Naw, B. You're still pretty." He snorted out a laugh.

Kit joined in. "Yeah, pretty fucking ugly."

"Seriously…" Bo gripped his shoulder. "…give yourself a break, man. And a facial or something, 'cause you got bags under your eyes." He chuckled.

Brendan nodded, snickering. "Maybe Chloe can hook me up."

"Maybe." Bo smirked.

He killed the whiskey in his glass and set it down on the table. "I've got some stuff to finish up in the office." Brendan stood. "Catch up with ya later."

Sitting at his desk, he kicked up his feet, and shot off a text to Dillon that he knew would go unanswered. Truth hurts sometimes. He wasn't trying to be an asshole. He'd never been in love, didn't plan to ever be either, still Brendan understood where Dillon's heart was at. His longing for…for the impossible.

'Always gonna love you, sweet girl.'

A sweet girl can fuck you up. Your head. Your heart. So he kept far away from them. Except for the one he never saw coming. And with just one kiss she'd been able to fuck with his head. He could still feel her. Taste her. Smell the sweet scent of jasmine.

Brendan thought he'd never see her again, except in his dreams, and she appeared in them often. But a few weeks after the eve of the solstice, well into July and the dog days of summer, there she was. He had just stepped out onto First Avenue after cutting through the park on his way to the club. The old man at the food cart put an Italian ice in her hands. He recognized her instantly.

She was beautiful in the dark, but that afternoon, with the brilliant rays of the sun shining down upon her she was breathtaking. Beguiling. Her long straight hair reached past the middle of her back. Its varying shades of blonde mixed together and swayed in the breeze like ripe wheat in the field. Long toned legs in a short denim skirt. Curves he already knew fit perfectly in his hands.

As if she had sensed he was there, she looked up at him with those enchanting eyes that were neither blue nor green, but the color of a turquoise sea. And she smiled. She stood on her tiptoes as high as she could reach and lightly kissed him beneath his jaw. Brendan remembered thinking for a fleeting moment that if any girl could bring him out of the dark it was this one. He reached out to touch her hair, but much like the sunlight, he couldn't hold onto it. The silky strands slipped through his fingers.

The door to his office burst open, interrupting his thoughts. Gillian stormed in with a bewildered-looking Matt right behind her. She threw her keys on his desk.

"I quit."

For fuck's sake.

You owe me a bartender, Dillon.

Two

I t was dark where he was. The air thick and dank. Suffocating. The blackness that surrounded him ominous and threatening, a malevolent entity that wanted to suck him into its void. He wouldn't let it, though. He clawed at it in his attempt to break free.

Off in the distance he noticed a pinpoint of light. He focused on it as it grew bigger and brighter, punching a hole through the darkness. The bright light was almost upon him and he sat up. He looked into it, but it didn't hurt his eyes like he thought it should.

She straddled his lap, encircling his neck with her arms, and softly kissed his lips. Along his jaw. His neck. He wanted to hold her, but his arms were just so heavy. Like lead. He couldn't lift them even though he tried. Her lips trailed down his chest. Her fingertips followed. She kissed and licked each ridge that defined his abs, her silky hair brushing through the precum that leaked from his pierced tip.

Kiss me there, sweet girl.

She looked up at him and smiled.

Take me in your mouth. Suck me.

He woke up to a knock at his door and his dick in his hand.

"What the fucking bullshit?" Brendan muttered to himself.

He thought about finishing himself off first, but the knock sounded again. And the doorbell immediately followed.

Scratching his head, he got out of bed and threw a pair of sweats on that he found on the floor. "I'm coming," he yelled.

Well, I would have been. Asshole.

With heavy footsteps, he trudged down the stairs and opened the door, not even bothering to check the peephole because it could only be someone who lived here on Park Place. Which meant it was one of the Venery boys or his cousins or…

"Chloe?" He cocked an eyebrow.

She pursed her lips, glancing up at him. "You do look like shit."

Brendan took the bags she carried as she strolled inside the house like she lived there. She practically did. Chloe was the closest thing he had to a lovable, though sometimes annoying, younger sister. But she was more than that to him. He could talk to her. She listened and she cared. Unlike most people, she wasn't intimidated by him. Not even a little bit. He could trust her to tell him how she saw things—not that he could have stopped her if he wanted to anyway.

Chloe lived next door and was married to his cousin—and his best friend. He'd been the best man at their wedding more than nine months ago now. In the eyes of the law she was Jesse's wife, but in their eyes and the eyes of those who knew and loved them, the three of them—Chloe, Jesse, and Taylor—were married to each other. They shared a love most people only dream of having.

"Good morning to you too, sweetheart." He leaned down to kiss her cheek, then carried the bags to the kitchen.

"It's afternoon, Brendan." Chloe looked him over, her perusal stopping at the more-than-obvious tent in his sweats and her pretty hazel eyes got big. "Jesus."

"What?" He smirked. "It's not like you've never seen it before."

She started unpacking the bags. "You should, umm, do something about that."

"I was, until you started banging on my fucking door." He rubbed the bulge in his pants. "Gonna help me out?"

Chloe shook her head with a grin and cracked some eggs into a bowl. "You need a girlfriend, Brendan. And a shower."

"Not gonna happen, sweetheart. I'll be back in five," he said over his shoulder as he left the kitchen.

She giggled and he heard her mutter under her breath, "I would have figured you were good for at least ten."

He took his time and came back twenty minutes later, sans hard-on, just to prove a point. Chloe had breakfast on the table for him, or considering it was past noon already, lunch. Had he really slept that late? He almost never did.

"So, what did I do to deserve all this?" Brendan sat down and tucked into the perfectly prepared meal Chloe made for him.

She gave him one of her mom looks, and considering Chandan wasn't even three months old yet, she was pretty damn good at it already. "It's what you didn't do."

"Oh?" He shoveled a forkful of eggs into his mouth and swallowed. "And what's that?"

"Oh, you know, just little things like eating an actual meal, getting some decent sleep—taking care of yourself, Brendan," she admonished him.

He chewed on a piece of bacon, not bothering to respond, because Brendan knew Chloe. And she wasn't done.

"You get what—maybe three hours of sleep a night? You think I don't see when you get home? I'm up feeding a baby, Brendan! Your fridge is empty, except for beer and leftover pizza. And Bo's right, you look like hell." She smirked then and held up a pink tote bag. "He suggested I give you a facial. Finish your breakfast, baby."

The fuck?

He decided Bo was an asshole.

"No fucking way." Then he added with a smirk, "Unless I get to return the favor."

As usual, Chloe somehow managed to get her way, though. She stood behind his head as he reclined on a leather chaise in his living room, rubbing some kind of goop into his skin and wrapping it in a warm wet towel. At least whatever she was using didn't smell all girly, and while he hated to admit it, someone taking care of him felt rather nice.

She massaged his scalp and his temples with slow, firm, circular strokes. "Mm, that feels good."

"See?" He couldn't see her, but he could feel her smiling behind him.

"How'd you learn how to do that?"

She wiped off his face with the towel. "YouTube. One day Jesse was saying that this was the best part about going to the barber, and we both know how often he and Taylor get haircuts."

He chuckled. "Jesse's always hated cutting his hair."

"So I wanted to be able to do this for him. And for Tay."

"They're both so lucky to have a woman who loves them the way you do."

"I'm the lucky one, Bren." Her fingers stilled on his skin. "And there's someone out there who will love you too."

He patted her hand on his face and smiled. "There isn't."

"There is." Chloe came and sat beside him on the chaise.

Brendan reached out for a lock of her hair, the color of nutmeg, and wrapped it around his finger. He thought of the girl with silky hair the color of ripe wheat and let it unravel.

He looked down at his empty fingers. "Not all of us are meant to have that, Chloe." And huffed out a sardonic chuckle. "C'mon, can you see a guy like me with a good little wife and two point five children?"

She didn't hesitate. "Yes." Then she giggled. "And no. Two or three children, maybe. You can't have half a kid." She paused. "Seriously though, Bren, don't you want that—a family?"

It's not that he didn't. Family was the most important thing in the world to him and he loved his fiercely. That's the only way he knew how. It's the way they'd been taught. Brendan and his cousins were closer than brothers. Chloe and Linnea. Venery. They'd been his friends his entire life. They were his family, and now they were lucky enough to all live here together on Park Place.

A private street that dead-ended at Coventry Park. Dillon negotiated the real estate deal of a lifetime for them when Hugh Brantley was forced to declare himself insolvent. As part of the bankruptcy proceedings, he had to liquidate his assets, sell off his properties. The investment company the four cousins owned together had done business with Hugh in the past and Park Place had ten vintage three-flat apartment buildings sitting on it. So they bought it, gated it, and converted the buildings into grand single-family residences for each of them—a family compound in the middle of the city. Who fucking does that?

Brendan smiled to himself. They did. Because that's just how tight they were, how fiercely they loved each other. It wasn't that he didn't know how to love, or that he wasn't capable of it, for he loved far more intensely than most ever could. That's the side of him Chloe knew. But he knew himself better. Most people outside his circle would describe him as cold. Unfeeling. An asshole. A deviant—depraved even. He knew he was fucked up. A man like him didn't get to marry the girl with the face of an angel and make babies. A man like him fucked a lot of women like Salena and ran a sex club. So, as much as he loved the thought of filling up this big house with a family of his own, it was just that. A nice dream. A fantasy. Nothing more.

And sometimes a fantasy is best left as just that.

"I already have that, sweetheart." Brendan pulled Chloe against him and hugged her close. He rested his head on hers and closed his eyes. She was soft and warm and smelled of milk and coconuts. "I've got all of you."

"That's not what I meant and you know it." She play-swatted his arm.

He chuckled. "I know."

The sounds of his front door opening and a baby crying saved him from elaborating further. Jesse strolled into his living room holding a very unhappy Chandan against his bare chest. The baby's head, covered in downy black curls, bobbed with his attempt to root for a nonexistent food supply from his father and Brendan couldn't help but laugh.

With his arm still around her, Chloe reached for her son and put him to her breast. The baby quieted and suckled eagerly. Brendan found his gaze drawn to the tiny hands that held onto his mother's plump breast and he swallowed. He'd seen her nurse the baby before, but never up close like this. It was beautiful.

Jesse sat on the other side his wife. He kissed her cheek and his son's baby curls before he joined Brendan with an arm around her shoulders. "Sorry, babe. I tried to give him the bottle of milk you left, but he wasn't having it. He wanted you."

"Do you blame him?" Brendan smiled.

Given the choice, who wouldn't prefer suckling from a lovely breast? He was certainly a fan of them.

"Nope." Jesse grinned. "Tay wants you to come over—we're gonna grill some burgers or something and watch the game outside while the weather's still nice."

"You mean you're going to watch the game. Nobody likes to watch the Cubs lose except you, Jess."

"It's football now, babe." Jesse smacked a kiss to her lips. "Everybody watches football on Sunday."

"Yeah, sure." He didn't have anything planned and the club was closed tonight. "I have some shit I need to run by Tay anyway."

"About the studio?"

No.

Brendan just smirked. The renovations across the street were the last thing on his mind. They were almost finished and Venery was almost ready to record their next album there—the first one under their own label. It was best if that's what his cousin assumed, though. For now.

"I'll call Linn. See if she and Ky want to come over—Dillon too."

"Already did, babe."

Dillon was a no-show. Brendan wasn't surprised. Knowing him, he was probably still pissed, and rather than face his shit went out to lick his wounds inside some random pussy. Not that he blamed him. He'd probably do the same. A tight, warm hole to wet your dick in made everything better, didn't it?

Usually.

He was kicked back on one of the patio loungers with a beer in his hand. Brendan wasn't really drinking it. Even though his gaze was on the outdoor screen, he wasn't really watching the game either. Kyan and Linnea cuddled together on one of the sofas. He trailed his fingers across her skin. Slipped them inside her shirt when he thought no one was looking. The happy trio shared the other sofa. Taylor had his back propped against the arm with some pillows. Like a triple-layer cake, Jesse lounged between his thighs and Chloe was wedged between Jesse's. He imagined they fucked that way too.

He shook the image from his head.

Why had he recently decided the club didn't need to be open seven nights a week? Because he was tired. Because after Salena, he didn't trust anyone. If he wasn't there, the red doors were closed. Right now, Brendan was kicking himself in the ass for it. His cousins held warm flesh while he held a warm beer.

'There's someone out there who will love you...'

Shut up, Chloe.

It was halftime when Linnea followed Chloe in the house to get her baby fix. Kyan had a dopey grin on his face, probably thinking of making his own babies—or practicing at it. God, he needed to get out of here.

"Someone outed the mayor to his wife," Kyan recounted with a smirk. "Ran into him when I was pulling permits at city hall on Friday."

That got his attention and explained why the mayor and his girlfriend hadn't been at the club. Yeah, the mayor had a wife *and* a girlfriend, but then the mayor was into some kinky shit and his wife was probably as vanilla as tapioca pudding. Not that Brendan condoned fucking around on your spouse behind their back. He didn't. At all. He hated liars and he hated cheats. Honesty was the only way to go. Either find a partner whose desires complemented your own or stay the fuck single like he did. But it wasn't his place to impose his morals on anyone else.

The only thing Brendan provided was a safe haven, a positive environment, for club members to explore their sexuality—their desires, fetishes, and kinks, whatever they might be. Explicit consent, safe practices, and discretion were the only rules. Members had the freedom to partake in whatever they wanted to. No recrimination. No questions. No judgment. They paid a helluva lot of money for the freedom they found, and to keep the secrets they guarded, behind the red door.

"Is that right?"

"Yeah," Kyan confirmed. "Apparently she got an envelope of eight-by-ten glossies in the mail and filed for divorce the same day."

Shit.

Taylor and Jesse both eyed him warily, but it was Taylor who spoke. "Salena?"

Kyan nodded. "Crossed my mind too."

"Maybe," he conceded.

"You think so?" Jesse leaned forward with his elbows on his knees. "C'mon, it's been a year now, man."

'This isn't the end, baby. It's foreplay.'

It may have been a year since he fired Salena and kicked her out of his club, out of his life, but she'd been making good on her veiled threats ever since. Brendan was almost certain she was behind all the baby-mama drama Jesse, Taylor, and Chloe went through. He just couldn't prove it yet. He would, though. Salena was conniving and manipulative, but she wasn't all that cunning. She'd fuck up again, just like she did with Linnea's message for Kyan. He was counting on it.

"I think it's a possibility." He took a swallow of warm beer and grimaced. "She did make an example of him at the masquerade ball."

"Revenge is a dish best served cold." Taylor nodded. "She still hanging onto Hugh?"

Kyan shook his head. "No, man. Hugh has dementia—something like that. His son put him in a nursing home. Heard he deteriorated pretty fast."

Taylor cocked his head. Apparently that news didn't sit quite right with him. "Hugh's not that old, is he?"

"He's in his sixties." Kyan shrugged.

Taylor glanced over at him. "That's not very old."

"No, but it's not entirely unheard of." Kyan let out a long exhale. "Poor guy. I liked him."

The French doors opened and his cousin's magnificent Berners, Roman and Timo, lumbered out to the patio with the girls and baby Chandan following right behind them. Chloe put the baby in his arms.

"Can you hold him for me, Bren?" She winked.

Not gonna work, Chloe.

He couldn't allow himself to even dream of such impossible things, could he? He gazed down at Chandan. The baby looked up at him with a big gummy smile and his heart melted. "Your mother put you up to this, didn't she?"

Chloe giggled. "You know what I always say, Brendan."

Let life happen.

"I need a girlfriend?" He chuckled.

She smirked. "I do say that, don't I?"

He nodded.

"She's out there."

I know.

Three

God, I loathe algebra.

Math had never been her strong suit, but it was a required class and she wanted to get it out of the way, so here she was. The professor stood at the whiteboard, marker in hand, droning on about linear equations in his monotone voice. Like white noise it was there but she didn't really hear it.

Katie sat in the very back row, in the seat closest to the window, which probably wasn't the best idea if she wanted to pass this class. Her gaze traveled from the whiteboard to the September sky outside the window. She counted the cotton ball clouds as they slowly drifted by. Memorized the view of the city from her vantage here in the third-floor classroom. Allowed her mind to wander.

So far, the city was everything she dreamt it would be. Even as a little girl she'd always known she'd end up here. Every year, in the summer and at Christmastime, her mother and her aunt Kelly would bring her and her younger brother, Kevin, on the train to the city. They'd go to the zoo, visit the museums, walk along the river downtown. Far different from the small town she grew up in a couple hours west of here, the city was a magical place that beckoned her to return every time she left it.

Her aunt, ten years older than her and the youngest of four sisters, must have felt the same. Kelly moved here the summer she turned eighteen and never looked back. It was a no-brainer then, when the time came to go to college. Katie came here too. And she didn't plan on looking back either. This was her home now.

Katie was so excited to come here that she refused to spend her last summer before college in the small town she grew up in with her childhood friends, surrounded by nothing but fields of corn as far as the eye could see. Right after her high school graduation, and five days after her eighteenth birthday, her parents moved her in with her aunt. She wanted to acclimate herself and explore the city before school started in the fall. Kelly was opening her new business the following month and she was going to work there, so the timing was perfect.

They lived in a big loft apartment on First Avenue, directly above where she worked. There was a huge park close by with food carts out front on the wide city sidewalk, the big trees and trails a welcoming green space in the midst of concrete, steel, and glass. She went there a lot. Something always seemed to pull her toward it. Maybe it was him.

"Miss Copeland?"

Shit.

Abruptly, she turned her head from the window to the monotone voice at the podium that called her name.

"Would you explain to the class what an inverse operation is?"

Double shit.

She had to know this. She just read the chapter last night. Properties of equations was pretty basic even for someone who hated math. After a shaky breath, she answered, "It's an operation that undoes another one—like an opposite, right? Addition and subtraction or multiplication and division."

"Right. Very good." He droned on. "You can perform the same inverse operation on each side of an equivalent equation without changing the equality."

She rolled her eyes and whispered to herself, "What the fuck did he just say?"

The boy in the seat next to her chuckled. She glanced over at him. While he had to be around the same age as her, he was no boy. Brown hair hung past his hazel eyes. She thought they were hazel anyway. Considering his muscled arms, she pegged him for a jock. He looked back at her and winked. She felt her cheeks heat and glanced away.

Minutes slowly ticked by, until finally class was over. She gathered her things and tossed them in her backpack. When she stood from her seat, the boy who was no boy, stood waiting for her.

"Hi, I'm Cam—Cameron Mayhew."

Cameron was tall. He had a nice smile and dimples.

"Katelyn, but everyone calls me Katie." She smiled back.

"Nice to meet you, Katie." He walked her out of the classroom. "Where's your next class?"

"Oh, um, that was my last one for the day."

They were hazel, his eyes. "Where you off to then? The dorms?"

Was he hitting on her or just making small talk? Katie wasn't exactly sure, and she wasn't sure which of the two she wanted it to be. He pushed the door to the stairwell open and held it for her.

"No. Work," she answered, hiking the backpack up on her shoulder. "You?"

"Football practice."

Jock. Knew it.

"Where do you work?"

He was behind her on the stairs. They reached the bottom and once again he pushed the door open for her. Fresh air and sunlight spilled into the vestibule as they stepped outside.

She shielded the sun from her eyes with her hand. "At my aunt's coffee bar. Beanie's."

He grinned. "I gotta go. See you, Katie Copeland."

Huh.

Beanie's Coffee Roasters was the new neighborhood spot to get your jolt of caffeine—or decaf, but then what was the point? Kelly and her girlfriend, Stacy, held their grand opening right after the Fourth of July. It was a trendy, happening place with a cool vibe, and it was fun—a Starbucks on steroids. Everyone from hipsters to college students to businessmen came in here. The work of local artists covered the exposed brick walls. Chalkboard menus. Sometimes in the evenings and on weekends, musicians played acoustic sets in the back. Katie worked as a barista and she loved it.

She pulled her hair up into a high ponytail and threw on the hideous low-cut knit shirt Stacy insisted they all wear. It was navy-blue with the Beanie's logo Kelly designed herself emblazoned across the chest. They were tight and showed way too much cleavage, not that she had a lot in that department, but she wasn't lacking either—a decent C-cup at least. Beanie's sure wasn't Hooter's, but Stacy had no issue with them using their assets, as she called them, to attract male customers. Funny, considering she and Kelly were lesbians and not attracted to men at all.

Tying the matching apron around her waist as she stepped behind the counter, Kelly bumped hips with her like they were at an eighties disco dance. "Hey, Katie-Kate. How was school?"

Her aunt was the only person left on the planet who still called her that like she was five. Katie wasn't ever going to tell her not to, though. She shrugged her shoulders. "You know. Algebra."

"Sorry." Kelly wrinkled her nose. "Make any friends yet? Meet any boys?" She looked hopeful. Then added, "Or girls."

Katie shook her head with a giggle. "Penises only need apply, Auntie. I keep telling you that."

"And I keep telling you not to call me Auntie. Makes me feel old."

Katie smirked. "Pushing thirty. You are old."

"Twenty-eight."

"Exactly. Old."

Katie giggled and replenished the paper cups and lids while there was a lull.

"So, you didn't answer."

And she wasn't sure if she wanted to. Yet. More like an older sister to her, she usually told Kelly everything, but she'd never told her about *him*. Only because that moment had been so perfect and magical that she wanted to keep it just for herself, as if sharing it would somehow spoil it. She never thought she'd see him again anyway, and now…well, now it didn't matter. So unless Cameron Mayhew turned out to be someone worth mentioning, she wasn't going to.

"Not really. It's only the third week of classes, though."

Maybe if she lived on campus or went to frat parties she'd have made a friend or two by now, but she didn't care to. She could pledge a sorority like Kelly had, but that didn't appeal to her very much either. It's not that she was antisocial or anything like that, she just didn't think watching a bunch of dudes chase pussy, chug beer, and puke was all that much fun. She'd seen all that in high school and she doubted it was all that different in college. Besides, she sucked at beer pong. The stuff tasted vile anyway.

She saw her first, pushing one of those fancy-ass strollers through the door. So, apparently there was a baby too? She had auburn beach waves to die for and was gorgeous, of course. What was her name again? Chloe. She sat down and waved at Katie, the diamonds on her left hand sparkling with the light, which only made her feel worse than she already did. She didn't know he was married when she'd kissed *him*.

She would have never, ever done that if she had known.

She was a piece of shit.

No. Scratch that. *He* was a piece of shit.

Katie frothed the milk for two soy lattes—nasty stuff—and prayed he didn't come strolling in behind Chloe. She'd seen him three times in her life, and that was three times too many. That magical night, the memory of which was now tainted. Then, as if fate ordained it, she saw him again a few weeks later. If love at first sight was a thing, she'd felt it that day. There was definitely something there. A connection. She thought he felt it too, but he ghosted her after that, and a few weeks later she discovered why.

He had a wife.

There were four of them that day. He was with her and another couple. Chloe introduced the other girl as her sister and some dude with long blond hair who looked just like the drummer in Venery. Hell, he probably was. She knew they were from this neighborhood and still lived here. The cheating motherfucker even had the nerve to stop before he walked out the door and turned around, looking at her all sorry and sad and shit. Then he just left. She was so dumbfounded, all she could do was stand there and stare after him like a fool.

Asshole.

Her prayers went unanswered. No sooner did she hand the two nasty soy lattes off to the customers who waited for them, when said asshole came through the door. Kelly was in the back so Katie had no choice but to take his coffee order when he reached the counter.

She could do this. Katie fixed her usual smile to her face and looked up at him.

Why did his eyes have to be so fucking blue?

"I'll have a large coffee, black…"

And why did his voice have to be so deep and smooth and sexy? The tiniest hint of an accent that she couldn't quite place.

"…and an—"

"Iced latte. Plain. No sugar. Whipped cream." Katie remembered.

"Yeah. That."

Of course, Kelly picked precisely that moment to reappear with a tray of pastries for the display case. "Katie-Kate, can you get…oh, hey, Brendan. How are ya?"

"I'm good, Kelly. You and Stacy doing okay here?"

"Great. Couldn't be better." Katie had just turned around to pour Asshole his coffee when Kelly pulled on her arm and dragged her back. "Let me introduce you to my niece, Katie."

She wanted to die.

"Katie, this is Brendan."

He extended his hand. She didn't want to touch him. Katie was afraid if she touched him that everything she was feeling would show on her face. But Kelly was watching and it would appear rude if she refused his greeting.

The instant his skin came into contact with hers she felt it. That connection. Blood coursed through her body. Butterflies tickled her tummy. She couldn't breathe and her heart was pounding.

He clasped her hand in his and brought it to his lips. He placed a light kiss on her knuckles.

"Hello, Katelyn."

He was the first and only person on the planet who'd ever called her that. Like she was an adult. A grown woman, not a child.

Katie didn't think she could speak. She really needed him to let her hand go to have a shot at finding her voice.

He let go.

"Brendan."

Then she turned around to prepare his order.

He sat down with Chloe. They talked and smiled and laughed like he hadn't just kissed Katie's hand. Like he'd never kissed her at all. How did the son of a bitch do that? And how did Kelly know him? She was going to ask her.

"Kell, who is that guy?"

She was bent over arranging the pastries. "Brendan?"

"Yeah."

"He's our landlord. Well, one of them. He and his cousins own the company that owns this building. We lease Beanie's and our apartment from them."

"The whole building?"

It was a converted warehouse that covered an entire city block.

"Yeah. They own Charley's, a club, and some other stuff too."

Great.

There'd be no escaping him. Maybe she would be better off at the dorms. Or in a sorority. Katie was legacy to Chi Omega thanks to Kelly, so she was likely to receive a bid to pledge. How godawful could it be?

She turned a blind eye to the table in the corner where he now held the baby in his arms to concentrate on the pour of steamed milk into espresso. The angle had to be just right to get that foam heart on a latte and she'd finally perfected it.

"Hey, Katie Copeland."

Katie glanced up to see hazel eyes and dimples leaning against the counter. She handed off the heart-art-topped latte.

"Hey yourself, Cameron Mayhew."

Seeing him didn't make her heart explode like seeing Brendan did, but then to be fair she hadn't kissed him either. Katie couldn't deny he was beautiful. Tall. Athletic. Ripped. He looked freshly showered in a long-sleeved gray T-shirt that was pushed up to his elbows. Perfect arm porn. His hair was similar to Brendan's. Short on the sides and long on top. Really long. He ran his fingers through it every time it fell into his eyes, which was a lot. She imagined he had a lot of girls at school vying for his attention, so why was he here?

"Can you make four quad-shot lattes for me?"

It was then she noticed the three guys wearing similar team shirts standing off to the side behind him. "Iced or hot?"

"Hot." He smirked. "And can you come to the game on Saturday? There's a party at the house after and I'd love to take you."

"Like a date?"

His smirk grew into a big smile, showing off his perfectly straight white teeth. "Yeah, exactly like that."

She glanced to her left where Kelly stood grinning, then right to the table in the corner. He was watching, and judging by the tick in his jaw, he was pissed.

Fuck you, you cheating son of a bitch.

She smiled back at Cameron. "I'd love to."

Four

"What's up with you and coffee girl?"

Shit.

"Coffee girl?"

He closed his eyes. Sunshine. White chocolate. Jasmine. Brendan hoped Chloe would drop it. He wanted to keep her in his dreams. To keep the memory of that kiss, and his sweet girl to himself. He knew she wouldn't, though.

"The pretty little blonde over there." Chloe smirked. "We caught you making puppy-dog eyes at her the last time we were here."

"Did you now?"

"Yeah, me and Linn both saw you." She grinned. "And just so ya know, she was looking too. So, who is she?"

He shrugged and rubbed his hand across his face. "A barista at Beanie's?"

"C'mon, Brendan."

"I don't know what you expect me to tell you, Chloe."

Chandan started to fuss. Chloe took him out of the stroller where he'd been napping and placed the baby in his arms. "Why don't you ask her out?"

"I don't date. I fuck."

"Try it once. What've you got to lose?"

Everything.

"Look at her, Chloe. How old do you think she is?"

Chloe glanced over to the counter, but he didn't follow her gaze. Unlike the light in his dreams, it hurt him to look at her. Brendan smiled down at Chandan in his arms instead.

"It's difficult to say for sure, but based on the football player flirting with her at the counter I'd guess she's in college." Chloe giggled. "Looks like he brought the team with him for backup too."

Brendan raised his gaze to see the kid leaning against the counter. Talking to her and flexing his muscles in a bid to impress her. More than a decade had passed since his wild college days, but he remembered the moves. The parties. All that fucking. He felt the tick in his jaw. The turbulence that swirled in his stomach. Rage simmered beneath the surface of his skin. But he knew he had no right so he tempered it.

"Jesus, Brendan, you should see your face."

"Don't, Chloe."

"Just ask the girl out," she implored. "It's obvious you like her."

"She's too young, too sweet, and way too innocent for someone like me." He shook his head and handed the baby to Chloe.

I'd tear her apart, and fuck me if I don't want to.

His dick began to swell. "There isn't much I won't do, but there's one line I can assure you I won't cross. I don't fuck little girls. And I'm not into the Daddy thing." He locked his gaze on Chloe. "She's only in college."

"Until a few months ago I was in college too, Brendan." Chloe nodded with a know-it-all smirk on her face. "And you're no older than Taylor, so…"

Eight days older, actually.

"That's different."

"How?"

"Because you're…" He stumbled for a word.

"And you're being ridiculous." Chloe shook her head at him, hazel eyes flashing with fire. "It's just a number, Brendan. I'm ten years younger than Tay, seven years younger than Jesse. So what?"

He glanced back at the counter. Katelyn smiled sweetly and nodded to the boy.

"If she's legal and you like her, then go for it. Afraid to catch real feelings instead of just fucking?"

Damn you, Chloe.

She'd hit the nail right on the fucking head.

Because that's exactly what he was afraid of.

He stood there on First Avenue watching her through the glass. She was alone. He waited until she locked the door and switched the lights off one by one. As Katelyn walked toward the back of the shop to the stairs that led to the loft above, Brendan unlocked the door and went inside.

She stopped dead in her tracks for the briefest moment, then turned to him. Fearless and unafraid. It almost seemed as if she knew it was him before she saw that it was. He locked the door and leaned back against it, pocketing his master key.

Katelyn took three steps in his direction and stopped when she got to the counter. Even so, she didn't look pleased to see him. "What do you want?"

You.

"I need to talk to you." Then he took three steps.

She crossed her arms over her chest, which only succeeded in pushing her beautiful breasts farther out of the low-cut shirt she wore, exposing more delicious cleavage to him. He ventured closer.

"Well, I don't need to talk to you. Go home to your wife…"

Wife? The fuck?

"…and your baby. Bastard. How could you?"

Did she think…? She did. He couldn't help it. Laughter rose from deep within him as he strode over to her the rest of the way. For whatever reason, his sweet girl mistakenly assumed Chloe was his wife and Chandan his son. He scooped her up and set her down on the counter.

"I'm not married."

He leaned in to kiss her, but she turned away from him. "Don't you dare touch me."

"I said I'm not married."

"Do you think you can play me? That I'm just some foolish girl?" Her head was cocked to the side, her brow raised. A storm brewed in her big turquoise eyes.

She was angry and he liked that she didn't hide it. Her fists were clenched at her sides like she was holding herself back from punching him. He liked that too. It meant she wasn't afraid of him and it meant she cared.

And that made his dick hard.

"I don't, so stop acting like one." He inhaled jasmine from her hair. It combined with the aroma of coffee. "Chloe is married to my cousin and my best friend. That baby is his son."

"Now I for sure know you're full of shit." She laughed. "You can't be married to two people. I've seen *Sister Wives*."

"Watch your mouth, sweet girl." He slid his hands up her thighs, covered in blue jeans, and encircling her slim waist he pulled her body closer to his. "I was the best man at their wedding."

Her lips parted but she didn't speak.

He dipped his head to inhale the flesh in the valley between her breasts. Salty and sweet. Sweat and perfume. His lips dragged across her skin to the warm curve of her neck, her jaw, the sweet spot beneath her ear, and he edgily whispered, "Who is he?"

She pulled her head back to look at him. "What?"

"Who is he?" To make sure she understood just what he was asking, he added, "Your boyfriend?"

"Cam is a guy in my algebra class." And she fucking laughed. "He's taking me to a party."

Brendan was well aware of what happened at college parties. Drinking. Fucking. He saw red. The turbulence came back with a vengeance even though he still didn't have the right to his feelings. Besides, that's what she should be doing. Going to parties. Dating boys her own age who can run a football down a field, but fumble flicking the button open on her jeans. Boys who can't find her clit or make her come. Who have no fucking clue what to do with the precious gift that she is.

He held her pussy, covered in denim, and squeezed it in his hand. "Has he touched you?"

She gasped. "No."

He traced her seam with his finger, applying pressure where he knew she needed it. "Has anyone ever touched you?"

"Never."

And no man ever will except me, baby.

"How old are you, Katelyn?"

"Eighteen."

Fuck.

'As long as she's legal and you like her…'

"Look at me." Her enchanting eyes locked with his. "I'm thirty-two."

He waited for her to recoil.

She just smiled.

With his hands on her knees he spread her legs on the counter. He popped the button on her jeans, lowered the zipper, and dipped his hand inside. She wasn't clenching her fists at her sides any longer. She held onto his shoulders as she gazed at his hand between her thighs.

He didn't penetrate her. Just ran his finger through her wet folds. She was soaked. "I'm touching you, Katelyn."

She tipped her head up and reached for his neck, bringing him to her mouth. It was Midsummer's Eve all over again. Every night for three months he'd dreamt of this kiss. Of his dick pulsing in time with her tongue. Tasting her. Smelling her. Feeling her. He needed her nipples in his mouth and her clit between his teeth.

He needed to make her come.

Mark her as his.

And one day, when she was ready and begging, she'd bleed for him. He'd wipe the mascara-stained tears from her eyes when he tore through her hymen, then after he'd clean their cum and the virgin's blood that dripped from her cunt with his tongue. Then he'd hold her. Forever.

Because once she was his he'd never let her go.

"I'm going to make you come, baby." He grabbed onto the waistband of her jeans. "Lift."

She did and he pulled the denim off her legs. Her shoes came off with them and dropped to the floor. He kissed her while he freed her tits from the silky cups of her bra. His thumbs skimmed over her nipples and she moaned into his mouth. The lightest touch and she was so fucking responsive to it. He did it again and once more she moaned.

"You like that, don't you baby?"

She answered him by holding his hands to her breasts and squeezing his fingers against her nipples.

"Fuck yeah, you do. Lie back." He lowered her onto the counter. She didn't resist. "I've got you, sweet girl."

He cradled her head in one hand and sucked a nipple into his mouth, circling it and flicking it with his tongue. She panted and wriggled. So sensitive.

"Fuck."

Not today, but soon.

His angel had a dirty mouth and he couldn't wait to teach her all the dirty things he wanted her to do with it. Pure and sweet and untouched. Only ever his. He'd never had that before and something about that turned him the fuck on. He wondered what would turn her on besides his fingers, his tongue, and his cock. He'd show her everything. Teach her everything. Give her anything she asked for.

But he'd never share her. No other man would ever fucking touch her.

He bit down on her nipple and moved to the other. He swore she would come from just this. Brendan lifted himself from her breast and eased his hand out from beneath her head. He gave her nipples a pinch and she bit her lip.

Yeah, she's close.

He placed her hands on her breasts. "Play with your nipples. Pinch them hard when you come."

His hand slid down her belly to part the lips of her little pink pussy. Beautiful and his. She was slippery and so wet it coated her thighs. He rimmed her tight hole with his finger, careful not to breach her. More of her sweetness copiously flowed out from it, covering his fingers with her. He brought them to his mouth and sucked. She twisted her nipples like he asked.

Holding her lips apart with one hand he gazed at her clit. Big and swollen, the perfect nub to suck on. Nibble. Bite. He took his fingers from his mouth and rubbed it with his saliva.

God, he wanted to be inside her. He could feel the hot precum leak from his aching dick. He retracted the hood of her clit. Time to make his angel fly.

She pinched her nipples so fucking hard.

My good, sweet girl.

"Katelyn," he whispered.

Then he bent his head between her legs and licked the cum from her thighs and her cunt. He was drowning in her sweetness.

"Brendan," she whimpered and pulled his hair.

He could love this girl.

Maybe he already did.

Five

"You really don't have to do this, Kelly."

Katie's aunt bared her shoulders, adjusting the white angora sweater in the mirror. It was so soft and had long wide sleeves. Katie tucked the front of it into her favorite pair of tight faded jeans.

"There. That's perfect, and stop saying that. I want to go." She handed Katie a crossbody bag while she put on her white ankle boots. "I haven't been to a game in years. They're fun. You'll see."

She was going to the game. So was Kelly. They were going to sit with her Chi Omega sisters. Katie supposed she should be grateful she wasn't going by herself. How pathetic would it look to sit in the stands all alone?

And after the game she was going to the party with Cameron.

And she wasn't going to waste one more minute thinking about *him*.

'*I'm sorry. I shouldn't have come here.*'

Katie wrapped her arms about herself to keep warm, huddled in her seat beside Kelly on the fifty-yard line. The last Saturday of September had turned crisp. She could smell fall in the late-afternoon air. Hot dogs. Beer. Popcorn. She wasn't the biggest football fan, but her dad and brother were, and she'd gone to plenty of games in high school. It was definitely more exciting sitting in the stands than it was watching it on TV.

But this wasn't anything like high school. This was much bigger. There had to be a hundred thousand people here in the stadium. A sea of navy blue and white. One of Kelly's ChiO sisters thrust a souvenir pom-pom in her hand to cheer with. Another handed her a beer. Kelly snatched it from her fingers. "You're not old enough."

'You're just too young.'

She didn't want it anyway and glanced over at the Jumbotron. The camera transmitted panned images of the crowd in the stands waiting for the players to make their entrance out onto the field. The band. The cheerleaders. Sports analysts in the booth. It was the first home game of the season and the excitement was palpable. Katie hoped that energy was contagious because right now she needed it to take her mind off...*him.*

"Here." Kelly passed her a Styrofoam cup of hot chocolate. "You look cold."

She shrugged.

"You okay, Katie-Kate?" Her aunt smoothed her hair over her shoulder. "Nervous about your date?"

No.

Should she be? Cameron didn't give her any reason to feel that way. He was sweet, kind, and attentive. Walked her to class. Held doors open. Obviously into her, there were no mixed signals from Cameron Mayhew.

'My sweet girl.'

So why didn't she feel anything? She should feel something, shouldn't she? Katie hoped Cameron would kiss her at the party tonight. She hoped his kiss would erase the memory of every kiss that came before him...every touch...of the man with the bluest eyes and the voice that haunted her dreams.

'I'm touching you, Katelyn.'

"Look." Kelly pointed to the Jumbotron. The team's intro video was starting. "What's Cam's jersey number?"

"Twenty-two."

Kelly squeezed her hand. "Watch for him."

In the middle of the video he flashed on the big-screen. Katie kept one eye on the Jumbotron and the other on the field as the video ended. The band, cheer squad, dance team—everyone was lined up on the field. The flags came out first, navy-blue smoke billowing from their staffs. Coaches. Finally the players in navy-blue jerseys and white pants emerged from the tunnel. Music blared. Pyrotechnics shot off from the top of the stadium, heralding their arrival.

There was no way Cam could see her from where she was, but she waved anyway as he ran by. She had to admit, he looked good out there. After their run across the field, he jogged over to the bench with his teammates and turned, gazing up into the stands like he was searching for someone. Was he looking for her?

There wasn't a girl on this campus who wouldn't want to be in her shoes right now. Cameron was everything she should want, right? If she hadn't kissed a stranger in the park that night Katie would have thought him perfect. But she had kissed Brendan. Let him touch her. He made her feel things. She was just going to have to unfeel them. Forget them. And *him*.

It was an insane fourth quarter. Cameron ran for two touchdowns. They had the win in the bag and Katie cheered wildly in the stands, Brendan's rejection temporarily forgotten, along with everybody else. After it was over, she and Kelly slowly made their way out of the packed stadium. She'd agreed to meet him at the west gate. Kelly insisted on waiting with her until he got there.

"Have fun and be safe." Kelly handed her a tube of lip gloss. "And don't drink the jungle juice—or any open drinks. You don't know what might be in it. I would tell you not to drink at all but I know better and that's not realistic. It's not that I condone you drinking underage but if you're going to, stick to beer and make sure…"

Her aunt was talking a mile a minute.

"Take a damn breath, Kelly." Katie swiped the gloss on. "You're rambling. I've been to a party before, you know." She handed the tube back to her. "And I don't like beer."

"You're so young, Katie-Kate." Kelly took her hand and worried her lip. "This isn't like high school, trust me."

"I am so sick and tired of people pointing that out to me." She snagged her hand back. "I'm eighteen, not eight."

"You know I didn't mean it like that." Kelly tilted her head with a sympathetic smile. "What's going on with you, sweetie?"

"Nothing."

Nothing she wanted to talk about anyway. Especially not now. Kelly could try to get it out of her tomorrow, but right now a certain running back was jogging toward them. Katie glanced over at Cameron. His eyes met hers and a smile spread across his face.

"Bullshit." Kelly followed her gaze. "Your date's here, so we'll have to finish this conversation later—but we will have it."

"I know."

Kelly squeezed her hand. "You know it's because I love you, right? I just don't want to see you make any mistakes."

"Isn't that how we learn, Kell?" She tilted her head to the side. "Making a mistake or two."

"Yeah, well, you always did have to learn the hard way." Kelly chuckled and leaned in for a hug. She held her tight and softly said, "Just try not to make one you'll regret, because they can last a lifetime."

There was a tap on her shoulder. Kelly let her go. Cameron stood at her side, his smile wide like he was actually happy to see her. "Hi, Katie."

He leaned over to kiss her on the cheek and she smiled. He was so damn sweet. Why didn't she feel butterflies? She so desperately wanted to feel them. For her breath to catch. Her palms to sweat. To feel that pull in her belly and her pulse beating between her thighs.

She just needed the ache he'd left her with to go away.

He didn't want her.

Cameron did.

Katie stood on her tiptoes to reach his cheek. She softly touched it with her lips and his arm came around her shoulders. Her aunt sighed. "You two are just too fucking cute."

Shut up, Kelly.

Cam grinned. "Ready?"

"Yeah."

There had to be at least fifty people in various stages of intoxication milling about on the lawn in front of the house. Cameron led her by the hand around the side to the backyard, which was just as crowded. A bonfire blazed from a pit in the center. Kegs of beer were stationed along the back fence. Music blasted from an upstairs deck. People danced with red Solo cups on a concrete slab that was an extension of the patio.

Cameron waved to a group of guys standing over by the kegs. "You want a beer?"

"No, thanks." She scrunched her nose. "I can't stand the way it tastes."

He chuckled. "C'mon, there's a batch of jungle juice in the kitchen." And with his arm around her waist, Cameron led her inside.

It was blue and it smelled like nail-polish remover. He took a sip first, grimaced, and took the cup she held out of her hand. "Er, no, don't drink that."

That was a relief. She really didn't want to, and not because Kelly warned her against it, but because after smelling it she thought it had to be even more vile than beer. Cameron rummaged through a cooler of ice that leaked onto the tile floor and pulled out a can of White Claw and a bottle of beer. He popped the tab and handed her the hard seltzer. Grapefruit.

Yum. This is more like it.

"Thank you."

Cameron took her by the hand and they went into the living room. More people dancing—though it looked like they were fucking upright with clothes on. There was a couple on a club chair in the corner that she would have sworn actually were. The girl's dress rode up her ass as she bounced on some guy's dick for everyone to see.

Oh my god, they are! What the actual fuck?

She looked up at Cam and he shrugged. They went back into the kitchen where he loaded up a box with more seltzer and beer. "Sorry about that." He hefted the box onto his shoulder and took her hand. "Let's get out of here."

They went through a door off the kitchen and up a set of stairs. He didn't stop at the second floor, though. Cameron opened a door to a narrow enclosed staircase and closed it again behind her. At the top was a small attic bedroom tucked beneath the eaves of the pitched roof. Exposed brick and wood framing. In front of the bed a panel of glass sloped down from the roof to join with the window. The night sky twinkled above and she could see the downtown lights through the branches of the trees in the backyard.

"Wow! This is so cool!" Her head tipped back as she gazed up at the moon through the glass. "Is this your room?"

"Yeah. No one will bother us up here."

Katie could feel him standing right behind her. "Football players got it pretty good, huh?" She turned around to face him.

He proffered a cute smirk. "Beats living in the dorms, I guess." Then he lugged the box over to the mini-fridge and stocked it with the beer and hard seltzer from the kitchen. "Freshman year I shared a room downstairs with three other guys."

"How'd you get this one?"

He grinned, looking up at her from his haunches. "I made first string and whipped some quarterback ass in a deadlift competition— five hundred pounds, baby! So this room is all mine until graduation."

"When's that?"

He stood and placed a fresh cold can of seltzer in her hand. "May."

"You're a senior?" Why didn't she know that?

"Yeah." He sat down on the bed and patted the space beside him. Katie sat down. "What are you doing in my algebra class?"

"I put it off." He shrugged.

"And I just wanted to get it out of the way." She giggled.

"What's your major?"

"No idea," she admitted. "What's your plan?"

"Law school."

That surprised her. "Not football?"

"Going pro is just a fantasy for most of us." He tucked a lock of hair behind her ear. "Maybe two percent of college players make it to the draft, so yeah, law school."

"But you looked so good out there."

He smiled. "Thanks. You want to watch a movie?"

"Okay."

Cameron tapped the can she clutched in her hand with the neck of his beer bottle. "To our first date, and I promise the next one won't be a house party."

Cheers?

Brendan curled his fingers around the railing in front of his upstairs office as he looked out at the main club floor. Members prowled about, drinks in hand, dressed to entice. Seduce. Subtle notes of plum, patchouli, black amber, and musk pumped through the ventilation system to blend with the heavy scent of arousal. Sex. He breathed it deep into his lungs, but it didn't stir him like it usually did.

Why did he unlock that door?

He glanced at his phone. Just after ten. Here, behind the red door, the night had barely even begun. She must be at that party with him by now. The game was over a couple hours ago. Brendan tried not to think about what his sweet girl might be doing. It was all he thought of, though. Was she drinking? Dancing? Fumbling in a dark corner with her tongue in his mouth while his hand slipped beneath her sweater? His gut clenched. He shook his head to break the chain of thought and reminded himself that Katelyn wasn't his.

He let her go.

Because it was the right thing to do. Not for him. For Katelyn.

And it killed him. Those stolen moments with her brought him to life. Woke up every dormant cell in his body. Katelyn made him feel things, and the things she made Brendan feel rocked him. Threw him off-kilter. He thought he could convince himself to overlook how much younger she was, but he couldn't ignore her innocence. Her light.

'*What kind of a grown-ass man preys on the innocence of a young girl? It's a sick fucking monster that does that.*'

And he'd be damned if he was the one to snuff it out. He could still see the shattered look on her face when he told her he'd made a mistake. Let her believe he was a dick. An asshole. She was better off fumbling with some inept jock in a dark corner of a frat house than for him to drag her into his fucked-up world.

Cuffing his sleeve, Brendan took the stairs down to the main floor. He didn't even glance over at the hedonistic display of naked bodies on the platform as he made his way to the booth by the bar. A bottle of whiskey sat waiting for him, along with Bo, Dillon, and Taylor. That surprised him. Taylor never came out to play anymore now that he had everything he wanted at home.

Lucky bastard. Must be nice to put your morning wood to good use every fucking day.

He couldn't help but hear them now that the nights were cool and windows were left open. And Chloe was loud. He wondered how baby Chand slept through it all. Sometimes, if the wind blew just right it sounded as if they were right there in his bedroom instead of in their own next door. Chloe would die if she knew how often Brendan jerked his dick to the sound of her screams. Taylor would punch his balls. He chuckled to himself.

"What's so funny?" Bo drawled.

Brendan took a seat next to his cousin and poured himself a finger of Glenlivet. "Nothing, man." He looked across the table to Taylor. "What are you doing here? Jess and Chloe come with you?"

"Hello to you too, mate." Taylor pretended to be offended. Brendan knew better. "Thought they could do with some together time, so here I am. We're all coming for the Halloween Ball, though." He winked.

At that, Dillon stopped scrolling through his phone to glance over at Taylor and he snickered, "Can't wait." Then returned to his scrolling.

What the fuck is up his ass?

Bo shrugged.

"Need help tomorrow, Bo? Kodiak's stuff all moved over to Linn's old place?" Brendan felt his cousin tense up next to him at the mention of her name.

"Thanks, Bren, we got it. Ky, Jess, and Tay here helped me with the moving part. The stairs in Linn's row house were a bitch—tight as a virgin's…"

"Indeed, but we sorted it. The girls did their thing behind us. Done."

"…pussy," Bo finished.

"Linn's fetching him from the airport and bringing him over for dinner. Chloe wants everyone there by six so he feels welcome," Taylor reminded them. "Dillon?"

He looked up from his phone. "What?"

"Dinner."

"If Chloe or Linn are cooking, you don't have to ask me twice." He winked. "I'll be there."

"Splendid." Taylor appeared annoyed when Dillon went right back to his phone. "Are we boring you?"

"No, asshole. Look." Dillon held it up so they could see what was on the screen. Three mug shots.

Taylor took it from him and read aloud, "Priest arrested for filming himself in an unholy trinity with two dominatrices on the altar of Saint—"

"Let me see that." Brendan snatched the phone from Taylor's hand. "An unidentified witness noticed stage lighting through the window of a church and observed the half-naked priest having sex with two women wearing corsets and high-heeled boots. The witness took video footage and sent it to police, who arrived to find the three with assorted sex toys…holy shit."

"Yeah, holy shit." Dillon raised a brow. "Isn't that Rourke?"

"It is," he confirmed the name the young priest went by here at the club. Brendan hadn't seen him in at least six months. Maybe more.

"Those girls look familiar too," Dillon added.

"Don't tell me that fucking priest is a member here, mate."

Brendan slowly nodded. "Was a member."

"Let me guess," Taylor intoned. "He played with Salena."

He kept nodding and rubbed his temple. "And those girls were friends of hers. They've been here too."

Bo smirked. "A priest, Bren?"

"We vetted him, same as everyone else. Not for me to judge."

Taylor swallowed his whiskey. "Salena doesn't have *friends*. I'd bet my new Gibson that cunt is the unidentified witness and she set them up."

"But why?" Bo questioned.

"Because she's vile and that 'unholy trinity' can be linked to here."

Dillon thrummed his fingers on the table. "Yeah, I can believe it." Then he turned to Brendan, a grin slowly spreading on his face, and said, "I'll fuck that bitch. And not how she likes it."

Not if I get to her first.

Hours later, after the club was empty, Brendan locked the red service door and stepped into the alley. Salena and sullied church altars were the last thing on his mind as he walked. He was too tired to think of much at all except getting home and falling into his bed. Sleep devoid of dreams.

Brendan was almost to the opposite end of the converted warehouse when he heard the sounds that made him turn his head. They weren't quite hidden in the shadows of the back stairwell, dimly lit by the lamppost in the alley. He was kissing her. She kissed him back. His hand left her waist and disappeared beneath her white sweater. She opened her eyes and saw him standing there.

For an instant her eyes locked with his.

He wanted to…

No.

He kept on walking.

Six

Sunlight streamed in through the slats of the blinds, painting stripes on her bedroom wall. Katie rubbed sleep from her eyes and reached underneath her pillow. She glanced at her phone, surprised it was already noon, but then she didn't get home until almost five.

In the morning.

And once she got in her bed she had a hard time falling asleep. She tossed and turned. Her brain just wouldn't turn off. It was all his fault, too. How was she supposed to forget about Brendan when he was everywhere?

He was too close, and there seemed to be no way to escape him.

The phone vibrated in her hand.

Cam: Good morning, beautiful! I hope you slept well.

God, why did he have to be so perfect, and at the same time not perfect at all? Katie liked him—she really did. What was there not to like? Tucked up together on his bed in the attic, they watched two movies. She fell asleep halfway through the second one and woke to fingers combing through her hair as the credits rolled on the television in the corner.

"Hey." Cameron sweetly smiled down at her. "You want me to take you home?"

"No," she whispered and shook her head.

Not yet. Katie had wanted him to kiss her, and gentleman that he was he hadn't yet. Or maybe he didn't want to? God, she hoped he wanted to because she really needed that other kiss wiped clean from her memory bank. Erased like it never happened. Gone.

The fingers that were in her hair reached around to grasp her nape. Cameron pulled Katie closer to him as he lowered his head and his lips touched hers. It was tentative at first, as if neither of them were certain what to do, which way to move. But then he gently caressed her mouth with his full soft lips. They were so warm. There weren't any butterflies yet, but it did feel nice.

He lifted his head a fraction and whispered, "I've been wanting to do that since the first time I saw you."

"Do it again."

And he did.

This time when his lips touched hers, his tongue slipped inside and he held her closer. Tighter. Where his first kiss was tender and sweet, this one was urgent and demanding. And it was just what she needed. The pull in her belly was faint at first, but with every sweep of his tongue grew more intense. Insistent.

His hand swept underneath her sweater. Fingers trailed over her skin. A thumb brushed over her sensitive nipple through the lace. Involuntarily, with a whimper she arched into him. Cameron groaned and pulled his lips from hers. He gazed at her with his hazel eyes, the pupils blown so big they were almost completely black. His hand remained beneath her sweater, his fingers caressed her breast.

Out of breath, he panted, "I want you so bad."

He wanted her.

Brendan didn't.

But he'd given her a taste of what wanting felt like. She wanted to feel that again. Katie grasped the bottom of her sweater and pulled it over her head. Cameron fixed his gaze on the mounds of flesh heaving with every breath inside the white lace cups of the strapless bra she wore. His fingers reverently swept down across her skin and over the lace, then his gaze returned to hers.

He licked his lips and rasped, "Have you ever…"

"No."

"You're still a virgin?"

Was that a bad thing?

She nodded.

Cameron dropped his face into the curve of her neck and nuzzled there. He kissed up the column of her throat until he reached her mouth. "I want to make you my girl, Katie. Only mine. In every way." He kissed her lips and pressed his fingers into her jeans, against the pulse that beat between her thighs. "I don't expect that to happen tonight, but I want to see you—all of you. To touch you."

'*I'm touching you, Katelyn.*'

Shut up, Brendan.

She bit her lip and nodded. "I want you to."

Her body responded to his touch. That was biology. She knew that. After he rubbed the orgasm out of her, the ache left behind from the man she had hoped to forget remained. Maybe with enough time it would go away.

She stared at her phone now, and imagined Cam staring at his, waiting for her reply. The perfect boy whose only flaw was that he wasn't someone else. She tapped out a text and sighed.

Do you really need butterflies?

Maybe not.

But she wanted them.

She held the metal pitcher of steamed milk intently in her hand as she carefully poured it into the thick espresso. Katie had the heart perfected, but the holidays were coming up and she'd been studying tutorials on YouTube for weeks. So while Beanie's hit its Sunday afternoon slump, she practiced her technique on a snowman, a pumpkin, and a ghost.

"Lookin' good, kiddo." Her aunt's girlfriend peered over her shoulder.

Katie rolled her eyes. She hated that. Being called 'kiddo' and someone hanging over her shoulder. She wasn't sure what Kelly saw in Stacy. She acted like she was better than everyone, Kelly included, and was a first-class bitch. Not that Katie planned on sharing that opinion anytime soon. She did have to live with the woman.

"Thanks."

"Now that you're here and it's slow, I'm gonna take off, 'kay?"

Ugh. 'kay.

Katie wrinkled up her nose. She hated that too. "Yeah, sure."

"All right then." Stacy patted her shoulder and she fucked up her snowman. "Kelly will be here in a few. Tell her not to wait up."

Whatever. Byeeeee.

It was thirty minutes before Kelly showed up. "Where's Stace?"

Uh-oh.

"Left about a half hour ago," Katie informed her as she wiped down the counter where she'd been practicing her latte art. "Said don't wait up."

What Kelly's reaction to that information was, Katie couldn't see since her back was to her. She wondered, though.

"How'd your date go?" Katie turned around to see Kelly smirking. "Must have been pretty fucking good being you didn't make it home until this morning."

"I had a nice time."

"Deets." Kelly was tapping her foot with one hand on her hip and still smirking. "Did you have sex with him? Not that I'm cool with you having sex, but I guess I can't stop you, can I? I remember when I was your age, so tell me if you are, because we need to get you on the Pill or something…"

Oh for fuck's sake.

"…can't have you getting pregnant on my watch. Your mother would never forgive me."

"Take a breath, Kelly." She rolled her eyes. "We didn't have sex. I didn't even see his dick, 'kay?"

"Ahem." A male voice cleared his throat.

A very deep male voice.

Nope. Not turning around.

"Hey, Bren. Taylor."

Katie kept wiping the already-clean counter while Kelly went to take his order, thankful he drank plain black coffee so she wouldn't have to look at him.

"Give me that coffee with the foam. Make it strong. And I want a heart on it."

Asshole.

"What do you want, Tay? I'm sure they have tea."

She turned around and narrowed her eyes. Then they went wide when she saw who was standing there with him. Venery's Taylor Kerrigan. Rocking a stroller instead of a guitar.

Kelly fucking giggled. "Katie can make you a matcha tea latte, then you can have a heart too."

That green shit is worse than soy.

Katie bit her lip and started on their drinks. Brendan stood right there watching her work. She wouldn't look at him but she could feel his eyes boring into her. Right in front of Kelly and the smirking rock star, he leaned down, kissed the spot below her ear, and breathed into it, "Hey, baby."

She fucked up the heart on his latte and handed it to him without a word.

"Hey, where's my heart?"

Katie cocked her head with a shrug. "Hm, I'd say you don't have one." And poured steamed milk into the hot matcha tea.

There. Perfect.

"Matcha tea latte." She gave Taylor his drink and waved at the baby in the stroller. "Tell Chloe I said hi."

"Right." Poor guy appeared so dumbfounded she almost giggled.

She went right to cleaning the frothing nozzle. Kelly sidled up to her. "You wanna tell me what that was all about?"

"Nope."

"Is there something going on between you and Brendan Murray?"

"I'm not talking about this now."

"Yes, you are. What's going on?"

Katie threw the cleaning rag down on the counter and turned around. It took every ounce of strength she had not to cry. She shook her head. "Nothing. Now will you just stop? Please?"

Kelly nodded, but the look on her face said this conversation wasn't over.

"I'm going to take my break now, 'kay?" Mimicking bitchy Stacy.

She quickly glanced at the corner table. His fucking bluer-than-blue eyes were honed in right on her.

He winked.

God, I need fucking air.

She spun on her heels and went out the back door to the alley.

"You're an arsehole, you know that?"

"I know." Brendan took a sip of his heartless foamy coffee—it wasn't bad.

Taylor tipped his chin toward the counter where his sweet girl was engaged in what looked to be a heated conversation with Kelly. "Is she the reason you decided you had to get a cup of coffee?"

Brendan shrugged with a smirk.

"What are you doing, Bren? She's just a kid."

He didn't know why, especially since he'd had the same thought himself, but Taylor saying it out loud made him angry. His jaw ticked. How dare he?

"Are *you* judging *me?*"

Taylor remained silent and sipped his tea.

"You, of all people, know me better than to think I'd…"

Taylor grinned. "I do know you better. Besides, Chloe told me and Jess all about your coffee girl."

"Fucker." He chuckled. "Your wife don't know…"

"What?"

Brendan took a long swallow of coffee before he answered. "I fucked up."

"How'd you do that?"

"I unlocked the door." Then he confessed everything he'd done to Taylor. "My conscience got to me, so I let her go, and I regret that I did."

"Tell her."

"Tell her what, man?"

"First off, that you're sorry for being an arsehole," Taylor chided with a smirk. "And that you want her."

"I shouldn't."

"Why not?"

Brendan shrugged and stood. "I'll be right back."

He found her in the alley. She stood with her back to the brick wall and her head tipped back to feel the sun on her beautiful face. What the fuck was he doing? He should just leave her alone, so why couldn't he?

"Go away, Brendan." Her eyes remained closed as she softly spoke, her face illuminated by the sun.

He moved closer until he stood right next to her, inhaling the scent of sweet jasmine. "I wanted to say I'm sorry."

"Okay, you said it."

They stood in silence for a moment, and when Brendan remained rooted in the space beside her, she angled toward him, opened her stormy blue-green eyes, and whispered, "What do you want?"

"You."

He pulled her hard against him and gripped the silky hair at her nape between his fingers as he lowered his lips to hers. He kissed her. Even though he was still at war with himself. Even though he shouldn't. He claimed her mouth, ravaging it with his lips and his teeth, pillaging it with his tongue. Brendan could no longer resist her.

Why do you have to feel so good, sweet girl?

He tugged on her hair, bending her head back, so he could get more of her mouth. With her palms against his chest, Katelyn pushed herself away from him.

She was bent over, gasping for breath with her hands on her knees.

"Katelyn. Baby—"

"You..." She stood, tears dripping down her face. "...don't get to do that." She took two steps toward him and poked her index finger into his chest. "You don't get to do that."

"I—"

"You don't get to play with my feelings just because you aren't sure of your own."

Then she went through the door, slamming it behind her.

Fuck.

Seven

Brendan opened the French doors and stepped out onto the brick patio. It wasn't quite six and the sun had all but disappeared, bringing a chill to the autumn evening. Summer was over. The leaves would change color and die. Tumble to the ground to lie in decay, disintegrating to nothing more than detritus. Seemed fitting.

He plucked a beer out of the tub of ice and popped the top. The door squeaked open behind him, but he didn't bother turning around. His gaze remained on the darkening sky until Jesse lit some kindling in the outdoor fireplace and Kyan appeared at his side.

"Less than two weeks now." He embraced his youngest cousin. "Linn and Kodiak here yet?"

Kyan checked his watch. "Any minute now, I guess. You hear about Rourke?"

"I did."

"It was her." Kyan reached across him to grab a beer of his own. "She set them up."

"You seem pretty sure about that."

He tipped the bottle back and drank. "Because I am sure."

"About what?" Jesse joined them.

"Salena," Kyan said. "Dillon told me about Rourke's arrest, so I called my old friend from high school—remember Billings?"

Jesse nodded.

"He started working for the state attorney's office after law school. Anyway, the witness who filmed the priest through the window is unidentified only because the footage was sent to the PD anonymously from one of those proxy phone numbers."

Jesse's eyebrows rose. "Fuck."

"Exactly. It was the same number."

"You sure?" Jesse asked.

"Yeah. I compared it to the texts we got back in February."

Chloe chose that inopportune moment to poke her head out the patio door. "They're here."

Kyan turned to him and murmured low, "We'll talk more later. I've got a plan."

Oh, yeah? Brendan couldn't fucking wait to hear it.

They all mingled in Chloe's enormous family room. It was easily the largest room in the house. Jesse's flat screen about covered an entire wall. Taylor's first guitar was mounted on another, along with a collage of framed gold records, album covers, and football jerseys. Photos of them all at the lake house. Charley's. Their wedding. Their son.

This room told their story.

This house was a home.

A family lived here. Loved here.

Nothing at all like the dark devoid dwelling Brendan occupied next door. For a moment he imagined blonde hair spread upon worn black leather, pale skin pushed against midnight walls. Holding her from behind in the kitchen. Her warm body nestled beside him in his bed.

He'd never shared his bed with anyone.

Or his heart.

Or his home.

Not once.

"You look lost in thought, my friend."

There wasn't a thing anyone could get past Monica Peters, so

Brendan wasn't even going to try. She could read you like a book. Probably why she was one of the best shrinks in the city.

He waved at her wife, Danielle, holding their baby son on her lap across the room. She waved back. His arm wrapped about Monica's shoulders, clasping her to his side. "You could tell, huh?" Brendan chuckled.

Monica chuckled in return. "How long have I known you?"

"Since college." He gave her shoulders a squeeze. "So fourteen years, give or take."

"Sounds about right." Monica smiled, looking up at him. At six feet, she was the tallest woman he knew, but still, he towered over her. "Penny for your thoughts?"

They aren't worth that much, but fuck it.

Brendan cleared his throat. "I can fuck a woman. Make her come." He smirked and then paused. "I'm not sure if I know how to love one, though. Especially a certain one."

Monica grinned. "Oh, I see."

"Trust me, you don't." He shook his head.

She's barely eighteen, barely been touched, and I already fucked it all up.

He was too ashamed of himself to admit any of that, though.

"Brendan, trust me when I say, you know how to love, and better than most. You love everyone in this room…"

He looked into her warm eyes with a smile. "You're all family. That's different."

"Is it? Love is love, no matter what form it takes." Monica tilted her head and pursed her lips. "I think you've got love and fucking mixed up, brother."

Brendan raised a brow.

"You have a gigantic heart and there isn't a person here that doesn't know firsthand how fiercely you love. And yes, you know how to fuck like the devil too, Mister." She winked. "So, what I think you're really saying is you're not sure how you fuck a woman you're in love with…because you've never done it. Am I right?"

He hadn't. "Maybe."

Monica turned in his embrace, her hands on his biceps. "Saying 'I love you' with your body is one of the most beautiful experiences there is in life, you sweet man. I'd hate for you to miss out on it."

"I'm not sweet." He smirked.

"To the people you love, you are."

Brendan felt heat bloom in his face, and that almost never happened.

Monica glanced over at Linnea and her brother who were talking with Dillon. "Kodiak looks good, doesn't he?"

He grunted with a nod.

She placed her hand on his forearm and smiled. "Now tell me all about this certain someone you're in love with."

"Did I say I'm in love with her?"

Monica grinned. "You just did."

Thirty minutes before closing time. She thrummed her nails on the counter. Beanie's was empty. After this afternoon, the only thing Katie looked forward to was crawling into bed and going to sleep. Kelly came around the counter from the back and planted herself there.

"Now that we're the only ones here, you wanna tell me what's going on with you and Brendan? And don't tell me nothing…"

Here we go.

"…because I'm not blind. That was something. And you come back from break with sad crying eyes and he takes off…"

Fuck it.

"Take a breath, Kelly." She sighed. "If it was something it isn't anymore, okay?"

"What happened, KK?" Kelly tilted her head, brows drawn in apparent confusion. "I mean you don't even know the guy."

"Yes, I do," she finally admitted. "I met him a few months ago at the summer festival."

Katie recounted that magical Midsummer's Eve night when

she ran into him on the path in the park. Their kiss. The butterflies she felt every time she saw him.

"Oh."

"And I thought…well, it doesn't matter now what I thought."

"I see."

She thought she did, but her aunt really had no idea.

Kelly wrapped an arm around her shoulders and gave her a squeeze. Katie fought the burn building behind her eyes.

"Cam is better for you anyway, honey," Kelly murmured as she smoothed the hair down her back. "Brendan's got to be in his thirties—way too old."

"That's what he said." She sounded pathetic, even to herself.

"He's a nice guy, but I don't think he's suitable boyfriend material for you…or anyone else for that matter." She gave her shoulders another squeeze. "Not to mention, he's way out of your league and *way* too experienced."

Katie turned her head. "What do you mean?"

"That club they own by Charley's, the Red Door—it's a sex club." And as if she needed to drive her point home, she added, "Brendan runs it."

Ohhh.

Katie didn't hear a word Kelly said after that. She didn't hear anything at all, even the jumble of thoughts swirling around in her head were nonsensical, until the bell on the door jingled. That made her look up.

Cameron.

Shit, shit, shit!

She'd forgotten.

He came toward her with that gorgeous smile on his face and a bouquet of flowers in his hand. Then he leaned over the counter to kiss her cheek. "Hey, baby. I ordered pizza for us."

When she texted him back earlier they'd made plans to hang out and watch movies together after she finished working.

Kelly stood there gushing. "Go on, you two. I'll close up. I'm heading out from here anyway."

Katie took him by the hand and led him through the back and up the stairs. As she reached up inside the kitchen cabinet to get a vase for the flowers, two strong arms wrapped around her waist from behind. Warm lips grazed across her skin. She turned in his arms and those lips found her mouth. They kissed right there in the kitchen, her body wedged between the hard edge of the counter and the hard bulge in his jeans, until the doorbell rang.

"Pizza's here." He went to get the door.

'Cam is better for you…'

Kelly was probably right about that, and yet…

'What do you want?'

'You.'

Katie brought her fingers to her lips that were swollen from Cameron's kisses. Brendan had kissed her too, though, and she couldn't help but wonder what else he'd wanted to say to her this afternoon in the alley.

If she'd given him the chance.

But she hadn't.

And now it was too late.

Eight

A sense of nostalgia gripped him. Brendan leaned against the railing on the back deck and gazed at the expansive lawn behind the house to the water just beyond it. Looking out at the tranquil lake never failed to evoke wistful childhood memories of the weekends spent here with his cousins.

He could see the four of them trampling through the grass, kicking at the crisp autumn leaves as they skittered by in the wind. Jesse holding onto Kyan's hand so he wouldn't fall behind. The earthy, heady scent of wood smoke. Roasting marshmallows. He could hear the raucous laughter of young boys.

Then he blinked and it was gone.

The bang of a hammer striking wood diverted his gaze. Workers erected a simple log arch amongst the towering oaks and lined up chairs on either side of a leaf-strewn path. Lights were being hung and strung across branches in accordance with Linnea's written specifications.

It was the eve of the wedding and Brendan had driven up to the lake house ahead of everyone to supervise. Bo came with him. Dillon and Kyan would join them later on tonight after he kissed his fiancée goodbye for the last time. She'd be his wife tomorrow. Linnea was superstitious, apparently, and took that whole bad-luck-to-see-the-bride shit seriously. She was going to have a girls' night with Chloe. The next time Kyan saw her she'd be walking toward him on the arm of her brother.

He never would have imagined *that* a year ago.

But then a lot can change in a year.

In a single moment.

A fraction of a second...

Brendan forcefully shook his head to snap himself out of the morose trajectory of his thoughts. He closed his eyes and let the mild October breeze wash over him. His nostrils flared as he inhaled and willed himself to think of something else. Anything but *that*. And he thought of her.

Of sunshine, white chocolate, and jasmine. Hair that slipped through his fingers like the finest silk. Lips that tasted of sweet spun sugar and melted on his tongue. Those aquamarine eyes that captured his own from the very moment he looked into them.

Katelyn.

She cried.

The last time he saw her beautiful face, tears dripped down her cheeks. She cried because of him. Because he was an asshole. Because he made her feel like shit when that was the last thing he wanted to do. Brendan had kept himself away from her since that afternoon in the alley. He'd walk right past Beanie's without stopping to get coffee on his way to the club. He told himself she needed her space. Time to think.

Who the fuck was he kidding? He's the one who needed it.

Because as much as hated himself for it, she was right. Except Brendan knew how he felt about her, and it wasn't his feelings he was unsure of. It was hers. She was only eighteen—and who the fuck really knows what they want out of life at eighteen? He was no Prince Charming. He was fucked up. He liked some fucked-up shit. She'd probably think so anyway. And sometimes he went to a place so dark, a place where even her light wouldn't be able to reach him. So he had to be sure that wanting her was right. That loving her was right.

Brendan had to be sure that *she* was sure. Because once his dick was inside her there'd be no going back. Not ever. For either one of them.

He'd never dared to dream of a happily ever after. Never thought he was meant to have one.

But Kyan found one with Linnea.

Jesse and Taylor got theirs with Chloe.

He was sure Dillon would get his one day.

So maybe, just maybe, he could too.

Footfalls crossed the deck behind him. Bo plopped his elbows on the railing and held out a beer. Brendan took it. "Thanks, man."

"I guess the girls don't want us to go hungry because they made us a shit ton of food for tonight and breakfast in the morning." He chuckled. "I unpacked it and put it in the fridge. There's even little notecards taped to all the containers with instructions."

Brendan smirked. "That would be Chloe."

"Darling, Red," Bo sighed. He turned toward Brendan and casually leaned his hip up against the railing. "I think I could be happy with a girl like her, ya know?"

Brendan cocked an eyebrow. "Not a guy like Kodiak?"

"Nah, it's not like that. Me and Kodiak are friends, B—like brothers." He shrugged. "Yeah, I know we've done shit together, but he's not even really bi and if I had to choose one over the other? A sweet young pussy wins. Every. Damn. Time." A grin spread across his face.

Brendan tipped the bottle back and let the cold lager bathe his throat. "How young?"

"What do ya mean?"

"The pussy," he clarified. "How young?"

Bo pursed his lips in thought and shrugged. "As long as she ain't jailbait, I don't fucking care. I'm still like a goofy kid myself half the time, so I can't picture myself with some chick who's like thirty, can you?"

"You're thirty-two, Robert."

"So?" Bo rubbed his finger back and forth across his chin. "It's just a number, B. It's what's in here…" He pointed to his head. "…

and here." Then he placed his hand on his chest. "That's what matters. And don't call me Robert. My dad is Robert. You know I hate that, man."

He smirked. "I know."

Brendan woke with a start. His hands scrubbed across his face and he sat up, pushing the sweat-soaked hair out of his eyes. The blinds were shut tight, but even so he could tell the sky was still dark. He tapped the screen on his phone. It wasn't quite six.

Fucking dreams.

They'd come again. He started having them right after the accident. In the beginning, he had them almost every night, but as time passed they became less frequent. Until lately at least. They weren't nightmares exactly. The dreams were disturbing more than anything, but they gnawed at him and left him feeling unsettled.

And for a man who craved control, Brendan did not do unsettled.

It always began the same. Dank, suffocating darkness that pulled at him. He might not remember every fucked-up fragment of the dream, but he always remembered that.

This time, his sweet girl appeared as she often did, punching a hole through the pitch black, but she didn't touch him. She didn't kiss him. She just stood there, tilting her head from one side to the other as she looked down at him like one would stare at a corpse in a casket, sobbing. Tears streamed down her face and he wanted to reach up to comfort her, but he couldn't move. Her mournful cries got louder and louder and her tears turned red. She was crying fucking blood and he couldn't do a goddamn thing to help her. Salena stepped out in front of her then. She just laughed.

Brendan didn't know what the dreams meant, or if they had any meaning at all. Weren't dreams just the mind's way of sorting through all the fucked-up thoughts and feelings stored in your subconscious? Maybe he'd ask Monica. Shrinks studied all that hooey shit, didn't they? Brendan couldn't shake off the sense of unease he woke up with, though, and the overriding urge to make contact with Katelyn.

Just to make sure she's okay.

Before he could talk himself out of it, he quickly tapped out a text and hit send.

Brendan: How are you?

He tossed the phone beside him on the bed and tipped his head back against the headboard, not really expecting her to reply. Because why would she? He'd been such a dick. It didn't matter that his motives were mostly altruistic because she didn't know that. They needed to talk.

Less than two minutes later, his phone vibrated on the mattress.

Katelyn: It's six in the morning. How do you think I am?

Not crying blood, apparently. Thank fuck.

Brendan grinned. She didn't take his shit. He was going to have a fucking helluva lot of fun with this girl.

Brendan: Would I have asked if I knew?

Katelyn: Why are you asking?

Because I miss you. Because you should be here in this bed with me. Going to this wedding with me...

He couldn't tell her that.

Brendan: Because I woke up thinking about you. And I want to know.

Five long interminable minutes went by before his phone vibrated again.

Katelyn: See me in your dreams, Brendan? LOL I'm fine, except for being woken up way too early on a Saturday.

You'll learn to like it, baby. Trust me.

He couldn't tell her that either. But the thought of how he'd like to wake her up seated itself in his mind and Brendan became acutely aware of the morning wood throbbing in his sweats. He reached inside them and gave his dick a firm tug.

Brendan: *Carpe diem*, sweetheart. You working today?

Katelyn: Yeah. I don't go in until this afternoon, though, so I could have slept some more.

Was she out last night? Was she still seeing that boy? He wanted to know, but he wasn't going to ask. If she was, he'd just put an end to it. Never mind that he only had himself to blame that Katelyn started seeing him in the first place.

Brendan: Sleep is overrated. There's more important things to do.

He squeezed the head of his cock.

Katelyn: Sleep is important.

Brendan: We need to talk. Can we do that, Katelyn?

Three dots appeared, disappeared and reappeared, only to disappear again. Then nothing.

He closed his eyes and leaned back against the headboard, languidly stroking himself just to maintain his erection. Keep himself on edge. He'd almost given up entirely on her answering when the phone finally vibrated beside him.

Katelyn: What do we have to talk about?

He smiled.

Brendan: Us

Katelyn: There is no us

Yes, sweet girl, there is.

Katelyn: I'm seeing someone and I'm not a cheater. We have nothing to talk about.

That answered that question, not that it mattered to him very much. It wouldn't be for much longer if he had anything to say about it.

Brendan: So he's your boyfriend now?

Katelyn: I guess so

His jaw ticked as he silently seethed.

Brendan: You guess so? Either he is or he isn't. He touch you?

Why the fuck did he ask her that when he already knew the answer? He saw them plainly enough in the alley that night sucking face. The sight of that guy with his hand up her sweater sliced through his gut.

Katelyn: What I do or who I see isn't your concern. I got your message loud and clear.

Wrong, sweetheart. It concerns me very much.

Brendan: You fuck him?

She better not have.

She was *his*. And so was that sweet virgin pussy.

The three dots did their dance across the screen again.

Brendan: Answer me

Katelyn: Would it matter if I have?

Yes.

Brendan: No

Katelyn: I haven't

Relieved, he expelled the air from his lungs.

Brendan: We're going to talk, Katelyn. So don't be giving some punk what's *mine*. And don't even think for a minute it's not, because trust me, sweet girl, it is.

She didn't respond to him after that. No dots. Just crickets. That was okay. He was certain she got *that* message loud and clear.

His dick sure fucking did.

With the thought of pushing his way inside her, he wrapped his fingers around his long, thick length and squeezed. He watched precum ooze from his tip and swirled it around the pierced mushroom head with his thumb, before bringing it to his mouth to taste himself.

He sucked the precum off his thumb, spit into his palm, and lubed his dick with a groan. "Fuck yeah, baby."

Then he fisted his cock and fucked his hand with a fury.

He was going to ruin that tight untouched pussy for anyone else. Obliterate it.

She was his, dammit.

And he owned that pussy.

Brendan was pounding his hand so hard his ass lifted off the bed. He pinched his nipple and thick ropes of cum shot out of him to land on his abs and chest. He squeezed his dick with an upward stroke until every last drop left his body, rubbing his cum into his skin just like one day he'd rub it into hers.

The truth was, Katelyn owned him. She just didn't know it yet.

But she would.

Real fucking soon.

Nine

Who the fuck does he think he is?

Katie stared at the text on her phone.

Admittedly, she felt somewhat triumphant reading his words, but at the same time she didn't think she should trust them and she was incensed that he thought he could tell her what, or in this case, what *not* to do.

'Don't be giving some punk what's mine.'

Pfft. As if…

She scrolled through their texts and read them again. Then she messaged Cameron.

Thirty minutes later she heard his soft knock at the door and got up to let him inside. He stood there, with mussed-up hair and a sleepy smile on his face. Her gaze traveled over him. Dimples, hazel eyes, and gray sweats. Then she took him by the hand and led him to her room.

"Everything all right, Katie?"

Okay, so it was a little out of character for her to text him first. To invite him over before the sun was even up—on a game day no less. What the hell was she doing?

"Yeah, I told you. I couldn't fall back to sleep so…"

"C'mere." Cameron pulled her into his arms and his mouth

crashed into hers. Fingers tangled in her hair as they fell backward together onto her bed.

Katie could feel his erection press into her bare thigh through his sweats. Her hands skimmed under his shirt and over the warm skin on his back.

"Fuck, Katie." His pupils were big black saucers.

He knelt between her legs and pulled his shirt over his head, tossing it to the floor. Then he pulled her up to sit and reached for the hem of her plain cotton cami. She lifted her arms and it landed on top of his shirt. Katie watched his eyes as he took in her nakedness in the muted morning light. Suddenly feeling self-conscious, she crossed her arms over her breasts.

"Don't." Cameron pulled her hands away. "You're beautiful." His hands swept up her arms. So gentle. He kissed her shoulder. Softly. Her neck. He whispered in her ear, "I want you, Katie Copeland."

'What do you want?'

'You.'

But did he really? Katie was afraid to even let herself believe it. Kelly was right. What would a man like Brendan want her for? She wasn't falling for it. He was just playing games with her and she sure as shit wasn't going to be his amusement.

She believed Cameron. Maybe he didn't give her butterflies, but he'd never given her a reason to doubt him.

"I want you too, Cameron Mayhew." She reached up to touch the cleft in his chin and he smiled.

"I'm going to make you feel so good, baby." He lowered her back down onto her pillow.

"Okay."

Cameron slid her boy shorts down her thighs. She was naked now. She'd been topless, but never totally naked in front of him before. Katie had the urge to cover herself, but she figured he'd just pull her hands away again.

"You too. I can't be the only naked person here."

He smirked. "Whatever my girl wants." He got up and stood beside the bed. "She gets."

Cameron pushed the gray sweats down his legs and stepped out of them. The head of his cock peeked out of the waistband of his boxers.

Oh, Jesus! Is that normal?

Katie didn't think a penis was supposed to be that big. It didn't seem as big when it was hard and hidden beneath a pair of jeans as it did now. She nervously swallowed as Cameron hooked his thumbs in the elastic waistband and took off his boxers.

Fuck. Me.

He fisted his cock in his hand. She squeezed her eyelids closed as he laid back down beside her.

"Are you nervous?"

She nodded.

"Open your eyes, baby. Look at me."

Slowly, she opened them. His face hovered just inches from hers. He smoothed her hair away from her face and softly kissed her lips.

"You don't have to be nervous. We're not fucking."

"We're not?"

Was she disappointed or relieved?

'Don't be giving some punk what's mine.'

"No. I told you I'm going to make you feel good." He stroked her hair. "I didn't bring any condoms with me. Besides, when we do I want it to be special and…"

Katie pulled his face to hers and kissed him. God, he was so fucking perfect—he deserved everything she didn't know if she would ever be able to give him. He deserved a girl who lost her breath when he looked at her, who got butterflies when he kissed her.

Like she felt with Brendan.

Give me fucking butterflies, Cam. I need them.

He glanced around. Every person he cared about was right here. Except one. She was in the city making frothy hearts in foam.

Linnea looked like a princess. A cloud of sheer voluminous ivory swished around her feet as they swayed to the music. Brendan held her close. Even with heels on she could barely reach his shoulders. Next to them, Jesse danced with his mother who still held Chandan—she hadn't put the baby down since she got off the plane.

The wedding had turned out just as Linnea planned it. Simple and beautiful. Small and intimate. Monica married them under the wood arch beneath the trees, the lake and fall foliage a stunning backdrop. Kodiak gave his sister away to Kyan and Dillon stood at his brother's side as witness to his marriage—the irony of that wasn't lost on him.

For the two men, both of them now her brothers, loving Linnea was akin to a glass splinter burrowed deep beneath the skin. It hurt. Neither man showed anyone their pain, but Brendan knew it had to be there.

A strand of Linnea's dark-blonde hair blew in the evening breeze. He smiled down at her and tucked it behind her ear. Brides are often described as radiant, and Linnea truly was. He squeezed his newest cousin against him a little tighter. "You're beautiful, sweetheart. No one deserves a lifetime of love and happiness more than you, Linnea Byrne."

"Thank you, Bren." She squeezed him back. "For everything."

"You know I love you."

Taylor and Chloe came up and wrapped their arms around them both, the four of them swaying together in a huddle.

"I love you too," Linnea choked out, getting all emotional. "All of you."

"Linnie, do you think you could help me steal my baby back from my mother-in-law?" Chloe giggled and Brendan chuckled with her. "If I don't feed him in the next five minutes, I'm going to ruin this pretty dress. You just married her favorite nephew. She won't refuse you."

"Hey now, I'm her favorite nephew," Brendan protested as Chloe pulled Linnea from his embrace. "Can I kiss the bride first?"

"Of course." Linnea grinned.

Brendan scooped her up in his arms so he wouldn't have to bend over a foot to reach her. "They say it's good luck, you know." He placed a soft kiss on her forehead, and then another on her lips. "And I need a little."

Okay, maybe a lot.

He set her back on her feet and Chloe pulled her away then. She and Linnea walked off in one direction. He and Taylor in the other.

"My wife is bloody brilliant. God, I love her." Taylor smiled to himself, casually resting a hand on Brendan's shoulder. "Come on, mate. Kyan wants us."

All of his cousins, along with Kodiak and the Venery boys, congregated on the deck where the bar was set up. Dillon poured fingers of Irish whiskey from a bottle of Redbreast as Kyan handed each of them a glass.

Taylor winked. "A gift from Colleen."

"And *this* is why I love Irish weddings." He chuckled.

Dillon raised his glass and turned to his brother. "*Go mairir is go gcathair. Sibh blur sail nua.*"

Taylor leaned over and whispered, "What'd he say?"

"An Irish blessing…may you live and may you wear it out. Enjoy your new life."

"*Sláinte*," Dillon toasted.

"Jonathan Swift said it better." Taylor downed the whiskey in one swallow. "May you live all the days of your life. Cheers, mate."

"Cheers, man." Brendan drained his glass. The twenty-seven-year-old whiskey an ambrosia to his palate.

Kyan gathered them all closer together. He looked at Brendan and murmured low, "I told you I have a plan."

"A plan?" Matt raised his brow in question. "What are you talking about, Ky?"

"To put an end to Salena's bullshit." Kyan smirked.

"Go on," Jesse prompted him. "We're listening."

Kyan slapped Kodiak on the back. "Tell 'em, bro."

Linnea's brother gave them a quick glance before he began to explain. He spoke in a hushed, unhurried manner. "Ky and Dillon filled me in on what's been going on. You won't be able to stop her unless you're a step ahead of her." He paused to pour himself another finger of whiskey. "And you can't get ahead of her unless you know what she's up to. Every move she makes. Where she goes. Who she talks to. The activity in her bank account."

Kodiak took a sip from his glass and shrugged with a grin. There was a gleam in his eyes as he swallowed.

"And how do you propose we do that?" Brendan queried.

Kyan and Dillon were grinning along with Kodiak. They flanked him on either side. Still grinning, the man pursed his lips to one side, then licked his bottom lip. "You can't, but I can. It's what I do—how I earn my living."

Well, that explains a few things.

"Heh," Brendan quietly sniggered.

Kit openly chortled. "What? You're like a spy or somethin'?"

Kodiak shrugged with that smirk etched into his face. "Or something."

Dillon's arm went around Kodiak like they were lifelong buds.

"The army trained me well. Communications intelligence. So it was a logical career choice when I got out—pretty lucrative too." He winked and drained his glass.

Kit cocked his head to the side. "So you hack into computers and shit?"

"I provide surveillance services among other things." He smirked. "Cheating husband? I can catch him for you. Need proof your business partner is embezzling funds? I'm your guy. Everything is electronic these days. Piece of cake."

And it was Brendan's turn to grin.

"I'll collect the intel. What you do with it is up to you."

He knew exactly what he was going to do.

Bye-bye, bitch.

Brendan felt lighter already and chuckled. "Dill, open up another bottle!"

Several hours and one too many shots of whiskey later, as the party wound down outside, Brendan found himself staring at the wedding portrait of his grandparents that hung on the wall. The wedding photos of their three children—his parents, aunts, and uncles—were mounted right below theirs. A portrait of Chloe, Jesse, and Taylor now claimed the once-empty space below Jesse's parents. He supposed he'd see Kyan and Linnea's picture hanging beneath Uncle Charley and Aunt Peggy the next time he was here.

When they were little, he and his cousins called it the wedding wall. As they got older, it became difficult to look at. After the accident, he couldn't bear to look at it anymore at all. By the time Uncle Charley was gone, no one came up to the lake house much. Until last year, when they all spent Fourth of July here together with Chloe and Linnea. When love breathed life and happiness into this place again.

He still avoided the wall, though. It hurt too much to look at it.

"I miss them too, *nia*."

Aunt Colleen came up beside him and took his hand. He interlaced their fingers and squeezed. "*Aintín*, I didn't hear you come in."

"I know." She chuckled. "I've been watching you stand here for a good five minutes already."

She reached out to touch the image of her sister, his mother, with the tip of her finger. A single tear rolled down her cheek. "She was so beautiful. And so damn funny."

He looked away.

"Just because you won't acknowledge it doesn't mean the pain isn't there, you know."

Brendan locked eyes with the woman beside him, the closest thing to a mother he had left. "You think I don't?"

She smiled at him. "I bet you still don't have one photo of your parents on display anywhere in your house—am I right?" Colleen squeezed his hand, nodding to herself. "You don't have to answer because I already know you don't. I bet you still have those nightmares too."

"They aren't nightmares, *Aintín*, just some fucked-up dreams."

"Language, Brendan," she chided him and then softened her voice. "I know what you're doing because it's what I did too, but you can't avoid it. Or run from it. Or bury your pain in somebody else."

She swiped beneath her eye. "In the end, what you do with your pain is up to you. You can allow it to break you, a little at a time, piece by piece, or you can use it to rebuild yourself even stronger. Suffering is a choice…so is letting go."

He blinked and sniffled away the tickle in his nose. "Sounds like something Uncle Charley said to me."

She laughed. "I think he said that to me too, or maybe I read it somewhere." She just shrugged and wrapped an arm about his waist. "I love you, Brendan."

"I love you too, *Aintín*."

She swatted his arm. "And fill up this wall, will you?"

"Sure, Auntie." He hugged her and chuckled. "I'll see what I can do."

Ten

Her phone buzzed.

Katie felt the vibration of it against her body. She pulled the phone out of her apron to glance at the notification on the screen and pocketed it again, ignoring this text just as she had all the others. She couldn't think straight, let alone figure out what to do, with him distracting her.

So she just wasn't going to let it happen.

She focused on mundane tasks to occupy herself with. Stocking supplies. Cleaning nozzles and wiping down stainless steel. Rearranging Halloween displays for the umpteenth time. Updating the chalkboard with tomorrow's menu.

Her phone buzzed again. Katie didn't even bother to look at the notification and turned it off completely. It wasn't Cameron, that she knew. They had an away game this weekend. He and the rest of the football team were currently on a plane to New Jersey. They had plans to see each other on Sunday. She had a lot to think about before then.

The voice in her head told her there wasn't anything at all to think about. Had she ever even dreamed of someone more perfect for her than Cameron? No. He was smart, athletic, and gorgeous. Kind, loving, and respectful—he treated her like a queen. He'd all but come right out and said he wanted more from their relationship—and he didn't mean sex. A future. Cameron talked about how he could stay here in the city another three years for law school instead of going to Harvard if he got in. They'd graduate at the same time. He wanted to go back to Montana afterward and set up his law practice there.

What did she want? She couldn't even decide on a major, for chrissakes. Katie knew she didn't want to leave the city, though. This was where she wanted to stay. It was home now. She'd grown up in Nowheresville, surrounded by nothing but cows and corn. She didn't know very much about Billings or the Treasure State. Cameron said it was beautiful. Glacier-carved mountains. Yellowstone. Blue open skies.

It shouldn't matter to me, should it?

But it did.

Because her heart told her that while she cared for Cameron, maybe even loved him, that she wasn't *in love* with him. Katie didn't feel the things she thought she should anyway. And she so desperately tried to. But you can't force a heart to feel what it won't.

Hearts are stupid. Stupid, stupid, stupid organ.

She wondered what her heart might have felt if she never kissed Brendan in the park that night, or if she had met Cameron first. Would he have given her butterflies then? It was silly to even think of, because she'd never know the answer to that question. And besides, do butterflies really mean anything anyway?

They don't last for long, do they?

Isn't that fluttering feeling in your tummy really just a rush of dopamine released by your brain when you're falling in love?

Biology.

Does true love give you butterflies forever?

Katie wasn't sure.

Cameron made her feel other things, though, and that was biology too. They hadn't had sex yet, but she knew he wanted to—a lot. Her lady bits were on board with the idea—oh, were they ever! Two weeks ago in her bedroom, he convinced them that he loved to lavish them with his utmost attention.

That morning, she'd gotten over her shyness being naked in

front of him the second his fingers grasped her nipples and his tongue found her clit.

Her pussy wept for him to sink his dick inside her as he rubbed her clit and lapped up her wetness.

Her head *and* her heart weren't quite ready for that, though. Not yet. And maybe that meant something too.

She glanced over at the counter. It had to mean something that on several occasions she'd attempted to recreate the sensations on her own with thoughts of someone else.

Stop it, Katie. This isn't about him.

Right. Who the fuck was she kidding?

Just as Katie wiped orange chalk from her hands, the door to the shop opened. Internally, she groaned. Only fifteen more minutes and she would have been home free. She plastered on a smile and turned from the chalkboard. There stood Chloe, sans stroller, perky as ever. She appeared to be alone, but Katie found herself discreetly glancing past her to see if anyone else was coming through the door.

Chloe giggled. "It's just me."

Katie relaxed. "Your usual?"

"It's chilly out there tonight." She ran her hands up and down her arms. "Can you make it hot?"

"Sure." Katie found herself smiling. "Plain, no sugar with whipped?"

"Yeah." Chloe nodded.

She went about brewing the espresso. Chloe leaned across the counter to watch her and smiled. Was she supposed to make small talk or something?

Why the hell not?

"How come you're out all by yourself?" That sounded invasively rude. "I mean, where's the baby?"

Chloe didn't appear put off in the slightest. "Chandan is at home with his daddies, hopefully still fast asleep." She smiled.

Katie nodded, surprised and yet not, that Chloe was so open about her child having two fathers. She steamed the milk for her latte, not sure how to respond. Chloe giggled—she did that a lot. "Go ahead and ask me. I can tell you want to."

"Ask you what?" Katie handed her the coffee.

"Come on." Chloe tilted her head toward the tables. "Sit with me."

She followed Chloe to the table in the corner and did just that. They stared at each other for a few minutes while Chloe sipped her latte, then she smiled and said, "You know, the usual questions. Do I know who my son's father is? What's it like being with two men? Do you take turns? How can you be married to both of them?"

"People really ask you that?"

"All the time." She smiled with a shake of her head.

Katie gasped a little. "That's incredibly rude. I'd have never asked you that."

"Maybe not." Chloe shrugged. "You'd always wonder, though, and since we're going to be friends let's just get it out of the way, shall we?"

"We're going to be friends?"

"Well, of course." She waved her hand in the air as if it were a foregone conclusion.

"Um…"

"Taylor is my son's biological father, there's nothing to compare to having two men love you, sometimes, and I'm legally married to Jesse but the three of us committed to each other in front of witnesses. We consider ourselves married to each other and that's all that matters—to us anyway." She took a breath and giggled. "Anything else you'd like to know?"

Before she could even think about it the words slipped out of her mouth. "Do you get butterflies?"

"Excuse me?"

Katie felt her cheeks heat. She must sound like an idiot. "You know, in your tummy. Do your, um, husbands give you butterflies?"

"Ohhh." Chloe grinned and nodded. "Yes, absolutely."

"Still?"

She kept nodding. "Always."

Katie pursed her lips and exhaled through her nose. "What if there aren't any?"

"What do you mean?"

"Butterflies." She picked at a loose thread on her sleeve. Maybe she did sound like an idiot, but it was too late anyway. "What if you don't feel them—like when someone kisses you?"

Chloe's head tilted slightly to the side and a look of understanding washed over her features. The corners of her lips upturned into a small sympathetic smile. She reached for Katie's fingers that were still picking at her sleeve and gave her hand a gentle squeeze.

"Maybe you're just not catching feelings, you know?" She shrugged. "I read an article about it once…ah, never mind. I wish I knew what else to say, sweetie."

Sunday came faster than Katie wanted it to. Cameron was picking her up in a few minutes and she was no closer to knowing what she was going to do than she was on Friday after her chat with Chloe.

Her head and her heart remained at war with each other.

She didn't know where they were going, or what Cameron had planned. He only told her to dress warm. Katie threw a thick, chunky sweater over her long-sleeved tee and swiped on some tinted lip oil. By the time she laced her boots, she heard his soft knock at the door.

He charged at her, hoisting her up into his arms the second she opened it. "I missed my girl." And he peppered her face with kisses, spinning her around the room.

Katie squealed and he set her down. "How was New Jersey?"

"We kicked ass!"

"I saw." She glanced up at his dimples on full display and smiled. He leaned in and kissed her forehead. "Ready to go?"

"Yeah, I guess so," she answered and grabbed her jacket and scarf from the back of the chair. "Where are we going anyway?"

"A corn maze." He rubbed his hands together and grinned.

Her brow arched. "They have corn mazes in the city?"

"No." He chuckled. "At least I don't know of any. One of the guys let me borrow his car."

Corn. I can't seem to get away from it.

Katie giggled. "All right then, let's do this."

He held her hand in the car. He'd glance over as he drove and smile at her. It would be so easy to just give in and go with her head, because being with Cameron was so damn easy. He took the exit off the highway and raised her hand to his lips, brushing them over her knuckles.

Nothing. Not even the tiniest flutter.

He held her hand inside the corn maze. Katie let Cameron lead her through the tall stalks, even though she'd been playing in cornfields ever since she was big enough to climb the fence into the Reilly's farm next door. Parents chased after shrieking young children. Couples purposely separated themselves from their friends to steal kisses hidden away in the corn.

They came to a dead end and stopped.

Cameron looked up at the stalks that stood a few feet over his head, then lowered his gaze to her. "We might be lost." He grinned.

"You think so?"

His arms circled around her waist and drew her in closer. He bent his head to nuzzle her neck. "Mmm…maybe."

It tickled. Katie tucked her ear against her shoulder and giggled. Cameron took her face in his hands and brought his lips to hers. Was there anything more romantic than being kissed while lost in a maze of corn? Maybe. But she couldn't think of what that might be right then. She tried to clear her mind, to empty her head of any thoughts, and just focus on Cameron kissing her. To let herself really feel it.

And nothing. Not even the faintest flap of wings.

Katie had no choice but to admit it to herself. If it hadn't happened by now, then it probably wasn't ever going to. And realizing that made her sad. She pulled back and ended the kiss. She tried to smile but the corners of her mouth wouldn't budge.

Cameron didn't seem to notice. She looked down at the ground as his arm went around her waist and he hugged her into his side. "I guess we should try and find our way out of this thing, huh?"

"Right or left?"

"What?" he asked.

"Pick one. Right or left?"

"Okay," he murmured. "Right."

"I grew up around cornfields, remember?" She winked. "Keep your right hand on the right side and just follow the path…"

Cameron leaned over and kissed her temple.

"…to the end," she whispered.

All the way home, Katie fought to keep the tears from falling. They'd been building, lodged behind her eyes, ever since he kissed her inside the corn maze. She stared out the window at the darkening October sky, focusing on the shards of blood-red orange that remained as the sun slipped away. She stared at it until spots danced in her eyes and her vision blurred.

How could she do this?

Her head told her she was about to make the biggest mistake of her life.

'Isn't that how we learn, Kell? Making a mistake or two.'

'Just try not to make one you'll regret, because they can last a lifetime.'

Her heart told her she was making the right choice. The only choice.

But she didn't want to hurt him. God, she didn't want to. It was hurting her to know she was going to. He'd always been so good to her, the last thing she wanted to do was bruise his big, beautiful heart. Cameron was everything a girl could ever want. And someone out there was going to be one very lucky lady, but it wasn't her. He deserved more. So did she.

Cameron took her hand and held it on his thigh as the lights of the city skyline came into view. Katie turned from the window and searched for the words she hoped would inflict the least amount of pain. Was she crying? Because she felt warm liquid seeping from her eyes.

He stole one brief glance at her and squeezed her hand. "What's wrong, Katie?"

Shit, shit, shit…

She shook her head and swiped at her eyes, then inhaled a deep breath. "I'm…you're so…" she stuttered. Everything in her head sounded so cliché. "…you're just so damn good. Amazing and wonderful." She sniffed. "Perfect, actually."

"Why are you crying?"

Katie couldn't look at him. And she couldn't answer him. She just couldn't do it. She let the tears fall and stared at the cars and shops as they passed them. Cameron pulled into the alley behind Beanie's and parked. He took both of her hands in his. She forced herself to turn and face him.

"I'm so sorry…"

He shook his head, then lowered it and stared at their joined hands. "Are you breaking up with me?"

"Yes," she whispered.

"I don't understand…why?"

"You deserve more." She squeezed her eyelids closed.

"I don't want more, baby." His hands cupped her cheeks, brushing her tears away with his thumbs. "Just you."

Why was he making this so hard?

She opened her eyes and tears dripped down her cheeks. "I'm sorry, Cam. I care for you so much and I…"

"Katie, I lo—"

"Don't say it, Cam. Please don't say it," she pleaded.

"Baby, you need to give us more time. It's only been a month." He held her against him, smoothing her hair and kissing her head. "We'll get there. And you're going to love me too."

Katie pulled back and held his face in her hands. She placed a soft kiss on his lips and looked into his sad hazel eyes—sad because of her. "But I do love you, don't you see?"

She reached for the car door and opened it.

"No, Katie, I don't." He sounded so broken and it was all her fault. "What more do you need?"

She hiccupped through her tears and got out of the car, closing the door behind her. Tires squealed as he peeled out of the alley. Then she shakily exhaled. "Butterflies."

Eleven

S
he wanted to throw her phone against the wall and watch it
break apart into itty-bitty pieces.

Katie must have ignored him one time too many.

Her phone remained silent and still.

Just as well.

She'd been in such a funk since ending things with Cameron.
He didn't sit next to her Monday in algebra, not that she expected
him to. On Tuesday, some cheerleader was rubbing up on him in
the student union. He seemed to enjoy her attention. Last night he
texted her. He told her that he missed her and asked if they could
at least be friends.

She wanted that. To be his friend. She missed him too.

"Quit staring at your phone and just call him, why don't you?"
Kelly hugged her around her middle from behind and rested her
chin on her shoulder. "Tell him you want him back. That you were
confused and made a mistake."

Katie slipped her phone back into her apron. "I didn't make a
mistake."

"But I liked Cam," her aunt protested, rocking her from side
to side.

"Me too."

Kelly let her go to pull a batch of pumpkin muffins out of the oven. The baking for the shop was usually left to Stacy—that was her thing, but she was conspicuously absent this morning. Katie didn't have classes on Fridays, so she agreed to come in early and help out. It wasn't like she had anything better to do, right?

"So, what's up with Stace?" Katie assembled the ingredients to make cream cheese frosting while the muffins cooled. "Where is she?"

Kelly let out a long sigh and perched herself on a stool. "I was going to tell you tonight." She blew at a lock of honey-colored hair that fell into her eyes. "Stacy's moving out."

"What?" Katie was stunned. She hadn't seen that coming. "But why?"

"We broke up." One shoulder lifted in a shrug. "That's all."

Katie set the bowl on the table and went to hug her aunt. Kelly's head rested on her shoulder and she combed Katie's hair with her fingers. How had she not known something was wrong? She never liked the woman, so maybe she just ignored all the signs.

"I've known for a while. She's, ah, opening a bed and breakfast in Door County with her new friend."

Ohhh.

"She has movers coming this morning." Kelly lifted her head from Katie's shoulder and gave her a wan smile. "I'm interviewing a baker—someone who can help you and me run this place, yeah?"

Katie nodded. "Yeah."

Considering Stacy and Kelly had been together for a few years, she would have expected her aunt to be more upset than she appeared to be, and for some reason it worried her that she wasn't. "You okay?"

"I'm fine, sweetie." She scooted off the stool. "You will be too."

Kelly went upstairs to the loft. Katie didn't know if it was to get Stacy's keys from her or to say goodbye, but she saw the moving truck roll out onto First Avenue about thirty minutes ago and she still hadn't reappeared. Maybe Kelly needed some time alone. She could understand that. It was that slow time in the afternoon anyway. Katie could handle things here without her.

She had just finished topping two hot chocolates with whipped cream for a lady and her little boy dressed up as Spiderman, when Chloe came through the door like a gust of wind pushing a stroller. It looked like the girl she'd introduced as her sister a few months ago was with her. Oddly, there was no family resemblance between the two of them whatsoever—like none. Zero. The only thing they had in common is they were both stunningly beautiful.

Chloe reached the counter, unwinding her scarf and out of breath. "Hey, Katie. Can I get my usual, hot, and an americano, please?"

"Of course." She peered over the counter to get a glimpse of the baby and smiled.

"You remember Linnea?"

Katie glanced at the tan blonde with Chloe. The blonde didn't speak, but raised her hand in a small wave. "Yeah. Hi," Katie said. "How are you?"

Chloe answered for her. "Linn just came home from her honeymoon in Hawaii. She married Brendan's cousin, Kyan, you know."

No, I didn't, but I guess that explains the tan.

"Oh, congratulations!"

"Thank you," Linnea said. Katie was surprised the girl was able to get two words in.

"Brendan caught the garter, didn't he, Linnie?" Chloe winked with a giggle. "You know what that means."

Nope. Not even going there.

Katie sniggered. Chloe didn't need any encouragement. "You going to drink these here or are you taking them with you?"

Chloe looked to Linnea who was rifling through a big tote bag. "I could use a breather. How about you?"

"Yeah, I could, but we still have a lot to do before this little guy decides he's had enough." She leaned down to coo at the baby in the stroller.

Chloe shrugged. "Shopping. We have a Halloween thing tomorrow."

"To-go it is then," Katie announced and started on their drinks.

"What about you?" Chloe asked.

Huh? What about me?

Katie arched a brow from behind the counter.

"What are you doing for Halloween?"

"Oh…um, nothing." She snapped the lids onto their coffees. "Just working, I guess."

Chloe leaned up against the counter. "Didn't catch any butterflies then, I take it." And she winked.

Katie pursed her lips and exhaled through her nose. "No, I didn't." She lowered her gaze and slid cardboard sleeves onto the paper cups.

Chloe took them and smiled. "Then I think you should text him back."

She looked up. Katie really didn't need to ask but she did anyway. "Who?"

"Brendan." Chloe giggled as she handed Linnea her coffee and wound the scarf back around her neck. "Be seeing you, sweetie. Happy Halloween!"

Linnea waved and Katie watched them push the stroller out the door onto First Avenue.

Should I?

It seemed to Katie that the window of opportunity to return Brendan's texts had already passed. Especially after she'd ignored him every day for two weeks. Then he stopped sending them altogether. Sighing, she scrolled through his texts and debated.

Blowing out a breath, she tapped out a text. She was about to press send when Spiderman's mother returned to the counter. Katie slid the phone back into her apron pocket. The lady just stood there, smiling oddly with her head tilted slightly to the side. The little boy still sat at the table, sipping on his hot chocolate.

"Can I get you something?"

"Hm." Her smile widened to a grin. "Yes. A large coffee, please. Black. To go."

"Sure thing." Katie got her the coffee.

"Were those girls friends of yours?" The woman gestured toward the door, apparently meaning Chloe and Linnea who had just left.

What an odd question. Katie didn't know what to make of it. She raised her gaze. The woman towered over her, but then she was wearing stiletto-heeled boots. Her long black hair was slicked back into a high ponytail and her eyes were an unusual golden color, like a cat's—contacts, obviously. She had a lot of makeup on too. Heavy winged liner. Big fake eyelashes. But then it was Halloween. Well, almost.

"They're customers, why?"

She handed her, what Katie thought at first glance was, a greeting card of some sort. Raised plum foil script on black vellum paper. "They dropped this."

"Oh." Not such an odd question then, was it? "Thanks. I'll return it to them next time they come in."

"You do that." The woman tapped her long manicured nails on the counter. "I hope you see them before tomorrow night, though. That's an invitation to the Halloween masquerade at the Red Door." She tilted her head again. "They won't let you inside without it."

"I see."

Katie almost laughed. Didn't Kelly say Brendan *and* his cousins owned the club? She wasn't about to tell this woman that Chloe and Linnea were married to two of them and they surely didn't need an invitation.

Hm, but…

"You're very young." She angled her head to the other side and softly laughed. It was rather odd and kind of creepy.

"Excuse me?"

"Never mind." The little boy in the Spiderman costume was there tugging at her coat and she turned her attention to him, patting him on the head. "Have you finished your chocolate, Payton?"

"Yes, ma'am."

"That's a good boy."

"What an awesome name." Katie reached into the case and handed him a sugar cookie decorated like a pumpkin. "Like Peyton Manning?"

"Thanks." He grinned. "No, like Walter Payton."

Bears. Of course. Duh.

"Even awesomer."

He giggled. "That's not a word."

"Come on, Payton." The woman took hold of his hand and they went to the door. After she pulled it open, she stopped to glance back at Katie. "Happy Halloween." She licked her bottom lip with a grin. "Have fun tomorrow."

So odd.

It was well past eleven by the time she and Kelly finished up at Beanie's and headed upstairs to their noticeably emptier loft. "What the fuck, Kelly? Bitch took half the furniture."

"We can get new stuff." She shrugged. "Look, I'm really beat and I just wanna go to bed. Sweet dreams." She leaned in for a hug. "I love you, Katie-Kate. Thanks for today."

"I love you too. Night."

Katie sat on her bed and blankly stared at the phone resting in her palm. The message to Brendan was still there, cursor blinking, waiting for her to press send. And she wasn't sure if she would. She saw him walk past the shop today.

Late that afternoon, as dusk approached and shadows lengthened on the avenue, she happened to look through the storefront window just as Brendan walked by on his way to the club—she assumed that's where he was going anyway. He didn't stop. Or slow down. Not even a quick glance toward the window. Nothing. He just looked straight ahead, keeping a steady pace as he went.

She wondered if he walked by every day and she just hadn't noticed before. Had he ever glanced through the window to catch a glimpse of her? Maybe. And maybe now he just didn't give a fuck.

Why should he? But then Chloe did tell her to text him back, and she didn't think Chloe would say that if he didn't.

Oh, fuck it.

She pressed send.

Now what? Katie didn't want to sit there and stare at the screen, waiting to see if he'd reply, so she stuffed the phone beneath her pillow and went to take a shower. She'd make it a long one too. Deep condition her hair or something.

An hour later she left the bathroom with extra shiny hair, smooth stubble-free legs and baby-soft skin. Katie reached underneath the pillow and retrieved her phone. Nothing. She opened up their text thread. Her message was still unread. Did she really think Brendan was just sitting around at a sex club checking his phone for a text from her? Of course he wasn't. What was he doing there? She probably didn't want to know.

Or did she?

Just because she'd never been penetrated by a penis didn't mean she was completely clueless. Katie had read her fair share of smutty novels, seen all the movies with red rooms and purple rooms, and a thirty-second scroll through Twitter was more than enlightening. Glory holes. Gang bangs. Dungeons and pleasure rooms.

Katie reached for the black vellum card she'd hidden between the pages of her English lit textbook. She traced the raised foil lettering with her fingertips. The idea had been brewing in the back of her mind since the odd woman put the invitation in her hand this afternoon.

'*Costumes are encouraged, though not required. Attendees must be en masque.*'

She could do it.

She even had a costume.

Before she ended things with Cam, they had plans to go to a huge Halloween bash on Greek Row—the theme was historical figures. She was going to go as Marie Antionette and Cam as Louis XVI. With a few adjustments it would be perfect.

She could pull it off.

She'd see for herself what was behind that red door.

Brendan wouldn't even know she was there.

She'd slip inside. Blend in. Have a glass of champagne—or two.

Katie giggled to herself.

Maybe, if she was feeling really adventurous and extremely brave, she'd throw caution to the wind. She'd walk right up to him and kiss him, just like that night in the park. Would he know it was her then? Would he recognize how her lips felt on his? Would he be angry and send her home like a naughty child or would he whisk her away and claim what he said was his?

Butterflies stirred inside her just thinking about it.

She was going to do it.

She was going to the ball.

Because butterflies don't lie...do they?

Twelve

Happy Halloween!

At first he thought he was seeing things, so he rubbed the sleep from his eyes and read it again. Three fucking weeks. It'd been three weeks since Kyan and Linnea's wedding, and that was the last time Brendan had gotten a response from her. No more of this text message bullshit. Time's up. He'd given her plenty. Tomorrow, he was going to walk his ass right into Beanie's to get some coffee—and his sweet girl.

Trick or treat, baby?

He grinned.

Whipping the covers off his naked body, Brendan swung out of bed with a burst of exhilaration that he hadn't felt in a very long time—maybe ever. He was pumped with a renewed sense of energy. Vigor. Of hope. An undeniable purpose. And that purpose was Katelyn.

Brendan glanced around his mammoth bedroom with its adjacent sitting room, envisioning her in it with him. It was decidedly dark and masculine, black being the predominant color, like most of the house. Ebony wood floors. Leather. He'd always found it too big for just himself, but now as he looked at the overstuffed sofas and chairs, the plush velvet hammock suspended from the ceiling, he thought it perfect.

In stark contrast to his dark bedroom, Brendan stepped into his en suite. Even though the space was twice its original size after the remodel, he'd managed to preserve the vintage aesthetic. The original white subway tiles and hexagon mosaic floor remained. Everything that was old looked new again, and everything that was new looked as if it had always been there—like it belonged. And that was exactly the way he wanted it.

Now to do the same with the rest of his life.

And it would all start tomorrow. The only thing that prevented him from going to her today was the masquerade ball tonight. Even though it was only late morning, Brendan was already behind schedule. Special events at the club required him to be there earlier than usual to deal with handling caterers and hired performers. At least Linnea and Chloe helped him with some of that now, but still, he had to be there and it was going to be a long night. Brendan wanted his focus to be solely on Katelyn when he saw her. So tomorrow.

Brendan got into the shower and as the hot water soaked his skin he laughed out loud to the tile walls. He might go to hell for this, but he didn't fucking care. Katelyn wasn't even old enough to step one foot inside his club, but she was old enough to get inside his head and his heart. His bed. And that's exactly where he wanted her to be.

By the time he made it to the Red Door it was already going on four. The guests would begin to arrive at seven and by ten the playrooms would come alive. There would be no demos tonight. Just as he'd arranged for their previous balls, they would be entertained with wicked exhibitions and erotic performances favorited by those members with more extreme preferences. Fear play. Sadism. Blood play. Electro-stimulation. Wax. The Halloween Ball was the one night of the year when the dungeon came upstairs. Though much of it was specially staged for tonight's event, like a horror movie, it probably wasn't for the squeamish or faint of heart.

It wasn't his thing, but it did make his dick hard to watch.

Linnea was upstairs in the VIP space directing staff who were stocking the private bars, setting up food stations, and draping gossamer webs on chandeliers. The club had been transformed into a haunted playground. She was so talented and any event she planned was incredible. Brendan strode right over to Linnea and wrapped her in his arms.

"Happy Halloween, sweetheart. You're fucking amazing." He kissed her cheek. "Everything looks fantastic—especially you."

She blushed as she often did. "Thanks, Bren."

He'd loved this girl from the start, knew they were meant to be her family from the moment he met her. Linnea was inherently beautiful and sweet and good. It was easy to understand why everyone loved her so much, but what was inconceivable to Brendan was how anyone could have ever hurt her as she had been. Both Linnea and her brother had suffered unspeakable cruelty by those who were supposed to love them the most. Knowing that brought out a driving need in all of them to keep her safe and protect her from anything bad and evil.

Her father.

Salena.

Brendan held her tiny frame to him even tighter and kissed her brow before he finally let go. "Where's Chloe?"

"Jesse called and she had to go." She shrugged. "She told me to tell you they'd be here before seven and something about not catching any butterflies…not sure what she meant by that."

He grinned.

Because he knew.

Brendan finished making his rounds, checking on his staff and greeting guests, then took the stairs up to the VIP space. Dillon and Kodiak stood at the private bar, their attention on the entertainment, sipping whiskey. Bo joined them as he approached.

"B, my brother." Bo clapped his back. "I'm digging the show this year, man. This is way hotter than the fuck-o-matic bull dude that was here last year."

"Minotaur." He chuckled, shaking his head.

Dillon placed a glass of Glenlivet in his hand. Brendan swallowed the smooth amber liquid and turned to face the platform. A sub with blue hair rocked back and forth on all fours. She wore nothing except ripped fishnet stockings held in place by a shiny latex garter and a studded leather collar around her neck. He could see her breasts quivering, her nipples stiff peaks, as melted wax slowly dripped onto her skin.

Would Katelyn allow him to do that with her? Would she like it? He hoped so. Brendan needed her to. He needed to hear her breath hitch in anticipation. To see the longing for him in her aqua eyes. To feel her body crave his. Her surrender to him. Her complete submission to every touch. Every caress. Only then would trust, and the bond he needed between them, come.

His cock swelled. Just thinking of her made him hard. Brendan rubbed himself over the smooth black fabric of his slacks. Any night before this one, he wouldn't have thought twice about sinking his dick inside any hot wet orifice he wanted—and he usually wanted more than one. Luckily for him they weren't in short supply here. Because he loved to fuck.

No, actually, for Brendan it was more than that. He loved every aspect of sex there was. Always had. He lost his virginity the summer he was thirteen. She was twenty. Couldn't tell you her name. Some college kids were having a party on the lakefront beach. He was always taller and bigger than other boys his age, so he looked older. She didn't ask him how old he was and he didn't tell her. The moment her tight wet cunt squeezed his dick he'd found his drug. Fucking was his high.

A natural, euphoric high. He relished in the heightened sensations, the sights, sounds, and the smell of sex. The chemical rush of endorphins and adrenaline as they coursed through his veins. Brendan loved sex more than most people did, or admitted to anyway, and so what? As far as he was concerned, his hearty appetite for pussy and pleasure was just as it should be. He had no inhibitions and few hard limits. There wasn't much he wouldn't do to feel pleasure or to make someone else feel it.

Throughout his adult years Brendan sought to learn everything he could about human sexuality, to develop and curate his erotic imagination. He went on retreats. He surrounded himself with like-minded people like Monica and embraced the sex-positive culture long before it was trendy. People are born as sensual beings. The human body was built for sex and human beings are naturally wired to give and receive pleasure. Sexual desire is innate. It was society that repressed it.

Brendan's attitude influenced his cousins to adopt the ideal that sex is beautiful in any form. He'd watched Jesse agonize over his bisexuality for such a long time—long before Jesse recognized it in himself. That his cousin and his best friend could love each other and share their love freely with Chloe made his heart swell.

He glanced behind him to see Jesse and Taylor kiss as they pleasured their wife together. Sweet Linnea lounged between her husband's thighs, her aroused gaze fixed on the blue-haired girl dripping in neon wax, lips parted as Kyan discreetly caressed her. It was fucking beautiful.

This is what it was all for.

Freedom to love whatever way felt right for you.

And that's what he wanted with Katelyn.

So on this night, the only solace he sought was in her. The only one he wanted was her. He'd fuck his own hand a dozen times tonight, and think of her when he did, because he didn't want to be inside anyone else. Ever. Katelyn was it for him. Brendan never thought he'd feel this way about anyone. He didn't think he was capable of it—hell, he wasn't capable of it before he decided he had to love her.

Brendan drained the whiskey from his glass and placed it on the bar. "I have to check on things. I'll catch you guys in a bit."

He went up to his office, closed the door, and sprawled out on the sofa. His dick throbbed in his hand. Closing his eyes, he squeezed it and tried to imagine what her innocent, unpracticed touches might feel like. Brendan had never felt that before. He'd only ever been with experienced women. He'd never taken anyone's virginity—not even in high school. Soon he would know what that felt like. Soon he would be the first man, and the only man, who would ever be inside her.

Fucking Christ.

He must have dozed off. His hand still held his dick, but a warm wet mouth sucked on its head, a tongue toying with the barbell that pierced it. Brendan opened his eyes to a head of long, rich-red waves. Instinctively, he gripped her hair at the nape and roughly pulled. She moaned and sucked him deeper into her mouth.

He yanked her head off his dick.

"What the fuck, Angelica?"

She was one of the vamp chicks. Tall, voluptuous, and pale, with a fetish for blood and knives. Angelica and her partner were doing an exhibition at midnight. They were the perfect coupling, dark and sensual. He'd watched them together many times. Played with them too, back when Salena was still around. Salena loved to eat cat, more than most men did, and she loved to play on the edge—that girl had no hard limits whatsoever. None. The more depraved something was, the more she desired it.

Brendan didn't see the appeal. So she did that shit without him. And he fucked her less and less often. Except when Kyan and Dillon were around. Then the viper would beg all three of them to fuck her together.

"I need a favor, B."

He still held her head up by her hair. "And what's that?"

"Milo can't get here." She licked her lips like she was nervous. "Someone slashed his tires and it's too late for him to get an Uber—he'd never make it in time. I need you to go on the stage with me."

He let go of her hair.

The fuck?

"No."

"C'mon, B. Why not?" She batted her thick black lashes and wrapped her fingers around his to stroke him.

"Did I give you permission to touch my dick?" He pushed her hand away. "Because I have a girl and your kink ain't mine, sweetheart. That's why not."

Angelica threw her head back. Her chin bobbed. When she came back up she was laughing. "You...wait a minute." She laughed some more. "I can't breathe. You have a girl? Since when?"

"Since now."

While that wasn't exactly true today, it would be tomorrow, and tomorrow was less than an hour away. So close enough.

"You're so full of shit." A wicked giggle erupted from her mouth. "Please, Bren? It's not like we use real blood—not in public anyway. It's a performance you've seen us do a million times. So I know you can do it."

He shook his head.

"It's not like I'm asking you to fuck me or anything." Then she winked. "Unless, of course, you want to."

"I do not." Her face fell and he felt bad that he might have hurt her feelings. "And don't take it personal. I told you I have a girl."

"So you said." She snorted. "Fine, no fucking. Will you do it then?"

He should say no.

But it was Halloween and everyone out there was expecting to see the vamps get freaky—even if it was just for show. Angelica was right. He could do it. He knew how to make it seem real.

Still, it just didn't feel right.

He should tell her no.

But he didn't.

Thirteen

Trick or treat, baby?

She looked at the text for probably the hundredth time today as she waited for her eyeliner to dry and giggled. Katie had already spent almost two hours making sure everything was flawless, from her costume to her makeup. It was almost eleven. She didn't have much time left before Kelly came home.

Her lashes popped on and stuck like magic, exactly as the ad on Instagram promised they would. Katie blinked a few times in the mirror, so amazed at the transformation that she almost didn't recognize herself. Then she breathed in a deep cleansing breath and got up from her vanity to dress.

The lace overskirt of her costume, called a polonaise in the days of Marie Antoinette, was hung up on the back of her door. It had a daringly low-cut tightly fitted bodice with a lace choker collar. The sleeves flared out at the elbows. The intricate floral lace pattern was sweet and delicate with a matching flounce trim and embroidered butterflies on the bodice—she took that as an omen. Designed to be worn over a petticoat and bustled, the garment was cut away in an inverted V shape in the front and draped to the floor in the back.

Katie had no intention of wearing the petticoat at all. She slid the snow-white lace over a white satin balconette bra and matching panty. The bra pushed up her breasts so high they threatened to spill out of the cups, crescents of pink areolae visible. She skimmed her fingertips slowly across her décolletage, gazing upon her reflection, seeing herself as Brendan would see her. A confident, sensual woman looked back at her. And she smiled.

She was ready.

Except she hadn't planned for a coat. She'd only have to walk a block, but it was cold, and she had a lot of skin exposed. She grabbed an old leather bomber jacket out of the hallway closet—and now she looked like a young Madonna. Giggling, with her aunt's ID (just in case), some cash, lip gloss, her phone, and the black vellum invite in a mini crossbody bag, Katie slipped out the door clutching her mask in her hand.

Katie didn't feel quite so confident walking down First Avenue as she had in her bedroom. Outside she became very much aware of her nakedness. At least there weren't that many cars passing by this time of night. Cold wind blew up her lace skirt, straight through the white satin. Her nipples pebbled into hard points. She prayed they let her right in or her pussy lips might freeze together if she had to stand outside too long. Not really, it wasn't that cold, but it felt like it.

With each tap of her spike-heeled booties on the concrete sidewalk her pulse quickened and she found it more difficult to breathe. Katie stopped when she reached Charley's. A cozy fire burned in the bar's brick hearth. Only a few patrons remained inside. The Red Door was on the other side of the restaurant, just around the corner.

She had to be out of her fucking mind. Why was she doing this again? She glanced over her breasts to her bodice.

Oh, yeah.

Butterflies.

With one last deep breath, she collected herself, put her mask on, and walked up to the red double doors.

A man dressed in solid black, a bouncer or security maybe, opened the door as soon as he saw her approach. With a brief nod he invited her past the portal and she exhaled. This was going to be easier than she thought.

Katie pretended to be nonchalant, feigning a lack of interest in the foreign surroundings she found herself in. It took every ounce of willpower she had not to drop her jaw and survey the sumptuous two-story lobby. A club mix of "E-Girls Are Ruining My Life!" by Corpse played on a loop, the bass vibrating through her body.

She could pick out scent notes of amber and patchouli through the tang of sweat and liquor circulating in the air. Katie wasn't sure what she was supposed to do next or where she should go now that she was inside. She took a step inside the lobby and a second man in black stopped her.

Shit.

"Welcome to the masquerade, miss." He led her gently by the elbow. "Member check-in is this way."

"Oh, thank you." Keeping her cool, she smiled with relief. "It's my first time here."

"I can tell." He smiled back at her. "Did you bring your invitation with you? You won't be permitted to enter without it."

They reached a desk and stopped. She pulled the piece of black vellum from her bag. "I did."

"Very good, miss. Axel will take care of you from here." He winked. "Enjoy the ball."

He was as big as a mountain—a mountain of solid muscle covered in skin. Did everyone dress in black here? Axel, as least she presumed that's who it was, came behind the desk that was more like an elegant hotel check-in counter. He gave her a quick glance and flipped a monitor on.

Double shit.

"Good evening, Miss…I don't know your name."

"Katie."

"Miss Katie, may I see your invitation, please."

Katie willed her hand to stop trembling and handed it to him. "ID."

She handed him Kelly's driver's license and crossed her fingers in her head.

He looked at it and then up at her masked face. "I thought you said your name was Katie. This says Kelly."

Shit. Shit. Shit.

"Uh…um…I don't go by Kelly. My middle name is Katherine." She paused. "Yeah. So, Katie."

He smirked. "I see."

The raise of his brow told her he didn't buy it, but he tapped on the keyboard and glanced at the monitor in front of him.

"Your name isn't in our member database…" He cleared his throat. "Miss, er, Katie. Who are you here as a guest of?"

And Katie was sure he already knew that. The man was fucking with her and enjoying it.

Asshole!

She couldn't say Brendan. Katie had a feeling that wouldn't go over with him very well. She had to give him a name quick. It just tumbled out of her mouth.

"Linnea."

Axel crossed his huge arms over his chest and grinned. "Linnea Byrne?"

Which cousin was she married to? Kayden? No. Ryan? No. Fuck!

"Yes, Linnea Byrne—she just got back from her honeymoon in Hawaii." Katie cocked her head and grinned back at him. "I'm her cousin."

Why did she say that?

He nodded. "Let me check your coat and I'll have someone escort you to VIP and your, um, cousin."

Katie shrugged out of her leather jacket and smoothed the flounced sleeves of her costume. The white lace glowed purple under the lights. She had no intention of going anywhere near Linnea or Chloe or any of the Byrne cousins. Then Brendan would find out she was here and she wasn't sure if she wanted him to know. Not yet anyway. She needed to stay incognito.

Axel returned with a claim check ticket and she tucked it inside her bag. "Your escort will be here in a moment."

She smiled with a slight nod. "Thank you."

A couple minutes had passed when Katie sensed someone was there beside her. She glanced over to see yet another man in black from head to toe. Even with half of his face hidden behind a mask she just knew he was beautiful. Purple light glinted in his long black hair and reflected in his ice-blue eyes. Eyes just like Brendan's. She gulped.

No. Please, no.

The man smiled at her. "Hello, cousin." He gave her his arm. "So happy you could join us. Shall we?"

She was so fucked.

His smile dropped as soon as they left the lobby. He backed her into the wall, caging her with an arm on each side of her head. "My wife doesn't have a cousin. Who the fuck are you? Because I sure as hell know you're not Kelly Matthews."

So much for staying incognito.

"I'm Katie…Katie Copeland. Kelly's my aunt."

The man, Linnea's husband and Brendan's cousin, whose name she couldn't remember, began to laugh. He took a step back and then he did the oddest thing. He hugged her.

"You're coffee girl." He grinned.

"Excuse me?"

"You know, Beanie's. Coffee girl. You're Bren's girl." He looked her up and down, then hooked his arm around her shoulders. "I'm his cousin, Kyan. C'mon. Nice outfit, by the way. He's going to love it."

Nooo. Fuck!

They came to a staircase and she stopped. "Look, Kyan, Brendan and I…I'm not his girl. He doesn't even know that I'm here."

He just smiled at her. "It's okay. He'll be happy you came to surprise him. C'mon." Kyan nudged her toward the stairs. "The girls are here and we'll introduce you to everyone."

Oh god. I can't. I look like an eighteenth century French whore.

"Is he up there?"

"Not at the moment." He chuckled. "Relax."

When they got to the top of the stairs Katie was finally able to take in the opulence around her. She'd never seen anything like it. Well, of course she hadn't. She'd never even been inside a regular dance club, never mind a club like this. Kyan slowed down so she could lean over the railing and look her fill.

"I feel like I'm at the X-rated version of the haunted mansion in Disneyland."

He laughed. "You're not too far off. Have you ever been to Disneyland?"

"I went to Disney World once." She giggled.

"Close enough." His arm went back around her. "Here we are."

Kyan took her arm and led her to an intimate space, sectioned off by gauzy draping that hung to the floor from dark wood beams suspended by chains in the exposed ductwork ceiling. A gigantic U-shaped plum sofa with oversized, comfortable-looking pillows and an antique chandelier centered over the seating area were the focal points of the room. Exposed brick. Flickering candles. Rich, luxurious colors. The eclectic mix of elements were magnificent. It was hard to imagine that at one time this entire building was an old dusty, dingy warehouse.

"Katie?"

Chloe jumped up from the sofa where she had been seated between two men. Of course she knew one of them was her husband, Taylor Kerrigan from Venery. *Matcha tea latte.* She'd met him briefly when he came into the shop with Brendan. The other long-haired man must be Brendan's cousin, who was also her husband. It was a bit confusing. She hoped she could keep it all straight.

Her new redheaded friend pulled Katie in for a hug like they'd known each other forever and not just a few months. "Holy shit! I can't believe you're here! This is wonderful—you and Brendan together at last!" Chloe smirked and playfully poked her shoulder. "I'd almost given up on the two of you—between you chasing the damn butterflies and him being such an ass." She hugged her again. "But here you are, and girl, he's going to die when he sees you!"

Katie gave her a weak smile. "Thanks, but…uh…me and Brendan aren't, um, together."

Chloe's brows drew together like maybe she hadn't heard her

right and Linnea came up to stand beside them. "I don't understand. How did you get in then?"

She worried her lip and then answered, "You dropped an invitation when you came in yesterday. Some lady picked it up off the floor and I was going to give it back to you, but then the lady who found it told me it was an invitation to the ball, and I figured you didn't need it and…"

"And you wanted to be Cinderella and see your Prince Charming?" Linnea hugged her, smiling from ear to ear. "Just like a fairy tale."

"Oh, god. I hope not."

Doesn't she know how sick and twisted fairy tales often are?

Linnea tilted her head to the side, the smile shrinking from her face.

"I'd hate to, you know, lose a shoe or turn into a pumpkin or something at the stroke of midnight," Katie quickly added, laughing at her own lame joke.

They must have found it funny, though. Chloe and Linnea both giggled in response.

Kyan put a glass of champagne in her hand. "C'mon, you need to meet everybody."

"Uh, Ky…" Linnea tapped his shoulder and spoke softly. "She's not old enough to have that."

And here we go.

Linnea's husband pressed a kiss to her lips and grinned. "If she's old enough for Brendan then she's old enough for a glass of champagne." He winked at Katie. "Maybe two. Don't tell me you never had a glass of wine before you turned twenty-one, princess."

Chloe giggled. "I know for a fact she did."

"I know she did too." He hugged her tighter and kissed the top of her head. "Let's introduce her to the crew."

Kyan swung her around and took a step to the space's private bar. Two men stood there sipping on drinks. One had long dark-brown hair, and the other blond. Both were gorgeous. "Katie, meet my brother, Dillon, and my brother-in-law, Kodiak. Guys, this is Brendan's girl, Katie."

Katie didn't bother correcting him. Everyone seemed deaf when she tried to. That she and Brendan were a thing seemed to be a foregone conclusion as far as they were concerned and she couldn't understand why.

Linnea's brother shook her hand, but Dillon leaned in for a hug. "Welcome, Katie. My cousin is a lucky guy, you're far too pretty for that beast."

"Um, thanks."

Then Kyan started at the far left of the big purple couch. She met all the band members of Venery without fainting, which she thought was a major accomplishment—well, they were famous and hella cute, weren't they? She said hello to Taylor and was introduced to Jesse—he hugged her too. Katie immediately understood why Chloe loved them both.

Finally, at the opposite end of the sofa were two women. They were obviously a couple, judging by the familiar way they touched each other—oh, and the matching wedding bands clued her in too. When she and Kyan reached them, a tall woman with mocha skin and hazel eyes stood up and clasped her hand in both of hers. Her smile was so friendly and warm, Katie immediately felt at ease.

Everyone is so darn nice.

"Katie, this is our dear friend, Monica, and her wife, Danielle. They're family." He clasped her shoulder. "Actually, all of us here are family. Monica and Brendan went to college together."

Monica squeezed the hand that was clasped in hers. "Hello, Katelyn. I'm so happy to meet the girl who's captured our Brendan's heart."

What?

"I did?"

"You did."

"Wait, you called me Katelyn."

She'd been introduced to everyone here as Katie. No one called her by her given name, except her mother when she was in trouble.

And Brendan.

Her eyes went wide as she looked up at the tall woman.

"I did." Monica nodded and winked. "He's a good man, but I think you already know that."

The house lights went dark, leaving the flameless candles on the tables as the only source of light. Chloe called out for Katie to join her by the bar.

"Go on, sweetie. I'm sure we'll be seeing each other."

Kyan took her hand from Monica. "Well, that's everyone. I'm sure Brendan will be back soon. He just went to check on things." And he brought her over to the bar.

Chloe handed Katie a cold glass of champagne and took the old one out of her hand. She'd barely taken a sip out of it. "Why'd the lights go out?"

"Oh." Chloe giggled. "It's showtime."

"Showtime?"

Chloe put an arm around her waist and they went to the railing that overlooked the main floor. "See the stage down there and that big-screen right in front of you?"

She nodded. "Yes."

"How do I put this?" Chloe pursed her lips. "Brendan can explain it better than I will, but this isn't a typical sex club—it's sex positive. That means that everyone's preferences, whatever they might be, are accepted here. And part of what the club does is teach people, um, how to do certain things safely. Since there's a party here tonight we're having kind of Halloween-themed, um…" She tilted her head from side to side while she thought. "…adult entertainment. Look, I know you're an adult, but…" Chloe paused.

"But?"

"I have to warn you, the entertainment can be pretty graphic— like X-rated explicit. Nothing is left to the imagination, get me? Tonight is all for show, but if you're not comfortable we can hang out somewhere you don't have to watch, okay?"

Now she was really intrigued.

"Look at me." Katie laughed. "I'm standing here in my

underwear. It can't get more uncomfortable than that. I think I'll be just fine."

"Okay then, but just say the word if you change your mind. I know it's a lot to take in." And Chloe hugged her, rocking her from side to side. "I'm so glad you came to see him."

Katie let out a brief chuckle. "My plan was to blend in and, um, observe. Not to see him, actually." She fiddled with the ruffle on her sleeve. "Unless I got very brave because I don't think he'd like it that I'm here. But I needed to know—to make sure."

"Know what?"

"What he does here…and…and if seeing him again." She stopped and glanced up to the dark void in the ceiling. "It sounds so stupid to say it out loud. If seeing him gave me butterflies."

Chloe grinned. Even in the dark Katie could make out her bright white smile. "Oh, I have a feeling with Brendan butterflies are guaranteed, sweetie."

The club music stopped and the hiss of a fog machine could be heard. Slow, sultry music with a dark hypnotic vibe began to fill the club as a red spotlight eerily illuminated the fog-filled stage. Venery's rhythm guitarist and shirtless drummer joined them at the railing.

"Isn't that the theme from *Vikings?*" Katie thought the music was familiar.

"It is." Matt winked. "Fever Ray. Great track, even if it is all synthesizer."

Says the guitar player.

"The vamps are next." Chloe was getting a little bouncy holding onto the railing. "I love all things vampire. I still mourn the cancelation of *True Blood*. It was my favorite show. And *The Vampire Diaries*. Until they killed that one too."

Bo nudged his way in between Katie and Chloe, putting an arm around each of them. "Vampires never die, baby girl. They exist forever on Netflix."

Katie couldn't help it. He made her laugh.

And once she started laughing she couldn't seem to stop. There she was, cast in a glow of red light, sandwiched between two rock stars she'd never have imagined meeting, in a sex club, barely dressed. The absurdity of it all wasn't lost on her.

Katie turned her head slightly toward Bo. His thumb casually skimming the skin on her neck. He just smiled. A wicked little smile on the face of a beautiful angel. She leaned forward a bit and noticed he was giving Chloe much the same attention on the other side.

Matt McCready casually leaned onto the railing with one booted foot. He rested his left elbow upon it, with his chin in his hand, and his right arm around her waist. Katie looked at him and he straightened, but he didn't let go of her.

His hand squeezed her side. "You okay?"

"I'm good, rhythm man." Katie smiled, swiping at the tears of laughter beneath her eyes as she nodded.

The music transitioned. It was different and yet the same. Deeper. Louder. Seductive. Angry-sounding strings, violin and bass, carried on with the notes of "If I Had a Heart" as two figures appeared on the platform below.

"Yeah!" Matt whooped, then he turned to her. "Hear that?"

Katie grinned.

"No synth. Pure strings, baby."

It was a man and a woman on the platform. The man was all in black. He was tall and wore a death cloak, his face concealed behind a hooded mask—or perhaps it was the cloak that was hooded. Katie wasn't sure.

The woman wore a similar cloak. Long waves flowed down her back. Everything about her was red, from her hair to her cloak to her full painted lips. The man came to stand behind her and parted her cloak. Red lace corset. Garter. Stockings. No panties. High-heeled boots. She untied the cloak at her neck and it fell to the floor, a crimson puddle at their feet.

The set on the stage was sparse. Only a stone altar with a silver bowl, candles and goblets placed on it, and a concrete slab—which she was sure was not actually made of concrete and stone, but from where she stood it looked like it. The scene reminded her of something out of an old Bela Lugosi film.

Katie glanced up to the screen over the stage, suspended from the ceiling in front of her. Large tattooed hands wrapped around the woman's throat and she tipped her head back to rest on his chest. Bo's thumb still slowly moved up and down, tracing the vein in her neck. Matt held her waist a little tighter. Or was she just imagining it?

One of the man's hands slid from the woman's throat to reach inside the red lace corset that hardly contained her ample breasts. He squeezed the flesh like he was angry with it and pinched her nipple until she screamed, then reached into his pocket and attached a clamp to her swollen nipple. A ruby-red gem, in the shape of a teardrop, dangled from it.

Matt squeezed her waist, his fingers caressing her hip. Now Katie knew for certain she wasn't imagining it. Was he just turned on or was he hitting on her? His gaze was riveted to the screen so she assumed it was the former. She couldn't say why, but it was getting to her too. It was getting too warm, tucked between him and Bo. Tiny beads of sweat erupted on her skin.

Where's Brendan?

Katie watched him from her peripheral vision. His gaze only moved from the screen to the stage below. The woman screamed again. Matt squeezed her hip. She returned her attention to the screen. A matching pair of blood-red gems dangled from her nipples, her corset gone. The woman appeared to be moaning, but the only thing Katie could hear was the hypnotic strains of the melody.

She felt his gaze on her and turned her head to look at him. Matt looked forlorn. Like she possessed something he knew she could never give him. His pupils were so dilated his eyes appeared black. He slowly licked his bottom lip and turned his head back toward the screen. His hand fell from her waist.

"Fuck," Bo muttered. "Red."

The hand around her neck disappeared. Bo was nudging Chloe on the other side of him and he leaned toward her, whispering in her ear. Katie glanced around to find everyone joining them at the railing. Jesse and Taylor on the other side of Chloe. Kit and Sloan took the spot next to Matt. Kodiak and Dillon stood behind Bo,

Kyan and Linnea sidled up behind her. Kyan put his hand on her shoulder. Monica and her wife were the only ones who remained seated on the purple sofa.

And where's Brendan?

Kyan squeezed her shoulder. He kindly smiled at her, almost like a parent would to reassure a child. "It's not what it looks like."

"What?"

She turned her head toward the screen. The woman was now totally nude, except for her boots, covered in blood. The man, kneeling at her feet, painted it on her thighs as she rubbed the red congealing liquid into her breasts. Katie, not quite sure what she was seeing, whipped her head back toward Kyan.

"If you're trying to tell me that's not real blood, I believe you, but it sure looks like it to me."

He released an exhale with a chuckle. "Corn syrup, chocolate syrup, and food coloring."

"I bet that's fun to clean up." She giggled.

From beside her, Matt muttered under his breath, "It can be."

Katie looked to the screen. The man was licking stage blood from the woman's thigh.

Ohhh.

Bo hooked his arm back around her shoulders. "Why don't we all get a drink and sit back down, yeah?"

"I'm all for that." Kyan gently pulled on her shoulder. "C'mon."

It all happened so fast. Katie thought it was part of the act at first.

The woman yanked the hood from the man's head, but Katie still couldn't see his face.

Then she pulled a knife from her stocking. The silver metal glinted red under the light.

The blade quickly sliced down the center of the man's chest, cutting his flesh.

Blood.

Oh my god!

There was so much blood.

She heard herself scream. Katie couldn't tell what was real and what wasn't.

The man peeled the knife out of the woman's hand and threw it to the floor.

With an arm across her throat, he held the woman down on the concrete slab and lifted his head.

Even contorted with rage, Katie recognized his face.

Blood dripped from the slash on his chest and the woman tried to catch it on her tongue.

"Katie."

She couldn't tell you who it was that said her name, but she knew it was Matt who hugged her to his side, who kissed her hair.

There's Brendan.

Fourteen

ucking bitch!

    He didn't feel the blade slice his skin until he looked down and saw blood bubbling to the surface. Brendan wrenched the knife from her fingers, tossed it to the ground, and grabbed Angelica by her throat. Was she on something? She laughed maniacally while he forcefully pushed her onto her back.

"What the fuck is wrong with you?"

She kept on laughing, writhing beneath him, covered in sticky red syrup, as he held her in place. Brendan lifted his head. Where was Axel? Blood dripped from his chest and she opened her mouth wide. He clenched his jaw so hard he thought the bone might crack. Rage consumed him. He wanted to choke the life right out of her.

"Go on. Fucking do it," Angelica rasped from under his arm as if she could read his thoughts. "I want you to."

She kept wiggling and writhing in the congealing mess, grabbing at his arms, her long nails daggers in his skin. He fought to maintain his hold on her. "Crazy bitch."

Angelica laughed. She let go of his arms. Her hands snaked up his chest, smearing the blood across his pecs. "Salena wanted me to give you a message…" And she sucked a bloody finger into her mouth.

Just the mention of her name. That's all it took for him to see nothing but red.

"…no more foreplay, baby. She's ready to fuck."

'This isn't the end, baby. It's foreplay.'

Brendan wrapped his hand around her throat, just enough to shut her up.

"Fucking cunt misses this big cock, does she?" He unzipped and snatched a condom from the silver bowl with his free hand, tore it open with his teeth and sheathed himself in black latex before he had time to think.

"I've got I message for you to take back to her." He grinned, flipping her over and pushing her face into the hard surface. "I'll see her in hell first."

He didn't touch her. Didn't prime her. Didn't even check to see if she was ready for him. Blind rage replaced all reason. Brendan hit bottom in one furious thrust.

And he didn't stop.

He did it again and again and again.

Salena was vicious, vengeful, and vile.

For Kyan and Linnea.

He closed his eyes and pounded into her messenger harder.

Salena hurt people he loved.

For Chloe, Jesse, and Taylor. Venery. Shelly Tompkins and her baby too.

He pounded harder and faster and harder and faster. Blood and sweat dripped from his chest to her back.

Salena threatened his family. His club.

For the mayor and the priest.

He was going to make the viper pay for everything she'd done.

No one fucks with my family. No. One.

Brendan pummeled Angelica's cunt with his cock. She moaned beneath him in ecstasy. Sucking on her fingers, fucking euphoric. The bitch cut him. She didn't deserve any pleasure from this.

'You wanna fuck, Sal?'

'We'll fuck, but you're not gonna like it.'

He stopped.

Brendan pulled the condom off and let it fall from his fingers.

"What are you doing?" Angelica lifted her head in protest. "I'm not finished."

"I am."

He walked off and left her in a bloody mess on the platform.

A member of his staff stood ready with a towel. "Jesus, she really cut you!"

"No shit." He wiped at the blood on his chest. "I'm going to shower. Tell Axel to get her cleaned up and bring her to my office. Got that?"

"Yes, sir."

"See? I tried to tell you I'm not his girl."

Chloe hugged her. "Sweetie, that wasn't what you think it was."

"It's exactly what I think it was," Katie snickered. "It's okay. I wanted to know what Brendan does here and I figured…well, now I know."

Linnea tried to take her hand, but she pulled it from her grasp. "Time for Cinderella to go home." She felt like such an idiot. "It's way past midnight and the ball is over. For me anyway. Goodnight."

She turned to leave, but Kyan stopped her. "Katie." He placed a gentle hand on her arm. "You should stay. Give Brendan a chance to explain."

He was so kind. Katie managed a small smile. "He doesn't need to explain anything to me, Kyan. Thank you, all of you, for being so nice. I really need to go home now."

"Then I'm taking you," Matt insisted, taking her hand. "I won't let you go alone."

She nodded. Tears rushed to burn behind her eyes. Katie blinked to keep them at bay. Crying was the last thing she wanted to do in front of these people. They reached the set of double doors that would take them outside. Matt threw his arm around her waist as the man in black opened it. The same man who had let her in.

"I hope you enjoyed the ball. Goodnight, miss."

Oh, yeah. Had a swell time.

When they got to the corner, Katie stopped to pull the mask from her face. She tossed it into the trash. Matt shook his head with a smirk. "So, what are you going to do now, Miss Katie?"

She responded with a halfhearted shrug. "I don't know. Take a long hot bath and go to bed."

"I know it's none of my business, and I'll probably kick myself for this later, but I think you should listen to Ky."

"And what?" She cocked her head at him.

His hand squeezed her side. "See what Brendan has to say." They were in front of Beanie's. "Is this you?"

"Yeah." Katie pointed up. "I live upstairs."

"How about you make us some coffee?"

Her eyebrows shot up.

"Just to talk," he added.

"Okay." She mustered up a smile. "Yeah, sure."

He followed her inside the shop and Katie locked the door behind him. She turned on a small light behind the counter. "What would you like?"

"Whatever's easy."

Matt leaned on the counter with his elbows and watched her prepare the French press. Five minutes later Katie pressed a cup into his hands and poured one for herself. He took a seat on one of the sofas that lined the wall and patted the spot beside him.

"Thanks." He took a sip of his coffee. "This is good."

He cleared his throat and turned in his seat so he was facing her. Katie wasn't in the mood to politely chat about the weather, or current events, or to talk about anything at all. She really did just want to wash this night away with a long, hot bath and crawl into bed. Matt had that look on his face, though—that look someone gets when they have something to say, but they're trying to come up with the words. The bath would have to wait. She probably wouldn't have been able sleep anyway. He opened his mouth to speak.

"We grew up together. All of us." Matt put his cup down and

took her hand. "I've known Brendan my entire life and what you saw tonight…that's not who he is."

"He owns a sex club, Matt. I'd say—"

"That's what he does, yeah, but he's so much more than that. Isn't there more to you than this cup of coffee?"

"He fucked—"

"Yeah, he fucked her. She cut him, and I don't think that was in the script either. Now let me finish." Matt squeezed her hand. "I'm not gonna tell you he's a saint, 'cause he ain't." And he chuckled. "Look at that, I rhymed there."

The guy's a poet and he…nah. I'm not gonna say it.

Katie chewed the inside corner of her lip instead.

"But I will tell you he's probably the best man I know. Works hard. Plays hard. Fucks hard." He smirked and gave her hand another squeeze. "But he loves hard too."

"Why are you telling me this?"

"I'm a musician in a pretty well-known band, and I know what it's like to be pre-judged for what you do and not who you are. I get to fuck a lot of women, but I never get to love any. Want to know why?"

Hearing that made her sad for him.

"Why?"

"No one ever gives me the chance." He lifted one shoulder in a shrug. "It's usually one of two things. Women either want to be with me for the money or the fame…or they assume, because of who I am, because I play in a band and all that shit, that I can't keep my dick in my pants. They get all paranoid and it's over before it even starts."

"So, you're telling me…"

"Give him the chance. Brendan would never betray anyone he loves. Not ever. I know I wouldn't," he implored before softening his voice. "Besides, if you don't, you'll always wonder if you should have. And that little piece of you that's left wondering won't be there for the next guy that comes along. That guy deserves to have all of you, every beautiful piece of you. Same as you'd want every piece of him."

Before Katie could even process what he'd said, Matt took her face in his palms and placed a sweet, gentle kiss on her lips.

"Goodnight, Katie."

He got up from the sofa. She let him out and relocked the door behind him.

She didn't know what to think and she had a lot to think about, didn't she? Then again, maybe she didn't. After tonight, she might never hear from Brendan again anyway. Would she be okay with that? Katie picked up the cups and the press pot and put them in the sink. She'd think about everything tomorrow.

She tiptoed up the stairs, careful not to make a sound, so she wouldn't wake up Kelly. If her aunt saw her dressed like this how would she ever explain it? Luckily, the loft was quiet and dark when she opened the door and made a stealthy beeline for her room. There was a note on her pillow from Kelly—she'd gone to a party of her own.

Stripping out of her costume, Katie threw a robe on over her white satin underwear, and checked Kelly's room to see if she'd come back. She hadn't. That meant Katie could have that bath without twenty questions about the Greek Row party she hadn't actually gone to. Was it her fault Kelly just assumed that's where she was going?

Yes, it is, Katie. When did you turn into such a liar?

Since she'd met a tall beautiful stranger with diamond-blue eyes, that's when.

Lies of omission are still lies, aren't they?

Filling the tub with hot water, Katie tossed in her favorite jasmine and soymilk bath bomb. After a soothing soak and a good night's sleep she hoped she'd find some clarity. Her head was a muddled mess.

She laid back in the scented water and closed her eyes.

But she couldn't unsee what she saw.

Like she couldn't unfeel what she felt.

And she let the tears fall.

Fifteen

He couldn't look at himself in the mirror.

Brendan turned the shower on and stripped off his soiled clothes. He threw them in the trash. Stepping into the small tiled stall, he adjusted the temperature of the water as hot as he could stand it. He was angry with himself. Disgusted. Maybe once he scrubbed the evidence of tonight's barbarity off his skin he wouldn't feel as repulsed in it as he did right now.

He turned to face the spray and hissed as the water hit the cut that ran down the center of his chest. It bled like a bitch, but he didn't think it needed stitches. Might leave a nice scar, though. Brendan took an angry fist to the shower wall and released a pent-up roar.

Salena.

How the fuck had he underestimated her?

Taylor and Jesse both warned him the night they all met her that she was no good. He laughed them off. In retrospect he should have heeded their warning, but he was twenty-six and thinking with his dick at the time. She was beautiful, she loved to fuck—probably more than he did—and she knew the club scene. And he'd had the idea for the Red Door long before then. Her knowledge and her contacts could prove useful.

Venery's first album had just come out and what would become their first hit song was finally getting airplay. They weren't famous yet, but they were definitely local celebrities. He, Dillon, and Jesse went to see them play at the Aragon that night, and ended up going to the gig after-party at a private club downtown.

Salena zeroed in on them the minute they passed through the velvet ropes. Then she followed them up to VIP and set her sights on him—well, she fucked him first. Brendan wasn't sure why, since he wasn't one of the future rock stars in the group. They hadn't been there thirty minutes when she took his cock out of his pants and enthusiastically sucked him off while everyone watched. Quite the show. Within an hour that VIP room was filled with naked rutting bodies, and they'd all taken their turn with her. More than once. Taylor and Jesse were the only exceptions.

And that was more than okay with him.

She wanted his dick.

He wanted her cunt.

Neither one of them wanted anything more than that.

He should have listened to Taylor, though. Brendan never should have trusted her and he should have ended their arrangement a long time ago. He should have noticed her obsession with Kyan, but he didn't, and by the time he did, it was too late. She'd already turned into a psycho bitch bunny boiler.

So the Salena shitstorm was all on him.

And it was up to him to end it.

He finished his shower and threw on a pair of jeans and a black button-up. Not exactly club attire, but he was done tonight anyway. After Brendan dealt with Angelica and saw his cousins, he was going home. He was dabbing some antibiotic ointment on the cut when he heard the blast of music as the door to his office opened.

As he stepped out of the small bathroom in his office, Angelica demurely seated herself on the sofa. Bare-faced. Hair wet from her shower. Dillon was perched on one arm, Taylor the other. Axel stood in front of the door.

Party's over, vamp chick.

Angelica folded her hands in her lap and lowered her gaze, attempting to appear contrite. He didn't buy it for a second. Brendan stood in front of his desk, and crossing his arms over his unbuttoned shirt, leaned back against it, stretching out his legs in front of him. He was still angry, but it was in check, his initial rage now tempered.

She cleared her throat and raised her gaze to his. "You don't have to tell me. I know I'm out of here regardless, but I'm sorry—"

"Sorry?" Dillon interrupted. "Look at what you did—you sliced him!" he yelled. "He should press charges."

"He'll be fine." Angelica smirked at Dillon. "I know what I'm doing."

"You want to tell us what that was all about?" Dillon threw his hands up in the air, then looked at Brendan. "And why were *you* out there? Where the fuck is Milo?"

Brendan winked at her with a grin. "Yes, Angelica. Tell him, and don't leave anything out."

She huffed out a breath and looked up at the ceiling. "Salena made sure he wouldn't make it here tonight."

Taylor's eyes widened. Brendan could see Axel struggling to keep his expression impassive. Dillon looked momentarily dumbfounded. He shook his head like maybe he hadn't heard her right, then smashed his fist on the side table. "What. The. Fuck?" He rubbed the side of his hand. "Spill it, Angelica. All of it."

"She called me yesterday. Said she needed me to do her a favor and get a message to Brendan." Angelica shrugged while her head bobbed from side to side, like she didn't understand what the big deal was.

Dillon's brow shot up. "And what was the message?"

"No more foreplay," Brendan supplied. "She's ready to fuck."

Dillon wouldn't get it. He wasn't at last year's masquerade ball when she uttered that threat, but Taylor was there. He looked at Brendan. No words needed to be spoken. Taylor got her message loud and clear.

Angelica allowed a wicked giggle to escape. "And she was quite insistent on exactly how she wanted the message delivered." She glanced up at him again. "Sal's my friend."

"Salena does not have *friends*," Brendan sneered. "She uses and manipulates people."

"You don't know shit, Bren. Sal has lots of friends. Important friends." Angelica winked. "I'm her friend. Besides, I got what I wanted—to taste you and fuck you." She swiped her tongue slowly back and forth across her bottom lip and grinned. "Just like she said I would. Win-win."

"She certainly sounds like she's sorry to me," Taylor said, rolling his eyes.

"I guess I'm really not," Angelica responded with a scornful smirk. "Well, maybe just a little."

Brendan had heard more than enough. He just wanted this girl out of his club and out of his sight. "Axel."

He didn't have to say anything else.

"Got it, boss."

Once they left and the door closed behind them, Taylor and Dillon slid off the arms to the cushions of the sofa. Brendan grabbed a bottle from his desk and poured a finger of whiskey into a glass.

"I need a drink." He turned to the sofa. "How about you?"

Taylor and Dillon exchanged a glance, then his cousin spoke. "Your, uh…your girl was here."

His mind blanked for a second.

My girl?

Fuck!

No, Dillon couldn't possibly be talking about Katelyn. He wanted her to be his, and after today she *was* going to be his. But Dillon didn't know that. No one knew that. She couldn't have gotten in here anyway. So who the fuck was he talking about?

"What?"

Taylor spoke up. "Coffee girl…Katie was here."

Brendan squinted his eyes shut, as if that could cancel out the words that followed. A lead weight dropped in his gut. He heard the door to his office open, but he didn't bother looking to see who'd come in.

"Bren." It was Chloe. She hugged him. "Are you okay?"

"Where is she?"

"Matt took her home."

His hands balled into fists at his sides. Brendan opened his eyes. "I have to go."

He snatched his keys and his wallet and his phone, stuffing them into pockets.

Chloe placed her hand on his arm. "Bren. Wait." She pointed to his chest. "Let me bandage that."

He silently nodded.

"I know you want to, Brendan, but don't go over there now," Chloe advised him as she wrapped him in gauze. "Katie needs time to…to think, and you need time to get your head straight and figure out what you're going to say to her so you don't make things worse."

He was going. His head was perfectly straight. Brendan could only imagine what must be going through hers.

Brendan buttoned up his shirt. "You don't need to figure out what to say when you tell the truth. And that's what I'm going to do."

She hugged him again. "I really like her, Brendan."

Me too.

It was after two in the morning.

Brendan realized it was way too late to be knocking on her door, but he couldn't let this wait. He'd always planned to be completely transparent and honest with her. About everything. His feelings. His parents. His past. His sexual ideology. The Red Door. All of it.

Baring not just your body and your mind, but your soul. Sharing your secrets and your dreams. Your thoughts and desires. Vulnerability. Acceptance. It was everything, wasn't it? What was the point of a relationship otherwise?

Trust.

Brendan understood he'd have to work even harder to earn that from her now.

But he would.

He tapped softly on her door.

Footfalls sounded from behind it. "Did you forget your keys, Kelly?" And it opened.

She was beautiful, standing there in an oversized T-shirt. Face devoid of makeup. Hair piled on top of her head in a tumble of messy waves. Her stormy eyes were red-rimmed, so he knew she'd been crying. Because of him. Again. Knowing that was a punch in the gut. Her lips parted, like she was going to say something, but no words came out.

Brendan didn't hesitate. He pulled her into his arms and held her tightly against him. "I'm so sorry." He kissed the top of her head. "You've got to know that. I'm so fucking sorry."

Still, she didn't speak. Her upper lip trembled.

"Can we talk?"

She just shrugged, but she didn't say no. Katelyn stepped aside to let him in, then she turned around and walked into the loft. He closed the door and followed her. She plopped onto her bed and hugged a pillow to her lap.

"Talk."

He sat beside her on the bed, pulled the pillow away, and took her hands in his. "What you saw at the club tonight—that wasn't supposed to happen. It wasn't planned. I just reacted, and badly." God, this was more difficult than he thought. "I'm not making excuses, but there's a lot you don't understand yet…"

"I understand more than you think." She pulled her hands out of his grasp. "And it's not like we're anything, so you don't owe me an explanation. I went there tonight because…" She looked up at the ceiling and shook her head. "…because I wanted to see what you do there. I guess I got what I wanted."

"That isn't true."

"What isn't?"

"Any of it." He pulled her onto his lap so she straddled him and ran his fingers through her silky hair. God, he loved how it felt. "I owe you more than a lousy fucking explanation because we *are* going to be something, sweet girl. Trust me, I wouldn't be apologizing if I felt otherwise. It wasn't my plan to put my dick in her—or anyone else."

"What was your plan then?" She gazed in his eyes, tension easing out of her muscles.

He kissed her forehead and grinned. "I was going to walk into Beanie's today for a cup of coffee and walk out with you."

"You would have been very disappointed."

Brendan could feel her smirk. "Oh? Why is that?"

"I'm off today."

He chuckled, brushing his lips across her brow. "Good."

"And why is that?"

"You have a date with your man today, sweet girl." He smiled against her skin.

Katelyn tipped her head back and glanced up at him. "I do?"

"You do."

Brendan held her face in his hands and brought his lips to hers, tender and sweet. So fucking sweet. Katelyn locked her fingers behind his neck and slipped her tongue inside his mouth. He wished tonight had never happened so he could just be with her—only her. She made him crazy. With every sweep of her tongue their kiss became more voracious. He brushed his thumbs over her T-shirt, where her nipples were pebbled beneath the fabric. She moaned at his touch.

"Fuck," she hissed. "Brendan."

He pulled the shirt over her head and gazing at her beautiful tits, he lightly touched her bare nipples. "I only want you, baby, and I'll tattoo your name on my dick to prove it to you."

"Can I watch?"

Yeah, he loved this girl.

"Absofuckinglutely."

"Brendan," she whispered and wriggled on his lap.

He tweaked her nipples. "Is this what you want, baby girl?"

Katelyn nodded and he latched onto her breast, sucking it hard into his mouth. She tumbled back onto the bed and he went with her, never letting go of her nipple. His fingers reached for the other one to find her fingers were already there. Twisting. Pinching.

Thatagirl.

Brendan lifted his head from her breast to watch her. As soon as he let her nipple go, her fingers found it. He pulled her panties off. She was so wet they were saturated with her arousal.

"Katelyn." Her eyes opened, but still she twisted her swollen nipples. "Touch yourself, baby. Rub your clit. I want to watch you come. Can you do that for me?"

She nodded.

"Words, baby. Always use your words, okay?"

"Okay. Yes."

"Good girl."

One hand left her breast to travel to her pussy. She parted her lips with two fingers, circled her clit, and bit her lip. "Can I watch you too?"

He unbuttoned his jeans. "You want to see what's yours?"

"Yes."

He unzipped and took his cock out. Brendan gave it a firm tug and let it slap his belly. He waited to see her reaction, for her eyes to widen or her jaw to drop—that's what he was used to seeing. It wasn't her reaction at all. Katelyn licked her lips and her pupils flared. She rubbed her clit faster and harder.

"That's it, sweet girl." He wrapped his fingers around his cock and squeezed. "Are you thinking about how good this big dick will feel inside you?"

"Yes."

"Only you, baby. Only you get this dick." He stroked himself. "Do you understand?"

"Yes."

She didn't yet, but she would.

He belonged to her.

She belonged to him.

He wanted to be inside her so badly. To make love to her. And once he'd earned her trust, when Katelyn truly believed that he was committed solely to her, he would.

Yes, he fucking would.

Sixteen

It's funny how everything feels so much better in the light of day.

Late-morning sunshine streamed in through the blinds. Katie woke to the sound of bells tolling from the church down the street. The day after Halloween was the feast of All Saints, wasn't it? Or was it All Souls' Day? Maybe she should have paid closer attention during those Saturday morning catechism classes when she was a kid. She still got them mixed up.

Whichever.

Brendan was picking her up at noon.

Was she happy about that? Hell, yes!

Katie was over-the-moon ecstatic, in spite of the reservations she had after last night's performance. She laid in her bed and thought about everything long after Brendan kissed her goodnight and slipped out of the loft. Kelly had returned from her party not five minutes later. And today, sitting on her bed that still faintly smelled of him, bathed in glorious sunshine, the world behind the red door faded into obscurity.

She was going to have to tell Kelly, though. Maybe not about the club, but she wanted her to know that she was going out with Brendan. Katie didn't want to sneak around or hide him from her. She knew what her aunt's opinion of him was, and maybe Kelly was right, maybe he wasn't *"boyfriend material,"* but Katie had a feeling Brendan was going to prove her wrong.

She hoped so anyway.

After showering, exfoliating, conditioning, and moisturizing, Katie sat at her vanity. Halloween was over, so no big fake eyelashes today. She wanted Brendan to see her authentic self, still it was their first date and she wanted to look pretty.

Now, what to wear?

Rifling through her closet, Katie didn't have a clue. Brendan had only told her they were going to one of his favorite places in the city and that they'd be outside. She opted for cute and comfortable with a big chunky V-neck cardigan over a delicate bralette top of scalloped silk, faded jeans ripped at the knees, and flat-heeled booties. She tucked the front of the sweater into her jeans.

There!

Kelly would approve of her outfit at least.

It wasn't quite noon when Katie ambled down from the loft to Beanie's. Kelly looked awfully chipper considering she couldn't have gotten more than a couple hours of sleep. She slipped behind the counter and started brewing some espresso. Brendan said he wanted to walk in there for a cup of coffee and walk out with her, so she was going to make that happen.

She was concentrating on pouring the steamed milk when Kelly made her way over to her. "Whatcha doin'?"

"Shh." She didn't want to fuck up his heart this time. "Ta-da! And *that* is latte art."

Kelly laughed while giving her the once-over. "Are you going somewhere?"

"Yeah, I have a date." Katie smiled as she snapped the lids on the lattes.

"Eek!" Kelly hugged her. "You and Cam got back together?"

"No," his deep, sexy-as-sin voice answered from the other side of the counter. "They didn't."

She and Kelly turned around at the same time to find him casually leaning against the distressed wood bar wearing a leather jacket and a lazy smirk. Katie handed him his coffee. Brendan popped off the lid to look at his heart. That smirk of his widened into a full-blown smile.

"Brendan is your date?"

"Hey, Kelly." He winked. "Car's parked out front, baby. Ready to go?"

Katie smiled wide to match him. "I'm ready."

Brendan brought her to the city zoo.

Katie had always loved coming here with her mom, her brother, and Kelly on their summer trips to the city. That this was one of Brendan's favorite places, and that he shared that with her, made her feel closer to him somehow.

They strolled by the lily pool. Brendan held her arm that was linked through his. The water, dotted with fallen leaves, reflected the trees with their brilliant foliage like glass. It was breathtaking and they stopped to take it all in.

"It's beautiful here." Katie glanced up at Brendan and smiled.

Brendan smiled back, his eyes sparkling even bluer than the brilliant November sky. He tucked her hair behind her ear. "So beautiful."

He gathered Katie in his arms and hoisted her up like he had on that magical Midsummer's Eve night. It felt like it was just yesterday yet seemed like forever ago. She wrapped her arms around his neck and her legs around his waist. He kissed her, right there in front of the lily pool, and she felt them.

Butterflies.

A kaleidoscope of wings took flight in her belly at his soft, tender kiss. Katie held onto him tightly. She found it difficult to catch her breath and inhaled deeply through her nose. Bergamot. Sandalwood. Amber and musk. Brendan. She kissed him like his breath gave her life and his lips nourished her soul. Because they did.

Her breasts pressed into his chest. She could feel her nipples harden beneath the delicate silk and wanted them in his hands. His mouth. He held her with one hand splayed between her shoulders and slid the other up her thigh, past her belly, to cup her breast over her sweater. He gently squeezed and then lowered her feet to solid ground.

He didn't let her go, though. Brendan held her close and kissed the top of her head, rubbing his nose in her hair. Katie closed her eyes. If this was just a daydream, she'd joyfully stay lost in it forever.

It was no dream, though.

It was blissfully real.

"C'mon." He took her arm and they left the lily pool behind them. "Let's go see the lions."

Brendan got them a table in the warmth of the sun with a view of the lion's den, though the lion himself was nowhere to be seen. He handed her a burger and sat down beside her. They shared a big basket of fries. He threw a fry up in the air and caught it between his teeth. Katie laughed.

He chewed it, then swallowed and grinned. "We used to have contests to see who could throw their food the highest and catch it."

"Oh, so it's not just French fries then?"

"Nope. Popcorn, peas, noodles, chips. Whatever was on the table." He laughed. "Dillon tried it with mashed potatoes once. Didn't turn out so well."

She snorted and Brendan laughed even harder. "Go on. You try it."

"Me?"

He nodded.

"Okay."

Katie tossed a French fry in the air and caught it. Half of it dangled from between her lips. Brendan leaned in and kissed her. He ate the dangling half and she swallowed the other.

"Good catch."

A cloud blocked the sun and Katie shivered. Brendan dumped their trash and took her hand. "Are you cold, baby?"

"A little."

"C'mon." He wrapped his arm around her and tucked her against him. "Let's go get you warm." They started walking. "We can come back at Christmastime when the zoo is all lit up, would you like that?"

Katie smiled up at him. "Yeah."

They got in his silver 'Vette and he cranked up the heat. It was a cool car, probably as old as her, though she didn't think it prudent to point that out, so Katie said nothing as she rubbed her hands together in front of the warm air blowing from the vent. Brendan took her cold hands and squeezed them between his own. Then he brought her hands to his lips and kissed them.

She didn't want the day to end. Brendan drove past First Avenue and Katie wondered where he was taking her. Then he turned onto Third. The back end of Coventry Park whirred by the window, and he slowed the car to a complete stop. A gate swung open.

"Where are we?"

"Park Place." He smiled at her from the driver's seat. The gate closed behind them. "I live here."

It was a dead-end street with five magnificent three-flat buildings on either side. Katie could see the edge of the park beyond.

"Wait…is that Chloe?"

Chloe and Jesse were coming through a small gate from the park with two big dogs. She turned in her seat to look at Brendan.

He shrugged with a grin. "We all live here, actually." He pointed to the buildings on the left. "That's me, Chloe, Jesse, and Taylor, Kit, Sloan, and Monica and Danielle." Then he pointed to their right. "Office/recording studio, Linnea and Kyan, Dillon, Matt, and Bo."

Holy shit.

"Those aren't apartments?"

He winked. "Not anymore." Then he turned into the alley on the left side and pulled into his detached garage.

They entered the house from the brick-paved patio into the kitchen. Katie's jaw dropped. Dark-stained wood floors. Black quartz countertops. White cabinetry. Old combined with new. All the modern conveniences with a vintage aesthetic, and it was magazine-worthy gorgeous.

Brendan's arms came around her waist from behind her. He bent his head and kissed her neck. "I've imagined doing exactly this from the moment I met you."

She turned in his arms. "Doing what?"

And standing in the middle of his kitchen he kissed her. "That."

"Oh." She smiled. "Yeah?"

"Yeah." He took her hand. " This is a first for me, you know. C'mon. Let me show you around the house."

Five bedrooms and she didn't count how many bathrooms later, they were back downstairs where they started. Katie followed Brendan into the family room off the kitchen. They got comfortable on the sofa and he flipped on the television. Neither one of them looked at it, though.

"You said this is a first for you." Katie glanced up at him from under his arm. "What did you mean? What's a first for you?"

"You." He pulled her onto his lap. "Us. All of this."

Katie rested her hands on his broad shoulders. She still wasn't sure what he meant. His hands moved up and down her back, over the silk and beneath her sweater. Her hands slid from his shoulders and down his back, pulling him closer, until their lips were just a breath apart.

"I want to kiss you again," she breathed.

He softly took her lips with his. "And I want to do more than kiss you."

That was quite evident. The erection in his jeans wedged against her bottom as she straddled his lap. Katie already knew that this was the man she'd give her virginity to one day. She'd known it the very first time she kissed him. But was she ready for it to be today?

"I never planned on you." He held her to him tightly, his lips in her hair. "Yet here you are. And I'm keeping you."

If ever there was a moment when a kiss wasn't just a kiss, it was this one. In a tenderly given gesture of force, Brendan gripped her hair in his fingers, and with an arm secured around her waist, captured her lips with his. His tongue took control of her mouth and Katie heard him speak a thousand words without having to say a thing. Want. Need. Craving. Desire. It seared into her core like a hot brand. And in that moment he claimed ownership of her but she'd never felt more free.

Seventeen

H e couldn't sleep.

It was after five in the morning, probably closer to six, and after another tedious night at the club Brendan lay there awake in his bed. Since when did he think of a night behind the red door as tedious? Since it kept him from spending time with Katelyn, that's when.

Yeah, he was fucked.

He hadn't planned on taking her to his house that day they went to the zoo, but then he couldn't have known just how much he wouldn't want that day to end. How much he'd enjoy her company. Just being with her. Talking to her. Kissing her.

Katelyn stayed until midnight. He ordered groceries and they cooked chicken piccata for dinner together. She told him funny little stories about growing up in corn country, as she called it, and her younger brother. How everyone in her family had names that began with the letter K. Then she fell asleep against his shoulder during the Bears game.

And fuck if he didn't like it.

But while Brendan was home all day, Katelyn was either at Beanie's or on campus. He'd stop in for coffee to see her on his way to the club every day, of course. Steal her away for breakfast or lunch or a walk in Coventry Park. But every night spent in the plum-velvet booth felt like time wasted. Drinking with the guys and watching Dillon go through pussy like a kid in a candy store. Coming home to an empty house and a lonely bed.

Not today though.

It was Sunday.

And that meant two things.

The Red Door was closed and he'd get to spend the day with his sweet girl.

Brendan managed to get in a few hours of sleep. Katelyn was helping Kelly and someone he'd never seen before arrange pastries and cookies in the display case. As soon as she looked up and saw him, she came out from behind the counter with a smile on her face that could light up the entire fucking world. It lit up his anyway.

Fucked indeed.

"And who is this tall and mighty fine drink of water?"

The unfamiliar voice was deep. Sassy. Each word delivered with sharp precision.

Katelyn giggled at the man behind the counter. He had black Shirley Temple curls that went past his shoulders and wore a wide headband with a bow, red lipstick, and dangling earrings that sparkled with rhinestones. "Leo, meet Brendan."

Leo?

"Ohh. Girl, now you didn't tell me he looked like that."

Katelyn stood high on her tiptoes and pecked Brendan on the cheek. "Bren, this is Leonardo Hill. Our new baker."

The flamboyant man fanned himself like it was a scorching summer day, never mind that it was close to freezing outside. "And assistant manager, thank you."

"That too." She grinned as she grabbed her coat. "Bye, Kell."

Kelly pulled her head out of the display case. "Bye, sweetie. Don't have too much fun now. You hear me?"

And laughing, Katelyn dragged him out of the shop.

Brendan looked back at the door, shaking his head. "Who was that?"

"Leo? Kelly hired him to replace Stacy. Isn't he awesome? I just love him!"

"Fabulous." He chuckled. "And what did Kelly mean? Don't have too much fun."

"Sex," she answered so matter-of-factly he raised his brow. "I think she imagines us in your red room or something."

"I don't have a red room." He grinned.

Not in the house anyway, but if Katelyn ever wanted to play, and perhaps one day she would…well, the club sat empty all day.

"You don't?"

"Did you see a red room?"

"Well, no."

Was that a pout? She almost looked disappointed, but he was still learning all her tells so he couldn't say for sure. Of course they hadn't had sex yet, and Katelyn had never had sex, so that was not a conversation for today. Soon, though.

Brendan pulled onto a side street, found a parking spot, and fed the meter. It was just a short walk from here to where they were going. He opened the passenger door and she glanced up at him, smiling as she always did. So beautiful. He helped her out of the low seat.

"Where are we going?"

"You'll see." He tucked her against his side as they walked to the theatre.

But it wasn't just any theatre. The Music Box was an icon, built almost a century ago, when silent movies were still all the rage, it was one of the first designed for talking pictures. As they turned the corner and walked toward the ticket window, Brendan watched her eyes light up as she read the marquee. He was taking her to a matinee screening of the old Jimmy Stewart film, *It's a Wonderful Life*.

They stopped at concessions for Cokes and a big tub of popcorn with extra butter to share. They actually melted real butter here. None of that artificial shit you got at the modern megaplexes in the suburbs.

"This place is incredible!"

Truth. There was no place else quite like it. It was said that each of the seven hundred seats inside the Music Box had a story to tell, and they were about to add theirs.

"Just wait until we get to our seats."

Santa, accompanied by an organist, was leading a sing-along. Brendan chose a row, and with his hand at the small of her back, guided Katelyn to her seat. Then he waited. It didn't take a minute for her to notice the ceiling with its twinkling stars and moving cloud formations. Her head tipped back, looking up at it in awe.

Brendan held her hand, like he was on a date in high school. Except he'd never bothered dating in high school, so this was a first for him too. "I used to come here a lot as a kid. Reruns of old classics with my mom. The annual sing-along to *White Christmas* with my cousins. *The Rocky Horror Picture Show* when we got older—we'll have to do that next year. I haven't been here since college, though."

Since the accident.

He squeezed her hand. *Next year.* He was already making plans for next year.

Katelyn laid her head on his shoulder. "Thank you."

He didn't ask her what for. He's the one who should be thanking her. Brendan put his arm around her and tossed a kernel of popped corn high in the air.

"Good catch." And she smiled.

George decided his life was worth living and Clarence earned his wings.

They filed out as the end credits rolled and as they walked through the lobby, near the concessions stand, Katelyn tugged on his sleeve. "Bren." She tugged again and tilted her head toward the line of people waiting for popcorn. "That's her—the lady who gave me the invite to the ball. There with that man and her little boy."

Get the fuck out of here!

Salena? And Eric Brantley?

Eric was Hugh Brantley's son. The little boy must be Hugh's grandson. Salena sure as hell wasn't anybody's mother. Did she move onto Eric as soon as he put his father in a nursing home or was he one of the important friends Angelica claimed she had? The little boy held onto his father's hand as he kissed Salena.

And that answers that.

Brendan wanted to get Katelyn out of there before Salena spotted them together. He didn't care to have an encounter with the viper, especially with a child present. Besides, he had the fridge and pantry stocked so he and Katelyn could cook dinner together again. He just wanted to enjoy the day with her and not have it tainted by that bitch.

They almost made it to the door before Salena turned around and saw them. She grinned that evil bitch grin. And then she waved.

He didn't acknowledge her. Brendan held Katelyn's elbow and ushered her out the door. She looked up at him, her eyebrow arched. "Do you know her?"

"I wish I could say I didn't."

He didn't sugarcoat it, but he didn't go into every little explicit detail either. Brendan recounted how he met Salena and how she'd been the hostess at the Red Door, until he let her go last year, as he made the short drive home. And once they were inside the house, standing in the kitchen, he didn't want to talk about Salena anymore. He knew this conversation wasn't finished, but he wanted to kiss his sweet girl.

Before she could take off her coat, Brendan scooped Katelyn up and sat her on top of the island. He caged her between his legs and brushed her hair back, the silky strands gliding between his fingers. Her turquoise eyes looked right into his, in a way no one had ever looked at him before. If he hadn't been struck already, he certainly was now. This girl was a fucking precious gift he didn't deserve, but he'd be damned if he ever let her go.

His thumbs skimmed along her jaw. Her lips parted as he lowered his mouth to hers. Pure sweetness. His dick pushed against his zipper, insistent and throbbing. Brendan wanted inside her. He pulled her hips closer so she could feel what she did to him. How much he craved her. He could fuck Katelyn right here in the kitchen.

He'd never shown such restraint. Ever. Never had to. So what the fuck was he waiting for?

Her.

When Katelyn was ready, he would know.

And the reward would be even sweeter.

Their kiss ended, both of them gasping for air. She held onto his shoulders and he helped her down from the island. Katelyn took off her coat and sat down in the family room. She reached for the remote.

"Are we watching the game?" She turned on the TV.

Yeah, she was fucking perfect.

It was a bye week, though, so there was no game he cared to watch today. Brendan sat against the arm of the sofa and positioned her between his legs, her back reclining on his chest. It felt nice.

She said it out of the blue. "She knew."

"Hm, what?"

Katelyn turned on his chest to look at him. "Salena must have overheard me and Chloe. She acted like she didn't know who Chloe or Linnea were, but she knew."

"Oh, she knows who they are all right." He ran his fingers through her hair. "What did she overhear?"

"Um…Linnea and Kyan got married…"

He chuckled. "That would do it."

"…and Chloe told me to text you back."

Brendan smiled. "Of course she did." He brushed his fingers across her cheek.

"She knew they didn't need that invite. She wanted me to show up at the ball, didn't she?"

"Seems that way. Explains a helluva lot."

"Why?"

"To send me a message."

Katelyn turned all the way over and straddled him. "Does she want you back? Is that it?"

He would have laughed if she weren't so serious. "What? No, we were never together like that."

"But you had sex with her."

Brendan was reminded that Katelyn was only eighteen—and innocent. It didn't matter how many books she'd read, or movies she'd watched, or stories she'd heard from girlfriends in the bathroom at school, sex was still an abstract concept to Katelyn.

"Everybody had sex with her. I've had a lot of sex with a lot of people, and that's all it ever was. Fucking and making love are two very different things."

Not that he had any experience with the latter. That would be a first for him too.

He soothingly stroked her arms and her hair. "Baby, I've never, and I mean never, been in a relationship with anyone before you. I told you, this is a first for me. Salena has never been in my home or in my bed. No woman has. Ever. Until you."

Her eyes darted, as if searching his for an answer, then she softly asked him, "How? How are they different?"

"The mechanics are the same, but fucking is purely physical. The only goal is pleasure. An orgasm. Feelings aren't necessary." He exhaled. "On the other hand, it's impossible to make love without them."

Her tongue peeked out to wet her lips and she nodded. Her mind was spinning. Brendan could see it.

"What are you thinking, Katelyn?"

Her lips parted to speak, but she hesitated.

"You have to be able to talk to me, sweetheart. That's how this works."

"I know." She lowered her gaze. "I'm trying to figure out how to say it."

"Look at me, baby," he said gently and tipped up her chin. "Just say it."

"Okay. Well, I haven't had sex, not really, and you've had a lot of it. I don't know what I'm supposed to do, and what if I don't like the things you like or what if I'm not any good at it? Like, the blood thing—what the fuck was that?" She only paused to take a breath.

Good girl.

That Katelyn felt comfortable enough to talk to him about this was just what Brendan wanted. It. Was. Everything. It meant she trusted him and he needed that from her.

He kissed her. Brendan grabbed her face and kissed her hard.

"Don't worry about the blood thing, baby—it's not my thing. I won't ever say no to period sex, though." He winked.

"What is your thing?"

"You." He spoke against her skin and kissed her forehead. "We'll figure out what *our* thing is together."

Brendan slid his hand beneath her hair to grasp the back of her neck and held her mouth to his. She opened for him and his tongue met hers. He didn't think he'd ever get enough of her sweet mouth.

"All your kisses are mine."

He lifted the sweater she wore over her head, tossed it to the floor, and gazed at creamy swells of flesh heaving inside pink lace cups.

"These gorgeous tits are mine."

With a flick of his fingers, he unhooked her bra, and the lace fell away. Ever so lightly, his thumbs brushed her nipples. He felt her thighs clench where she straddled him.

"Fuck, Brendan," she whimpered.

He tweaked them and twisted them, pinched them and pulled them until she rocked on his lap.

"See how sensitive your nipples are?"

She nodded and rocked. His dick throbbed in his jeans beneath her.

"I love that." Brendan kissed and licked her swollen nipples. "You know what? Mine are too." He reached behind him and pulled his shirt off. He took her hands and placed them on his pecs. "Go on. Touch them. Pinch them."

She was hesitant at first. Light touches with the pads of her fingers. Brendan watched her pupils flare as his nipples hardened to small beads. Katelyn grasped them between her fingers and squeezed. His cock surged and he groaned.

"Bite them if you want," he encouraged her. She was licking his nipples just like she had in his dreams. "See how it works, baby?"

Katelyn bit him then, gently, but it was enough. Brendan pushed her back onto the sofa, unzipped her jeans and yanked them down her legs. Her pink lace panties matched the bra on the floor. He slid his hand inside. She was soaked.

"This pussy is mine."

He took her hand and held it on the hard bulge in his pants, rubbing back and forth.

"And this cock is yours. Do whatever you want with it. The what or the how doesn't matter. I'll love it because it's you doing it. Understand?"

She nodded again.

"Words, baby. I need to hear you say it."

"I understand."

"Good girl." He pushed his fingers farther inside the pink lace, coating them in her wet heat. "These panties look pretty on you, but they'll look even prettier on the floor."

Flimsy little things. With one swift yank they were gone.

Brendan gazed upon his precious gift, naked and beautiful and his.

Katelyn had no idea what she was capable of yet.

But he knew.

And he couldn't wait to show her.

Eighteen

Pink lace sailed to the floor.

Wait. Those are my panties. How…

Katie watched Brendan stand and strip out of his jeans. His heated blue gaze never left hers. He was so big his boxers couldn't contain him. His cock jutted out of the waistband, past his navel, the silver barbell that pierced the wide head flashing at her like a neon sign. He rubbed himself as he sat back down, then pushed her feet back until her heels touched her buttocks.

"Drop your knees."

His voice, rich and buttery, compelled her to comply. She felt herself open, cool air connecting with warm wet flesh. Fingers slowly moved through her slit.

"That's my girl."

Katie felt the tickle of hot fluid trickling from inside her down between her cheeks. Brendan leaned forward and kissed her inner thigh, her hip, up her ribs to her shoulder and along her collarbone. Her arms came around him, fingers pressing into his back, and he sucked the skin at the curve of her neck.

The slow up-and-down movement of his fingers in her pussy stopped then. His thumb softly circled her clit while a fingertip lightly rimmed her opening. Brendan pressed his lips against hers and spoke into her mouth. Warm. Luscious.

"Relax for me, baby." He kissed along her jaw to her ear. "Just like that."

His thumb still circled as the tip of his finger pushed inside her. Katie bit her lip at the unfamiliar sensation. Teeth grazed her neck. A hand tugged on her hair. His erection pressed into her thigh, the curved barbell digging into her flesh, precum leaking onto her skin.

Brendan pushed his finger in a little bit more and her muscles involuntarily tensed. She closed her eyes. It's not that it hurt. It didn't. It was just that no one had ever touched her quite like that before and it felt strange and wonderful and forbidden all at once.

"Look at me," he commanded in that butter-rich voice.

Katie opened her eyes to piercing blue irises. His finger dipped deeper. It pinched and stung as it delved into her, making its full presence known. Still, she wanted more of it. Because it was him.

A squeak of sound came out of her and he retreated, circling her entrance with his fingertip. Massaging it. His gaze stayed on hers, as did his thumb on her clit. Her body was on fucking fire and she wanted to scream at him to put his finger back inside her. She wanted it there. No, she needed it.

She raised her hips from the sofa and the corner of his lip turned up. He gripped her hair tighter. "Whose pussy is this?"

"Yours."

Brendan brought his hand up to her mouth and traced her lips with his finger. She could smell herself on him. Then he parted her lips and she sucked his long, thick digit inside her mouth without having to be told.

"My good, sweet girl."

He slowly pulled his finger from her mouth and placed her hand on his giant cock against her thigh. She couldn't wrap her fingers all the way around it. Brendan brought her other hand to her breast. She pinched the nipple and heard herself whimper. Then his fingers found her pussy again and he tugged on her hair.

"Tell me again, baby. Who does this pussy belong to?"

"You," she breathed.

His thumb was back on her clit. His thick finger pushing its way into her. And out. And in. Going a little deeper every time. She could hear herself bleat out a sound with every slow dip of his finger.

"I'm taking what's mine, sweet girl, and my finger's only half-way in. Relax."

That's it?

It felt like his whole hand was inside her.

"I'm trying."

"Such a good girl," he praised her. "Hold my dick. Squeeze it. Play with your nipple."

She squeezed his cock and he groaned. It was a helluva lot bigger than his finger. She tried to imagine him pushing that inside her as he pushed his finger all the way in.

"Shh, shh, shh."

Did she scream?

She gripped his cock in her hand and twisted her nipple.

Brendan let go of her hair and leaned over her pussy. Saliva fell from his lips to her clit as his thumb rubbed over it, back and forth. Katie watched as he pushed a second finger inside her.

Oh, fuck!

He groaned. "Whose pussy, baby?"

"Yours." She wasn't sure how she managed to speak.

"I'm going to ruin it for anybody else."

His eyes bored into hers. Those two fingers didn't move. They remained still, lodged inside her. Waiting.

"Go ahead. I only want you."

Only then did they move. Slowly at first, a gentle rhythmic push and pull. In and out. The thumb on her clit kept time with them.

Brendan groaned with each thrust of his fingers inside her. "So fucking tight. Feel that?"

Katie felt like she was dying. Her body hummed, limbs shaking.

"Mm, fuck, Brendan."

He quickened his pace. Both hands on her pussy now. The fingers of one thrummed her clit while the other pushed in and out of her.

"That's right, Katelyn, my fingers are fucking you. It feels good, doesn't it?"

"Yes."

So good.

She closed her eyes.

"Look at me."

She opened them.

"But I'm loving you."

He claimed her mouth and she exploded.

'My fingers are fucking you…but I'm loving you.'

"Katie. You in there…hello?"

Fingers snapped in front of her face, bringing her out of her reverie. Leo wore a cheetah-print scarf with his Beanie's shirt today. He insisted on wearing the same low-cut style Katie, Kelly, and the other girls wore, instead of a regular T-shirt. She couldn't decide if he looked more like Prince or Lenny Kravitz, but if they'd somehow been able to make a baby together, Katie was sure he'd look just like Leo.

She looked at him and went back to wiping chalk off the menu-board. How long had she been standing here?

"What?"

"Baby girl." He paused, raising his brow. So dramatic. "I don't know where you been the last ten minutes, but I wanna go there too." He nodded for emphasis.

Katie laughed and picked up a piece of chalk.

"You're blushing." He pinched her cheek. "So I know where your mind was. You seeing that helluva fine man of yours today?"

Katie smiled. "Yeah. He should be here pretty soon."

The sound of a throat clearing caused them both to turn around.

"Wow. Replaced me already? Or did you know I was standing here?" Cameron winked. "Hey, babe."

Shit!

He stood at the counter with a couple of his teammates. And a couple cheerleaders. They looked like cheerleaders anyway. Cameron didn't seem to be attached to either of them. He looked sad even through his smile. His dimples hardly showed.

Leo sauntered over to them and took their order while Katie readied the cups to prepare it. Why did she still feel bad about ending things with him? Now more than ever she knew that her decision was the right one, but she still felt like shit that she hurt him. Overhearing her and Leo, especially when they were trying to remain friends, was like pouring salt on the wound and that made her feel even worse.

"Stop it," he said. She glanced up to find Cameron leaning against the counter, watching her steam milk for their lattes. "You have this look on your face like you just kicked a puppy."

"I'm sorry, Cam. I…"

"It's okay, babe. We're still friends."

She glanced up.

Double shit.

"Katie's coming, isn't she?"

Chloe stood at the island, mixing something in a bowl, baby Chandan attached to her with some kind of contraption. It couldn't be very comfortable. He looked like he was about to cry.

"Yeah, I'm going to get her in a little bit." Brendan plucked the baby out of the thing.

Everyone was coming over to Chloe, Jesse, and Taylor's place today for a football Sunday potluck. Brendan was going to pick Katelyn up from work and bring her to the house first so they could whip up Italian meatball sliders as their contribution. That was another thing he loved about Sundays now. Having Katelyn in the kitchen with him. Cooking together. Sharing stories.

"I meant for Thanksgiving, Bren."

Oh.

It's not that he didn't want to spend the holiday with her. He did. Brendan wanted to spend every minute of every day with her.

But he couldn't invite Katelyn without Kelly, and he didn't think Kelly approved of their relationship very much. If it were anyone else, he wouldn't give a shit what they thought. But Katelyn loved her aunt, so the woman's opinion, and her approval, mattered to him.

"What do you think, Chandan?" The baby grinned up at him, displaying two bottom teeth, drool dribbling down his chin. "I'm not sure what her plans are, but I'll ask her."

"Yay!" Chloe clapped her hands together. "I love the holidays. We have to figure out who's hosting this year."

"I will," he volunteered. "Me and Katelyn."

Why not?

He was closing the club for the holiday weekend and Katelyn would be on break from school. They'd have all that time to spend together. In the kitchen. And perhaps other places. Besides, Linnea hosted the previous year. His house was first and going forward they could just go in a circle around Park Place.

Brendan liked an order to things.

And that meant next year Thanksgiving would be here at Chloe's. He chuckled to himself. It would be another three before they had to worry about getting food poisoning from Sloan.

Chloe made her I-told-you-so face and grinned. "Maybe you and Katie would like to come with us the day after to get a Christmas tree? It'll be fun."

Brendan hadn't bothered with any of that in years. No reason to. He had one now.

"Yeah, I think she'd really love that."

Who was he kidding? He'd really love that. Because he'd get to do it with Katelyn. And she was his reason for everything.

Brendan kissed Chandan's soft baby curls and handed him to his mother. "Time for Uncle B to go." He kissed Chloe on the cheek and hugged her tight. "We'll be here in time for kickoff."

He started for the door and then winked over his shoulder. "And thanks."

There was a crowd at the counter when Brendan walked into Beanie's. Leo had his hair back in an Ariana Grande ponytail, rocking a cheetah-print scarf, taking orders at the counter. He didn't know this guy's story yet, but he got a good vibe from him.

"You have this look on your face like you just kicked a puppy."

"I'm sorry, Cam. I…"

"It's okay, babe. We're still friends."

Don't even try it, frat boy.

Brendan winked at Katelyn. Leo coughed behind his hand. Kelly chose the perfect moment to come out from the back.

"Brendan's here for you, KK." He figured Kelly said it more as a warning for the boy at the counter. "I've got it."

The boy turned around then. Brendan actually almost felt sorry for him. He'd seen that look before. He did look like a sad, lost puppy.

That's what losing a sweet girl did to you.

And Brendan sure as fuck never wanted to know what that felt like.

Nineteen

"Is that snow?"

Katie craned her neck to see better out the shopfront window. The foot traffic on the sidewalks of First Avenue had dwindled, most of the shops closing early today in preparation for the holiday tomorrow, followed by the busiest shopping day of the year on Friday.

"Looks like it's starting to." Kelly joined her at the window. "Why don't you go ahead and take off."

"Are you sure?"

"Yeah." Her aunt hugged her. "It's slow. Leo and I can close up. Besides, I know you're itching to get out of here. You've been watching the damn clock all day."

Truth.

Katie texted Brendan to let him know she was leaving work early. They had a lot to do to get ready for tomorrow and she was so excited to do it with him. She'd searched Pinterest for recipes and tablescape ideas. Brendan gave her the login for his shopping app and she ordered everything they needed. Tonight they'd prep and cook. Tomorrow they'd celebrate their first holiday together—with his entire family. Like a Hallmark movie. And yeah, she was kind of nervous about it.

But the best part was, since they both had the entire weekend off, Katelyn was staying with Brendan. At his house. As in sleeping there. In his bed. With him. And yeah, she was kind of nervous about that too.

Brendan texted her that he'd be right there to pick her up. It was only a few blocks. She could have walked, but Brendan always insisted on driving her. Just like he opened doors, and held her hand, and always walked on the street side when they were together.

"I'll see you tomorrow then." She kissed Kelly on the cheek.

"Two o'clock?"

"Two o'clock, Auntie."

"I would tell you not to have too much fun, but I think that ship has already sailed," Kelly sighed. "And I told you to stop calling me that."

"Never." Katie giggled. "And you can't ever have too much fun, can you?" She winked, not bothering to inform her they hadn't had too much fun. Yet. Let Kelly think what she wanted.

Brendan was leaning against the 'Vette, waiting for her in the alley. He took her bag from her and tossed it in the trunk.

"C'mere."

Then he pulled her into his arms and kissed her. Slow and deep. Tiny dots of snow falling all around them. Before this man, Katie only imagined what being this happy could feel like. She realized she hadn't even come close.

Brendan brushed a melting snowflake from her nose and kissed it. "Let's go home."

Butterflies.

Yeah, he said that.

It was after midnight by the time they finished their Thanksgiving preparations and Katie stepped out of the en suite into Brendan's bedroom. He lay there, eyes closed, hands clasped behind his head, until she got under the covers beside him. Two strong arms encircled her and tucked her against his chest. Warm lips skimmed her neck.

"It feels so good to have you here like this," he whispered. "To hold you."

Like a reflex to his voice, Katie felt the corners of her mouth pull up.

It did feel good. It felt better than good. Here, in Brendan's arms, was right where she wanted to be. Where she was supposed to be. Katie felt it deep in her soul. Her head, her heart, and her body all on the same page.

She loved him.

It was as simple as that.

Katie turned her head and kissed the corner of his mouth. Those two arms squeezed her tighter and he kissed the top of her head. Then she felt his muscles relax and his breaths slowed to a steady, even rhythm.

He slept.

Now, while admittedly, a part of her, namely that part of her between her legs, wanted to wake him up and have too much fun, the rest of her was relieved to see him sleep. Not because she was nervous or afraid to have sex, though she was a little, but because she knew how much he needed it. He had to be exhausted. All the hours of work he put in, and not just at the club.

Katie knew all those days they had breakfast together, that he'd stayed up after a night at the club just to spend time with her before she went to work or school, only to go to the office afterward and work some more with his cousins. He'd get a few hours' sleep after lunch and then he was back at the Red Door and the cycle would start all over again. How long could he keep that up?

Sweet dreams, baby.

Katie nestled against Brendan and closed her eyes, content to be cocooned under the covers with him. Surrounded by his hard, strong body. Breathing in bergamot and cedar as snowflakes gently tumbled from the sky.

It sounded like she imagined a bear might sound with its paw caught in a trap. Something between a roar and a whimper. A deep guttural sound came from beside her on the bed. Brendan wasn't holding her anymore. His head thrashed on the pillow. He'd kicked off the covers. Goosebumps rose on her skin.

Obviously caught in the throes of a nightmare, Katie sat up and cautiously leaned over him. "Brendan."

A gentle caress. "Wake up, baby."

She combed sweat-dampened dark-auburn hair away from his face with her fingers. "Shh, it's just a bad dream."

The anguished sound ceased, the thrashing stopped, and his arms came around her. He just held her like that for a moment, the room quiet except for the sound of his heart beating rapidly in his chest. Then he lightly stroked her back with his fingertips.

She kissed the spot where his heart beat. "Are you okay?"

"Yeah. It was a dream, that's all." Brendan kissed her hair. "I'm sorry I woke you."

"More like a nightmare, I'd say." Katie pulled the blanket back over them and scooted up higher on his chest, fitting her face against his neck.

"Maybe," he said with a shrug. She felt the movement of his shoulder. "I usually don't remember much."

"You get them often?"

"I don't know." He squeezed her. "Now and then."

Taking Katie with him, Brendan sat up against the leather up-holstered headboard. She straddled his lap, hands clasped behind his neck, her thumbs rubbing his skin. His blue eyes were hidden in the shadowed room, but she could feel them looking into hers. He leaned forward and softly kissed her lips.

"I've had dreams on and off since the accident."

"What accident?" He'd never mentioned anything about an accident to her before.

Behind her back his fingers played with her hair. He took an audible breath. "My parents were killed in a car crash fourteen years ago."

"Oh, my god…I didn't know…I can't imagine how…" Katie stammered and hugged him tighter. "I'm so sorry, Brendan."

That was the last thing she expected to hear. He'd never even mentioned his parents. She was stunned, and the words she spewed sounded so trite, but she didn't know what else to say.

"Fourteen years ago you were only…"

"Eighteen," he whispered.

The same age she was now. Katie didn't want to think about how horrific that must have been for him. She'd never experienced the death of a loved one. Your parents are supposed to be with you until they're very old and you've given them a bunch of grandchildren to spoil and fuss over. Just the thought of losing her parents crippled her, yet he'd lived it.

"It was raining. Semi missed the stop sign."

Katie squeezed her eyes shut.

"They were going to dinner, and I, uh…" He sniffed. "Told my mom I had to study, but the truth was I didn't feel like going. She called me from the car to see what I wanted her to get for me to bring back. I heard everything…then nothing."

The fingers playing with her hair tugged at the long strands. "Sometimes, I still hear it. Uncle Charley—Kyan and Dillon's dad—lived upstairs from us at the time. We got in his car and headed to the restaurant they were going to. It's the only time I can ever remember praying. But as soon as I saw the flares, I knew."

She did the only thing she knew to do. Katie gripped his neck and held him tight while he held onto her hair like it was his lifeline.

"Cops had the road blocked off, but my uncle talked to them and they let us through. No one had to tell us they didn't survive. All I could smell was metal and blood and gasoline. We stood there in the rain until they cut them out of the wreckage and…"

Jesus.

His fingers stopped moving. "I was supposed to be with them. I shouldn't even be here."

She opened her eyes because she didn't want to imagine the horror of it all. Katie felt warm liquid stinging her cheeks. She quickly swiped at her eyes and laid her head on his shoulder. "Tell me about them. Your mom and dad."

"They would have loved you." She felt his smile in the dark.

"Yeah?"

"Yeah." He kissed her forehead. "My dad, his name was James, came here from Dublin to go to college—Uni he called it."

She laughed. "Ohh, that explains it."

"Explains what?" He squeezed her in his arms.

"That trace of an accent you have." She nodded.

"It's easy to pick up. Just wait until you meet my aunt Colleen—Jesse's mom. She's my mom's younger sister. She lives in Ireland."

His voice was lighter now, the abject horror momentarily forgotten, as Brendan remembered his parents as they were, instead of how they tragically died. "Anyway, my mom and dad met at school. Bumped into her in the library. Love at first sight, my dad said. They got married a year later and I came along a year after that."

"That's so romantic."

"Yeah." He brushed the hair out of her face. "Just like us."

"We didn't meet at school, Bren."

"The other part, sweet girl."

Then he smiled and he kissed her.

"It's perfect, sweetheart."

"Are you sure?"

"The thermometer says it is." Brendan playfully swatted Katelyn on her behind and bent over to pull the bird from the oven. "I'm sure."

Not to mention it was the fourth turkey they'd roasted since yesterday. How many people did she think they were feeding anyway? "You do know there's only sixteen of us, right?"

"Twenty-six and two babies. So I rounded it up to thirty."

"How do you figure?" He shook his head and grinned.

She smirked. "You boys count as two—that's twenty right there."

They were both laughing. Brendan pulled her to his chest and gazed into her enchanting eyes, the eyes he could see his future in. He bent his head to kiss her and the doorbell rang.

"That has to be Kelly," he said and swiftly kissed her on the lips. "Anyone else would have just come on in."

Brendan opened the door to Kelly holding four apple pies. Kodiak was coming up the porch steps with Kyan and Linnea directly behind him. House by house, everyone who lived on Park Place—his family—gathered in his living room. Dillon was the last to arrive. If Katelyn was apprehensive or nervous at all, you'd never know it. She was the perfect hostess, right at home with that beautiful smile for everyone.

She was perfect.

She was home.

And just the thought of that made him smile.

"So, did the two of you meet at Beanie's?" Dillon asked in between mouthfuls of mashed potatoes during dinner.

Katelyn watched him with her lips pressed together, containing a giggle, like she was waiting for him to toss a spoonful into the air. Brendan winked at her.

"Um, no. We met before the coffee bar opened. I bumped into him in the park," she supplied.

Brendan looked at his cousin and smirked. "During Venery's concert."

"Midsummer's Eve." Dillon dropped his spoon to his plate and laughed. He took on an Irish brogue. "And what did I tell ye, cousin?"

"Watch out for the faeries." He chuckled, rolling his eyes.

Katelyn smiled in spite of her confusion. "Faeries? Huh?"

Jesse and Kyan exchanged a knowing glance. They started chuckling too.

"See? It was the fair folk that put you in each other's path." Dillon regaled Katelyn with the Celtic folklore of midsummer. "And there's no avoiding your destiny."

Brendan still didn't believe such things.

But whatever brought them together on that path in the park, whether it was the faeries, serendipity, or divine intervention, he was thankful for it.

So fucking thankful.

Twenty

He didn't want to move, not even to stretch.

Light was just beginning to seep inside the dark bedroom. Brendan couldn't remember the last time he slept so soundly as he did with Katelyn wrapped in his arms, her bottom tucked up against him. He opened his eyes. She was still asleep, unaware of his hard dick wedged between her cheeks. All he could think of was slipping those itty-bitty panties to the side and sliding home. Fucking her until she was raw and begged him to stop.

He knew in his gut she wouldn't ever want to stop. Once they started, Katelyn would be a force to be reckoned with. Brendan could see the hunger in her, an appetite for carnal pleasure that he sensed matched his own. It was about time they talked about practical things like condoms and birth control. They could discuss limits and safe words and all that other shit later, when she was ready to discover her sexual self and try different things with him. For now, though, he needed to get her on the Pill. Something. Because he needed his dick inside her. Bare.

And that would be another first for him.

He'd never felt the inside of a tight, hot, wet pussy with his bare dick.

Not that he intended to wait for Katelyn to get on the Pill or whatever to fuck. He filled an entire drawer with condoms and he'd use every last one of them before this weekend was over. His ready dick twitched.

It was barely dawn. There was time before they were supposed to be next door for breakfast and to go pick out a Christmas tree with Chloe, Jesse, Taylor, and baby Chandan. Time to show his sweet girl why sleeping in was overrated.

Kissing her shoulder, he nudged her from behind as his fingers reached inside her tiny tank to grasp her nipples. Her eyelids flew open as she pressed her lush ass into his hard dick and a sweet sound escaped her lips.

"Good morning, sweet girl," he whispered as he kissed along her collarbone to the skin at the curve of her neck.

Brendan sucked on the flesh there, nipping at it with his teeth. Tugging on her nipples until she squirmed. Katelyn held onto his forearms for leverage, rubbing her ass up and down on him, seeking friction.

Bad girl.

He was not about to come in his boxers like some pubescent boy. Brendan turned, so he hovered over her, and he took her mouth. He took it hard. Katelyn held his face in her hands. He was fucking starving for her. She made him insane.

"I want you naked."

He pulled the tiny tank top over her head. Brendan didn't look to see where it landed. His gaze was fixed on those perfect tits, her hard swollen nipples. He took off her panties and brought them to his face, breathing in her delicious scent, hungrier than he'd ever been. She looked a bit startled, her eyes wide and her lips parted, at seeing his nose in her underwear.

He smirked.

"Get used to it, baby. I love how you smell…" He pushed a finger deep inside her and pulled it back out. Coated in her wet sweetness, he sucked it into his mouth. "…and I love how you taste even more."

To prove the sincerity of his words, he spread her thighs wide and slowly dragged his tongue through her slit up to her clit, clamping it between his teeth. Then he sucked. He sucked until her thighs were shaking and she pulled his hair while she screamed.

His dick throbbed in his boxers, twitching to break free of the knit cotton. Brendan could feel precum leaking onto his skin, dampening the fabric. He removed them and with one knee on the mattress he reached for her nipple. Katelyn reached for his cock.

Warm, slim fingers circled his shaft and squeezed. Two knees on the mattress. She bit her lip and a wet tongue peeked out from between them, sliding across the bottom one. One hand in her hair. She kissed the head and licked the precum from her lips.

"Suck me, beautiful."

Those eyes that he loved looked up at him as Katelyn opened wide and tentatively took him in her mouth. Her tongue toyed with the barbell. Exploring his flesh. Brendan could tell she was a novice. Hell, maybe she'd never had a dick in her mouth before. And fuck if that thought didn't please him.

His fingers razed through her hair, holding her head to his dick. It felt like fucking heaven in her mouth. He eased his hips forward, sliding himself inside just a bit farther. Just enough to make her gag a little, but not enough to scare her off him.

She still gazed up at him. Pretty eyes glassy. Lips stretched thin. Did she have any idea how beautiful she looked to him like that? Katelyn sucked on his head like a straw in a milkshake. Brendan wanted nothing more than to fuck her mouth at that moment. Come down her throat. He knew his sweet girl wasn't ready for that. Not yet.

"What a fucking good girl you are," he praised and gently eased her from his dick. "Spit on it."

"What?"

"You heard me, baby." He traced her lips with his thumb. "Spit on my dick."

Katelyn did as he asked and he slid her bottom to the edge of the bed. Brendan leaned over her, his wet cock resting between her breasts. He kissed her mouth.

"Push your tits together for me."

She cushioned him with her supple flesh.

"Yeah, stay just like that."

A slow, gentle thrust.

"So fucking beautiful."

And another.

And another.

And another.

His weeping head touched her lips with every upward thrust. Her tongue darted out to catch a taste of him. She wanted his cum. He wanted to give it to her. This beautiful girl was so fucking his.

"So fucking mine."

His hand went to her throat.

She pinched her nipples as she held her tits together. Mewling. Licking.

"Fuck," she cried out. She twisted her nipples and let go. "Gimme."

Katelyn grabbed ahold of his cock with both hands and sucked it back into her mouth.

She wanted him.

"My sweet girl."

And with one thrust he gave her what she wanted.

They were cutting through the park, walking along the path through the trees, on their way to the Christmas tree lot. Chloe, Jesse, and Taylor were pushing Chandan in the stroller behind them. Brendan stopped, took her hand, and pointed to a big oak tree. There wasn't anything special about it, stripped of its leaves, it stood naked with the rest.

"See that tree?"

"Yeah."

"This…" Brendan hoisted her up into his arms and she wrapped her legs around his waist. "…is the exact spot where we met."

"Oh yeah?" She grinned, gazing into his crystal eyes that

sparkled like diamonds against the overcast sky. "How can you be sure?"

"That tree." He leaned in to kiss her lips. "And the bench across from it."

Katie held onto his neck and laid her head on his shoulder. *You beautiful man.*

Chloe and her boys caught up to them. Brendan set her back on her feet and they walked holding hands the rest of the way to the lot. There were rows of freshly cut trees catching snowflakes in their branches. Wreaths and mantelpieces fashioned from boughs were strung all around. The market lights that framed the perimeter were alight even though it was daytime. Katie breathed the smell of spruce and pine deep into her lungs.

Brendan put a paper cup of hot cocoa in her hand and clasped the other in his, lacing their fingers together as they inspected the row of trees, looking for the perfect one to bring home.

"There's nothing wrong with this one, Jesse," Taylor insisted from the next row over. "It's ace."

Katie glanced at Brendan and giggled.

"See one you like?" he asked her.

"I like them all." She shrugged. "I don't know anything about picking out a tree."

Brendan gave her a sexy smirk. "Well, first you just look at it and see if the trunk is straight." He ran his fingers down her spine. "If it's full and lush, it's shape pleasing to the eye." His hands skimmed down her arms. "Perfect."

"Brendan." She felt her cheeks heating in spite of the cold.

"Then you check to make sure it's fresh." He kissed her. "Yeah, I got the best one right here."

Katie bit her lip, her insides turning to goo.

He stepped back and surveyed the tree in front of them. He shook a couple branches on the nine-foot fir and inspected the cut edge of the trunk, then he looked at her. "This one?"

She nodded.

Brendan picked her up and spun her around, kissing her.

Chloe was standing there with a big grin on her face when he put her down. "You found one, yeah?"

"Yeah," Brendan answered with a grin just as big. "You?"

"Two." She giggled. "Taylor's ace tree and Jesse's taller, greener, fuller one."

"I heard that." Taylor put his arm around Chloe from the right and he kissed her.

Jesse linked his arm with Taylor's behind her from the left. "Well, it's true." He kissed her too, then, and turned to his cousin. "Hey, we're doing our carriage ride downtown to see the tree tomorrow—want to come?"

Brendan kissed the top of her head before he answered, "Thanks, Jess, but Katelyn and I already have plans. Maybe next year."

We do?

He winked at her.

I guess we do.

The lot attendant wrapped up their trees and Brendan arranged to have them delivered along with fresh wreaths and boughs for the mantels. Chandan started to fuss so they said their goodbyes and headed in opposite directions on the avenue.

"Where are we going?" Katie asked.

"Shopping."

"Oh." Katie was not about to question shopping.

He took her to a quaint little gift shop on a side street off First Avenue. It was one of those stores filled with a colorful array of anything and everything you could imagine. A large decorated tree, filled with ornaments of all kinds, stood in the center. Brendan took her by the hand and led her to it.

"We need to pick out an ornament for our tree."

She tilted her head toward his. "Just one?"

"Just one." He winked. "You'll see."

They looked at angels and snowmen, candy canes and stars. Every ornament was exquisite and unique and artistically crafted. Then she came across a handmade little guy with filigree leaves for wings and an acorn hat. Katie tapped Brendan on the shoulder.

"Babe, is this a…"

"Faerie. It is." An old woman with white hair approached them. "Hello, Brendan. I haven't seen you in here since forever. How are ya?"

"Aggie!" Brendan hugged her, rocking from side to side. Her head barely reached the center of his chest. "I'm good. How are you?"

"Old." She chuckled. "I'm fine, dear."

"You're beautiful, Aggie." Brendan kissed her short white curls. "This is my girlfriend, Katelyn."

The old lady turned to her then. "Hello, Katelyn." Aggie pinched Brendan's side. "Watch out for this one. He's the dickens, I tell ya. Known him since he was no taller than my knee, and now look at him." She chuckled with a shake of her head. "I'll be up front when you're ready."

Katie watched the old lady make her way down the aisle. She still held the faerie with filigree wings in her hand.

"Is that the one?"

She didn't think Dillon actually believed in faeries, and she didn't either, but unexplained things happen every day, don't they?

She nodded. "Yes."

'There's no avoiding your destiny.'

Now *that* she believed.

And Brendan, he was hers.

Twenty-One

He sat on a dusty old chair, a cardboard box on his lap, alone in his basement. Katelyn was upstairs in the kitchen, making dinner out of Thanksgiving leftovers, while Brendan dug out boxes of Christmas stuff that hadn't been opened since they died. The box was tattered and worn from age, the packing tape that sealed it stiff and cracked. His hands rubbed gently over the top, reverently touching the surface his mother once had.

He missed her.

He tried not to think about her too much. Fourteen years hadn't dulled the pain of their loss. When he thought of them, remembered them, it was as sharp as ever. It seared into his gut as if he stood in the rain just yesterday. Flares burning on wet pavement. Twisted metal. It was easier not to think of them.

But things were different now.

Now he had Katelyn to think of.

He wanted to share a life with her. He wanted to share *his* life with her, and he couldn't do that if he kept the first eighteen years of it sealed up in a box. Katelyn would never really know how fucking amazing they were. She wouldn't come to know them at all if he didn't share his memories with her. Even the ones that hurt.

Uncle Charley had a quote for everything. He loved to throw sage wisdom at you like he was Confucius. Not too long after the accident his uncle said to him, "Brendan, sometimes your world is such a dark place you might think you've been buried, but you've actually been planted. Trust me, son. Good things will grow."

Brendan wasn't sure who actually said it first, or what his uncle meant by those words at the time. He thought perhaps he got it now.

He stacked the old Christmas boxes to take upstairs.

Then he added one more.

Because his *aintín* was right.

Katelyn wasn't in the kitchen when he came up from the basement. Something sure smelled good, though. He carried the boxes to the family room where the tree stood naked in its stand by the fireplace and he couldn't believe what else he saw there.

She'd built a tent—a childlike fort of sorts—out of blankets and pillows and sheets, and strung it with white Christmas lights. Their dinner was on a tray on the coffee table beside it, along with a bottle of his Glenlivet, and champagne Linnea had brought over yesterday chilling in a silver bucket. He chuckled to himself and grinned.

Where is she?

"Sweetheart?" He put the boxes down by the tree. "Katelyn?"

"I'll be right there." Her sweet, gentle voice came from upstairs.

Brendan added a log to the fire and sat on the floor. She was barefoot, her toes painted burgundy. Plaid lounge pants tied at the waist. One of those tiny tops she wore to bed. It was white. He could make out pink areolae through the fabric. Beaded nipples. Wheat-blonde hair hung in loose waves to her breasts. He looked up at the face of an angel, his angel, smiling down at him.

He smiled back. "What's all this?"

Katelyn took a seat beside him on the floor. "My mom calls it Thanksgiving leftover pie. It's kind of like a pot pie, or a shepherd's pie," she explained. "I made fried mashed potato balls too. You dunk them in the gravy. Sooo good…"

Brendan was almost speechless. This girl. What had he ever done to deserve her?

"…and there's still plenty of cheesecake and pumpkin…"

He grabbed her and kissed her. Fuck, he was starving and not for dinner.

"All this." He gestured to the pillow fort.

"Oh, that."

She glanced down at her lap and shyly smiled with a shrug. Then she looked up at him again. Twinkling white lights danced in liquid pools of aquamarine. Cheeks tinged with pink. God, he was so fucking in love with her.

"Well, every year after we finished decorating the tree, me and Kev watched Christmas movies in a tent we built in the living room. So I thought…"

"I love it, baby." He did. "Let's eat some leftover pie and get that tree done, yeah? What's your favorite Christmas movie?"

"*Miracle on 34th Street,*" she answered as she made him a plate. "You?"

"Um, it's a tie between Chevy Chase and Macaulay Culkin. *Christmas Vacation* or *Home Alone*—the first one."

She rolled her eyes with a giggle. "Why am I not surprised?"

They ate the delicious meal Katelyn prepared, sitting on the floor. Brendan brought the tray of turkey pie and plates to the kitchen. She was staring at the bottle of champagne in her hand when he came back. A glass of whiskey, filled close to the brim, sat on the table. He hid a snicker behind his hand.

Trying to get me drunk?

Not tonight, baby.

"I can't figure out how to open this." Katelyn held out the bottle.

Legally, she wasn't old enough to drink it, but fuck it. They were home where she was safe. What was the harm in it? If Katelyn wanted to celebrate their first tree together with some champagne, he wasn't going to tell her no.

He took the bottle from her and popped the cork.

She held up two glasses and he poured.

They didn't toast. Katelyn took her glass and walked over to the tree, sipping along the way. "This is good." She took another. "Really good."

Uh-oh.

He grinned with a shake of his head.

"So, shall we get started?" Her hand rested on top of the box, fingers smoothing over the cracked tape.

A warm feeling of nostalgia came over him. He was filled with a sense of how right all of this was. With Katelyn.

It was time to let the suffering go.

"Yeah."

She opened the box, and one by one, Katelyn gingerly took out the ornaments he hadn't seen in fourteen Christmases. Every year his mom would take him to Aggie's shop on Maple Street to choose a special ornament to add to the tree. Blue baby booties from the year he was born. A wedding bell. He held an Irish Santa made of glass in his palm.

"Now we can add our faerie." He nodded. "Go on. Find a good spot and hang him up."

Brendan took a step back and watched her. Katelyn carefully placed the ornament on a branch in the front and when she turned around her smile was so big and so bright—like he'd given her the world. He was giving her his. He only hoped it was enough.

Katelyn leapt, actually leapt, into his arms, almost bowling him over. She held onto him tightly, her arms around his neck and her legs around his waist, like a monkey clinging to a tree. He liked the way it felt. Like she needed him. Like she couldn't get close enough. She pulled her head back and gazed into his eyes.

"It's the most beautiful tree ever!"

She kissed him.

And she didn't stop.

Her nipples rubbed against his chest through her tiny top and his Henley. Brendan could feel them just as surely as if the hard points were grazing his bare skin. Katelyn was making those sounds that made his dick hard—like she couldn't get quite enough air even though she was breathing.

His hands were clasped behind her back, holding her up on his waist. He let one slide down her ass. Felt the damp fabric between her legs. And that was it.

He laid her down inside the tent and pulled the plaid fabric down her legs. She wore no panties underneath. Brendan fixed his gaze on her pretty pussy, bare and ready to welcome his fingers, his tongue, and his cock. He peeled off his Henley and popped the button on his jeans. His eyes never leaving hers.

She knew. The look in her eyes, the flare of her pupils, told Brendan that Katelyn knew exactly what his intentions were. More than that, she wanted what he did. He lowered his zipper and shucked off the denim. Naked, he knelt beside her under a ceiling of white cotton sheets and Christmas lights.

"Take it off," he rasped.

Katelyn yanked the little white top over her head. Brendan studied her naked form. Memorizing every freckle, dip, and curve of her body. He held her foot between his palms, slowly rubbing it, pressing his fingers into the sole.

"There isn't a part of your body I won't kiss…" He sucked her toe into his mouth. "…or love or touch."

His hand skimmed up her calf and her inner thigh until his fingers came to her pussy. Katelyn parted her thighs for him. She was wet and he could smell how much she wanted him. Brendan pushed two fingers inside her and she spread her thighs wide, gripping them in her hands to hold herself open.

If she only knew the visions running through his mind. Rope. Cuffs. A spreader bar. Yeah, he could see it. His sweet girl had a dark side and she'd want to play. Maybe he should build them a private playroom in the basement.

One day.

Right now her pretty pussy was gripping his fingers like a vise. Katelyn was so tight Brendan actually worried how he was going to get his dick inside her—at least without hurting her too much. He'd heard chicks tell their first-time stories. There was no avoiding it, he supposed. But he wanted it to be as pleasurable for her as he could possibly make it. He wanted her first-time story to be a good one.

He leaned forward and kissed her. Two fingers weren't enough. As tight a fit as it was, she had to take more before he pushed his way inside her.

"Baby." He sucked on her neck and spoke in her ear. "Let go of your legs now and just look at me."

Katelyn turned her head on the pillow. Eyes glazed. Lips parted. So beautiful.

He pressed his thumb into her clit, fucking her with his fingers. He pushed in as deep as he could go, until the knuckles of his hand met her flesh. She moaned. He pulled back and did it again. Her moans urged him on. He twisted his hand to the opposite side, his palm facing up, and he did it again, hooking his fingers to stimulate her G-spot.

She lifted her hips.

"More, sweet girl?" It wasn't really a question.

"Yes." She gasped in air. "Everything."

Brendan sat up and worked a third finger in, rubbing her clit with his other hand. She whimpered, her eyes squeezed shut, thrashing her head on the pillow.

"Am I hurting you? Do you need me to stop?"

"No. Don't stop." Her head thrashed some more. "Please, don't stop."

He stilled his fingers to let her get used to the sensation, lightly circling her clit, until he felt her muscles relax. Her head stopped moving on the pillow and she opened her eyes.

"Good girl. Keep them on me."

Only then did he move his fingers. In. Out. Twist. Tears leaked out from the corners of her pretty eyes, dripping down her temples and disappearing into her hair. He rubbed her clit faster. Her lips formed an O and her eyes rolled back in her head. Then she screamed.

Brendan laid down beside her and pulled her into his arms. He just held her, smoothing her hair and kissing her face, as she came down from her orgasm. He was out of his element here, the irony of it almost laughable, but he wasn't sure what the fuck to do with a virgin.

She kissed him then.

Her fingers reached for his dick. "Stop thinking, Brendan."

"You're my angel, baby," he whispered, his fingers strumming through her pussy. "The only light in my fucked-up world, and my ticket straight to hell."

"Then I'm going with you, Brendan. Don't you know you're my everything?"

He held her to him and kissed her brow.

"That's what I want to give you. Be for you. Teach you." He eased a finger inside her. "Everything."

"Then give it to me. Please."

He stopped thinking then. His brain and his body focused on one thing. Giving them what they both wanted.

Brendan rolled over on top of her. He stared into her pretty eyes as he notched the head of his dick at the entrance of her pussy. She winced.

"I don't want to hurt you, baby, but I'm going to."

She kissed his lips. "I know."

He eased his hips against her softly, trying to gently nudge his way inside. Katelyn bit her lip, he was sure to stifle a cry. She gripped him so tightly, her nails dug into his ass. He took her face in his hands and kissed her, then with one powerful thrust he drove all the way home.

And Katelyn screamed.

"Shh, baby." He tenderly kissed her lips. "I'm sorry."

No going back. She was his now.

Brendan didn't move. He held her face and kissed away her tears, his dick pulsing inside her torn tissue.

Jesus. Fuck.

He'd never felt anything like this before. Spongy wet walls of hot slippery flesh consumed his cock. He was dying here. Katelyn shifted her hips beneath him.

"Wrap your legs around me, sweet girl. Can you do that?"

She nodded, her cheeks stained with tears.

"Words, baby." He kissed her again.

"Yes." And she did.

He moved. Brendan slowly withdrew and she sucked in air through her teeth. He pushed back in and she exhaled. He did it again. And again. And with each thrust the sounds coming from her changed. A hiss. A squeak. A whimper. A moan. He watched her metamorphosis with awe.

Soon she was meeting him thrust for thrust. Rocking with him. Adjusting her pelvis, seeking friction from the barbell that pierced his dick. Sweet fucking moans coming from her mouth.

Brendan sucked on her nipple, her neck, her lips, wanting this incredible maelstrom of pleasure to last forever.

He wouldn't last much longer, though.

She felt too good.

Reaching between their bodies, slick with sweat, his fingers sought her clit. He grasped it and pinched as he sucked hard on her nipple. The violent pressure in his balls burst free while he heard her cry out his name.

Brendan felt the cum jettison from his cock, but he kept thrusting, not wanting to leave her yet. When he felt himself beginning to soften, he lifted his mouth from her nipple and gently eased himself out of her.

His dick was streaked with her blood. Cum, tinged in red, covered her thighs and dripped from her battered pussy. He licked his lips and his eyes flicked up to hers. There was no pain in them. No remorse. Only love.

Brendan took her face in his hands and brushed his lips over hers. "You're mine now." He kissed her, slow and deep, imprinting himself on her. "And I'm yours. Always."

Katelyn held him tight, burying her face in his neck. He thought he heard a sob.

"Are you crying, sweetheart?"

Warm wet drops rolled onto his skin.

"Are you hurting?"

She shook her head and sniffled.

"Why are you crying then?"

Katelyn shrugged and lifted her face from his neck. Cheeks wet with tears and sweat, stormy eyes blazing with newly awakened passion. He'd never seen her look more beautiful.

"I don't know. It's like I was flooded with these feelings all at once and…I can't explain it." She held him tighter. "I didn't know it could feel like this."

He didn't know it could either.

His fingers swept over her damp skin. She shivered. He began to kiss his way down her body starting with her lips. The column of her throat. Between her breasts. He kissed and licked each nipple until she wiggled beneath him. Down her belly. Her clit.

He licked up her slit, tasting the blood, his cum and hers, while his fingers massaged the wet mess into the skin on her thighs.

"Oh, shit. Brendan, I'm bleeding."

"You did a little." He grinned from between her legs. "You're not anymore."

He kissed her clit and leisurely circled it with his tongue.

She moaned. "You said blood isn't your thing."

"It isn't, sweet girl, but you are."

Every drop of you.

Katelyn was the only thing he needed.

Just her.

Always.

Twenty—Two

He scooped her into his arms, blanket and all, and carried her up the stairs. They never did get to watch Christmas movies. And she didn't care.

Katie was in her own movie. Either that or a fantastic dream. That's what it felt like anyway.

Brendan set her down on the bed. He leaned over and softly kissed her mouth. The butterflies took flight once more.

"Stay right here." He turned on the bedside lamp and disappeared into the en suite.

The blanket was cold and wet beneath her. Katie unwrapped it from her naked body to see if she looked any different now that she'd given up her v-card. Nope. She was swollen and tender down there, her lips puffy, but other than that everything seemed normal. That's when she noticed it.

Shit!

Yeah, she was in a movie all right. She stared at it horrified. The blanket looked like it had been used at a Freddy Krueger pajama party. Smears of blood. How do you get that out of white cotton sateen? She'd have to google it.

Brendan came out of the bathroom, took one look at her face, and rushed to her side, crouching in front of her. "Are you okay? What's wrong?"

"I bled all over the blanket."

With a smile, he took her hands in his. "It's a blanket, sweetheart."

An expensive one by the look and feel of it. The tag said L.L.Bean. Down-filled ultra-plush fleece on one side, cotton sateen on the other. Cozy, soft, and snuggly. Now it was just a ruined mess.

"Come on." He picked her up from the bed, cradling her in his arms. "I made you a bath."

Steam rose from the big clawfoot tub. An aromatic blend of patchouli, rosemary, lavender, eucalyptus, and sage permeated the air. Brendan lowered them into the hot water, tucking her against his chest. He dipped a sponge into the fragrant water and began washing her.

"Mm, it smells good."

"It's a recovery body soak I use after a heavy workout." He kissed the top of her head. "Dead Sea salt, arnica, and essential oils. This should soothe any soreness and achy muscles." Brendan ran the sponge between her breasts. "Did it hurt very much?"

"It, um, hurt like hell. More than I thought it would."

No exaggeration. Brendan was a helluva lot bigger than two of his fingers—bigger than three even, maybe four. It felt like she'd been ripped open. Flayed by a fire-hot poker driven deep inside her body. The initial discomfort gradually subsided, leaving a sensation of incredible fullness. She thought she could feel the pulsing of his cock in her pussy that throbbed with a heartbeat of its own. Even now, she could still feel him inside her, as if he'd branded her somehow.

"And then it didn't."

She'd wrapped her legs around him, holding on for dear life through the stinging burn of tissue being stretched for the first time. For a fleeting moment Katie wondered how any woman could like this, but then his mouth was on her nipple and his barbell grazed her clit. A fireball burst in her core and the heat of it spread and bloomed, proliferating through her body. She looked into those eyes that were so fucking blue looking into hers and melted into him. Became a part of him, just as he was a part of her. There was no other way to describe it.

"It was beautiful and wonderful and magical." She turned over and straddled him in the tub, wanting to see his face. "I didn't know you could be so connected to another person. Is it always like that?"

"No."

Brendan took her face in his hands. He brought her mouth to his and slipped his tongue inside. Fingertips skated down her spine and cupped her bottom, pulling her in even closer. Her nipples beaded against his wet skin. Immersed in warm water, breathing in patchouli, eucalyptus, and Brendan. She wanted to stay just like this. Always.

"But it's like that for us." He combed the hair out of her eyes. "See, that's the difference between making love and fucking."

He finished washing every inch of her, even her hair, dried her, and carried her naked to the bed. Brendan climbed in beside her and Katie snuggled into him. She reached for his lips with her own. His hands pressed her into him. She felt his cock stiffen against her thigh.

"Is it bad that I want you inside me again?"

"No, sweet girl." His lips brushed the column of her throat. "That's right where I want to be. Are you too sore?"

"I don't care about that." With the tips of her fingers, Katie stroked the hard length pressing into her thigh.

Brendan rolled over and reached inside the drawer of the bed-side table.

"What are you doing?"

"What I should have done in the first place, but in the heat of the moment I didn't." He tossed a bottle and some foil packets on the bed.

Katie picked up the plastic bottle. It was lube.

"Not that I'm making excuses. It was careless and irresponsible of me, and I'm sorry," he said, leaning over her to kiss the top of her head. "I always use condoms and I got tested after the ball. I'm clean. You know I haven't been with anybody since."

She took his hand and smiled. "I know. I trust you."

"We have to get you on some birth control. I'll have Chloe hook you up with her doc because I need to feel you bare, baby." He pulled her hand to his lips and kissed it. "But, for now, let me show you how to wrap me up."

Katie watched Brendan tear the foil packet open with his teeth. He placed the condom in her palm. It looked like a little hat.

"Pinch the tip between your thumb and index finger."

She did as he instructed.

Brendan placed his hands on top of hers, guiding her, showing her the amount of pressure he liked, as she slowly rolled the condom down his thick shaft. "Yeah, just like that."

He picked up the lube, and squirting some into his palm he fisted his sheathed cock. Slippery fingers strummed through her pussy and a lubed finger entered her.

"Does it still hurt?"

"A little." Katie opened her legs wide to give Brendan easier access. "I love that it does."

"Yeah?"

"Yeah."

And he kissed her.

Snoring softly, his breath ruffled through her hair. Katie blinked her eyes open to a solid wall of man. *Her* man. She smiled to herself, tracing the ink on his chest with her fingertip as he slept. His nipple beaded in response. Her tongue peeked out to lick it, nipping him with her teeth. Brendan groaned.

Her lips trailed down his chest. Her fingertips followed. She kissed and licked each ridge that defined his abs, the taste of him tantalizing her tongue. Katie held his hard girth in her hand and wet her lips, bringing the pierced head to her mouth. She sucked him.

"Fuck, baby."

Fingers pressed down her back, then up again, reaching into her hair. Holding her head to his dick. Tugging on her scalp. She felt a pulse beat in her clit and she tried to get more of him past her lips.

Brendan pulled her off his dick and yanked her up to him, mouths crashing together. He sucked on her bottom lip, grazing it with his teeth as he let it go. One hand reached for the bedside table while the other squeezed her breast. Tipping her head back, she closed her eyes.

When she opened them he was sitting up beside her, tearing a foil packet with his teeth. In the second it took her to raise up onto her elbows, Brendan sheathed himself.

He sat cross-legged on the bed and patted his lap. "Come here."

Katie wasn't sure exactly what he wanted her to do, how to approach him. He crooked his finger and smirked, his lusty eyes glowing like diamonds in the gray morning light. She got up off her elbows and sat across from him, knees touching his.

Brendan took her hands. "Climb on top of me."

She seated herself on his thighs, facing him.

"Good girl. Hug me like a koala does a tree and cross your legs behind my back."

Katie did as he asked. Her arms came around his back, and his held her. They were nose to nose, chest to chest. She gazed into his diamond eyes. He stared into hers.

"Breathe with me, Katelyn." He inhaled deeply and then exhaled. "*Yab-yum.*"

She didn't know what that meant, but synchronized her breathing with his, connecting with his energy. It flowed into her like an electrical current.

His forehead touched hers, fingertips lightly skated up and down her back. "The full embrace in tantra."

They stayed like that for a time. She wasn't sure how long. Staring into each other's eyes. Breathing together. Lightly touching. Was there anything more intimate than this? The feeling started at the base of her spine, and like a coiled snake awakened from its slumber, slowly traveled upward. Katie didn't think. She just let herself feel it.

Never taking her eyes off his, she reached beneath her and notched him to her entrance. He slowly pushed all the way inside her. Katie gasped at the welcome invasion. Cried out at the stretch of already-tender tissue.

"That's it, baby." He kissed her lips. "Now rock back and forth."

Katie set the pace. Brendan didn't move. He sat solid, holding her, supporting her as the energy danced between them, overtaking her. With each rock of her hips, the barbell grazed her clit and carried her away.

She was flying.

Soaring.

The floodgates opened and she surrendered all of herself to him.

Her eyes closed then, head tipped back.

She exhaled with a stuttered sob and laid her wet cheek on his shoulder. Brendan held her steady. What the fuck just happened?

Divine bliss.

What else could it be?

Brendan smoothed her hair from her face, combing it with his fingers. Katie took a deep cleansing breath and lifted her head from his shoulder, gazing into his beautiful blue eyes. His forehead touched hers and he softly kissed her.

"Good morning, my sweet girl."

Katie smiled.

Good morning, indeed.

"Shall I make us some breakfast?" She went to get up from his lap, but her flexors were tight and she couldn't move. "You told Jesse we have plans today."

"We do." He rubbed the tops of her thighs and winked. "Right here. All weekend."

She was on board with that.

Brendan gently straightened her legs and got out of bed. "And I'll make breakfast."

He made them French toast and sausage. Katie made the coffee.

Afterward, they curled up together under a blanket on the soft leather sofa. Brendan picked up the remote and flicked on the TV.

Miracle on 34th Street.

Katie noticed a box from the basement they hadn't opened sitting on the floor beside the tree.

"Babe, we missed one." She sat up, getting out from beneath the blanket. "There's another box of ornaments."

"There aren't any ornaments in there."

Katie watched Brendan carry the box over to the sofa. "What's in there then?"

He carefully opened the flaps of the worn cardboard box and sifting through packing paper, he lifted out a frame wrapped in tissue and handed it to her. She flicked her eyes up to his and he nodded for her to open it.

Three faces smiled at her. One obviously Brendan. Younger. A teenager, and already devastatingly gorgeous with his dark-auburn hair and striking blue eyes. No ink yet, though. A man and a woman posed with him, leaning against his silver Corvette. The woman was beautiful with dark hair and the same blue eyes as Brendan. The man, a handsome ginger.

His parents.

Katie glanced over at him. His eyes were glassy and she looked away to the framed photo on her lap.

"That was taken on my sixteenth birthday. They got me the car." He smiled at the memory of it. "My dad said if I made honor roll I could have any car I wanted." He chuckled. "I never brought home anything but As on my report card, so that was a given. I almost flunked out of my first semester of college when they died. Would have, too, if it weren't for Uncle Charley keeping my ass in line. But I packed away all the pictures, that way I didn't have to be reminded they were gone."

Katie squeezed his hand and gave the photo back to him. "And now?"

"I want to remember they were here." Brendan got up, and dusting off the frame he stood it on the shelf. "Sometimes it feels like they still are." He paused and turned around. "All of them. Uncle Charley. Aunt Peggy. Uncle Tommy."

Katie glanced at the photo on the shelf. Their tree beside the fire. The man she loved with every fiber of her being. And she smiled. *Miracle on 34th Street* played in the background, a young Natalie Wood on the screen.

I believe, I believe, I believe.

Twenty-Three

I t's funny how everything looked so different now, brighter, yet was still the same.

Brendan glanced at the painted black walls with crisp white molding, the tree twinkling in the corner, the photos on the shelves. He and his cousins at the lake house the summer before last, a fangirling Chloe and Linnea posing with Taylor at Charley's, his mom and dad. Thanks to Jesse, a new photo of he and Katelyn at the Christmas tree lot stood next to it.

Old and new. Past, present, and future together. Side by side, just as they should be. Exactly the way he wanted it.

The front door creaked open. Brendan felt the cold rush of December air come in with Dillon from outside. His cousin strolled into the room, coat hanging open, Hugo Boss beneath it.

Ready to fuck.

Course, he was.

Dillon plopped his ass down on the arm of the sofa. "Anything you need to fill me in on before I go?"

"Don't think so." Brendan smirked. "Just keep your dick out of the help. You already cost us one bartender."

"Fuck off, man."

"Kidding." He clapped Dillon's shoulder. "Thanks for covering tonight, man."

"Sure." He smirked. "I'd be hangin' out there anyway. Go have fun with your girl."

Katelyn was going to spend a few days with her parents for Christmas, so Brendan was taking her to the zoo to see the lights. They'd have a holiday celebration of their own. He was going to meet her family and bring her back home in time to ring in the new year.

Brendan grabbed his gear. "C'mon, I was just going to leave to pick her up. I can drop you off at the club on the way."

Katelyn came bustling out of Beanie's, bag in hand, wearing a wool knit cap and dressed in warm layers, just like he'd told her to. It was cold and there was a good chance they'd be getting more snow. He didn't want her to get sick, besides he was looking forward to peeling off each and every layer when they got home later.

Yeah, he had plans.

He jumped out of the car and took her bag. Kissed her there at the curb and waved to Kelly who was watching them through the window, then he tucked her into the passenger seat and buckled her in.

"She likes to watch us, huh?"

Katelyn giggled. "Who?"

"Kelly."

"Oh." Katelyn waved it off. "Kelly just…I don't know. She worries about me and I don't think she trusts men very much."

"You mean she doesn't trust me."

"No." She shook her head emphatically. "Not you in particular. Men in general."

He put the car in gear and muttered under his breath. "She was okay with frat boy, though, wasn't she?"

The zoo was a different place in the dark, transformed into a holiday wonderland. Lights danced and flashed everywhere in synchrony to music. Another amazing spectacle to see at every turn, and Katelyn stopped at each one. He watched her eyes light up, the sparkle in them, as she took delight in every festive display, her arm linked with his.

Brendan had always loved this place, found it magical in every season. Like the lake house, it was special to him, and that she loved it too made it even more so. Katelyn was shivering in spite of the layers she wore. He couldn't keep her out here much longer.

He pulled her closer against him. "Want some hot chocolate, sweetheart? Warm you up a little."

"Yeah, that sounds good."

She drank it as they walked away from the crowds and all the lights. Brendan stopped when they reached the lily pool. He wrapped his arms around her and they swayed to the music playing far off in the distance.

It had to be here. Right here in front of the lily pool.

Brendan took her face in his hands. He brushed his thumbs across her cold cheeks, and gazed right into those eyes that were neither blue nor green. "I love you, Katelyn."

He'd been wanting to say it for weeks, but it had to be here.

Her lips parted with a silent gasp and a tear slipped out of her eye. Brendan hoisted her up to him like he always did. She held onto him so tight.

Katelyn spoke through her tears. "I love you too, Brendan. I'm so happy."

That's all he wanted. To love her. To be happy with her.

Brendan kissed her slow and deep and sweet, holding her in front of the lily pool. Then he set her down. "Close your eyes and no peeking."

Katelyn did as she was told. He took the vintage bracelet out of his pocket. An aquamarine, the color of her eyes, set in platinum and surrounded with diamonds. It reminded him of her as soon as he saw it.

He fastened it to her wrist. "Merry Christmas, sweet girl."

She opened her eyes and gasped. "Oh, Brendan, it's beautiful!" Then she threw her arms around him. "You said no presents."

"I lied."

"But I don't have anything to give you."

He leaned down to kiss her. "Sweetheart, you just did."

Katelyn still shivered beneath her layers and her scarf and her knitted cap. "Still cold?"

"A little."

"Let's get some dinner and go home."

They went for pizza pot pies. It was an hour wait for a table, but it was her favorite place, so Brendan didn't mind. She came first.

When they were boys, he and his cousins had been taught that. It had been instilled in them by word and example, from the men of the family—his father and his uncles. Family first. Above all others, your love and loyalty belonged to them. Traditional in that sense, it's the reason they were as tight as they were today. And Katelyn was his. His to love. To keep safe and care for. She was his family now.

After dinner and the zoo, with their bellies full, comfortable and warm, they snuggled together under a blanket on the hammock bed suspended from the ceiling in the sitting area of the bedroom to watch a movie. Brendan had thought it ridiculous when the interior designer first suggested it, but now, with Katelyn curled up flush against him, he thought it perfect.

Yeah, this night was just beginning.

Under the blanket, she wore one of her tiny tops that he loved and a pair of boy shorts. He stroked her soft skin, from shoulder to thigh, as they watched the movie. Happy and content just to be with her. Breathing her in. Edible and sweet. Candy and flowers. White chocolate and jasmine.

Katelyn rested her hand on top of his, the bracelet sparkling on her wrist, as it moved up and down her body. She locked her fingers with his and held him to her breast. Brendan heard her breathy sigh and squeezed the mound of supple flesh through thin cotton. His cock stirred in his briefs.

He squeezed his eyes closed, face nuzzled in her neck, he felt compelled to tell her again. And again, and again, and again. "I love you."

"And I love you," her sweet voice answered, turning to face him. "So much."

Brendan brushed the hair from her face and his hand dipped

beneath the thin cotton, her warm flesh in his fingers. "I have something else for you." He squeezed her bare breast. "Do you trust me, baby?"

"Of course I do."

He reached under his pillow, retrieved the small wrapped box, and set it in her hand. Katelyn tilted her head with a smile as she held it. Brendan sat back to watch her reaction as she tore off the paper and opened it.

She looked confused at first. Realization dawned on her face slowly as she gazed at the pair of nipple clamps, adorned with dangling butterflies, nestled on a cushion of black velvet. He didn't miss the flare of her pupils, the flush to her cheeks.

"Butterflies," she whispered, gazing up at him from beneath her lashes. "Why butterflies?"

"Because I love that I'm the man that gives them to you." He winked. "And I always will be."

Her eyes widened and she gasped. "You knew?"

"I knew." He took her in his arms. "Don't be mad. Chloe was looking out for us, that's all."

"I'm not." Katelyn smiled and flicked the little butterflies so they danced on the clamps. "That girl at the club that night, you put them on her."

How he regretted that night ever happened, but it had. Brendan was giving the clamps to Katelyn for reasons besides what Angelica, and others, used them for.

"I did," he admitted, not that he had to. She'd been there. "They were used as prop, part of the exhibition and purely for physical pleasure—just like fucking."

"Oh."

Brendan kissed her brow and lightly stroked her skin. "For us, the clamps can be more than just an enhancement to pleasure. We can use them to increase intimacy between us. Trust. Vulnerability. A bond. Do you understand?"

"Kind of."

"Sex always requires a certain level of vulnerability, but when you love someone, being vulnerable builds trust and creates a deeper bond. Closeness. Intimacy. You can't have one without the other, and that's what I need to have with you."

"And these will do that?"

"They're a device that can be utilized to enhance that—just like tantra." He squeezed her shoulders. "And anything else we might want to try together in the future."

She nodded.

"Sweetheart, do you know why I always tell you to use your words?"

She shrugged. "Not really."

"Communication is key. I have to know when you want something or when you don't, when it feels good or if it doesn't. When to stop. When to keep going. Faster. Slower. Harder. Softer. Less. More. That you understand." He kissed her lips. "Okay?"

"Okay."

"Good girl."

Open communication would spill into every aspect of their life together, not just sex. Brendan didn't need to tell her that, though. They'd just have a better relationship for it.

"Do you know why I chose nipple clamps for you?"

"No." But Katelyn was smiling. He guessed she had a notion.

Brendan slowly ran his index fingers down her chest and over her nipples as he spoke. "Because your nipples are extra sensitive, sweet girl. You enjoy when they're played with, pinched, when I bite on them. With the clamps we can stimulate them while my hands and mouth are…" He paused with a wink. "… occupied elsewhere."

Katelyn bit her lip. Yeah, she got the idea.

He lifted the little shirt by the hem and pulled it over her head, exposing her luscious breasts to him. Creamy swells of warm flesh. Areolae, pink and puckered. Ripe nipples just waiting for his touch.

Tenderly, Brendan took her lips with his. He slipped inside and savored her sweetness, their tongues in a soft slow dance. Unhurried. This wasn't a race to the finish, climax would come soon enough. This was for her.

With the pads of his thumbs he lightly caressed her nipples as he kissed her. A barely there touch, yet she arched her back, pushing her breasts into his hands. He smiled against her lips and kissed down the column of her throat, stopping to suck the skin at the curve of her neck.

His hand reached inside her boy shorts, seeking out her cunt with his fingers. Slick and wet. Brendan bypassed her clit and easily penetrated her, delicately massaging her G-spot. He teased a nipple with his tongue, licking it while he touched the other. Katelyn began to make her little squeaky noises in between panting breaths.

He stopped, and sucking her from his fingers, he sat up. Brendan pulled her panties down her legs, then he reached for the clamps.

"Katelyn. I'm going to put the clamps on now, baby." He traced his fingers soothingly up and down her thigh. "I want you to touch yourself. Rub your clit. Can you do that for me?"

Her turquoise gaze was on him. She swallowed. "Yes."

Brendan watched as she spread her legs, and holding her lips open with one hand, began to rub circles on her clit. Displaying her pretty pussy for him. He attached a clamp to her right nipple in its most open position, slowly tightening the screw without applying pressure, only to the point the clamp could hold on its own. Then he did the same on her left.

"That's my good girl." Black crystal butterflies dangled off her nipples. So fucking beautiful. He gave his dick a firm tug. "Keep touching yourself."

He stretched out beside her and lavished attention on her clamped nipples, licking each one, then he tightened the screw one turn and licked them some more. Her squeaks turned into breathy moans.

"How does that feel, sweet girl?"

"Good."

Brendan tightened them a second time. Katelyn moaned louder. He licked and laved her nipples, pointing his tongue and then flattening it while he watched her work her clit. She was rubbing it faster, the circles smaller.

"Still good?"

"Yes."

Then he tightened the screws a third time.

"Fuck," she cried out and began rubbing her clit in a frenzied motion.

"Easy, baby." He pushed her hand off her pussy and spread her thighs wide. "I've got you."

He feasted on her wet cunt, lapping up the delicious honey that flowed from inside her. Katelyn alternately whimpered and called out his name, holding his head to her pussy, pulling on his hair. And he was just getting started.

Brendan penetrated her with two fingers, crooking them inside her to stimulate her G-spot while his tongue moved to her clit. Light circles contrasted with the intensity from his fingers. All the while, the clamps provided constant stimulation to her nipples.

He applied more pressure with his fingers and tongue, licking and circling and sucking on her clit. Pressing into her G-spot harder and faster. She tugged on his hair and screamed, bathing him in a fountain of her glorious cum.

Katelyn was in another space, and before she could come down from it, Brendan removed the clamps, sheathed himself, and swiftly entered her. Their sex was on fire. He fucked her hard and fast in the hammock bed suspended from the ceiling. He fucked her until they both dripped with sweat and she screamed once more. Then after, he held her to him, combing his fingers through her sweat-soaked hair, kissing her face, as he wrapped them in a blanket.

He'd never been as close to another human being as he was with her.

Not ever.

And he knew in his soul he never would.

Twenty-Four

I will always despise algebra.

She sat in the same seat, in the very back row, closest to the window. Her gaze traveled from the test questions in front of her to the dismal December sky outside. Thankful that once she was finished with this exam she'd never have to sit in this third-floor classroom or listen to that monotone voice at the whiteboard ever again. Thirty minutes and solving a quadratic equation were the only things left between her and three weeks of freedom.

Katie forced her attention back to the paper on her desk. Cameron sat in the seat next to hers, scribbling away on his answer sheet. Things were still kind of awkward, but somehow they'd managed to remain friends.

"Fuck this," she muttered under her breath.

Cameron sniggered from the seat beside her. She was done with finding the value of x, coefficients, and graphing quadratic functions. Katie set the pencil down on her desk. She'd never use any of this shit in real life anyway, so what was the point in making her brain hurt?

Being in the back had its disadvantages. She and Cameron were the last ones out the door when the bell finally rang. Katie stopped in the hallway to put on her coat before she reached the stairwell. He stopped with her.

"Was that your last exam?"

Katie paused mid-sleeve and grinned. "Yeah."

"Me too." He helped her with her coat. "You staying here for Christmas?"

"No, I'm catching a train this afternoon to visit my folks." She wound her scarf tighter around her neck in preparation for the arctic blast when they opened the door to the outside. "Are you going home?"

They'd lost the playoffs. There'd be no bowl game. No chance at the pros.

"Got a flight out to Billings in the morning." He smiled, a hint of dimples showing, and opened the door. "Going skiing."

"Have fun with your family and Merry Christmas," she said, smiling. "I'll see you next year."

How corny was that?

"We don't have any classes together next semester, so I probably won't see you much." He looked kind of sad. Why did he have to look like that?

"Oh, I'm sure I'll still get to see you."

"Maybe." Cameron leaned in and hugged her. "Hope so."

He kissed her on the forehead and took a step back. "Merry Christmas, Katie Copeland."

Then he smiled and walked away in the opposite direction on the icy sidewalk.

Merry Christmas, Cameron Mayhew.

Hours later, on a train headed west, Katie mused on how much had changed in the six months since she'd left her childhood home. How *she* had changed. Would they notice? Everything was so different now. She'd met Brendan. Fell in love. She saw a future with him—a life. A beautiful life.

Kevin was waiting when she got off the train. She'd expected to see her dad, and for a second there, she'd almost mistaken him for their father. He must've grown half a foot and had filled out some since she saw him last. He had stubble on his face that hadn't been there before. Her brother looked more like a man than a sixteen-year-old boy.

"Kev!"

She dropped her bags on the platform to hug him, then ran her fingers through his shaggy blond hair. Taller than she was now, Katie tilted her head back to look up at him. She'd never had to do that before and it felt weird.

"Hey, sis." He gave her a squeeze. "I've missed you."

"Oh, I've missed you too." She had. A lot. Katie hugged him again. "You should come visit me and Kell for spring break."

"Yeah. That'd be cool."

Katie glanced around the small station. "Where's Dad?"

"Back at the house." He picked up her bags. "Shit, Katie, what the hell did you pack in here?"

"Presents mostly." She smirked. They started walking outside toward the gravel lot. "I can't believe Dad let you take his truck and come get me."

"Um, he didn't exactly." Kevin stopped in front of a brand-new Ford F150 Raptor. "Came to get you in my own."

What. The. Fuck?

She'd had to beg to borrow her mother's Volkswagen. Getting a car of her own had been out of the question—a big fat '*no*' any time she'd brought it up. How did Kevin rate a fucking sixty-thousand-dollar truck?

"This is yours?"

"Yeah." Her brother loaded her bags in the back of the shiny red cab and helped her into the passenger seat.

"Did you win it or something?"

It was the only explanation Katie could come up with. She breathed in winter, leather seats, and new car.

"Nope. Dad went to trade his old truck in on a new one. Left the dealership with two." He chuckled with a shrug. "You buckled in?"

She sat there with her mouth hanging open and reached for the seat belt, latching it into place. Kevin just turned sixteen in July. He was a junior in high school, for fuck's sake. Katie spied some familiar foil packets in the cubby below the touch screen.

Oh, Jesus!

"Kevin, please don't tell me you've been fucking girls in the seat I'm sitting on."

"Nah." He smirked and tipped his head behind him. "There's more room back there."

Kevin pulled into the snow-covered drive of their house on the outskirts of the small town they lived in. Lit with multicolored lights for Christmas. Same as every year. The Reillys' farmhouse beyond was dark, their winter fields barren. A black truck she'd never seen before, she presumed it was her dad's new one, and her aunt's blue Tahoe were parked off to the side.

He turned off the ignition and Katie looked over at him. Kevin could read her face. He always could. "They're all here waiting on ya. Mom made all your favorites for dinner."

Which one?

Katie didn't have one mother. She had four. Not really, but her aunts—her mom's younger sisters—were all mother hens who liked to think she was still five. Kelly was the youngest, and if it hadn't been for her already living in the city she probably would have never been allowed to leave the cornfields to go to school.

Her brother looked at her like he felt sorry for her. "I should probably warn you. Kelly told them all about your boyfriend."

Thanks a fucking lot, Kelly.

She knew better. As the youngest of the four sisters, Kelly had to know the inquisition Katie was going to walk into. Her mother, Kristie, was the eldest, followed by Kim and Kara. Kelly, who was teasingly referred to as the *'oops'* baby by her siblings, was six years younger than Kara—twelve years younger than Katie's mother.

"Great." She unlatched her seat belt and took a deep breath before she got out of the truck to prepare for the onslaught. "What did she say?"

Brendan was coming for dinner to meet her family and bring her back home on Sunday. It's not like her parents didn't know about him, for chrissakes, but Brendan had a point. Kelly was still judgmental when it came to him, and she wasn't sure why that was.

"Not sure." He shrugged, pulling out her bags. "I only heard Mom going on about him being older."

"He's thirty-two and he's a wonderful man."

Kevin helped her down from the truck and held her hands in his. "Listen, don't let them get to you. If he's good to you, then I like him."

"He's so good to me, Kevin. I love him." She squeezed her brother's hand. "And he loves me."

"That's all I needed to hear. C'mon, I got your back, big sister." He kissed her cheek.

"You're bigger than me now."

He snickered. "Yeah, how'd that happen?"

They were all waiting for her in the family room. Her mom and her aunts sat together on the sofa, her dad dozing in his recliner. He got up as soon as she and Kevin walked in.

"Honey," her dad called out, and extending his arms he wrapped her in a giant hug.

It started as soon as he let her go and lasted all the way through dinner. Brendan was the sole topic of conversation and Kim led the inquisition.

"So, what exactly does your boyfriend do?"

Katie smiled politely. "Brendan and his cousins have their own investment company—real estate mostly."

Kim nodded. "Uh-huh. He was a business major then?"

"Yeah. Actually, he's a CPA." Her aunt looked at her funny. "An accountant."

"Don't be flip, young lady. I know what a CPA is." Kim shook her head, still looking perplexed. "Kelly said something about a restaurant and a nightclub."

"Yeah, well, they own those too."

Her mom cut in. "Are you going to major in business too, then?"

Why would she think that? Because Brendan had?

"Uh, I don't know yet."

Kara locked her eyes on the bracelet that dangled on her wrist and remained silent.

Kevin and her dad just stared across the table at one another, snickering and shoveling spoonfuls of mashed potatoes into their mouths. They knew better than to even try to get a word in when her mother and her sisters were going at it. Katie smiled at her father.

"So, Dad, how's the store?"

Her family owned the hardware store in town. Business must be pretty darn good if the new trucks in the driveway were anything to go by.

He swallowed a mouthful of potatoes. "All right."

"Katie, honestly, you really should know what you want to do with your life by now. Your father and I pay a lot of money for your tuition."

Not really. She had a scholarship, but she didn't feel like wasting her breath to point that out. It would fall on deaf ears anyway.

There was a moment's silence. The sisters cut into their food and chewed. Her ears were vibrating from their incessant chatter. Katie closed her eyes and prayed they would just stay quiet and keep eating.

Kara finally spoke up. "It's serious, huh?" Her gaze was back on the bracelet.

Katie just looked at her.

"It's not serious. Katie's only eighteen. She's too young to know what she wants," her mother scoffed.

"You expect me to know what I want to do with the rest of my life, but I'm too young to know who I want to spend my life with?" Katie threw her napkin down on the table. "Yeah, that makes a lot of sense."

Five unblinking pairs of eyes stared at her. They were speechless now that she had spoken. Katie glanced around the table and stood.

"It's been a really long day and I'm tired. I'm going to unpack now, take a shower, and go to bed."

She left the room.

Kevin must have carried her bags upstairs. They were in her bedroom by the door. Katie grabbed her stuff and trudged into the bathroom. Even she was surprised at herself for losing her temper like she had. She was used to her mother and her aunts. She loved them. That's just how they were, how they'd always been. So why was she so out of sorts?

She missed him.

Even when they weren't together, she was comforted knowing he was close by.

The city, and Brendan, were two hours and a hundred miles away.

Katie stripped off her clothes to shower. There was blood in her panties. She looked under the bathroom sink for a box of tampons.

Maybe she was just hormonal.

And it had been a long day.

After her shower, she snuggled under the covers in her childhood bed and texted Brendan to say goodnight. She knew he was at the club, but he'd asked her to, and she promised she would.

His reply was immediate.

It warmed her heart to know he'd been waiting for her text.

She smiled and closed her eyes.

Dream of me, sweet girl.

I love you.

Twenty-Five

One more night.

One more night behind the red door. One more night until his sweet girl was back in his arms where she belonged. While Brendan knew he was going to miss Katelyn, it came as a surprise to him just how much he'd missed her. How empty the house felt without her. He wanted to wake up beside her every morning. Fall asleep holding her every night. He knew some things were going to have to change for that to happen, but he was more than ready for it.

Brendan waved at Kelly and Leo through the window as he walked past the coffee bar on his way to Charley's. He was meeting Kyan and Dillon for a beer and a burger before he had to be at the club. Marcus, who managed the restaurant, rushed to greet him when he came in the door.

"They're waiting for you. Usual table."

"Thanks, Marcus." Brendan patted him on the shoulder as he walked past and headed toward the side of the restaurant where the bar was.

His cousins, along with Kodiak, were seated in a private booth near the fire that burned in a hearth of exposed brick. A welcome respite from the bitter cold outside. Brendan slid in next to Kyan. Dillon and Kodiak had their noses buried in menus, which made him laugh. They damn well knew what was on it and ordered the same thing every time they were here anyway.

Dillon looked up. "What?"

"Menu hasn't changed since we opened the place, Dill." Brendan shook his head, still chuckling. "You're just gonna get a cheeseburger and wings. Kodiak will order the ribs. So why in the hell do you even bother looking?"

The server took that opportune moment to appear. Dillon grinned. "Ribeye, medium rare. Loaded baked potato and the asparagus." He paused briefly. "Oh, and give me an order of hot wings too."

Brendan snickered, pouring himself a beer from the pitcher on the table. "Change is good, Dill."

After the server left with their order, Kyan got their attention and spoke in a hushed tone. "Get this. Looks like Salena is keeping exclusive company with…" He elbowed Brendan in the ribs. "…Eric Brantley."

"Uh, I think I already knew that."

"How? Kodiak just told me…"

"Katelyn and I ran into her at the Music Box. She was with Eric and his son." Brendan shrugged and took a pull of his beer. "I didn't know they were exclusive, though."

"They seem to be," Kodiak added. He started scrolling through his phone. "When was that, Bren?"

"November. Before Thanksgiving."

"Wish you'd have told me." Kodiak cocked his head. "I'd have started digging into this dude sooner." Then he grinned. "Know of any reason Senator Rollins might be depositing ten grand into Salena's bank account every month?"

The fuck?

Brendan could think of several. A friend of Salena's, and he used that term loosely, State Senator Mitch Rollins was one of the club's original members. The press would have a field day, and his political career would be over, if that alone ever became public knowledge. But Rollins belonged to several private clubs, not just the Red

Door. He was into pain and degradation. His preferences bordered on the extreme.

He nodded. "Blackmail comes to mind."

"She has a few other hefty monthly deposits coming in, but I haven't figured out the sources of those yet." Kodiak cocked his head to the opposite side, still grinning. "Rollins isn't very smart. The funds went directly from his personal account into hers."

"Is that right?"

"He's been paying her off for years, from what I can tell, but I only went back five."

Interesting.

"That's before the club even opened," Dillon interjected. "She's been playing at this gig a long time. What the fuck?"

"How much?"

"She's taking in about half a mil a year." Kodiak shrugged. "That's pocket change to guys like Rollins."

Whatever Salena was up to, it was bigger than her obsession with Kyan or Dillon, more than revenge against him, and reached further than the Red Door.

Yeah, he'd underestimated her.

"It's not adding up. We're missing something." Brendan rubbed his finger back and forth across his lip. "What's she doing with Brantley?"

"That's what we're gonna find out."

When Katelyn said she lived in Nowheresville, she wasn't kidding. He was almost in Iowa, for fuck's sake. Not really, but it seemed like it. He'd seen nothing but snow-covered corn fields since he got off the interstate.

Brendan came to a four-way stop. His GPS told him to turn right. He'd gone about a mile when a house strung in multicolored Christmas lights finally came into view. Big front porch. Trucks in the driveway. The mailbox said Copeland.

He pulled in behind a red Ford Raptor and Katelyn came running out the front door. No coat. He got out of his car and wrapped her inside his. She hugged him like they'd been apart five years and not just five days.

"Sweetheart, you're going to catch pneumonia out here like that."

They swayed from side to side on the driveway in his coat. She felt good. Warm. His.

"I couldn't wait one more second." She squeezed him tighter. "I missed you."

"I missed you too, baby." He kissed her crown. "Let's get you back inside."

"Wait." She smiled from beneath her lashes, shivering against him. "I want to give you something first." Katelyn scooted around to the passenger side and they both got in. She handed him a small wrapped box.

"We agreed, sweetheart. No presents."

"I lied." She winked. "Kevin helped me. It was supposed to be for your birthday."

Thin bands of braided black leather were attached to a small hammered plate of silver. There were numbers engraved on it. Coordinates.

41.9398° N

87.6589° W

She fastened the bracelet to his wrist as he had done with hers. "The coordinates of Coventry Park. Where we met."

"God, I love you."

Can a heart explode? Because it felt to him like his could. This girl. She kept right on squeezing that muscle in his chest. Brendan took her face in his hands and kissed her. He would have hauled her over the console into his lap if he could've.

"And I love you," she whispered.

Katelyn brought him in the house and hung up his coat. It was a modest home, from what he could see. Neat. Comfortable and cozy.

She took his hand and whispered, "My mom and her sisters are in the kitchen, but my dad and Kevin are in the family room."

"Why are you whispering?" he whispered back.

Then she laughed. "I don't know."

"Nervous?"

She raised one shoulder and pursed her lips. "Maybe a little."

"It's your family." He kissed her forehead. "I love you."

"I love you too."

He overheard a woman from another room say in a hushed voice, "He's here."

Katelyn blushed pink. "That would be my aunt."

"Shall we then?" He chuckled and wrapped an arm around her waist. "C'mon."

Kristie Matthews Copeland and her two younger sisters stopped their chatter the instant he and Katelyn entered the kitchen. Blonde, blue-eyed, and pretty, it was obvious they were related. They probably weren't much older than him—mid to late thirties, if he were to guess. That was awkward, but they were pleasant enough when Katelyn made the introductions. Not overly friendly. Just polite.

Her father and brother came into the kitchen. He presumed that's who they were anyway. Brendan towered a good eight inches over both of them. Wearing a football jersey, her father's vibrant green eyes stood out with his tousled brown hair. He guessed him to be about forty. Still in decent shape. Katelyn's brother looked a lot like her. Hair the color of wheat. Blue-green eyes. Worked out. He appeared to be older than the sixteen years Brendan knew him to be.

"Whoa, how tall are you?" Katelyn's brother looked up and extended his hand. "I'm Kevin."

"Six-eight." He grinned, shaking his hand. He got asked that a lot. "Brendan."

"I'm Katie's dad, Drew."

He seemed like a nice enough guy. They joined her father and brother in the family room to watch football until Kristie announced dinner was ready. Katelyn still seemed nervous. She held onto his arm as she led him into the dining room.

Brendan couldn't say what prompted the outburst. He, Drew, and Kevin were discussing how the NFC playoff picture was shaping up in between bites of cheesecake. Next thing he knew, Katelyn was pressing her fingers into his thigh.

Kristie pointed at her daughter with her fork, waving it. "You know nothing of yourself at eighteen." Graham cracker crumbs flying. "You can't even pick a major, for chrissakes."

"Really, Mom? Again?" Katelyn calmly set her fork down on her plate and stood.

Brendan glanced around the table.

She never raised her voice, yet spoke with conviction.

"So what if I haven't decided on a major yet. I know I like working at Beanie's with Kelly. I know the city is my home now—my heart is there. It has been since the first time I can remember getting off the train downtown when I was a little girl. And I know I love Brendan—the same as you love Daddy. If anything, you should trust me on that. It was you and Daddy who taught me what love is supposed to look like after all."

You could have heard a pin drop after that.

Brendan stood and took her hand in his. "Sounds like Katelyn knows herself pretty well to me. We have a long drive back and they're predicting snow. Are you ready to go, sweetheart?"

"Yeah. Let me grab my things."

"Sorry, man." Kevin shrugged and got up from table. "I'll help you, sis."

"Thank you for dinner. It was, um, nice meeting you folks."

She was quiet most of the ride back to the city. Katelyn gazed out the window. Brendan sensed she needed a little time to process and she was probably embarrassed, but she never had to feel that way with him, and he needed her to know that.

As the lights of the city skyline came into view, Brendan took her hand and held it on his thigh. Katelyn turned from the window.

He could feel her gaze on him and lacing their fingers together he rubbed her palm.

"Do you want to talk about it?"

"Nothing to talk about." She squeezed his hand. "Sorry you had to witness that, but my mother—hell, my aunts too—need to realize that I know my own mind. I'm not a little kid anymore."

"No, you aren't, but you are the first one to leave home." He rubbed her hand up and down his thigh. "And I imagine that hasn't been easy for them. Letting go, you know?"

"I suppose."

"Feel better now, sweetheart?"

"Not yet." Her hand left his thigh and traveled to his groin, cupping him over the denim. "Are we almost home?"

He groaned and reflexively pushed himself against her hand. *Not close enough.*

"Take me out."

Katelyn popped the button on his jeans and lowered the zipper. She reached inside and pulled his dick free, watching it fill in her fingers. Then, slow and firm, she began to stroke him. A drop of precum beaded at the tip. She rubbed it around his head with her thumb and brought it to her mouth.

"Baby, just you wait until I get you home."

He didn't even wait until they got inside the house.

Brendan pushed her onto the hood of the 'Vette, pulled her jeans down her legs, and buried his face in her warm, wet cunt. He fucked her with his tongue, clamped her clit between his teeth, mercilessly sucking on it until she screamed.

"Feel better yet?"

"Not yet," she panted.

He reached into his back pocket, pulled a condom out of his wallet, then tossed it on the hood. "I'm gonna fuck you right here then."

Her jeans were stuck on her boots, puddled at her ankles. Brendan lifted her legs, folding her in half, and with one thrust he was all the way inside her hot, wet heaven.

"I missed this tight, little cunt on my dick."

He pounded into her, got off hearing her little whimpers with every slap of flesh.

"Fuck, Brendan." She clung to his arms. "Yes, fuck."

He stopped to let her legs down and pull off her boots and her pants.

"No, baby. Don't stop." Tears ran down her cheeks. "Put it back in me."

"Sweet girl."

He ran his fingers through her slit and plunged back inside her. Brendan slid his hands under her back and lifted her from the car, impaling Katelyn on his cock. He moved her body up and down on it as he backed her into the garage wall, caging her with his body.

Then he thrust up inside her as far as he could go.

"Yes," she mewled, thrashing her head on the wall.

He thrust again. Harder. She bit her lip and moaned.

"That's my good girl." He thrust again. "Take it."

She did.

Brendan let himself go, plunging inside her soft pussy again and again and again.

Katelyn was home.

And he was home inside her.

Twenty-Six

"Did we just fuck?"

Brendan gently eased her away from the garage wall and lowered her to the floor.

"Baby, with us it's never gonna be just fucking, but I'll make love to you when we get upstairs." He winked and patted her behind.

He made love to her in the shower, and again on the hammock bed. Katie lay in the crook of his arm, sheltered by the warmth of his body, as he played with her hair. With Brendan, she felt safe, loved, protected—not that she ever felt unloved or unsafe before. But her place in the world made sense when they were together. And with him is where she wanted to be.

She felt his kiss on her crown. "I'm going to start looking for someone to help manage the Red Door."

"What?" Katie turned over in his arms. "Why?"

"Because the club takes me away from you six nights a week." He pulled her up on his chest until their noses met. And their lips touched. "One night with you isn't nearly enough."

"No?"

"No." His hands held her face and his thumbs skimmed her cheeks. "I want every night."

Warm lips caressed hers, gently coaxing her to open, and his tongue slipped inside. Katie wanted the same thing. More time together. Just like this. Soon, the holidays would be over. She'd start the new semester, juggling Beanie's and classes. Between his schedule and hers, they'd only have stolen moments and Sundays. Brendan was right. It wasn't enough.

Katie felt it all too keenly the next morning when he took her home and she kissed him goodbye. She didn't want to. Not that she wouldn't see him later. Brendan would stop in for coffee on his way to the club like he always did, but being in love is like an addiction, and he was her drug. She wanted…more.

Kelly had her AirPods in, humming along to whatever song she was listening to, as she sat at a table close to the counter doing paperwork. It was annoying. Leo had a couple days off now that she was back, so it was just her and Kelly here today. Katie glanced over at the clock.

Ugh.

It hadn't moved much since the last time she looked at it. That was another thing. Why did minutes seem to fly by when they were together, yet dragged when they were apart? Katie figured First Avenue would be bustling the Monday after Christmas with the sales and all—she'd at least be occupied then. She figured wrong.

"Shit, you've got it bad."

"Got what?"

No longer humming, Kelly looked at her from the table and smirked. "Lovesickness. Whatever you want to call it." She shook her head. "Kim called me and told me about the shit you said before you even left the driveway."

Katie rolled her eyes in response. "Why am I not surprised? I don't care what Aunt Kim…"

"Shut up, KK." Kelly gathered her papers from the table. "Everyone liked him—even if we all think you're too young."

"Too young for what, Kelly?"

Her aunt wouldn't meet her gaze. She kept her eyes cast down to the paperwork in her hands and shook her head. "Just…too young."

"Can I ask you something?"

That got her to look up. "You can ask me anything, tell me anything. You know that."

"Would you think that if I was still with Cam?"

Crickets.

Of course not.

"That's what I thought."

Why the fuck did it matter how young she was, or how old Brendan was, or how many years separated them? She loved him and he loved her, and nothing else mattered. If Kelly, or her parents, or her aunts, or anyone else had a problem with it, it was their problem. Not hers. Not Brendan's.

"Katie, it's just…never mind." She released a loud exhale, shaking her head.

"No. What?"

Kelly came behind the counter. "Remember what I said about making a mistake you might regret?"

Katie tucked her hair behind her ear, her eyes flicking to her aunt. "Yeah, they can last a lifetime."

"Well, for your sake…" Kelly smoothed her just-tucked hair. "…I'm going to hope Brendan doesn't turn out to be one of those."

He won't.

She would never regret him. Not ever. He was her forever.

Her gaze cut to the window right as Brendan walked up to the door with Dillon on his heels and her lips instantly rose in a smile. The winter air rushed inside with them. Katie rubbed her arms, wishing they had a fireplace in here or that she'd remembered her sweater.

He looked so fucking delectable. Wool overcoat hanging open over a shirt that hugged his abs. Slim-fit pants. All black. All custom tailored. And all hers.

Katie had his coffee poured before he reached over the counter to kiss her. "Mm, sweet girl."

Dillon grinned at his side. Kelly rolled her eyes and took his order. Handing Katie the cup, she cocked her head at Brendan.

"Are you stealing my niece for New Year's Eve or do I get to spend at least one holiday with her?" She pursed her lips and brought her index finger to the corner of her mouth. Then she smirked. "Never mind. You'll be *busy* at the Red Door, won't you? She's mine."

Trying to start shit, Auntie?

Well, it wasn't going to work.

Katie knew Brendan had to be at the club that night and had already resigned herself that she'd be watching the ball drop alone on TV. Was she thrilled about that? Of course not. But right now she was more pissed off at Kelly for bringing it up—so she would second guess herself, she was sure—than she was upset that she wouldn't be able to kiss him at midnight on New Year's Eve.

Brendan raised his brow and grinned. He licked his bottom lip. "Actually…"

Dillon interrupted, "It's my birthday, and you and Katie are both invited…" He winked at Kelly. "…to come."

Oh, Jesus. Is he hitting on her?

Katie fought to keep a straight face. "Your birthday is on New Year's?"

Dillon looked her way. "New Year's Day, yeah." His smile was dazzling. "So everyone has to kiss me at twelve. It's a rule. Right, Bren?"

"Right," he snickered.

"Are you out of your fucking mind?" Kelly leaned over the counter. "I cannot. I will not bring my eighteen-year-old niece to some sleazy sex club."

Uh-oh.

Katie spied the tick in Brendan's jaw before it disappeared, replaced by his trademark lazy smirk. "Then I guess she'll be there without you."

Her eyes darted from Brendan to Dillon to her aunt. This could go bad very quickly.

"C'mon." Dillon took Kelly's hand in his, stroking her palm. "It's my birthday, and the club is nothing like you're imagining, I assure you. Just ask…"

Katie felt her eyes go round as she looked at Dillon and slowly shook her head. She never did tell Kelly she went to the ball there on Halloween, and now was not the best time for her to find out.

"…anyone." Dillon caught her eye and winked.

"Katie's underage." Kelly crossed her arms over her chest and popped out her hip. "She can't get in a bar."

"It's a private club and we'll have our own VIP space," Brendan explained. He cleared his throat. "I know Katelyn's been to frat parties and we both know just how *sleazy* those are, don't we, Kelly?"

Her aunt opened her mouth, but no words came out.

Dillon grinned. "Wear something black and slinky for me."

Kelly turned abruptly and left.

"Your aunt is hot."

Katie handed Dillon his americano. "You do know she's a lesbian, right?"

He smirked with a wink. "I can change her mind."

Shaking her head, Katie giggled. Because if anyone could, it'd be him.

"I can't believe I let you talk me into this." Kelly pulled three black dresses out of her closet and threw them on top of her bed. For someone who was bitching about going, she sure was putting an awful lot of effort into getting ready.

"I didn't talk you into anything," Katie reminded her, and she snickered. "You must really want to kiss Dillon."

Holding a dress to her body in front of the floor-length mirror, Kelly glowered, her deep-blue eyes shooting daggers. "No, I really, really don't."

Katie shrugged. "If you say so."

"I say so." Kelly stepped into the dress. "He's a gorgeous man, but since he owns a penis I'm going to pass."

"Maybe you should try one."

"What makes you think I haven't?"

Nope. Not going there.

Kelly adjusted her breasts inside the dress. It had a plunging V neckline and spaghetti straps. Black and slinky, just as Dillon requested. Katie opted for a sparkly rose-gold surplice wrap, ruched-front bodycon dress. Short. Long sleeves. Daring low-cut neckline. The sequins were itchy, but she had to admit it looked hella good on her.

"Whatever." She rolled her eyes and turned to leave her aunt's room. "You almost ready? Because the car is going to be here for us any minute."

"We could have walked. It's only a block, you know."

Katie swung back around. "Brendan wants to make sure we're safe. He's thoughtful like that."

Not to mention it was fucking cold and who wants to walk on an icy sidewalk in six-inch heels? No, thanks. Kelly didn't think of that, did she? Brendan did.

The town car pulled up to the Red Door. Brendan stood waiting for them. No coat. He opened the door and assisted Kelly out first, then his hand reached for hers and Katie was in the shelter of his arms. If there was a better feeling than that, she'd yet to find it.

They bypassed the velvet ropes and crossed the threshold. This time, Katie looked her fill. The lobby, which wasn't quite the right word for the space, was magnificent. It was a cavernous two-story area where members checked in and met up. Sumptuous sofas of deep plum, rich mahogany wood, exposed brick, and crystal chandeliers.

Champagne was being served. Everyone had a flute in hand as they hugged and conversed and milled about. No masks tonight. No costumes. The people here were dressed to kill. To seduce. Sleek. Chic. Louboutin and Armani. Black, once again, the predominant color. Katie stood out from the rest, sparkling in rose gold.

She recognized the mountain of a man who canvassed the room from where he stood near the check-in desk. What was his name? Axel. With his hand on the small of her back, Brendan guided them toward him and took their coats.

"Axel, this is my beautiful girlfriend, Katelyn, and her lovely aunt, Kelly." He winked, passing off their coats to an attendant.

He did one of those chin-tip nods, the movement almost imperceptible if you weren't paying attention. "Miss Katelyn. Miss Kelly."

She looked at her aunt, feigning nonchalance as her gaze flitted all over the place. Katie knew the feeling. The Red Door was out of this world. It was a lot to take in.

Brendan led them out of the lobby and down the wide passageway where Kyan had backed her into the wall to the obscure stairway that would take them to the VIP space, to a bright new year.

Like a rerun of Halloween, Dillon and Kodiak flanked the private bar. The Venery boys, sans Taylor, loitered on the U-shaped silk sofa. Katie waved to Matt. Bo and Matt returned her greeting.

She looked up to Brendan. "Where's Chloe?"

"Today is their first wedding anniversary, sweetheart." Katie loved how his eyes twinkled gazing down at her. "She, Taylor, and Jesse are celebrating on their own." He winked. "Linnea and Kyan should be here soon, though."

Brendan softly ran his fingers through her hair. He was always touching it, like it soothed him somehow. She loved that.

Dillon came over from the bar with glasses of champagne. Looking at Kelly, Katie took a sip, daring her to say anything. She pursed her lips, but remained silent.

"Me likey," Dillon announced, surveying her aunt's sexy black dress.

"I'm going to show Katelyn around." Brendan kissed her temple and possessively wrapped his arm around her waist. "C'mon."

They left the VIP space. Brendan stopped and pulled her into a hidden corner. His hand grasped her neck and he leaned down to kiss her. Softly at first, inciting the butterflies in her belly, the pulse between her legs, with every sweep of his tongue. Fingers trailed up the back of her thigh and he lifted her up, deepening their kiss.

He paused to catch a breath. "I wanted to get you alone so I could kiss you hello without your aunt watching."

She giggled. "What about everyone else?"

"Let them watch." His thumb reached beneath her dress and brushed her nipple. "She bothers me."

"Because she's my aunt?"

"Maybe."

He kissed her again. Wild and hungry. Katie held onto him, wishing they were in his room on the hammock bed without any clothes between them. His lips trailed down her neck.

"I love you, baby."

She squeezed him against her. "And I love you."

Gently, he set her down on her heels and took her by the hand. "Let's go."

He led her down a hallway and pointed out the stairs to his office loft. They stopped when they got to the railing that could be seen from their VIP space on the other side of the club, which was between the pair of grand staircases that flanked the stage below. Brendan gave her his arm and they descended the stairs, but they didn't stop at the main club floor.

Katie didn't know what she was expecting, but it didn't look like what she thought a dungeon would at all. It was dark and decadent. Forbidden. And just as swanky and posh as it was upstairs.

A large black X mounted to the wall was the focal point in the room. Her breath hitched. She knew what it was. Brendan looked at her with that sexy, lazy smirk and his smoldering crystal-blue eyes.

"Is this your thing?"

"I told you what my thing is." Both hands reached inside the neckline of her dress, pushing it apart. "It's you."

"You know what I mean, Brendan."

He tweaked her nipples. "I do. And I remember telling you we'll figure out our thing together. We have an entire lifetime to do it."

Her knees went weak and her heart pitter-pattered when he said stuff like that.

"I wanted to bring you down here while it's relatively quiet, so you can freely explore."

"We're alone?"

"No, but there's a party going on upstairs. People won't come down here to play until after we ring in the new year. The rooms down here will fill up after that."

She walked up to the cross on the wall. "You like using this?"

Brendan stood behind her. "Yes."

"Why?"

"Control."

She pulled her sleeves down and lowered her dress. Katie stood before him, naked except for her panties and heels. He thrust his hand inside the wisp of silk. His finger combed through her wetness.

"My pretty pussy's all wet for me."

"Uh-huh."

Brendan cuffed her wrists above her head and slid her panties down her thighs, then stuffed them into his pocket. He latched onto a nipple and sucked it hard into his mouth.

"You make me fucking insane, baby," he crooned, kicking her feet apart. "The things I want to do to you."

"Do them," she panted.

He hadn't even started and already she was dying. For his cock and his cum. For all the wicked, dirty things he wanted to do with her. And she didn't care what they were. Every cell in her body was on fucking fire. Katie burned for this man in a way she'd never imagined possible.

Then he secured her ankles to the restraints. She was spread-eagle on the cross, her empty hole gaping between her legs. She could feel the cool air inside her hot pussy, but it was his dick she wanted him to fill it with. Or his fingers. Something. Anything. He twisted her nipples and she cried out, wishing she'd brought her clamps.

This man could read her mind, or maybe he just knew her body. Brendan reached into an armoire and pulled a silver chain from a drawer, nipple clamps attached to each end. She smiled.

Katie moaned as Brendan secured the clamps to her nipples. "Tight enough, baby?"

"More, please."

He turned the screw until they pinched hard and she cried out. "Mm…you don't know how much I love you, sweet girl." He kissed her and placed the chain between her teeth. "If you need more, pull on the chain. If you need something else, tell me. Understand?"

"Uh-huh." She nodded.

She needed his dick inside her, but with the chain in her mouth she couldn't tell him that.

Two fingers filled her pussy, stimulating her G-spot. His tongue flicked her clit. Katie yanked on that chain over and over. The sting in her nipples went straight to her clit only to be soothed by his wet tongue. She felt it building in her core.

It was one of the most delicious sensations in the world. To be totally at the mercy of the man you love. Restrained. Safe. Her pelvis began to undulate against his mouth. His fingers. She opened her eyes. The mountain of a man stood in the shadows at the back wall. Axel was watching them.

"Baby, I'm gonna come." The chain dropped from her mouth.

Brendan pulled his fingers from her pussy and tapped her clit. "Not yet."

His wet finger circled her ass. He'd never touched her there before. "Please, baby. I'm dying."

He nudged his finger against her hole. "One day I'm going to fuck you here."

"God, yes," she cried out. "Fuck me."

Brendan pushed his finger all the way inside her ass. It burned, but fuck if it didn't feel good. As he stroked in and out of her she imagined what his beast of a cock would feel like there. Then he pushed two fingers from his other hand inside her pussy and sucked on her clit.

Holy…mother of…shit!

Katie didn't see stars or fireworks. She felt her eyes roll back in her head, maybe she even blacked out. When she opened them again, Axel was gone and Brendan was releasing her wrists from the cuffs.

He took care of her afterward, and held her against him in a big overstuffed chair. "Dominance…being in control." He paused. "For me, it's really all about building that inseverable bond between the two of us. Trust. The connection is my thing. Mediocrity will never be in the cards for you and me, sweet girl. I'll fuck you so hard we break the damn bed and make sweet love to you too."

It was after eleven by the time they returned upstairs. Kyan and Linnea had arrived in their absence. The stage was filled with people throwing confetti and blowing horns, the video on the screen over-head cut back and forth from an orgy to the midnight countdown.

Katie looked at Brendan and raised her eyebrow.

He shrugged with a smirk and handed her a glass of champagne. "Sometimes pleasure is a team sport."

Linnea passed out noisemakers and those silly paper hats to everyone. No one was sitting on the big purple couch now. They all stood waiting to kiss the old year goodbye and bring in the new one. The four Venery boys had a couple girls between them. Kelly stood, smiling and sipping on champagne, between Dillon and Kodiak. She looked…happy.

Katie beamed up at Brendan. "I'm so happy I'm not watching the ball drop on TV."

Ten, nine, eight…

He gathered her in his arms and brushed her hair from her face, kissing her forehead. "Sweet girl, you were always going to be right here with me. Did you really think I'd want to end this year and start the new one without you?"

…four, three, two, one…

"Happy New Year, baby. I love you."

Confetti rained down on them from the ceiling. Brendan held her face in his hands and brought his lips to hers. Her first New Year's kiss, and it was the best kiss ever. Overcome with emotion, she might have been crying. Katie felt warm liquid escape from the backs of her eyes.

She held him tighter. "I love you, Brendan. Happy New Year."

"Happy birthday, Dillon," someone chanted. She thought maybe it was Kit.

Katie turned in Brendan's arms to see her aunt making out with Dillon *and* Kodiak. Not just kissing. They were swapping spit.

Dillon had his hand under her dress, fondling her breast, while Kodiak palmed the other.

What. The. Fuck!

Kyan and Linnea came over to them then. Hugs and cheek kisses.

One by one, Bo, Kit, and Sloan did the same.

Matt alone stood in front of her. The beautiful, sweet man no woman had ever given a chance. He smiled and opened his arms. Katie stepped into them and hugged him. He leaned in and kissed her lips. It wasn't more than a friendly New Year's kiss. He didn't force his tongue in her mouth or anything, but perhaps his lips stayed on hers a bit longer than they should have. She felt his erection press into her and took a step back.

"Happy New Year, Matt."

He patted her shoulder and winked. "Happy New Year, Katie."

Glaring at Matt, Brendan tugged on her hand. He took her over by the bar and held her in a tight embrace, cupping her mound in a way no one else could see.

"This pretty little pussy is mine, sweet girl, all mine. I claimed it. You bled for *me* and no other cock will ever know what's mine. Do you understand?"

Was he jealous? Of Matt?

"Yes."

"It's just you and me, Katelyn. No one else."

She got up on her tiptoes and kissed his cheek. "You don't have to be jealous of Matt."

"You're a brat. You need a spanking." He squeezed her shoulders and swatted her bottom.

"Do you want to spank me?"

"Naked across my lap, baby."

Katie looked up at him and grinned. "Let's go home."

Twenty-Seven

"Love is a severe mental illness..."

The psychology professor droned on from the lectern to an auditorium filled with second-semester freshmen. Katie thought she might vomit. Heat was blasting through the vents, making the air dry and breathing difficult. She glanced at the time on her phone.

Fifteen more minutes.

She'd get through it.

Maybe.

"...curable only with time. That's what the great philosopher Plato said. What say you?"

"Who'd want a cure?"

The professor looked at his seating chart and cleared his throat. "Miss, er, Copeland?"

Oops. I said that out loud, didn't I?

She looked up. "Yes."

"Unrequited love. Misplaced love. Abandoned love. Lost love." He nodded. "There are plenty of reasons people might want to be cured of it. Love, if not returned, can be a very painful condition indeed. If you've never felt that pain, trust me, one day you will."

The bell rang and she was the first one out the door. Sometimes being in the back row had its perks.

Katie walked backward down First Avenue, keeping the brutal January wind off her face when she got off the train. Even with a scarf over her nose and mouth it hurt her lungs to breathe, like tiny little daggers of ice were stabbing at her air sacs. Chloe was already waiting for her inside Beanie's. The thought of having to go back outside made her wish she could reschedule her appointment with Doctor Torres, but they'd waited six weeks to get this one. And she was just as keen to get rid of the condoms as Brendan was.

Kelly and Leo were behind the counter. Chloe waved from her seat at the table in front of the window. She had to be freezing sitting next to the cold glass. Katie held up her index finger to signal she'd be there in a minute. She needed something hot to warm her insides.

"Fuck, Kelly, we need to get a gas fireplace or something put in here. I feel like I'm never gonna thaw out. Can you make me a latte?" She batted her eyelashes. "Please?"

Even Leo wore a turtleneck underneath his Beanie's shirt. "I feel you, girl."

"Gotcha, KK."

The door to the shop opened. Katie felt the burst of frigid air right to the bone. Two arms wrapped around her from behind. Warm lips kissed her neck. His nose was cold. She turned around.

"Sweetheart." And those warm lips met hers. "I thought you and Chloe might have left by now, but I was hoping I'd catch you."

She grabbed her latte and a cup of black for Brendan from Kelly, then they joined Chloe at the table by the window.

Chloe looked at her phone. "We've only got five minutes before we have to go."

The door burst open again. Katie didn't pay any real notice to the couple that came in and walked up to the counter arm in arm. She and Chloe were sucking down the last dregs of coffee, almost ready to leave. Brendan leaned in to kiss her goodbye when she felt a presence standing next to their table.

"Well, would you look at that. Hello, Jesse's girl."

She knew that voice. Her hair was stuffed under a woolen cap, but there was no mistaking her amber eyes.

"Brendan," she tsked, shaking her head. "Everyone knows how fucked up you are, but robbing the cradle is just so twisted—even for you." She cackled. "How old is she, baby? Sixteen?"

He ignored her, instead addressing the silent man beside her. "Eric, if you know what's good for you—and for her—you'll get her out of here."

The man just shrugged.

"Honey, are you letting him put that big ol' dick of his in you?" She smirked. "He used to put his whole hand inside of me. And other things. Didn't you, baby?"

The man flinched. Brendan's jaw ticked. Chloe visibly paled.

"Eric," Brendan's voice boomed.

He was going to blow. She felt his hand ball into a fist, his muscles tensed, and he clenched his teeth.

"I bet they told you all sorts of lies about me. Don't believe a word from him." She looked at Chloe. "Or any of them. Trust me, you will never be able to satisfy Brendan and you'll ruin your life trying. After five years in his bed I would know."

She lies.

"I like you, little girl. And Payton liked you because you gave him a cookie. You're sweet and innocent, too young to know any better. So I'm going to do you a favor and just give you a warning to stay the fuck away from him. I wouldn't want to see anything bad happen to you. Am I clear?"

"I'll fucking kill you." Brendan stood up and in the blink of an eye he flipped the table over onto the floor. He turned to the man and bellowed, "I said, get her out of here!"

Kelly and Leo rushed over. He pulled out his cell. "I'm callin' the po-po."

The man finally found his voice. "No need. We're going."

He led Salena out the door.

Brendan picked up the table. "Sorry, Kelly." He turned to Katie then. "Are you okay?" Before she could answer he pulled her into his arms, kissing her hair. "I'm sorry, sweet girl, and I'm going to make sure you never have to set your pretty eyes on that vile bitch ever again."

"We gotta go, Bren." Chloe pecked his cheek.

"I'm not going to the club. Bring her to the house after your appointment." Hugging her tight, he gave her another kiss. "I love you."

Chloe whisked her to a blue Rover parked at the curb. It was warm inside, the engine already running. Katie was still shaken. Her friend squeezed her hand. "Something dark and turbulent that rages beneath a calm surface. That's Brendan." Then she put the Rover in gear and pulled out onto the avenue.

They were late getting to the doctor's office, but she was running behind so it didn't matter anyway. The nurse called Chloe back first.

"Chloe Nolan?"

She stood and feistily corrected her. "Kerrigan Nolan. No hyphen." Then she turned to Katie. "You can come back with me. I don't mind. Beats sitting here looking at old magazines."

That's how Chloe came to be sitting beside her, holding her hand, when it was her turn with Doctor Torres.

Tiny woman. Looked like she was no older than Katie.

"When was your last period?" she asked her, scribbling on a clipboard.

"Um, right before Christmas. I was visiting my parents."

The doctor looked up with a furrowed brow. "Was it a normal period?"

"Uh, yeah, I guess." Katie glanced over to Chloe, who shrugged.

"And your period before that one?"

She tried to think. Was it before Halloween? After? "I'm not sure. They've never been very regular."

"Have you ever had unprotected sex?"

Fuck.

"Once."

She felt Chloe squeeze her hand.

"And when was that?"

One time. Her first time. In the tent under the Christmas lights.

"The day after Thanksgiving. Black Friday."

Katie squeezed her eyes closed. She felt the tears building behind her lids.

Doctor Torres patted her arm. "Your urine sample is positive for hCG, which tells me you're pregnant."

She opened her eyes and felt the tears escape down her temples. Chloe held her hand with both of hers. Katie looked to the little doctor. "Are you sure? It was my first time!"

"I'm sure, but we're going to draw some blood and do an ultrasound to confirm it. Okay?"

The probe was cold and uncomfortable, but Katie held onto Chloe's hand, her eyes on the black and white screen.

She heard the heartbeat.

She saw the tiny speck of life floating in the sea of her womb.

And she still didn't believe it.

"What is it with you girls and Black Friday?" Katie didn't get it. "That's definitely when you conceived your little bean here, which gives you a due date of August twentieth."

Chloe got a little bouncy in her chair. "Oh, I hope you have him on the twenty-fourth, then the baby can share a birthday with his uncle Jesse!"

I'm having a baby.

How was she ever going to tell Brendan? Would he be mad or glad? She wasn't even sure how she felt. Katie thought he wanted kids one day, but they'd never really talked about having babies or…anything.

It wasn't supposed to happen now.

Not like this.

She tucked the sonogram in her bag. "Chloe, you can't tell anyone. Not until after I figure out how to tell Brendan, and he should be the one to tell his cousins, you know?"

Chloe took her hand in hers. "Sweetie, I would never betray a confidence like this one. I know what you're feeling, and trust me when I tell you everything is going to be okay—more than okay. Brendan loves you. He's going to be so happy when he finds out he's going to be a daddy."

Maybe.

She hoped so.

As soon as she figured out how.

Twenty-Eight

There was no chugging sound, just the strained grinding of wheels on the elevated track. As each second passed, the train brought him closer to satisfying the darkness that permeated his soul. To easing his hunger, quenching his thirst. He could feel his pulse quicken in anticipation, the blood pumping and coursing through his veins.

The city, frozen in winter's icy clutches, flew past. A muted blur through the cold glass, but he didn't notice. She flashed in his mind. How had he fallen for her lies? He let her in and allowed himself to be caught in her web of seduction.

Restless. He needed off this train. Then the sophisticated games he had choreographed in his mind could finally be played. Every detail was perfect. He rifled through his bag one more time, fingering the leather of the whip, the silken bonds, the objects of pain that brought pleasure.

He could almost feel her petal-soft skin, her fragile wrist, as he let the silk slip through his fingers. She would struggle, and the bonds would tighten, cutting into her delicate flesh, bruising her unmarred skin. The thought made him smile. He would tenderly caress the markings of her bondage, sweeping his fingers over every inch of flesh. She would quiver and moan as sweet sensations swept over her body, as she undulated within the bonds in readiness for him. Yes, she would like the game to begin that way.

The fantasy flourished in his mind. He swallowed back his own saliva, but it was her essence, her thick, salty-sweet blood that he tasted. He imagined the terror that would fill her eyes when she saw the blade, when it cut into her thigh, and the crimson nectar welled from the wound. And just as the blood began to trickle down, he would lap it slowly, savoring the feel of it and the taste of it on his tongue. His cock was hard now, as hard as forged steel, its length and girth increasing in proportion to his lust.

She owed him.

He rubbed himself through his clothes to heighten his arousal. He didn't want to come, just to keep himself on edge. He couldn't wait to pour his seed into her dripping cunt, explode inside her hot little mouth, her tight ass. He had come this far, and had to play the game to its conclusion. The train reached his stop. He wouldn't have to wait much longer.

Only a thickness of rich mahogany wood stood between them. He tapped on the door and heard her footfalls padding toward it.

"Oh, it's you." She held a glass of red wine in her hand.

"You lied."

She smirked. "I did." And with a shrug, she drained the wine from her glass.

He already knew that, of course, but the admission of her deceit rocked him. His anger and sense of betrayal boiled just beneath the surface.

"Why?" He looked into her amber eyes for the truth, but it wasn't there.

He pushed past the door and turned her to face him. Startled. Her eyes went big and wide. That pleased him. He held her head firmly between his hands and lowered his lips to hers, brushing them softly, before plunging his tongue inside her hot mouth. He wanted to devour her.

He kissed her mouth until he was her breath, until her knees threatened to buckle out from underneath her. Abruptly, he pulled his lips away and grabbed a fistful of her long black hair, forcing her head back roughly, exposing her neck to his hungry mouth. His fingers trailed over her creamy skin, tracing the pulse that beat just beneath its surface.

"Bitch!"

He slapped her with such force that she was knocked against the wall, falling into a crumpled heap upon the hardwood floor. She brought her hand to her cheek, and before she could stand on her own accord, he grabbed her by the hair again and dragged her to the foot of the bed.

She looked up at him stunned. Dazed. He wanted her to feel his anger with every contact of his boot against her ribs. And when his fist slammed hard into her gut, she sat bolt upright and doubled over, clutching her belly, but she didn't scream. She didn't cry. She didn't make a sound. There was pleasure in the pain he brought her.

Standing over her, he watched as she sat with her arms crossed over her stomach, her chest heaving up and down. He thought how it must hurt her to even breathe, how every inhalation and expiration of precious air caused her pain.

It wasn't enough.

She didn't hurt enough.

She, the woman he once needed, and he, the man she once craved. Still, he hungered. He would give her all that she craved, everything she deserved, and more.

Without conscious thought, his carnal impulses, his dark urges, took over. He hauled her up from the floor, and casting aside the bonds of silk, he reached for the coarse rope and tied her wrists to the foot posts. It annoyed him that she didn't try to squirm out of his hold, that she didn't struggle in her captivity, that she didn't even utter a sound.

The whip rested gently in his palms. He traced it delicately with his fingers and breathed in the scent of leather, before gripping the handle is his right hand. He drew his arm back and snapped the whip. He loved the feel of it, the sound it made when it connected with flesh. He loved to watch the perfection of skin glowing hot and pink and then red. The welts as they rose and then bled. She had a nice ass. High and round, with delicate skin.

The ropes jerked. She flinched as the leather made contact with her flesh. He saw her stiffen, bracing herself for the next sting of the whip. He cracked the whip again, searing her skin, branding her with his anger. And still, it was not enough. The lash came down again and again and again, until she began to cry and scream. Until she was silent.

Her body was shaking with violent tremors when he finally stopped the flogging. The once-pristine skin of her buttocks glowed a fiery red, and raised, angry-looking welts oozed with blood, trickling down her backside. He threw the whip to the floor and stood behind her. She hung her head so he couldn't see her face, or the salty tears running off her cheeks onto the mattress.

For a moment he forgot her duplicity, and once more she became the woman who held his dark desires in his heart. Almost lovingly, he traced the welts on her skin, smearing the blood. He brought his fingers to his lips and tasted her. Instantly, his cock surged, and he knelt behind her, licking the rivulets of blood that trailed down her flesh.

One finger became two, and then three. He slid his fingers in, and then out, of her body. And with every thrust, the juices dripped from inside of her, coating her thighs, running down her legs. She arched her back to meet every thrust.

He released her wrists and flipped her over onto the bed. Kneeling between her thighs, he crushed his mouth against her, relishing her delicious cunt. He licked and laved voraciously, drank what flowed into his mouth freely, like a man who had found a quenching oasis in an arid desert. His tongue flicked over her swollen clit, teasing it, taunting it, until she cried out his name with her orgasm.

No.

His eyes narrowed, the brows coming together, as he saw, really saw, the woman who lay before him. This woman who had deceived him. Tricked him. Betrayed him. She'd duped him into thinking she was the perfect woman.

She wasn't. Not at all.

Eyes that he once found so beautiful closed as he held his engorged cock in his hand. He stroked his shaft, squeezing the head, and sheathed himself. His balls felt as if they could burst. He was close now. Close to the edge. He wouldn't waste it.

Reaching into his bag, he felt for the blade and found it, carefully placing it behind him. He leaned over her then and brushed away the long dark hair that clung to her wet, mascara-stained cheeks. Tracing the curve of her brows with his thumbs, he placed a featherlight kiss on each of her closed eyelids.

And then he plunged himself inside her, deep inside, so deep he could feel his cock against her womb. He thrust fierce and fast. Furious. He wanted to fuck her hard. So hard. So deep. He wanted to split her open and see her entrails spill upon the bed.

He wanted.

He wanted.

Fury burned his eyes. Hatred. Her eyes opened and she looked up at him. He was hurting her. She reached for his face with her hands. Grabbed at his hair. She tried to make him stop, but he didn't. He wouldn't. Blood flowed from her cunt, glazing his cock as it disappeared and then reappeared from inside her body.

"Why are you doing this to me?" She spoke on a muted sob.

He ceased his movement, holding himself still inside of her. "This is what you wanted, isn't it?" He smiled then, really smiled, as if nothing else could make him happier. "Welcome to hell, you fucking cunt!"

And then he threw back his head and laughed from deep within his throat.

"What do you want?" The words were spoken so softly he almost didn't hear them.

Then very slowly he lifted his head and looked directly into her amber eyes. He saw the terror there and it pleased him.

The words that came from his lips were slowly spoken, low and deep.

"I want your blood all over me."

She didn't see the blade. He plunged it into her belly, as his blood-covered cock plunged back inside her body.

Euphoria filled him.

He looked down upon the traitorous bitch as he thrust his dick into her. Hot blood spewed forth from the gaping slit in her belly, the dark-red puddle in the hollow of her abdomen spilled over onto the white linen sheets. He cupped his hands and filled it with her blood. His hands rose to his mouth. He drank her in, filling his mouth with the sweet nectar, loving the thickness of it. Loving the taste of it.

But it was a thirst he would never completely quench. No matter how much he drank, he would always want more. It would never be enough, he thought, as the hot rush of his orgasm filled her lifeless body.

If only she hadn't betrayed him.

He boarded the train that would take him back. He took his seat and opened a book to read. In spite of it all, he felt sated and satisfied. Relaxed. And as the train pulled out of the station, he closed his eyes and saw her as he'd seen her last.

Not one drop of blood dirtied her chalk-white skin, for he'd bathed her body and then hacked through her torso, severing her in half. She was an aesthetic vision, artfully arranged on the big white bed. He'd brushed her long black hair and gently placed a pillow beneath her head, before giving her a final kiss.

And when his warm lips touched hers that were cold, he smiled.

Goodbye, Salena.

Twenty-Nine

He got off the train at Wabash and made the short walk to Jewelers Row. He supposed he could have gone to Tiffany's or a myriad other stores, but Brendan wanted something created especially for Katelyn that was as perfect, beautiful, and unique as she was. And there was no better place than the city's diamond district to do exactly that. Glancing at his watch, he pulled open the heavy glass door and stepped inside.

The jeweler stood hunched over behind a glass case, lighting strategically illuminating the brilliant gems displayed on mid-night-blue velvet. He straightened as he sensed Brendan approach.

"Oh, you're early, my friend."

"I know." He half shrugged with a smirk. "Is it ready?"

He answered with a wink, "Indeed it is."

It was snowing when he stepped back outside and headed for the train to take him home. Brendan pulled the velvet box from his pocket and looked inside. He smiled. The future he'd never dared to dream of was in the palm of his hand. One chance encounter, one serendipitous kiss, had irrevocably altered the course of his life.

Not that he had much of one, he realized, until Katelyn came crashing into it. Sunshine and sugar. Rainstorms and whiskey. Each of them were just what the other needed. She smoothed out all his rough edges. He was her safe harbor. Together they were everything.

By the time the train reached the Coventry Park station the weather had turned to complete shit. Snow was accumulating quickly, coming down in big, heavy flakes. Gusts of wind blowing it in drifts. Visibility next to nothing. He sent Katelyn a text to let her know he'd pick her up from class and started the trek home to get his car.

Katelyn: I grabbed an Uber. A storm is coming, so they canceled classes. Snow day!

Brendan: Good girl. Have the driver bring you here. I love you.

Katelyn: Ok. ILY!

To keep himself occupied, he threw fixings for dinner in the crock pot. He sent off texts to let everyone know the club would remain closed tonight. Who'd want to go out in this shit? He lit a fire so the house would be cozy and warm when she got there.

Then he paced.

Brendan looked out the window, watching for approaching headlights. He could barely make out the gate through the swirling mass of white. It had been an hour since her last text. On a normal day it would be a fifteen-minute trip.

She's fine.

Logic told him traffic was a nightmare, travel slow and treacherous. He didn't have to worry. Not yet. But in the back of his mind flares burned on wet pavement.

He shook the image from his head. It wasn't until headlights finally appeared and he gathered a slightly frozen Katelyn in his arms that the heaviness in his chest dissipated so he could breathe.

"Thank fuck." He kissed the top of her head, dusting flakes of snow from her hair. "Let's get you warmed up."

She raised a brow, her aqua eyes heated, and grinned. "I fucking love snow days!"

"Yeah?"

"Yeah."

"Well, I fucking love *you*." He swatted her behind.

Katelyn stood on her tiptoes and kissed him beneath his chin. "That's a good thing, because I love you too."

Brendan tipped his head and took her mouth.

A very good thing.

After a warm shower, Katelyn came down the stairs in a pair of leggings, fuzzy pink socks, and one of his old sweatshirts. Fucking adorable. He could get used to days like this. Hell, if he wasn't looking forward to a lifetime of them.

"Something smells good." She twirled into the kitchen, her fuzzy socks gliding on the wood floor.

Yeah, she fucking twirled. Adorable.

"I've got dinner going in the crock pot."

"Oh?" Katelyn backed herself into the island, pushing up on top of it. She did that a lot so she could reach him better, and he loved it. "Whatcha makin'?"

Brendan stepped between her thighs, and wrapping a strand of silky hair around his finger, leaned in to kiss her on the nose. "Your favorite."

"Mississippi roast?" She smiled big. "Please tell me that's what I'm smelling."

"Mmhm." Releasing the strand of hair, he watched it unravel.

Her arms tightened around his neck and her legs squeezed his thighs. "You are the bestest boyfriend in the whole entire world."

Brendan planned on being more to her than that. So much more. Soon.

"You deserve nothing less, sweet girl." He leaned in and kissed her, and scooping her off the island, he carried her up the stairs.

"Where are we going?"

"Bed."

Brendan lowered her onto the mattress, his lips seeking hers. Katelyn was his. She was here, she was okay, she loved him. He loved her. This overwhelming need to be inside her came over him. And it had to be right now.

His lips trailed down her neck, his nose nuzzling in the warm, sweet skin. "Do you have any idea what you do to me?"

He reached inside his sweatshirt that she wore and grasped her nipples firmly in his fingers. Her lips parted on a gasp and he claimed her mouth, grinding his erection into her thigh so she could feel exactly what she did to him. How much he needed her. Wanted her. He'd never felt desire such as this with any other woman ever before. He knew in his soul he never would again.

She held his hands to her breasts over his shirt. Katelyn was right there with him, her desire matching his own. That got him. Every. Damn. Time. There wasn't anything sexier, nothing turned him on more, than her confidence in herself. Showing him that she wanted him. What she needed.

He pinched her nipples and lifting his mouth from hers, pulled the sweatshirt over her head. Her nipples enticed him to suck on them. Brendan dragged his teeth over his lip. They stood taut and swollen on supple mounds of quivering flesh. Edible. Luscious. Made for him. He knew it the very first moment he held her in his palm that night in the park.

"I love these gorgeous tits."

Brendan sat against the headboard and pulled her to sit on his thigh, spreading her legs apart. He leaned over her shoulder, an arm around her waist, sucking a sweet nipple into his mouth, while his hand reached inside her leggings.

His mouth left her nipple to kiss her. He opened the lips of her pussy with his fingers, brushing them through her wet slit, then he brought them to her clit and massaged it in light, slow circles.

"How many times can I make you come?"

Katelyn softly whimpered and his fingers moved faster. He alternated between sucking on her nipple and sucking on her tongue.

"How many, baby?"

Drawing her nipple deep into his mouth, he rubbed her clit hard and fast until she mewled and cried out with her first orgasm. Then he pushed her down onto the bed, and pulling the leggings off her body, he ravished her cunt with his mouth. Fucking her with his tongue. Swallowing every drop of her sweetness.

He penetrated her with two fingers, pressing up into her sweet spot. Brendan knew her body as well as he knew his own. He flicked across her clit with his tongue, back and forth, over and over again. He sucked on it. Gnawed on it.

Katelyn clutched his hair in her fingers. Pulling and tugging as she panted and moaned, cried and begged.

"Please…" Her head thrashed from side to side on the mattress. "…fuck."

Soon, baby.

Using the muscles in his forearm, he pressed firmly into her hot, wet wall. Her pussy fluttered on his fingers. Contracting and releasing. She was almost there, right where he wanted her. He did it again. And again. Repeating the motion until her walls spasmed, then he clamped down on her clit and sucked. His sweet girl rewarded him with her cum. Drenching him in it. He lapped her up, her thighs trembling against his head.

When her legs stilled and her screams quieted to gasping intakes of breath, he kissed his way up her body, his cock dripping precum on her skin. He ached to be inside her, longed for that connection he shared only with her. Glancing at the floor mirror in the corner, he angled her body toward it.

"I want you to see how your pussy stretches to take my cock."

Brendan strummed his fingers through her slit, slick and wet from cum and saliva, and notched himself at her entrance. He painted her lips with a fingertip and she sucked it into her mouth. Slowly, so Katelyn could see, he nudged the head inside.

"Look how fucking beautiful that is, baby."

Her pussy welcomed him inside, the lips stretched shiny and taut to accommodate his girth. She watched, her head turned toward the mirror, mesmerized by the sight of him slowly disappearing inside her.

"Look at me."

Katelyn turned her head and her aqua eyes gazed into his. He could see all the love she had inside their depths and it was his turn to be enthralled.

"I love you." He held her to him, and bringing his lips to hers, pushed himself all the way inside her. The spark she ignited in him all those months ago would never extinguish. It burned brighter with every passing day.

With every touch.

Every kiss.

She fucking consumed him.

Brendan couldn't tell where he ended and she began anymore. He pumped in and out of her, faster and faster, skin slapping skin. Sweat dripped from his face, his hair, his chest, to join with hers and trickle in rivulets down her breasts. He caught one with his tongue and suckled on her nipple. *

Katelyn burned inside him. She pumped through his veins and singed every cell in his body, leaving her indelible mark. So lost in her, he didn't notice the sensation at the base of his spine until it was too late to stop it. His balls drew up and painfully tightened as the orgasm ripped through him with a roar. It was like she siphoned the cum right out of his body into hers, leaving him weightless. Boneless. Weak.

He just held her. Stroking her hair down her back, he held her until he caught his breath and his heartrate slowed. He kissed her crown and closed his eyes. How lucky was he to have her to love?

To be loved by her.

Brendan wasn't sure how long they slept. The snow was still coming down when he opened his eyes to a dark room. Katelyn was burrowed beneath his arm, under the blanket. He watched her breathe until her eyelids fluttered open.

"Hey, sleepy girl."

She smiled.

Ping.

He grabbed his phone from the pocket of his jeans on the floor. Dillon. A link to a newspaper article accompanied three little words.

Salena is dead.

Thirty

"**A**pparently she'd been dead for a while." Dillon shrugged. "Didn't find her until the neighbors started complaining about the smell."

Brendan shuddered to think of the ghastly sight they must have encountered when they opened the door to that apartment.

It'd been a couple days since the near-blizzard storm dropped a foot of snow on the city. He, Taylor, and his cousins sat in their Park Place office, ruminating the news of Salena's death. The newspaper article, a short blurb with her photo, didn't tell them much, other than her death was being investigated as a homicide.

"How long do you have to be dead before you start stinking up the place?" Dillon wanted to know.

Taylor pursed his lips in thought and shrugged. "That would depend on a lot of things, like ambient temperature and the manner of death, but with the heat on I'd guess not too long. A few days, perhaps. A week at most."

Everyone just looked at him. Everyone except Jesse, that is. He shook his head and rolled his eyes with a smirk on his face.

"What?" Taylor responded to the roomful of stares. "I watch all those bloody true crime programs on the telly."

"You're morbid, Tay."

"And yet you watch them with me, don't you, love?"

"Don't you think someone should've noticed before that?" Kyan held his chin with his thumb, rubbing his temple with his index finger.

Dillon looked at his brother. "Before what?"

"Before she putrefied."

Taylor's distaste was evident. "I guess she really didn't have any friends."

"Yes, she did." Kyan rose from his chair to refill his coffee. "Brantley."

Odd.

After that, they didn't talk about Salena anymore. Not here. Not at the club. Besides that brief mention in the paper, there hadn't been another word of her. It was almost as if she'd never existed. Brendan was sorry her life ended like it did, but he wasn't sorry that he wouldn't have to worry about Salena fucking with his family ever again.

"If the groundhog sees its shadow, does that mean an early spring or six more weeks of winter?" Katelyn pondered between bites of her cheeseburger. "I can never remember which it is."

"It means six more weeks of this shit."

They were having a late lunch at Charley's before she went to work and he headed into the club. While it was as cold as a witch's tit on this second day of February, the sun was shining and there wasn't a cloud to be seen in the pale-blue sky. If Punxsutawney Phil was to be believed, spring wasn't coming anytime soon. Of course, here winter could last until May—felt like it anyway.

"Do we have any plans for this Sunday?"

"No, sweetheart." Brendan reached across the table for her hand. "Is there something you want to do?"

"Yeah." Lowering her lids, Katelyn stared at her plate and squeezed his hand. "I want to stay in and make some lasagna. Talk and stuff. You know, have a quiet, lazy day."

"That sounds good to me."

She still stared at her plate. He'd noticed Katelyn hadn't been quite herself the past couple of weeks. She seemed preoccupied, but he figured it was the new semester at school.

"Everything all right, baby? Classes going okay?"

She looked up. "Yeah."

His cell vibrated in his pocket. It was Murphy, a friend since childhood, who was a detective with the police department, so he answered it. The call was brief and he wasn't sure what to think of it. Katelyn was watching his face.

"Friend of mine at the PD." He shrugged like it was no big deal. He didn't want to give her any reason to worry. "They, um, want to ask me some questions about Salena."

"They're probably contacting anyone who knew her, don't you think?"

"Probably," he agreed, nodding. "Calling my attorney anyway."

By the time Phil Beecham met him in front of the station two hours later Brendan was fucking glad he had. His phone had blown up since he'd gotten the call from Murphy. His cousins, Linnea, Chloe, Venery, Axel and his staff at the club, Marcus, and even Jason, the kitchen boy from Charley's, had all called or texted him because they'd been asked to go down to the station too.

What the actual fuck is going on here?

The churn in his gut told him something was fishy. And whatever that something was, it stunk.

Murphy approached him in the lobby. He had a hangdog look on his face, lips pressed together in a straight line, as if he were uncomfortable about having to be here. They'd known each other since kindergarten. He was his go-to guy at the department whenever Brendan needed one, like when the black van was camped out by Park Place. When Linnea was missing. Murphy was very much aware of all the troubles Salena had caused. Her machinations. Her threats.

"Hey, Bren," he greeted him with a backslap and a bro-hug. "Phil, how are ya?" He shook the lawyer's hand.

Phil answered with a nod and Murphy smiled. Not really. It was sheepish. He motioned them over to a corner where they wouldn't be overheard.

"Look, Bren. They took me off the case because we're friends, but I gotta tell ya, someone has it out for you." He worried his lip. "And I can't say who."

Stinks like a putrefied corpse.

Murphy turned to Phil then. "I'm glad you're here. I'll be in there, but be careful. Don't let him lose his cool, get me? We'll talk later." He winked and walked away.

"This is fucking outrageous, Phil," he exclaimed. "I haven't had anything to do with that woman in well over a year." Brendan began to pace. "I've run into her maybe twice in all that time."

"Then you have nothing to worry about, Bren." Phil placed a reassuring hand on his shoulder. "Relax."

"I don't need this shit, Phil." His thoughts went to Katelyn. "Especially now."

Brendan hoped that after he answered their questions today, that it would be the end of it—as far as he was concerned. He did not want Katelyn to be caught up in this bullshit with him. She was young. Innocent until he got his hands on her. All he wanted was for the two of them to have a happy, peaceful life together.

Is that too much to fucking ask?

Funny thing is, at one time even he thought that it was.

And now, it was the only thing he wanted.

A door opened down the hall. Angelica came out of it, dabbing at her eyes. Dressed conservatively and her face devoid of makeup, Brendan almost didn't recognize her. A detective patted her shoulder in what looked to be a comforting gesture. She walked past him, without even a remnant of a tear, and smirked.

'Sal's my friend.'

Brendan glanced to his lawyer and shook his head. "I think we're going to be here a while."

It was another fifteen minutes before they called him in.

The room was small, maybe ten by twelve feet, with a square

conference table in the center and a single window covered with cheap slatted blinds. Beige walls. Linoleum tile floor.

An older, overweight man with a shiny bald head sat on one side of the table. Tape recorder in front of him. Brendan hadn't seen one of those in years. There was probably a camera hidden in here somewhere too. Murphy stood over by the window.

"Have a seat." The detective who called him in patted a chair directly across from the bald guy with the recorder.

He sat. Phil sat in the chair beside him. The two detectives sat together. Murphy remained standing.

The bald one glanced at Phil and said, "This is a non-custodial interview being conducted for information gathering purposes in relation to the homicide of Miss Salena Dara. I need to advise you that this interview is being recorded."

Brendan looked up to the ceiling and spotted the camera in the corner. He nodded.

"State your full name, please."

The guy was reading off a sheet of paper. He didn't even look at him.

"Brendan James Murray."

"Date of birth."

"Four. Twenty. Eighty-eight."

"And you knew the decedent, Miss Dara?"

"Yes."

"How long did you know her?"

"I met her six years ago. Seven, maybe."

"And what was the nature of your relationship?"

Brendan looked to Murphy, then to Phil. "She, uh, used to work for me."

"And where was that?"

The guy still hadn't looked at him.

"The Red Door."

"Were you intimately acquainted with Miss Dara?"

Here we go.

Phil interrupted. "Define intimately acquainted." He placed his hands on the table. "For the record."

"Did you engage in sexual activity with Miss Dara?"

He wished he could say no. Never. He couldn't say that, though. "Yes."

"And when was the last time that occurred?"

Demo. Third anniversary party at the club. They didn't fuck, only his hand was inside her.

"Maybe a year and a half ago."

"Were you romantically involved with the decedent at any time?"

Hell to the no.

"No."

"But you had sex with her? For what, five years? Is that what you're saying?"

Yeah. People do it all the time, asshole.

"That's exactly what I'm saying. Yes."

"You sure about that?"

He arched a brow. "Positive."

The other detective whispered in the bald guy's ear and he nodded.

"When did Miss Dara leave your employ?"

Day after the anniversary party.

"A year and a half ago."

"I see."

What the fuck do you see?

"And how did she leave?"

Is he kidding?

Brendan was getting tired of this nonsense already. He rolled his eyes. "I don't know. In an Uber?"

"Think you're funny?" Baldy scoffed. "Did she quit? Get fired?"

Did it matter?

"Her services were no longer required. She was terminated."

Baldy smirked to the other one then looked back at him. "You have records to back that up?"

Brendan felt the tick in his jaw. "I do."

"We're gonna need to see those because that ain't the story we got."

Brendan shrugged. "Well, that's the truth."

"Did you ever see Miss Dara after she left your..." He cleared his throat. "...employ?"

"Ran into her a few times."

"When and where did you see her last?"

Brendan didn't like where this was going. Not one bit. He wanted to keep Katelyn, Kelly, and Beanie's out of this if he could. His fingertip rubbed over the coordinates etched on hammered silver.

"Maybe two or three weeks ago in a coffee shop."

"Why don't you take a look at these." Baldy slid a manilla folder across the table.

Brendan opened it. His stomach roiled. Bile rose in his throat. He swallowed it.

Salena, photographed in a state of grotesque decay. Naked. Swollen. Her skin looked waxy, slimy, and had a greenish tinge to it. Purple veins. Brown liquid seeped from her ears, mouth, and nose. Were those maggots? She'd been...he covered his mouth with his hand...cut in half. Hacked through the center of her torso like a magic act gone horribly wrong.

"Isn't that the last time you saw her?" Baldy was looking at him now.

"No."

Don't lose your cool, man.

"The truth is she ended a romantic relationship with you and walked out on you a year and a half ago, isn't it?"

Is this guy high?

"No."

"That's enough," Phil interrupted. "Are we done here? My client has answered your questions."

"For now. We'll be subpoenaing those records."

Thank fuck.

Phil led him by the arm out of the interview room. "Not one word until we get outside."

They got into Phil's Mercedes and drove to a nearby parking lot. "Tell me everything, starting with the first time you met Salena Dara—and I mean everything."

So Brendan recounted the night they all met Salena after Venery's gig until the day he fired her from the club. Her fucked-up obsession with Kyan. Her threats. How he suspected she was behind all that shit with Taylor. The mayor. The priest. Angelica. Her extreme kinks. Her relationships with first, Hugh Brantley, and then his son, Eric. The senator and the money going into her bank account. The last time he encountered her at Beanie's. Her threat to Katelyn.

"I'll be goddamned." Phil tapped out a text on his phone. "Fuck."

"What?"

"And they're looking at you?" He shook his head. "Too bad we can't hand them that info."

"Why can't we?" Seemed reasonable enough to him.

"One, we don't have solid proof." He shrugged. "Two, we can't tell the police you hacked into her bank account." He paused. "But if you found it, hopefully so will they."

"Whoever sent the texts to us during the whole Taylor thing was the same person who sent the video of Rourke to the cops." Brendan pounded his fist on his thigh. "Same number. I know it was Salena."

"The priest?"

"Yeah."

"Hmm."

There was a knock on the glass. Murphy was at the driver's side door. Phil unlocked the car and he got in the back.

"Listen up, you know I can't be seen here talking to you guys so I gotta make this quick." He let out a loud breath. "Two witnesses said Salena told them if anything ever happened to her...it was you. And almost everyone they've interviewed so far said...that you said you'd kill her."

"That doesn't make him a murderer," Phil sneered.

"No, but it's enough to make him a suspect in a homicide."

"Did the coroner give you guys an estimate on the time of death?"

"She was too far gone for that, man. The body was washed after she died and laid out like that, so there's very little forensic evidence to go on. No semen. No fibers. No fingerprints. No sign of forced entry. She knew her killer, whoever it was. I can tell you she was sexually brutalized—extensive lacerations in the vagina. She was beaten. Broken ribs, ruptured spleen, welts on her buttocks. Stab wound to the lower abdomen killed her. Coroner estimates death occurred sometime between January twentieth and twenty-second."

Jesus. What kind of fucking monster…

Poor Murphy was sweating. "Neighbors were no help. They only said she wasn't very nice." He wiped his brow. "Look, I gotta get back."

"Are they charging him?"

They were talking as if he wasn't sitting right there. Brendan shifted in his seat. He was starting to get agitated.

"No, but they want to. They don't have enough to charge him yet." Murphy clasped his shoulder and squeezed. "Sorry, Bren."

"Yeah, man." Brendan patted his hand. "Thanks."

Then he got out of the Mercedes and left.

Phil pounded on his steering wheel. "We need those interview transcripts."

"You're my attorney. Can't you get them?"

"No. Not unless they charge you."

Well, fuck.

"So what do we do then?"

Brendan wasn't sure if he was caught in *The Twilight Zone* or a bad episode of *CSI*, but he wanted out. This was a shitshow that he didn't play a part in. Did he despise Salena for everything she'd done? Yeah, he did. No denying it. But whoever did this was sick. He might be fucked up, but he wasn't a goddamn psychopath.

"You go home and try not to worry about it. They don't have anything. This is going to blow over." Phil patted his shoulder.

God, if one more person does that...

"I'm going to see what else I can find out. Murphy will keep me posted. Trust me, this is the end of it."

Except that it wasn't.

And as much it killed him inside, he knew what he had to do. For her.

Thirty-One

Sundays.

God, how he looked forward to Sunday every week. And not because it was his only day off or because it was game day. Brendan really didn't care that much about watching football on TV. It was watching it with Katelyn, just being with her, that he looked forward to the most. Until today, he hadn't realized just how much.

Today would be the last football Sunday for a long time. Jesse was having everyone over for the Super Bowl. Katelyn wanted to stay here. Just the two of them. Cook up some lasagna together. Snuggle and watch the game. And that's what Brendan wanted too.

It might not sound like much to most people. A typical Sunday spent at home. But to him, it was everything. He was going to lap up every fucking minute of today. Savor it. Appreciate it. Because it's the ordinary moments that make a life extraordinary. Beautiful. Wonderful. Joyful.

That was his sweet girl. She was all of those things and more, his little wisp of a thing with the beautiful face of an angel. Sunshine. White chocolate. Jasmine. God, he just loved her so fucking much. It hurt inside his chest. That's how much he loved her. So today he was going to forget about everything else and spend every fucking minute of it loving Katelyn.

A day of ordinary moments.

Because he didn't know if they'd have tomorrow.

Brendan came up right behind her, wrapped his arms around her waist, and squeezed her tight as she layered noodles and cheese in a pan. It was one of his favorite things. To hold Katelyn like that. To feel her softness sink against him. He leaned over, his face nuzzling into her neck, and kissed the tender spot beneath her ear that tickled. Just so he could hear her laugh. She had the cutest laugh.

"Bren." She giggled and turned around in his arms.

Barefoot, in leggings and a sweater, her head only came up to his pecs. She kissed the space between them and gazed up at him with those enchanting blue-green eyes of hers and the most beautiful smile a woman could ever give to a man. This girl. His gift.

He kissed the top of her head. She finished assembling the lasagna and put it in the oven while Brendan cleaned up the kitchen and watched her. Ordinary moments.

"C'mere."

Taking her hand, he spun Katelyn into his arms. They crashed together. Brendan held her face in his palms and gently, tenderly, so he could savor the taste of her sweet mouth, he kissed her. Their tongues caught up in a slow lovers' dance. Couldn't they just stay like this?

Brendan lifted her up and she wrapped her legs around him. Another favorite thing. It always brought him back to their first kiss on the eve of midsummer. The night she came crashing into his life and changed it forever. He squeezed his eyes shut.

Fuck.

Blinking, he opened them, and with his lips on hers, carried her to the sofa. Gently, he laid her upon it. Katelyn looked up at him. Brendan stripped off his clothes and stood naked before her. He'd shown her not only his skin, but his soul, and still she loved him. He knew all along he didn't deserve her, but he loved her anyway. How could he not?

Katelyn pulled the sweater over her head. He peeled the leggings down her thighs. Brendan knelt at her feet. He picked up her right foot and cupped the heel in his palm. Softly, he kissed up the tender sole and sucked her pink polished toes into his mouth. He loved and lavished each one with licks and kisses. Then he held her foot on his erect cock, only to pick up the left and repeat the process all over again.

Brendan kissed the backs of her calves, behind her knees, and the sweet skin inside her thighs. He'd told her once, there was no place on her body he wouldn't kiss. Wouldn't touch. And that's what he intended to do. Love every square inch of her.

He kissed her palms, sucked on her fingers one by one, kissed each wrist and brushed his lips up her arm to her shoulder. He watched the goosebumps rise on her skin. Heard her sighs. Felt her breath hitch.

Nice.

His fingers swept through her silky wheat waves to cradle her head. Brendan kissed her hair, her eyelids, and each cheek, before settling his lips on hers. Urgently taking her mouth. Swallowing her breath and giving her his. Trailing kisses down her neck, he inhaled her scent so deep into his lungs it would never leave him.

Then he took those gorgeous tits, one in each hand, and squeezed them. He suckled on a nipple, rolling the other between his fingers, listening to her soft whimpers. Her tiny cries urged him to suckle the other. And once she was squirming beneath him, he lifted his head from her breast.

"I love you, Katelyn."

Always.

She reached out to touch him, fingertips trailing down his chest, his abs, and she stopped at the root of his cock.

"I love you, Brendan."

Then he notched his head inside the pretty pussy he'd ruined for anyone else but him. He held her against his chest and kissed her, pushing his way inside. He told her just how much he loved her with every slow thrust, every caress of her delicate skin. Every breath. Every touch. Every kiss.

Brendan didn't want this moment to end. He kept the pace of his thrusts unhurried and slow, his movement inside her easy and gentle, to make it last as long as he could. When his dick urged him to fuck faster and harder, he ignored it. Stroking her skin. Kissing her mouth. But ultimately the body wins. He couldn't hold off any longer and reached between them, rubbing her clit as he thrust, so she could come with him.

Katelyn cried out with her orgasm as he poured himself inside her. He held her after, brushing his fingers through her swollen, wet lips. Pushing his cum inside her. He wished they could've made a baby, but he didn't dare to dream of those things now.

Because what if…

He wasn't going to think about that today.

Today was for Katelyn.

The what-ifs could wait until tomorrow.

They snuggled on the sofa watching the game, plates of lasagna on their laps. He watched her yell at the players on the field as if they could hear her. He watched her get teary at a sappy commercial with a cute puppy. Ordinary moments. The moments that turn into the most precious memories. He glanced at the framed photos on the shelves.

His phone vibrated on the table. Phil. He answered it. Murphy was on the line with him. He just listened, letting their words register. Brendan didn't say anything except goodbye and then ended the call.

Fuck.

She was cheering at the TV. Carefree and happy and smiling. He watched her for a minute. That's all he'd ever wanted her to be.

He couldn't give her that now.

Not anymore.

Tomorrow came early.

"Katelyn." He clicked off the TV.

"Bren, what…" She looked at him, and when she saw the expression on his face, her smile fell in an instant. "…what is it? What's wrong?"

He rubbed the hammered silver plate on his wrist. "That was

my attorney on the phone." Katelyn took his hand in both of hers. "I'm, uh, going to be charged with Salena's murder."

She sat stunned and began to slowly shake her head back and forth. "No."

He saw the tears pool in her pretty eyes. Again, he was the one to put them there, after he promised himself he'd never be the reason that she cried.

Katelyn shook her head faster. "How can they do this? You didn't do it!" Her tears were falling in earnest now. "I know you didn't do it!"

Brendan held her in his arms against his chest, smoothing her hair down her back. "Shh, shh. Don't cry, baby."

Please don't cry. You're fucking killing me.

He knew it was a futile plea. The dam had broken. It was only going to get worse.

She sniffled, nodding her head. "It's gonna be okay. You didn't do anything. We'll get through this."

Maybe.

But he wasn't going to do that to her. He couldn't put her through what might be years of legal bullshit. A trial. She'd end up with a man who'd once been charged with murder and got off, the shadow of suspicion dogging the rest of his days, or a man who would spend the rest of his life in prison. He couldn't be selfish. Katelyn deserved better than either of those options.

Fuck. Fuck. Fuck.

Brendan took a deep breath, trying to get air into his lungs. He squeezed her hand in his and shook his head. "No, we won't."

"What do you mean?" She tilted her head. "Of course we will, baby."

That muscle in his chest was squeezing. It hurt. It fucking hurt. She had to see it in his face because hers was crumpling.

Fuck you, Salena! I'm glad you're dead and I hope you rot in hell for this, you vile fucking bitch!

"I mean I'm not letting you go through this." Brendan kissed her, tasting the salt of her tears on her lips. Already missing the sweet. He forced himself to pull away, holding her wet cheeks in his hands, wiping away her tears with his thumbs. "I love you too much."

He kissed her forehead, holding his lips there as he choked on the words. "So I'm letting you go."

She just sat there. Dazed. Blinking the tears from her eyes.

He stood. "I'll call you a car."

Katelyn glanced up then. Stormy aqua eyes, bloodshot and red-rimmed. He saw the pain, the hurt, the confusion he put there.

"No." She quickly got off the sofa and grabbed her coat. Her bag.

"Katelyn."

She ignored him and put on her boots.

"Katelyn."

She looked at him then, her expression blank. "It's Katie."

She didn't even put on her coat before she ran out the door.

I'm so sorry, sweet girl.

The little box was hidden away in his desk drawer. Brendan took it out. He opened the box and gazed at the engagement ring he'd gotten made for her. Diamonds sparkled on velvet of midnight blue. He had it all planned…Valentine's Day was next week. But that's the thing about plans, isn't it?

And dreams.

The dream he once held in his palm was gone now.

He closed the lid and put the box away.

Thirty-Two

"I love you too much."

No, this isn't happening.

Brendan pressed his lips to her forehead. She felt the end in his kiss.

Don't say it. Please, don't say it. God, please. I'll do anything. I didn't even get the chance to tell you...

"So I'm letting you go."

...we're having a baby.

Katie sat there for a minute. Too stunned to even cry. It felt like her heart had seized in her chest, deciding whether or not to take another beat. She wasn't sure what she was supposed to do.

"I'll call you a car."

She looked up at him, into the eyes of the man she loved that were so fucking blue. He was really doing this.

"No."

She couldn't think straight. Too many emotions all at once, Katie couldn't think at all. She shot off the couch and grabbed her things.

"Katelyn."

She laced up her boots on autopilot.

"Katelyn."

Katelyn? No.

Her mother called her that when she was in trouble.

But then she was in trouble, wasn't she?

"It's Katie."

And she scrambled to get out of his house.

The house she'd begun to think of as home. Would he come after her? Katie darted through the backyard and out the gate to the alley. She could hear everyone next door at Chloe's whooping at the TV. Boisterous laughter. She felt sick.

Not here. Please, not here.

With her hand over her mouth, sobbing, Katie hurried down the alley. She just had to make it to the end of the street and slip through the gate into the park. She thought she was behind Sloan's house, or maybe Kit's, she wasn't exactly sure, but she couldn't stop it. Holding onto the icy trunk of a tree, she clutched her belly and violently retched, emptying the contents of her stomach into the snow.

She felt a hand on her shoulder. Another rubbed her back. They weren't Brendan's hands.

"What's wrong, Katie?"

She began to cry at the sound of Matt's voice. Katie didn't want him to see her like this. Heart shredded, sick, a fucking mess. She didn't want anyone to see her.

"I threw up."

Standing behind her, Matt pulled her hair back. "I see that."

Squeezing her eyes closed, Katie wished she could just disappear, crawl away like the wounded animal that she was. She needed to get away from here.

"Let's get you inside."

"No," she sobbed, shaking her head. "Please, I just need a minute. Go back to the game."

"Katie." Matt turned her around. "Talk to me. What's wrong?"

Everything.

She felt her lip tremble, her chin wobble. She inhaled a stuttering breath. "They're charging him…" Her eyelids closed. "…and he broke up with me." Hot tears stung her cheeks in the cold evening air.

"Fuck." Matt's hands clasped her shoulders. "Katie, now listen to me. Brendan loves you. He's just…"

"I'm pregnant."

Katie just blurted it out. Two little words. Three syllables. She'd kept them to herself for weeks, trying to figure out a way to tell Brendan. Today was supposed to be the day she finally did, but it didn't turn out that way.

"And he broke up with you?" Matt looked angry. "That motherfucker."

"He doesn't know, Matt." She rested a hand on his chest. "I never got the chance to tell him."

The muscles in his face relaxed and he took her hand. "C'mon. I'm taking you back. Brendan needs to know—"

"No." She shook her head, tears spilling down her face. "Not now. Not like this."

"Katie." Matt pulled her against him and hugged her. "Please go talk to him."

"Promise me you won't say anything to him. It needs to come from me. Okay?"

He hesitated. His mouth opened like he was going to say something, but changed his mind. Then, in a quiet voice, he simply said, "Okay."

Katie sat on her bed hugging her knees, and unseeing, watched the sky change color through the window. It gradually lightened from the darkest black to a bleak gray. She was thankful that it wasn't fucking blue.

She hadn't slept, didn't even bother to try, even though she was physically drained. Emotionally exhausted. Empty. Broken. Luckily, Kelly wasn't home when she got here last night. Katie heard her come in around two, and presuming, thankfully, that she was still at Brendan's, went right to her room. She wasn't ready to talk to anyone.

The door to the loft opened, and then closed. Katie heard her aunt's footfalls recede down the stairs and left her bed. She padded into the bathroom and got in the shower. That's when her tears began to silently fall. Then they tumbled, cascading down her cheeks with the warm water. She covered her face with her hands and cried, choking on her own saliva. Gasping for air between sobs.

Her hands slid down her body to her belly. She rubbed over the skin. Her baby was in there. Brendan's baby. What the fuck was she going to do now?

The only thing she could think of.

That afternoon, wiping at her swollen eyes yet again, Katie bumped into Cameron as she left the registrar's office, pulling the door closed behind her. He'd been right. They'd hardly seen each other since the end of last semester. She'd seen him on occasion in the student union, or they'd pass one another on the quad and wave, but that was it. Cameron took one look at her and glanced at the door she just came out of.

His hand shot out to grab hers. "What the fuck did you do?"

Keeping her gaze on the toes of her boots, she answered him, "I withdrew."

"You what?"

"You heard me." She still wouldn't look at him. "I quit school."

"Fuck, Katie." He gently raised her chin. "Why?"

She bit her lip so she wouldn't cry, and shrugged. "I'm going home."

"Katie, no." He pulled her into a hug. Her head rested on his shoulder simply because she could reach it. "What happened?"

"I don't want to talk about it." She shook her head, bursting into tears. Again.

She hated this. How long would it be before she stopped crying? Katie had never experienced the loss of a loved one before, but she imagined this is what it felt like. Unimaginable grief. It was like mourning for someone who'd died, yet they weren't dead. How would she ever get over this?

She wouldn't.

'Love is a severe mental illness curable only with time.'

'Who'd want a cure?'

'There are plenty of reasons people might want to be cured of it.'

"Sometimes, talking things over, just having someone listen, can give you clarity." He took her hand and led her outside. "Let's go."

"Where are we going?" She abruptly stopped walking and he spun around. "Don't you have a class to get to?"

"My place." He tucked her hair behind her ear. "And I'm skipping it."

She was too exhausted to argue and went with him. Back inside his attic room under the eaves, Katie glanced up at the panel of glass in the ceiling. The sky was still heavy and gray. It would probably snow. It was fitting, she supposed. She wondered how many girls had been in this room since she'd been here last. When was that? Four months ago?

"None." Earnest hazel eyes caught her gaze. "I can still tell what you're thinking."

Wringing her hands, Katie sat down on the edge of the bed and stared at the misty downtown skyline through the window. She could see it now, without the leaves on the trees impeding her view as they had in October.

"You want a drink? I still have some of that seltzer you like in the fridge."

"No, thanks." She looked down at her lap. "I, um, can't."

"Water?"

"Yeah, that'd be great."

Cameron got her the water and sat beside her. "Tell me what happened. Why are you leaving school?"

"I'm…" *Just another statistic.* "…having a baby, Cam."

"Oh." Now he was looking at his lap. "You don't have to leave school because you're pregnant, you know."

"I know, but…"

"But?"

She was silent for a minute because she really didn't know how to put her thoughts and feelings into words yet.

"What happened?"

Once she started talking, though, the words just tumbled out. The story sounded like a fucked-up romance novel gone wrong, even to her, and it was her story. Boy meets girl. Boy and girl fall in love. Girl gets knocked up. Boy is accused of murder. Boy and girl break up. No happy ending.

"So, now you understand why I just can't stay here."

"Not really." His arm came around her. "You know, I don't like the guy. But in all fairness, seems to me like he's doing what he thinks is best for you."

She arched her brow. "How do you figure?"

"If they convict him he gets prison for life, babe."

"He didn't do it," Katie vehemently insisted.

Cameron brushed his fingers through her hair. "Look, you're reacting, and I don't think you should be making any big decisions right now—like quitting school."

She scoffed. "I hadn't even picked a major."

Cameron chuckled and squeezed her shoulders. "You've got time."

"Not anymore." It was starting to get dark. She could see the lights turn on in the buildings downtown. "It's getting late. I should go."

"Stay."

"I can't."

"Yes, you can," he insisted, tilting his head with a smirk. "Got anywhere else you need to go?"

She didn't, but Katie wasn't sure if staying here with Cameron was such a good idea. Then again, it was better than going to the loft and facing Kelly. She would know something was wrong right away, and she sure as hell wasn't ready for that.

"No, but…"

"Then you're staying. We can order some take-out and watch a movie. Or talk some more. Whatever you want, but you're staying."

Apparently, he wasn't going to take no for an answer. "Okay."

Cameron smiled, his dimples showing. "Pizza?"

Katie wrinkled her nose. The thought of pizza didn't agree with her. She was hungry, though. She hadn't eaten since yesterday, and that ended up in the snow. "Um, can we get Thai?"

"Sure, babe." He ruffled her hair. "I told you, whatever you want."

She ate half of her chicken pad thai and made it through the first thirty minutes of *Guardians of the Galaxy* before she fell asleep. Katie wasn't sure how long she slept or what exactly woke her, but when she blinked her eyelids open the TV was still on. Cameron was the big spoon behind her, lightly stroking her arm.

"I got into Harvard." He kissed her hair. "I want you to come with me."

What?

She turned over, stunned. "Cam…"

"Shh." He held his finger to her lips. "Just listen."

"Okay."

He caressed her cheek and combed his fingers through her hair. "I love you, Katie. Never stopped. And I'll love this baby too. We can get married, and after I graduate in May we'll go right to Boston and get a place. We can be settled before the baby comes and law school starts."

Her eyes searched his. He was serious. That was the last thing she expected him to say. Katie was so stunned she couldn't speak.

"You don't have to give me an answer right this minute. I know it's a lot to think about. But for me it's always been you, Katie. I don't mind being second-best right now, because I know that eventually you'll love me too."

Nooo.

Tears welled in her eyes. She bit her lip. Didn't he know she never saw him as anything less than perfect?

Her fingers reached for his face, tracing his cheekbones. "Oh, Cameron. I do love you. You're wonderful and perfect." She pushed the hair off his face that constantly fell into his eyes. "You were never, ever second-best. It's just that I didn't meet you first. I tried to fight it, but it was too late. My heart was already taken. I just didn't realize it at the time."

If she had met him first they wouldn't be having this

conversation. Her life would have taken a different course. Cameron could have been the one to give her butterflies instead. She rubbed her tummy. But then her little bean wouldn't be here.

Cameron cupped her cheeks in his hands, and lowering his lips to hers, he softly kissed her. "Sleep, baby. We'll talk some more in the morning."

It didn't take long before Cameron's even breathing signaled he was asleep. She couldn't possibly think about agreeing to what he asked, could she? Katie felt for Brendan's bracelet on her wrist. It gave her comfort to feel it there.

Her sweet, wonderful Cameron. He wanted to do right by her and it wasn't even his baby. He was right too. Katie knew he loved her. He'd always shown it. And he was selfless enough that he'd love this baby just the same as he would've if he'd been the one to make it. They could have a happy life. But she didn't want him that way.

Brendan didn't even know he was going to be a father. If he did, Katie knew he'd want to do right by her and his child. She knew way down deep in her soul, felt it in her bones, that he loved her. He was selfless enough to let her go so she could live a happy life. As soon as he found out about the baby, he'd want her back. She didn't want him that way either.

Katie didn't want to be an obligation to anyone. Even someone who loved her. And maybe that's why she found it so difficult to tell Brendan in the first place.

Cameron slept peacefully beside her, his arm protectively around her waist. He was a good man. So fucking good. She eased out of his embrace at the first sign of light and softly kissed his face.

I love you, Cameron.

Then she quietly slipped out the door.

Kelly was already downstairs in the shop when she got to the loft. Katie took a quick shower and packed a bag. Then she called for an Uber to take her to the station. She descended the stairs to the alley. Leo was tossing trash into the dumpster.

Leo saw her, bag in hand. "Wasn't you gonna say goodbye, girl?"

"No."

"I'm guessing this has something to do with that gorgeous man of yours." He wrapped her in his arms and hugged her tight. "Listen to Leo. Everything's going to be all right. Time has a way of fixing things, you know. I love you, girl."

The Uber pulled up.

"I love you too, Leo."

Katie boarded the train that would take her back to Nowheresville. She watched the city skyline through a veil of tears as it got smaller and smaller, then it disappeared, and she couldn't see it at all anymore.

Her heart was still there.

'Love is a severe mental illness curable only with time.'

Sad part was, she didn't want a cure.

Thirty-Three

"**A**re you sure, Bren?"

Kyan pushed the button on the Nespresso machine. The smell of coffee brewing made him want to punch his fist through the wall. He closed his eyes for a second and saw Katelyn behind the counter at Beanie's, her little pink tongue peeking out, as she poured steamed milk into espresso to draw a heart in the foam. What was she doing right now? Did she make it to class this morning?

"Phil and Murphy called me last night." He shrugged. "That's what they said."

"When?" Dillon asked.

"Today. Tomorrow. This week." Brendan worried his lip. "I don't know. As soon as they get the go-ahead from the prosecutor, I guess. Murphy said he'll try to let me know when they're coming."

"Fucking railroad job is what it is," Kyan scoffed. "There's bigger fish than you out there celebrating that they don't have to make monthly deposits into her bank account anymore. So, the question is, which of them did it? Because it has to be one of them."

"Maybe."

Kyan nodded, blowing on his coffee. "I'm sure of it."

"Ky's right, Bren," Dillon added. "And they had to have looked at her bank account. So you have to wonder why they're targeting you. Either they're too lazy to do their jobs, they don't give a shit, or…"

"Someone wants to make sure Bren takes the blame for it?" Kyan finished his thought. Those two were always doing that.

"Yeah." Dillon eyed his brother.

"Who?" Brendan glanced to the ceiling, tapping his hand on his thigh as he pondered. "And why?" His gaze moved to his cousin.

Kyan swallowed his coffee. "We would've had a better shot at figuring that out if Kodiak had been able to identify where all the money was coming from."

"Besides the senator?" Dillon asked, reminding him that according to Kodiak, Salena was getting income from multiple sources.

"Yeah," Kyan affirmed with a nod.

"I saw the photos, and trust me, it wasn't him." Brendan shuddered, a cold chill running through him as the pictures flashed in his head. "Mitch likes to beg for a flogging. He doesn't give them."

Dillon got up from his chair. "We can't just sit around and hope they—"

The front door swung open, halting whatever Dillon was going to say. Brendan froze for a second, thinking they were here to arrest him, but then he remembered even the police had to buzz the gate to get inside.

Chloe stormed into the room. Jesse, Taylor, and Matt followed in her wake. She stood right in front of him, hands on her hips, glaring at him with that look. Eyes narrowed. Lips pursed. Brendan hadn't seen her look this mad since…well, since that time she insisted she was an entrée, not a side dish. On any other day he might've given a shit why she appeared to be so angry, but not today. He had his own shit to deal with.

"You…" Chloe wagged her finger in his face. She looked like she was about to cry. "…are such an ass."

Brendan sat back in his seat. He knew what was coming and why she'd barged into the office like that. He hadn't told anyone about him and Katelyn yet. Obviously, Chloe must have spoken to her.

They're friends, idiot. Of course she did.

"Uh-oh." Dillon chuckled at her. "What he do?"

It wasn't Chloe who answered, though. "Big man, here…" Matt sneered with a tip of his chin. "…dumped Katie."

Everyone looked at Brendan. He looked at his hands in his lap. "It wasn't like that." And he looked up. "I love her, you know."

"Then why would you do that?" Her voice rose an octave. "I don't understand, Brendan."

"For exactly that reason, Chloe. I'm not dragging her into this shit."

"But—"

Using a curt tone, Brendan cut her off. "I don't want that for her."

Chandan began to cry. "You made a huge mistake, Brendan. Huge!" Chloe retrieved the baby from Jesse's arms.

Matt shook his head. "Did you ever think to ask Katie what she wanted?"

No.

Brendan never got to answer.

Matt walked out the door, slamming it behind him.

Katie stepped onto the platform.

No one knew she was coming home. She hadn't bothered calling before she left the city. Then she'd just have to explain twice. Once on the phone and again when she walked in the door. She figured once would be difficult enough.

She retrieved her bag, psyching herself up for the short walk to her dad's hardware store here in town. Katie never expected to see Kevin standing there when she turned around.

"Kev?" She flung herself at her brother, tears flowing, hugging him so tight they swayed on the platform. "How did you know I'd be here?"

"Kelly called this morning." Kevin put one arm around her and picked up her bag with the other. "You got a bunch of people worked up back there. Who's Leo?"

"He's our…I mean Kelly's assistant manager at the shop."

"Well, the story I got from mom was some guy…I forget his name…plays football? Anyway, he shows up at Beanie's looking for you and Kelly tells him you're at school. Guess he told her you ain't, 'cause you quit or some shit, and when he woke up this morning, you were gone. That's when Leo informed them you got in a car with your suitcase." He shrugged then put her bag in the back of the Raptor. "They're all freaking out. I knew this is where I'd find you."

Kevin helped her into the passenger seat. He got in on the driver's side and started the truck, but he didn't pull out of the parking space. He turned in his seat.

"Now, before we go home, wanna tell me what's going on? And why you spent the night at some guy's house who ain't your boyfriend?"

She sniffled, wiping her eyes. "It might take a while."

"That's okay." He leaned over the console and hugged her. "Not going anywhere, big sister."

"You're bigger than me now, and I hate it."

"So you keep reminding me." He laughed. "Spill it, Katie. You're gonna need backup when we get home, trust me."

"I'm not sure where to start."

"Try at the beginning." He winked.

So she began her sordid tale of woe—because what else could she call it? Her life had become some fucked-up Shakespearean tragedy. After hearing the story of how she kissed a stranger in a park, the masquerade ball, Salena's murder, loving Brendan and how Cameron fit into all of this, her brother commented on only one thing.

"Wow!" He was grinning. "I'm gonna be an uncle?"

"Yeah."

"Mom's gonna shit." Kevin chuckled, shaking his head.

That was the understatement of the year. Her mother was going to have an apoplectic fit, and her aunts? She dreaded the thought of walking through that door, but what other choice did she have?

Katie sighed. "Yeah."

"I think you best leave some parts out when you tell Mom

and Dad." He reached over, giving her a noogie. "They don't need to know all that."

He made her laugh, sad as she was. "Which parts?"

"You know, sex clubs and stuff." He leaned back against the seat, put his hand on the shifter, and turned his head toward her. "Better make it G-rated, sister. Venture into NC-17 territory, and you're asking for trouble. Mom found my condom stash, so trust me on this."

The closer they got to the house, the more difficult it became to breathe. Katie felt nauseous, whether it was from anxiety or little bean, she couldn't say. She leaned toward the former, since she hadn't gotten sick until she puked lasagna in the snow.

Kevin pulled into the driveway, grabbed her hand, and squeezed it. "It's going to be okay. You know I got your back, Katie. I tell you that all the time."

As it turned out, apoplectic fit was the understatement of the year. Katie sat alone in her room, staring at the hideous flowered wallpaper she'd picked out in sixth grade, while her mother wailed to her aunts in the kitchen—like her being pregnant was tantamount to being diagnosed with a terminal disease.

"My life is so *not* over," she whispered to the flowers on the wall, even though it felt like maybe it was.

Katie turned her phone back on. She'd turned it off when she got in the Uber this morning. She sifted through the notifications. Kelly, Cam, Chloe, and even Matt had texted her. Nothing from Brendan. She didn't read the messages. That would make the tears start all over again when she'd finally gotten them under control. Maybe.

The tap that sounded on her door was soft, which meant it wasn't her mother or one of her aunts. "Come in."

Andrew Copeland sat beside his daughter on her bed. He didn't say a word. He just put his arm around her, patting her head that rested on his shoulder. They stayed like that for a time, supported in the silent comfort he gave her. Why couldn't the women in the family be like her father and Kevin?

"I love you, honey." Her father rested his head on hers and stroked her hair. "I just wanted you to know that."

"I love you too, Daddy."

Her rock. She felt like a little girl again, crying over Missy Reilly not wanting to be her best friend anymore. He'd done the same thing that day. Just held her. Her father never said much. God knows, her mother did more than enough talking for the two of them. But his hugs said a thousand words without him having to say anything at all.

"Everything is going to be just fine, Katie. I promise." He gave her shoulders a squeeze and lifted his head from hers. "Now I'm going to tell you, as a man, it's in our nature to protect the women we love, even from ourselves. I could tell that Brendan loves you, and it wasn't the pretty bauble on your wrist that told me that."

She nodded. "I know he does."

"He deserves to know he's going to be a father. Keeping that from him isn't right, honey."

A lie of omission is still a lie.

"I'm going to tell him, but now isn't the right time."

He stood, his hand on her shoulder. "There's no such thing as the right time. His troubles could last for quite a while, but knowing he has a baby on the way could affect the decisions he makes."

"That's just it, Daddy," Katie said, glancing up at her father. "I don't want it to."

"It's going to, whether you want it to or not. And he's going to find out, whether you want him to right now or not. Wouldn't you rather he heard it from you?" He gave her shoulder a final squeeze and left the room, softly closing the door.

Was she wrong? It's not like her intentions were to keep it a secret forever, just until...

Until when?

Until after the arrest? The trial?

Her father was right. There would be no right time.

She only knew it wasn't now.

Thirty-Four

A day became a week. One week became two.

And still he waited.

Every time his phone went off, Brendan expected it to be Phil or Murphy with the news that today was the day. That hadn't happened. So he sat on pins and needles. Waiting. Worrying about Katelyn. Wondering how she was. Missing her.

He'd picked up his phone to call her countless times, and stopped himself from doing it just as many. He didn't go anywhere near Beanie's so he wouldn't be tempted to go in and see her, or even catch a glimpse of her through the window. The photo of them still sat on his shelf. Brendan looked at it often. That was painful enough.

Dillon was helping him out at the club every day. Most days he didn't want to go in at all, but everyone insisted, and Phil agreed, that he keep to his usual routine. They'd been looking at candidates to manage nightly operations, and there was an Austrian couple that looked promising, so at least there was that. Brendan was trying to tie up as many loose ends as he could in the time he had to ease the burden on his cousins.

Venery was downstairs in the lower level studio. Brendan could hear the music as soon as he stepped inside their Park Place office. They had a small gym set up downstairs too. Brendan made use of it daily, releasing his aggressions and pent-up frustrations in there. He skipped it this morning, and went into the lounge for a cup of coffee.

The lounge, as Taylor dubbed it, was a casual space on the main level that resembled a living or family room, probably because it was once. It was where they worked together and spent the majority of their time—more than they did in their individual offices on the second level. It was comfortable, with overstuffed chairs, cushy sofas, and low-set tables. Enlarged photos in sepia hung on the exposed brick walls. Vintage buildings they'd bought and restored to their former glory. An old framed map of the city.

Jesse and Kyan were already here, seated on the eggplant velvet sofa and thumbing through Kyan's drawings for their latest renovation project. Oddly, Kodiak was here with them. Lazily sprawled in a club chair with his feet kicked up on an ottoman, he tapped away on the MacBook in his lap.

"Hello, Bren." Kodiak looked up from his screen with that sinister-looking smirk of his, like he was up to no good. It would be off-putting if he didn't know the guy.

"Kodiak." He tipped his chin as he headed over to the coffee machine. "How's it going, man?"

He chuckled. "It's going." And he winked. Maybe he was up to no good.

Brendan sat down in the vacant club chair and set his coffee on the table. Kyan pushed his drawings to the side. He looked up with a smirk. Jesse had a grin on his face too. He wasn't sure what the fuck everyone looked so happy about.

"What?"

"Expect a call, Bren." Kyan's smile widened. "I spoke to Billings about an hour ago. The investigators are bringing Eric Brantley back in for questioning today."

"Why?"

Kodiak set the computer to the side and straightened, his feet now on the floor. He cocked his head to the side, still grinning. "I might have sent them some information they couldn't ignore. A copy went to the prosecutor's office too. Anonymously, of course."

"What information?"

Kyan answered, "All of it, Bren."

"What do you mean, all of it?"

"Well, I dug a little deeper into the Brantleys," Kodiak said. "And it sure looks like Daddy Hugh's financial troubles weren't of his own making…" He steepled his fingers and grinned wider, raising his brow. "…and when you look at the paper trail it's pretty easy to see Eric was stealing assets right out from under Daddy's nose. With Salena's help, if I were to guess."

"Is that right?"

"Backfired on him, though," Kyan added, shaking his head. "Poor Hugh had to claim bankruptcy and liquidate his holdings because of his own son."

"Wait." Brendan knitted his brow. Was he missing something here? "What do you mean with Salena's help? She didn't start seeing Eric until after he put Hugh into the nursing home, right?"

"That's where you've got it all wrong, my friend." Kodiak was positively gleeful. "I'd say they've been together for quite some time, considering he paid the rent on her apartment for the last three years."

"The fuck?" That put Eric with Salena when she was still his hostess at the Red Door, so why didn't he know this? Hugh visited the club often, mostly to network with business contacts, but Eric? Brendan could count on one hand the number of times Eric had been to the Red Door. "Are you saying, Eric had Salena fuck his own father to get to his money?"

Because if that's what Kodiak was implying, this was all kinds of fucked up.

"Hugh couldn't get it past half mast, remember?" Jesse winked. "That's what Matt told us anyway," he explained.

"Yeah, I seem to recall that conversation." He wrinkled his nose in distaste, then chuckled. "And I told Matt I did not want to know how he knew that."

"See?" Kodiak smacked his hands on his thighs and stood. "She just had to pretend to like him. Show him a little attention." He walked over to where the mini-fridge was and got a bottle of water. Turned around. "So they got all the documentation that apparently led them to the same conclusion, considering Eric's been called in, plus her financial records, call and chat logs—which connect her to the priest and the senator, by the way." He looked to the ceiling. "Oh, and Hugh's medical records. They were a bitch to get ahold of too."

Should I even ask?

"What was so important about getting those?"

The guy was in a nursing home with some sort of early onset dementia, for fuck's sake. They'd heard he deteriorated quite rapidly. Didn't even know what day it was anymore. Brendan couldn't imagine why Kodiak thought he needed to get his hands on them.

"It didn't sit right with Taylor," Jesse explained. "Hugh's only sixty-two."

"Not to mention, the timing of his…unfortunate diagnosis." Kodiak tapped his finger against his temple. "I'm no medical expert so I did a little research. There are drugs that can mimic early onset dementia. Feed him those. Put him in a facility where they're probably pumping him full of psych meds. Declare him incompetent. Following me?"

"Christ."

"So"—Kyan came over and hugged him—"I think you'll be hearing from Phil or Murphy before too long."

"I hope so." Brendan chewed his lip. Dare he even begin to hope? "That proves Eric is a nasty piece of shit. Doesn't make him a murderer, though."

"No?" Kodiak shrugged. "He all but ended the life of his own father. Regardless, it's more than what they think they got on you, which is what? A whole lot of nothin' if you ask me."

"I don't think he killed her."

"Does it matter? The only thing that matters is taking the target off your back, brother." Kyan gripped his shoulder, squeezing it hard. "We can't let you get charged with this bullshit. Besides, it's already done."

Another week went by without a word.

Brendan still sat on pins and needles, and he would be until they either made an arrest or told him he was cleared, but at this point at least no news wasn't bad. As much as he feared this could still go horribly wrong, as each day passed that tiny inkling of hope grew. Perhaps one day soon this nightmare would finally be over, and when that day came the first thing he was going to do was see Katelyn.

And bring her home.

For keeps.

He hadn't seen her, or touched her, or heard her sweet voice in three miserable, hellish weeks. Besides all this shit hanging over his head, Katelyn was all Brendan thought about. How he'd managed to exist before her, he didn't know, because he wasn't much more than an empty shell without her now.

His phone signaled a text. Taylor telling him to come over for dinner. He wasn't all that hungry, but he could use the company and he figured he should probably eat.

Linnea and Chloe were cooking together in the kitchen. Chloe was still angry with him and gave him the cold shoulder. Didn't she get it? He was hurting too here. Linnea turned from the stove and flung herself at him. At least she was happy to see him.

"Sweetheart," he crooned, hugging her.

She looked up at him. "How are you, Bren?"

"Hanging in there." He walked over to Chloe at the island and swatted her behind. "Red."

Taylor, Jesse, and Kyan had the hockey game going on the big-screen in the family room. Brendan sat down with them to watch it. Maybe he'd get tickets. Take Katelyn to a game. She'd love it. Nobody did hockey better than this town, never mind that the season was pretty much already in the toilet.

At the end of the first period his phone rang. His cousins and Taylor all turned their heads toward the sound.

"It's Murphy."

Chloe and Linnea left the kitchen. He picked up the phone, hoping for the best and expecting the worst, but he sure as hell didn't expect to hear what Murphy called to tell him. He looked at his family, who anxiously waited with bated breath.

"Eric Brantley shot himself."

"What does that mean, Brendan?" Chloe squeaked out. She looked close to tears. He missed giggling Chloe.

Linnea turned to her and said, "I think it means he's dead, sweetie."

"Yeah, he's, um, dead." Brendan nodded.

"But what does that mean for you?"

He shrugged. "No idea."

"Fucker couldn't live with himself after what he'd done, I bet." Kyan pounded the table. "Probably knew an arrest was coming and offed himself."

Brendan looked at his youngest cousin. "I still don't think it was him, but I guess we'll never know now."

"They won't come after you again, will they?" Chloe sounded almost frantic and hugged him.

"I hope not, but they haven't cleared me yet, so I don't know, sweetheart."

Jesus Christ, will this ever fucking end?

"I'm gonna call Billings." Kyan stood from his seat. "See what I can find out."

Two days he waited. Forty-eight agonizing hours. That might not seem like very long, but after weeks of this hell, with his future and Katelyn hanging on the line, it was brutal. Finally, Phil called and said he and Murphy were coming by to see him. He wouldn't say anything more than that on the phone.

His three cousins, Taylor, Chloe, and Linnea were all gathered in his living room to lend their support and wait with him. Brendan knew just how fucking lucky he was to have them as family. He wouldn't have made it through these past weeks without them.

"Why are they dragging this out?" Chloe was chewing on a

fingernail. "Why couldn't they just say whatever they needed to tell you on the phone?"

He'd been asking himself the same question since this afternoon. Was it bad news? After all this were they coming to arrest him?

"Stop fretting, cherry cake." Taylor held her to his side on the sofa, attempting to soothe her. "Everything's going to be tickety-boo. You'll see."

But Brendan could tell that Taylor was worried. They all were. He gazed at six anxious faces. They tried to hide it with tentative smiles, but it was there in their eyes. Their nervous gestures. Chloe still chewed on her manicured fingernail. Linnea was wringing her hands until Kyan held them to still her. Jesse bounced Chandan on his knee. Dillon poured himself a shot.

"Anyone?" He held up the bottle.

Everyone shook their heads.

The buzzer for the gate sounded. Dillon got up to let them in. Brendan glanced to the photo of Katelyn on the shelf, and tracing the coordinates on his wrist, he silently prayed that he'd get to see her tomorrow.

Thirty-Five

Every day she went online to see if there was any news about Brendan or the case. And every day she found nothing. Katie even tried googling his name. *Nada*. It'd been weeks, so she couldn't understand why there hadn't been some news of it by now.

Just call him.

She was going to have to eventually, wasn't she? And yet, somehow it didn't feel right. This was something Katie needed to say in person. Brendan deserved that. Maybe she'd ask Kevin to take her to the city this weekend. He could visit with Kelly while she talked to him. She needed to get the rest of her things from the loft anyway, right?

This sucked.

Everything just fucking sucked.

Katie whipped the covers off and forced herself to get out of bed before her mother came knocking on the door. Kevin would be at school by now and her dad at the store, which meant it was just her and her mother without a buffer between them. It wasn't as bad as when she first got here. At least her mother seemed to have resigned herself to the fact she was going to be a grandmother before the age of forty. She couldn't hide her disappointment, though. Katie saw it in her face every single day.

Her mom was in the kitchen, digging through the freezer.

Deciding what to take out for dinner, Katie supposed. She plunked a package of frozen pork chops on the counter.

She spoke without turning to look at her. "I thought we could go into town this weekend. Pick out some new paint for your room. We'll have to rearrange the furniture in there to make space for a crib."

"Okay, but I was gonna ask Kevin to take me to the city this weekend."

That got her to turn around. "Why?"

"I have to talk to Brendan." Katie was an adult. Why did she feel it necessary to explain herself? "About the baby. And I need to see his face when I tell him."

"Honey, now why would you want to do that?" Looking upon her with pity, her mother pulled her into a hug. "He'll just hurt you again."

"No, he won't." It was going to rip her to pieces just to see him. "And you don't tell someone they're going to be a father over the phone."

"You're going to do what you want anyway," she sighed. "You always do."

"It's the right thing to do, Mom."

"We'll go paint shopping another day then." She shrugged and changed the subject. "Aunt Kim is coming for dinner."

Great.

Katie refrained from rolling her eyes. She could handle her mother when it was just her, but her mom and her aunts together were an entirely different animal. Fierce. Opinionated. Overbearing. And Kim was the worst.

"Aunt Kara too?"

"Not expecting her."

Maybe it wouldn't be so bad.

She thought she was home free, seeing as they'd made it to dessert in relative harmony, that is until her mother had to mention she was planning to go to the city this weekend. Why was that any of her aunt's business anyway? Kevin squeezed her knee under the table in a bid for her to hold her tongue. Katie put another forkful of chocolate cake in her mouth.

"Kelly told me that football player wants to marry you." Kim looked from her to her mother. "He's going to law school. Did you hear? Got accepted to Harvard."

Katie rolled her eyes. She couldn't stop herself this time.

"Cameron." Her mom gushed like she actually knew him. "He visits Kelly every day to check on Katie. He really cares for her."

"When's the last time you heard from your baby daddy?" Her aunt looked at her all righteous and smug.

Katie wanted to slap that look off her face. But she couldn't. The truth was she hadn't heard one word from Brendan in all this time, and everybody here knew it. Maybe if she didn't respond at all, her aunt would just drop it.

"You should marry him."

"No…"

"If you're even thinking of sitting around and waiting for Brendan, then you're foolish." Kim sat back in the chair and folded her arms across her chest.

Wasn't anybody going to help her out here? Someone needed to shut her aunt up before she lost her temper.

"That's not what I'm thinking."

Kim wagged her finger. "You're not thinking at all. What kind of options do ya think you're gonna have around here, especially after that baby comes? None, I tell ya."

Options? What the fuck was she talking about? Katie knew what love was, and as far as she was concerned there were no other options.

"I don't love Cameron that way and I don't want to get married just because I'm pregnant."

"You'll learn to love him." Kim shook her head. "Kristie, you need to talk some sense into your daughter…"

"Stop it."

Her aunt continued as if she wasn't sitting right there. "…before she throws her whole life away."

"I said stop it." Katie spoke louder.

"Katelyn," her mother used a warning tone.

Oh, am I in trouble?

Katie smiled as she spoke in the most pleasant voice she could muster. "With all due respect, Auntie, gossiping about me with Kelly or Kara or my mom just isn't right, and whatever my *options* may or may not be, are none of your concern."

Her aunt's mouth hung open. "Are you going to let her talk that way to me, Kristie?"

"I am." Her father stood up from his seat at the table, dropping his napkin. "Katie doesn't have to marry anyone. You're thirty-seven, Kim. Might want to start thinking about options of your own."

Thank you, Daddy.

Kim was out of line, but she did have a point. There weren't any options for her, or little bean, out here in Nowheresville. Isn't that why she left in the first place? Maybe she should have stayed in the city with Kelly, but that really wasn't an option either. She was just going to have to suck it up until she came up with a viable plan for the future.

A future on her own.

With a baby.

And without Brendan.

Dillon led Murphy and Phil into the living room. Brendan couldn't read their faces as they nodded at everyone and took a seat.

"Well?"

"They closed the case, Bren." Murphy finally cracked a smile. "It's over."

Clasping his hands behind his neck, Brendan let out his breath in a loud rush and lowered his head to his knees. The enormity of the weight that had been lifted left him lightheaded. Hands rubbed his back and squeezed his shoulder. He couldn't tell you who they belonged to.

After a few deep breaths he lifted his head. "You're sure."

"Yeah." Murphy patted his shoulder. "There's no actual physical evidence against you, Eric, or anyone, but in light of what we do know…and Eric's, uh, suicide, the investigators and the prosecutor agreed to close the case."

He looked to Phil, who nodded and patted his briefcase. "I have it right here."

They stood then. "Well, we don't want to keep you." Phil winked. "You have a life to get back to."

He had to get back to Katelyn. She was his life.

Brendan reached for the leather on his wrist. He needed to go see her right this minute. Hold her. Celebrate.

"I have to go," he announced and went to get his coat.

Dillon held a bottle of champagne in his hand. "Bren, where the fuck you going?"

"To get a cup of foamy coffee with a heart on it." He winked.

"Um, Bren." Chloe slowly walked toward him, chewing on her lip. She placed her hand on his forearm. "She's not there."

Thirty-Six

"What do you mean she's not there?" Chloe knocked the air right out of his lungs when he'd only just gotten it back.

She looked to Jesse and back at him, wringing her hands. "Um, she left."

That didn't tell him shit. He didn't have an ounce of patience left. Not after almost a month of this hell. Brendan needed his sweet girl and he needed her right the fuck now.

"Where. Is. She?" Each word spoken was louder than the one before it.

Chloe stared down at her shoes. "She went home, I think."

"You think? Have you talked to her?"

She glanced up to his face. "Yeah, a few times."

"Why didn't you tell me?"

"I tried, Brendan," she implored. "Remember?"

Did she? He didn't remember. Brendan had a sinking feeling that he'd fucked up. Big time. He couldn't wait. He had to go fix it.

"What're you doing, Bren?" Chloe still wrung her hands.

"Going to get some answers from Kelly."

When he'd given himself permission to imagine an end to this fucking nightmare, he never once thought he'd be walking into another one. He only thought of her. Everything he did was for her. She had to know that.

It never occurred to him that Katelyn wouldn't be here. Why would she leave? What was she thinking? What about school and Kelly and Beanie's? It didn't make any sense.

Nothing made any fucking sense.

He shrugged into his coat and went out the front door. Early March wind bit into him, cold and damp, chilling him to the bone. Brendan slipped through the gate into the park, and passing the spot on the trail where he first saw her, he felt for the hammered silver plate on his wrist and hurried his steps.

Kelly and Leo were behind the counter. He could see them through the window. And was that frat boy? What the fuck was he doing here? Brendan felt the tick in his jaw before he even opened the door.

Leo noticed him first. He elbowed Kelly and tipped his chin in his direction, then she noticed him too, and her face took on a scowl. Frat boy leaned against the counter, oblivious to his arrival.

"Brendan." She cocked her head.

Frat boy turned around.

"Kelly." He didn't have time for bullshit. "Where's Katelyn?"

"She isn't here." Kelly held her hands out to emphasize the fact.

"I know she isn't here." He shook his head, exasperated already. "She with her folks?"

She crossed her arms over her chest and didn't answer.

He moved closer to the counter. "C'mon, Kelly. You know I'm just going to drive out there anyway."

"I wouldn't do that if I were you. My brother-in-law just might shoot you on sight."

Drew likes me. He wouldn't do that, would he?

Brendan could understand Kelly being upset with him, but this seemed like more than that. She was downright venomous. "Why did she leave? Is she okay?"

"Why do you care?"

He wasn't getting anywhere with Kelly. If she wasn't Katelyn's aunt he'd have told her to fuck off by now. What the fuck was he wasting his time here for? He should just go, get in his car, and get his girl back. Why did he feel like he had to make her understand?

"Kelly, you know I love her."

"Really? Is that why you tossed her out like trash?" she spat out.

Is that what she really thought? Is that what Katelyn thought? Because nothing was further from the truth. God, she had to know that.

"That's not what happened."

Kelly popped her hip. She didn't try to mask her disdain. "Sure seems like it to me."

"What would you have had me do, huh?"

Tick. Tick. Tick.

Brendan was really getting pissed now. He should go.

"Not what you did, you bastard. You ruined her life, just like I told her you would. And I hate you for it." Kelly choked on her words and began to cry. "She didn't tell me she was going. She didn't even say goodbye."

Why did she have to go and cry? She made him feel like the bad guy here even though he wasn't.

He took her hand. "Kelly, I'm sorry. I'm going to go get her and bring her home."

"Leave her alone, Brendan." She pulled her hand from his grasp.

"Can't do that."

Leo nudged her side. "Girl, you gotta tell him."

"Tell me what?"

"Shush, Leo. If Katie wanted him to know, she'd have told him."

"Tell me what?" he yelled.

"He has a right to know." Frat boy finally spoke.

Straightening himself, he stood toe to toe in front of Brendan. "Katie's pregnant."

Pregnant?

Did he hear that right?

The world seemed to stop for a moment and he forgot to breathe. He was vaguely aware of his hands shaking and his eyes burning. A baby? Why didn't she tell him?

Because he shouldn't have found out this way.

Those words should have come from her.

It shouldn't have been like this.

He didn't need anything else from these people. Katelyn and his baby—God, he was trying to wrap his head around that— were waiting. He had to go.

"You say you love her, yet you let her go," Frat boy said. "How could you do that? I don't know. Maybe you thought you had a good reason. Maybe you thought she was better off without you. She probably is," he added, nodding. "Well, guess what? I love her and I won't ever let her go. The way I see it, part of loving someone is letting them love you back. Sharing the good *and* the bad together. You didn't do that, though, did you?" Frat boy shrugged. "I've asked Katie to marry me and I'm taking her to Boston."

Over my dead fucking body.

"That's my baby."

Frat boy smirked. "That's just genetics."

Brendan's fists curled at his sides. It took everything in him not to punch the daylights out of this fucking punk. "That's my baby and my woman."

Kelly came out from behind the counter and stepped between them. "You should probably go now, Brendan." She exhaled a breath. "If you really love her like you say you do, you'll leave her alone."

He didn't remember the walk home. Too many thoughts flooded

his mind. How long had she known and kept this from him? Brendan knew the exact moment they made that baby. There was only one possible moment it could have been. On the floor, in a tent made from blankets, under twinkling white lights. And that was more than three months ago.

Admittedly, he didn't know a whole helluva lot about girls and their periods, except they got one every month or so. He didn't know shit about pregnancy tests or how any of that worked, but Katelyn went to the doctor for birth control in January. It was the same day as that last awful encounter with Salena and Eric Brantley at Beanie's.

Katelyn had to have known at least since then. She said they didn't need to use condoms anymore and he just assumed...why the fuck didn't she tell him right then? Did she think he'd get mad? That he didn't want to be a father? What? He'd never given her a reason to think any of those things so he couldn't come up with a reasonable explanation for her to keep it from him.

Brendan was angry. At her. At himself. At Kelly. At that punk kid who had the audacity to think he could just step in, take his girl, and be a father to his child.

Make your own baby, asshole. Get your own girl too.

Was Katelyn still his?

In his mind she was. His heart would always belong to her. Did she give up on him? He almost couldn't blame her if she did.

Chloe was right. He did let her go.

He'd made a huge mistake.

Jesse was sitting alone on the sofa in his living room when he returned. Everyone else had apparently gone home. Brendan didn't say a word. Blowing out a breath, he sat next to his cousin, tipped his head back, and stared at the ceiling.

Jesse didn't say a word either. He poured him a finger of Glenlivet and put the glass in his hand. Brendan downed it in one swift swallow.

"Talk to Kelly?"

"Yeah." Brendan poured himself a second shot.

"And?"

He shrugged. "And nothing."

"Are you going to get Katie?"

He shrugged again. "Not sure yet."

"I have something to tell you." There was no sense of urgency in his voice. Jesse spoke in the same calm, easy manner he always did. "But you can't get angry with Chloe. She couldn't betray a confidence and it wasn't for her to tell. I didn't make any such promise, though, and you need to know."

Brendan was pretty sure he already knew what Jesse had to tell him. Who else knew about the baby before he did?

"I got it out of her once you left. She was acting funny, wringing her hands and shit, so I called her on it. I know my wife." His cousin took a breath. "Katie's having a baby, Brendan. You're going to be a dad."

Brendan poured a third shot and turned his head toward Jesse. His cousin was smiling. He swallowed the whiskey.

"Katie's pregnant, Bren," Jesse repeated, like maybe it hadn't sunk in the first time he said it.

"I know."

Jesse appeared truly flummoxed. "I don't understand."

"What don't you understand, cousin?"

"Why you're sitting there pouring shots instead of jumping in the 'Vette to go get her."

"You poured me the first one." He shrugged.

"Are you scared, Bren?" Jesse put his hand on his shoulder. "It's normal if you are. I remember I freaked the shit out when Chloe first told us she was having a baby—and you should've seen Tay."

"That's the thing, Jess." He waved his empty glass in the air. "Chloe told you. You didn't get the memo from her ex-boyfriend."

Jesse swallowed. His mouth frozen in a silent O.

"She went to him, not me." Brendan shook his head. "Have any idea what that feels like, Jess?"

"No." Jesse took the glass from his hand and set it on the table. "But I do know that girl loves you."

They sat there for a minute, staring at the flickering flames in the fireplace, listening to nothing except the crackling logs. Jesse took his cousin's hand and squeezed it, then he stood to leave.

He took a step and turned around. "You gave me some advice once, when I thought Chloe and me would never get to be where we are now. You told me I couldn't be a coward and be in love. That I had to choose one. It was good advice." He smiled then. "Choose love, my brother. I know you're not a coward."

He loved her.

That wasn't in question here.

He poured himself another shot.

Thirty-Seven

Brendan woke up on his living room sofa in the same position he'd passed out in. An empty bottle of whiskey sat on the table. His head pounded and his tongue stuck to the roof of his mouth, sticky and fetid with the remnants of alcohol-induced sleep. The fire in the hearth had long since gone out, leaving a chill in the air. He pulled the throw on top of him and closed his eyes against the early morning light.

One of the few perks of passing out in a drunken stupor was if he'd had any dreams, he certainly didn't remember them. Brendan was more than good with that. He'd gone months without having any, the last one he remembered was around Thanksgiving, but with Salena's death they'd come back.

He was too old for this shit. After Jesse left last night, with an open bottle of Glenlivet, his only purpose was to slow his racing thoughts, numb the pain, and drown his sorrows. It seemed like a good idea at the time. This morning it sounded fucking pathetic, even to him. Brendan was going to be thirty-three next month and he'd made it through every fucked-up thing life had thrown at him so far. He had a baby on the way, for fuck's sake. Yeah, he was way too old for this shit.

There was a gentle tap at the front door, then it opened. He really should remember to lock it. Keep the well-intentioned busybodies out. Namely Chloe. In all likelihood, it was her. She was lucky he loved her ass something fierce, because he was none too pleased with her at the moment. By not betraying Katelyn's confidence, she'd betrayed him. Kept his baby a secret from him for what—close to seven weeks now? It was going to take him a bit to get past that.

He felt the shift of the cushion beneath him when she sat down on the edge of the sofa. He could smell her freshly washed hair. Milk and coconuts. His head was still pounding, so he refrained from opening his eyes. A soft hand touched his.

"Brendan?" She tentatively spoke his name in a voice almost too quiet to be heard. "You know I love you the most. Well, after my husbands and my son, that is. I love you and I'm so sorry, but I promised. Please, you have to forgive me."

"Is that what you came here for?" His eyes remained closed.

"Um, yeah."

"Okay." He tried to roll over, but she was in the way. "You can go now."

She shook his arm. "Brendan. It's not like you think. Katie wanted to tell you herself and she wanted you to be the one to announce it to everyone."

Why didn't she then?

"I only knew because I was at the appointment with her. See, I told her to come back with me so she wouldn't have to sit in the waiting room all by herself and then when it was her turn I just stayed. Good thing too, because she was so not prepared for that unexpected news, let me tell you…"

Now that Chloe started, she'd keep going until she recounted every last detail or ran out of breath to speak. He couldn't tune her out even if he wanted to.

"…total shocker. You should have seen her face. She spotted at Christmas and thought it was her period, I guess. I mean, I could understand what she was feeling and all. She walks in to get a script for the Pill and walks out with samples of prenatal vitamins." Chloe giggled.

He didn't find it at all funny.

"She kept asking Roberta—she's our doc—if she was sure, until she heard the heartbeat and saw your little bean on the screen anyway. There was no doubt after that."

Brendan cracked his eyes open. "Little bean?" He sat up. "You saw my baby?"

"Yeah." Chloe smiled. "Katie got pictures for you."

I should have been there.

She hugged him. "She was scared, Bren, and that's a normal thing to feel. But she asked me not to tell anyone and I promised I wouldn't. I know she was going to tell you, and then the Salena thing happened…and she didn't want to come over for Super Bowl because she had it all planned to tell you that day and…" She shrugged in his arms.

And he got the phone call that changed everything.

He was an ass.

"Brendan?"

"Yeah."

"I love you, baby, but you stink." She patted his back. "Go take a shower. I'll fix you some breakfast."

Brendan needed a shower, to drink a gallon of cold water, and swallow eight hundred milligrams of ibuprofen before he'd even come close to resembling a functioning human again. He just wasn't sure if he possessed the energy or the capability to get off the couch. But he pushed himself, and while a hot shower wasn't the panacea for a hangover, at least he didn't feel quite so disgusting.

Chloe had breakfast waiting for him as promised. Chocolate chip pancakes, scrambled eggs, bacon, and orange juice sat at a place on the kitchen island. Brendan appreciated the gesture, but he wasn't in the mood for company or conversation. He had a lot to think about and he required solitude to do that.

"Feel better?" She smiled at him.

And she was too damn perky for him to be around too.

"Eh."

"Eat." Chloe stood, tucking into a pancake of her own. "Carbs and chocolate make everything better."

He scarfed down his food in silence with the hope that the faster he ate, the sooner she'd go home. She had husbands and a nine-month-old waiting on her over there after all.

"Do you think you'll be back in time for dinner?"

Huh?

"Back from where?"

"Getting Katie." She swallowed another mouthful of pancake. "Because we can do stir-fry or something if you want to come over and…"

"Whoa, I don't know that I'm going anywhere."

That was the bulk of what he needed to think about. To work out in his head. Katelyn. The baby. Yesterday, it required no thought at all, but he wasn't as sure today as he was then.

"What makes you think she wants to be gotten?"

"Stop it, Brendan. She loves you. You love her."

"I hear she's going to Boston." He smirked.

Chloe shook her head with a giggle. "Shut up, Brendan."

"You shut up, Chloe."

It was almost too quiet after she'd gone, leaving him alone with only his thoughts for company. That's what he wanted just an hour ago, though, wasn't it? Why was his head such a fucked-up mess? He could blame the after-effects of the alcohol, he supposed. Stress. God knows, he'd had a lifetime's worth this past month. Brendan had to admit it was none of those things. It was Katelyn. Everything was fucked up without her.

Go get her, idiot.

He opened the French door and stepped out onto the brick patio. Patches of snow interlaced with mucky puddles covered the backyard, as if nature itself was stuck somewhere between winter and spring. Death and rebirth. He took a deep breath of cold, clean air in through his nose. It smelled of wet earth, budding life, and the promise of things to come.

What the hell was he doing? Why did he hesitate? Brendan

didn't have a ready answer. He only knew if he went over there today, fueled by shit he hadn't fully processed, things could go horribly wrong. He needed everything to be right. His future with Katelyn was too important to risk fucking it all up.

If he hadn't fucked it up already, that is.

He couldn't accept that.

He wouldn't.

Their baby would grow up in this house, chase leaves in this backyard, learn to ride a bike without training wheels on Park Place. They'd spend weekends at the lake house watching all the kids play while they grilled burgers. Snow forts. Lightning bugs. Skinned knees. They'd build a tent in the living room every year and make love under twinkling white lights—perhaps make more babies too. They'd add another ornament to their tree.

Rubbing his arms, Brendan went back in the house. Dillon was sitting on his sofa. He really needed to remember to lock the damn door.

"Hey, cousin. I, um, just wanted to check on you before I took off to the club." He threaded his fingers through the long blond hair on top of his head, pushing it out of his eyes.

"It's that late already?" Brendan rubbed the beard on his chin. "Hadn't noticed."

"Yeah." Dillon angled his head, studying him. "You good?"

"Yeah, man."

"Good." He blew out a breath and smiled. "I still say she's much too pretty for an ugly beast like you. You're lucky, bro."

"I know. I don't deserve her."

But I'm going to keep her anyway.

"Oh, Hans and Brigitta accepted our offer. They start Monday."

"Thurner, right? The Austrian D/s couple."

"Yeah, you still good with the administrative stuff and special events?"

"Definitely." He couldn't let the club go completely. The Red Door was his baby. He'd still oversee administrative operations, plan special events, and such. Put in an appearance now and then. Hans and Brigitta came highly recommended. The club would flourish in their hands.

"Congrats, your evenings are your own then." Dillon winked. "Until the baby comes anyway."

"You knew too?"

"Nah, we all heard Jesse wrangle it out of Chloe."

Brendan chuckled at that. It was the first time he recalled laughing in weeks.

"Okay, I'm out."

"Thanks, Dill." He hugged his cousin. "For everything."

"Family, Bren." He pounded his chest. "It's what we do."

One less thing on his plate. Brendan went to bed feeling a little bit lighter, and a little bit closer to making the life he dreamt of a reality. With thoughts of Katelyn, he closed his eyes.

He could see the dark void off in the distance. Like an approaching thunderstorm, it was there. Waiting. Brendan stood in the light, staring at the darkness. Salena walked past. She didn't see him, at least she didn't acknowledge him if she did. He watched her go until she disappeared into the dark void ahead.

So long, Sal.

Uncle Charley stood beside him, shaking his head, arms crossed over his chest. "Didn't I always say that every storm runs out of rain, son?"

"Maya Angelou said that, Charley."

He chuckled. "Yeah, well, she got it from me."

"We miss you, old man."

"Who you calling old?"

He turned his head to reply but no one was there, and he returned to staring at the black void. As if by looking at it, watching it, he could keep it from getting closer. He couldn't turn his back on it.

Brendan woke in a cold sweat, in the dark, alone in his big bed. Leaning over, he switched on the bedside lamp. It was clear in his mind what he needed to do. He could stand at the edge of darkness or take a step back into the light. He could dream of his future or build one.

Katelyn was his light in the dark.

His future.

Everything he wanted.

He just had to go get her.

Thirty-Eight

The house was far too quiet.

And cold.

Ever since the disastrous dinner with Kim, her mother had hardly spoken, and not just to her, but to anyone. Katie felt bad that her father and brother had to suffer the silent treatment along with her. In a way, the silence was even more deafening, it spoke volumes louder than her incessant chatter ever did.

Katie was sure they still talked about her, they were just a little more discreet about it now, keeping their gossip to when she was out of earshot. Kelly sent her a text to say she was sorry. Kim and Kara said nothing at all.

Katie prepared herself for yet another day of nothing but more of the same. Same side-eyed glances. Same whispers in another room that she couldn't quite hear. Same bullshit. Same boredom.

The days ticked by slowly out here in Nowheresville with nothing to break up the hours of monotony stuck inside the house. No classes. No job. No car. Not that there was anywhere to go except town, and there wasn't much to be had there either.

Tomorrow would be better. She told herself that every day. At least tomorrow Kevin was taking her back to the city for the weekend. Katie was anxious to see Brendan after almost a month of not seeing him. She missed him so fucking much that most days it felt like she was slowly dying. The only thing that kept her from going insane was the little piece of him she had inside her. In the midst of chaos and uncertainty, maybe knowing their little bean existed would keep him sane too. She hoped so.

According to the baby tracker app on her phone, today marked sixteen weeks, not that you could tell that by looking at her. Katie gazed at herself in the mirror over her dresser, running her hand over her belly. There wasn't a bump yet, but she definitely felt a thickening there. She sighed and wondered if her little bean was a boy or a girl with eyes of the bluest blue.

Katie got dressed in a pair of leggings and Brendan's big old sweatshirt. The fabric was warm and soft and worn. It swam on her, falling to her knees. She wore it a lot, much to her mother's chagrin. Somehow it made her feel close to him, like he was giving her a hug. She put on a pair of fuzzy socks with bright-pink stripes and threw her hair into a messy topknot. She didn't bother with makeup at all these days, because who the fuck cared what she looked like?

Padding into the kitchen, Katie expected to find her mom there, and was surprised when she did not. The room was empty. A note propped on the counter. She was alone.

"Well, how do you like that?" she muttered into the open refrigerator, grabbing the juice. "That's okay. Not like I wanted to go anyway."

Katie poured herself a glass of juice and popped some bread into the toaster. Thrumming her fingers on the counter as she waited, she thought she heard a knock at the door. She figured she was hearing things, going plum stir-crazy or something, because hardly a soul ever bothered coming all the way out here. Except the mailman, and he could leave the package at the door.

Then she heard it again and she knew she wasn't crazy.

She opened the door and her eyes instantly flooded with tears.

Six feet eight of solid man in an open black peacoat stood in front of her, a big shopping bag in one hand, a bouquet of flowers in the other. He was the most beautiful thing she'd ever seen. Katie didn't hesitate. She catapulted herself into his arms.

"Sweet girl."

That voice. God, how she'd missed hearing it. She clung to him like a monkey to a tree, her face pressed into his neck, breathing in his bergamot smell. Tears freely flowing. Shaking. Afraid if she let go he'd disappear, that this was just some crazy dream.

"Sh, sh, sh." He held her with the flowers in his hand behind her back. "Don't cry." But he sounded choked up too. Gently, Brendan eased her down. "It's too cold out here for you. Can we go in?"

"Yeah." She swiped the wetness from her face. "No one's here."

He picked up the bag, followed her inside to her room, and closed the door. "C'mere."

Then he swept her back into his arms and lowered his mouth to hers. Butterflies that had lain dormant swooped and dove like a flock of birds, making her dizzy. Katie touched his face with shaking fingertips, tracing his cheeks and his jaw, while her tongue urgently sought to be reunited with his.

He lifted his head from hers and sat her on her bed, then kneeling in front of her, he laid his head in her lap, his hands skimming up and down her back. She combed her fingers through his auburn hair.

"Is everything okay, Brendan?"

"It is now." He pressed his fingers into her skin.

"What happened?"

"A lot happened. I'll tell you all about it later. The only thing that matters is it's over. They closed the case."

Upon hearing that, she burst into tears again, pure and utter relief washing over her.

He rose from his knees and sat beside her on the bed, taking her hands in his. "We have a lot to talk about, don't we?"

Sniffling, she nodded.

"I'm so happy about the baby."

She froze. "Chloe told you, didn't she?"

"No, she kept your secret." He leaned over to kiss her forehead. "Which I'm mad at her for, by the way."

She worried her lip. "Matt?"

"Matt knew too?"

She shrugged and wrinkled her nose. "Well, he got to watch me puke lasagna in the snow."

He hugged her. "Oh, baby, I'm so sorry." His hand left her back to touch her belly, slowly rubbing back and forth. She could have sworn she saw a sheen in his blue, blue eyes. "When?"

"August." She smiled.

"Why didn't you tell me?" He was still rubbing her belly.

"I was going to and then…" She shrugged. "Kevin was actually taking me to the city to see you tomorrow."

"I wish I had known." Brendan looked both awestruck and disappointed at the same time. Disappointed in what, though? Himself? Or her?

"Why? Would it have changed anything?"

"Yes, of course it would have."

Hearing that struck a chord in her. Would knowing there was a baby have made her worth keeping?

"It shouldn't make a difference," she implored. "I was capable of being there for you, standing by your side, pregnant or not, but I wasn't given the choice."

Brendan looked right at her, apology etched into his face. "You're right. My only excuse is I wasn't thinking clearly, but you know I was only trying to protect you."

She knew that to be true. Katie never doubted for one moment that he loved her, but he was wrong to make decisions like that without letting her be a part of them.

"I know that's what you thought you were doing, but you hurt me. You had a month to think, but I never heard one word from you in all that time." Katie wasn't trying to be accusatory or start an argument, especially when they'd just been reunited, but it was what it was. She wanted him to know how she felt. More than that, she needed to be sure it wouldn't happen again, because she wouldn't survive it a second time.

"Every day I picked up my phone to call you, and every day I stopped myself because I didn't want to hurt you more than I already had. Every. Day." He gripped her shoulders. She could see it in his eyes. Brendan had suffered too. "I love you, Katelyn, and I'm sorry. But we're the same, you and me. See, I was capable of being there for you too, only I wasn't given a choice either. You've known we're expecting a baby for almost two months now and never said a word in all that time." He paused, rubbing her arms. "I understand, though."

He was right. God, he was fucking right. She'd been guilty of the same and hadn't they both suffered enough?

"I'm sorry too." She straddled his lap and hugged him. "I love you, Brendan."

"Let's go home, baby."

It didn't take her long to pack her things. She'd only brought one bag with her when she boarded the train that took her away from the city. Katie scribbled out a note and propped it on the counter.

Everything looked different, yet everything was exactly the same. This house was her home now.

Brendan carried her bag upstairs and she unpacked her things, putting them away in drawers left empty for her.

"I'm going to have to go see Kelly. Ask for my job back and I've got more stuff to get at the loft."

Katie turned around and the look on his face could best be described as a sneer. Contemptuous. She was almost afraid to ask what happened with Kelly in her absence. Thinking of that dinner with Kim, she had a pretty good idea.

Nope. Not going there today.

"All of that can wait, sweet girl." He combed his fingers through her hair. His features relaxed. "But this can't."

She was still in his sweatshirt. Brendan lifted it over her head and stared at her standing there in just her bra and leggings. He licked his lips. It wasn't even one of her pretty lace ones. Just plain white cotton that was a bit too snug because her breasts had gotten larger.

Oh.

His fingers lightly skimmed her décolletage, leaving goose-bumps on her skin. Lowering the straps from her shoulders, he kissed her crown. "I love you."

With a flick of his fingers he unhooked the clasp and plain white cotton fell to the floor. Brendan knelt in front of her, and cupping a breast in each hand, he kissed and licked the space between. His thumbs brushed over her nipples and she bit her lip at the delicious sensation. She could tell he was holding back, trying to be gentle with her, but after a month without his touch she needed to feel everything.

Katie placed her hands on top of his and squeezed. "And I love you."

Brendan smirked. "Look at these gorgeous tits." He pinched her nipples and she whimpered in appreciation. They were even more sensitive now. "Not sure I'm ready to share them, even with my kid."

"You better take advantage of the next five months then, huh?" Katie took his face in her hands and brought his mouth to her nipple. His tongue peeked out to lick it. Then he drew it into his mouth and suckled. Her body hummed in response.

She closed her eyes and held his head to her breast as he sucked, her pelvis rocking against him. His lips moved to latch onto the other and her fingers sought the wet, swollen nipple he left behind. Pulling. Tugging. Twisting.

"Do you have any idea how hot that is?" He sat back on his haunches, watching her.

Katie took hold of both nipples, rolling them in her fingers. She felt his fingers slip inside the waistband of her leggings and he lowered them to her ankles. He lifted one foot, then the other, and spread them wide.

"Who does this pussy belong to, baby?"

"You."

"Better fucking believe it."

Already wet, he slid two fingers in to the hilt. Katie yanked on her nipples with a moan. Brendan pumped in and out of her, fluid gushed with a squelch of sound, to run down her thighs. His thumb mashed into her clit.

"That's it, make it messy for me." He leaned in and licked up her thigh. "Cover my face with your sweet cum. That belongs to me too."

Brendan pulled out his fingers and dipped his head between her legs, covering her slit with his mouth, fucking her with his tongue. Slurping and sucking at her opening. Her thighs were shaking and her knees threatened to buckle. Katie let go of her nipples to hold onto his shoulders as his tongue found her clit.

He loved on her clit with slow, easy circles, sliding his fingers back inside. Massaging her wall with firm, solid strokes that urged her to let go, to give him what he wanted. His lips clamped down on her and sucked.

"Fuck," she cried out.

God, she'd missed this. Katie couldn't imagine feeling this with anyone else. Being close like this with anyone else. Sharing this with anyone else. And she didn't ever want to.

His strokes became fast and relentless. He sucked her clit like he was sucking her soul from her body in his quest to pluck the orgasm from her. She felt the heaviness, the tickling throb, and gasped in a breath. A jolt of electricity arced through her body and she let go.

Brendan caught her and lowered her to the floor on top of him. He peppered her face with kisses. Big, strong hands skimmed her back, holding her close against him. She listened to his heart beating beneath his hot, sweaty skin. She traced the ink with her fingertips, breathing in bergamot and cedarwood, and smiled.

She was home.

Thirty-Nine

What the ever-loving fuck?

He didn't even open his eyes. His fingers flew to tangle in her hair. Brendan tugged her head even closer. Katelyn had him in a tight vacuum seal, sucking like she was dying for his dick. Her tongue toyed with the silver barbell. The noises she made, humming moans, vibrated against the stainless steel. That alone could make him come.

She gagged on his girth. Saliva dripped from her mouth to cover his cock and she gripped him with both hands. Her left hand twisted right, and her right twisted left, like she was trying to wring the cum right out of him.

You keep on doing that, baby, and you're gonna get more than a mouthful.

And wring it out of him, she did.

Messy. Sloppy. Noisy. Beautiful. But then that's a perfect blow-job, right?

Every man should wake up like that on his birthday. Blowjobs and fucking are two very different things, and every man needs both. He was the luckiest man on the planet.

Katelyn sat up, licking the cum that dribbled from her lip, with a satisfied smile. "Happy birthday, baby."

"Get over here."

She crawled naked up his chest, her gorgeous globe-shaped tits and her little baby bump brushing his skin along the way, and he kissed her. Tasting himself in her sweet mouth. His spent dick twitched back to life, wanting to sink itself inside her warm, wet pussy. That would have to wait until later. He had plans for today.

"I love going all gluck gluck on you." She giggled. "Would you say that was a three thousand? Or a nine? I'd say it was a nine, but it's your opinion that counts."

"Nine, baby. That was definitely a nine."

Yeah. Luckiest man on the fucking planet.

"So, what do you want to do today, birthday boy?"

He'd taken the day off from working at the office and she had the day off from Beanie's. Katelyn didn't need to work at all, and honestly, Brendan didn't want her to. Especially with Kelly. She was still frosty and he hadn't quite forgiven her yet. But it was Katelyn's decision, and she loved Beanie's. Besides, it was only a few days a week and she'd be home once their little bean arrived.

"We're going car shopping."

"Why?" She glanced at him from where she rested her chin on his sternum.

"We can't strap a baby to the back of the 'Vette, now can we?" he said with a smirk.

Her eyes widened and she lifted her head off his chest. "You can't get rid of the 'Vette. You love that car."

Got it on my sixteenth birthday, seventeen years ago today.

"Did I say I'm getting rid of it? Hell, no." Brendan wrapped his arms around her. "The new car is for you."

Semantics. Since, technically, he'd be driving it too.

"Me?" Her jaw dropped. "Do I get to pick?"

"Of course." He grinned because she was so happy. "You can even choose the color."

Brendan saw the wheels turning, a dreamy look on her face.

"Oh, I always wanted a Dodge Challenger—it's my dream car!"

He chuckled. "Sorry, sweetheart. That isn't very baby friendly."

"But you said I could choose." She stuck out her lip in a pout. So fucking cute.

"You can." He smacked a kiss to her lips. "Beemer or Benz?"

Call him paranoid, but the safety of his family was paramount. Brendan needed to be sure he was putting them in the safest vehicle possible. After much deliberation, Katelyn chose a sexy-as-fuck white Mercedes-Benz AMG GLS 63 SUV. With 603 horsepower, it had an engine that rivaled the 'Vette's. His sweet girl had good taste.

After signing all the paperwork, he shook the salesman's hand. "Can you deliver it to the house tonight? We'll be home by dinner."

"Sure thing, Mr. Murray. I'll give you a call when we're on the way." Then he turned to Katelyn and shook her hand too. "Congrats on your new ride. She sure is pretty."

On the way out she whispered, "Why do you men refer to cars in pronouns like they're people?"

"Aren't they?" he snorted. "C'mon."

They'd spent three hours at the dealership. It was well past noon, he needed to feed her, and they were already behind schedule. He helped her fold into the passenger seat of the 'Vette. No way was she going to be able to do that in a few months. The Benz was a smart purchase.

"Where to now, butterfly man?"

He grinned at that.

"Does that mean I still give them to you, baby?"

Katelyn leaned across the console and kissed him. "All the time."

"I thought we'd get some lunch at our favorite spot."

She cocked her head like she was trying to think of where that could be.

He tsked. "You'll see."

They sat at the same table with a view of the lion's den,

chowing down burgers and sharing a big basket of fries. The lion himself was still a no-show. She threw a French fry in the air and he caught it.

"Good catch."

It was a mild day for April. You could smell spring. The grass was starting to green and trees were beginning to bud. The tulips would open up soon. They strolled hand in hand through the zoo. Every once in a while she would stop to look at something. He would hold her from behind and rub her little baby belly.

This wasn't how he originally planned it, but that's the thing about plans, right?

They walked to the lily pool and gazed out at the water. "It's still beautiful here," she whispered.

He tucked a wheat-colored strand behind her ear and smiled. "You're beautiful." Then he took her face in his hands and kissed her. "This has always been a special place to me, and it's even more dear to me now. It's the first place I brought you. I told you 'I love you' here..." With his hands holding hers he got down on his knee. "...and this is where I'm going to ask you to be my wife. I rehearsed the words in my head for months, but I can't remember them now, so I'm just gonna ask...Katelyn, I love you, sweet girl. Will you marry me?"

She smiled through her tears. "Yes."

He slid the ring he'd had made specially for her on her finger. A three-carat brilliant round solitaire surrounded by pave diamonds sat on a diamond band. It reminded him of a solar eclipse, when the moon passes between Earth and the sun, blocking out its bright light. That's when the glowing corona can be seen.

Sometimes it takes darkness to see the light.

That's how he saw her.

Katelyn was his light.

Brendan lifted her in his arms and kissed his wife-to-be, the mother of his child, right there in front of the lily pool. He was indeed the luckiest sonofabitch on the planet.

Easing her down, he gazed at her beaming, beautiful,

tear-stained face. She glanced up at him. "It's your birthday and I'm getting all the presents."

He wiped her cheeks. "You just gave me mine. The only thing I wanted was to spend all of my birthdays with you as my wife."

Once, he'd dreamt of a girl with long hair streaked in gold by the sun. It gently fluttered in the breeze. The beautiful face of an angel. Lips swollen from his kisses. Cheeks flushed pink. Eyes neither blue nor green, but the color of a stormy tropical sea.

She stood in front of him now.

And she was real.

She was his.

Forty

Holy Mary, *mother of fucking God!*
Does it count as blasphemy if you don't say it out loud?
He sat in the chair, gritting his teeth while Katelyn held his hand.

A promise is a promise…

She said she didn't want a big to-do, that she didn't need a wedding. Brendan may not know a lot about girl shit, and heaven help him if they were having a daughter, he was in fucking trouble. But he'd been around Chloe and Linnea enough to know that every girl dreams of her wedding, so he got Linnea started on it before he even popped the question. If anyone could make Katelyn's dream a reality, it was her.

Brendan only told her the wedding had to take place on Midsummer's Eve at the exact spot in Coventry Park where they met. What a difference a year makes, right? They could have a backyard reception after. He wanted Katelyn to have everything—the dress, the flowers, the party. So with that, he left the details up to Linnea and his beautiful bride.

And Chloe.

And much to his chagrin, Kelly. She was Katelyn's maid of honor.

On Friday, two days before the wedding, his aunt flew in from Dublin to celebrate not only his nuptials, but baby Chandan's first birthday the following day. Brendan was bummed they were going to miss his birthday party, but in lieu of a honeymoon, he and Katelyn were going to enjoy a week at the lake house, just the two of them. At seven months along, she didn't want to travel, so Paris would have to wait—probably until their kid was in college.

On Saturday, the day before the wedding, God help him, Katelyn's family arrived. Her parents and Kevin were staying with them, and that was cool. Brendan got along really well with her father and brother. He'd have to learn to tolerate Kristie, but if she did or said one thing to make Katelyn feel anything less than beautiful, they were going to have words. Fortunately, the aunts were staying at Kelly's. He didn't think he could stomach all of them together under his roof.

The summer festival was going on out there beyond Park Place. Venery took an earlier time slot than usual and played their annual hometown gig. They all watched the concert together and did the rehearsal thing in the park, then headed over to Chloe's. She was hosting a wedding eve backyard soirée, as she called it.

By this point, Brendan wanted nothing more than to fast-forward twenty-four hours and be alone with Katelyn at the lake house.

His aunt brought him a glass of whiskey and took a seat beside him. "*Aintín*, I am your favorite nephew, aren't I?" He savored the aroma of the ruby port cask whiskey that she'd brought with her from Ireland.

"One of them." Colleen winked. "Your Katelyn is just lovely. I can't help but imagine my sister smiling down on the two of you. I know she'd have loved her and I'm sorry she can't be here for ya, but I'm so happy that I can." She hugged him then. "I feel her, though."

He quickly swiped beneath his eyes and nodded. "I do too."

"After that baby comes, I want all four of you boys to take a trip to Ireland. You hear me? Maybe next summer?"

"Yes, *Aintín*." He wasn't going to tell her no.

It was a nice little shindig in spite of Kristie and her sisters, hovering in a corner, whispering and ogling the Venery boys like a gaggle of teenaged groupies. Brendan actually found that rather amusing. Katelyn sat nestled between his thighs. Little bean kicked beneath his hands that rubbed slow circles on her belly. He kissed her neck. He couldn't wait to marry her.

Her mother left the gaggle and came over then. "Let's go, Katie. It's almost midnight." Then she flicked her eyes to him. "Kiss her goodbye now. You'll see her at the wedding tomorrow."

Is she fucking serious?

He chuckled. "We live in the same house, Kristie."

She smirked. "You're staying here tonight."

Superstitious nonsense. Katelyn giggled.

Brendan scooped her up and set her on the table. He moved to stand between her thighs and took her face in his palms, skimming her soft cheeks with his thumbs. Slowly, he lowered his lips to hers and kissed Katelyn Copeland for the very last time. She'd be Katelyn Murray when he kissed her again tomorrow.

"Goodnight, sweet girl." He kissed her forehead. "I love you."

As soon as Katelyn and her parents left, Chloe took the vacant seat beside him. She was grinning from ear to ear. "I've just got to say this. I told you so."

She did. He didn't believe her then, but she'd been right.

Shut up, Chloe.

You shut up, Brendan.

"Brat."

He didn't think he'd be able to sleep without Katelyn in Chloe's guest bedroom, but he woke up the morning of the wedding feeling fucking fantastic. Brendan looked out the second-story window into his backyard below. A crew of workers had already begun transforming it for the reception later.

"It's a beautiful fucking day," he shouted as he came down the stairs.

Jesse was flipping pancakes. Taylor was feeding Chandan his breakfast, more like he was wearing it. Brendan snickered.

"Laugh now, mate." He wiped oatmeal off his chest. "Your turn's coming."

"Where's Chloe?"

"Your house." His cousin put a plate in front of him. "She left us with instructions to keep you occupied until it's time." He grinned. "You're ours for the next six hours, so eat up."

It all kind of buzzed by in a blur. One minute he was eating pancakes in Jesse's kitchen and the next he was walking that familiar trail through the park. An arch had been constructed in front of the tree that marked the spot where he'd met her one year ago this very day. It was constructed of oak logs and branches, decorated with greens and fresh flowers in shades of cream and blush and burgundy. Bohemian and whimsical. A crystal chandelier hung from its center.

The only remaining bachelor, and the second eldest of the cousins, Dillon stood at his side with Monica. Brendan fidgeted, not because he was nervous, but because he couldn't wait to see her. Chloe waved to him from the front row, baby Chandan imitating his mother from where he sat on her lap. Brendan waved back.

Kevin came down the walkway with Kristie and sat beside his mother. He winked at Brendan. That was the signal apparently. Taylor and Matt began to play. He couldn't tell you what song it was. He'd never heard it before.

Kelly appeared first in some slinky satin number. Dillon apparently liked it because he couldn't seem to take his eyes off her, or rather her cleavage. He elbowed his cousin in his side and Katelyn's aunt took her place across from them. Then he took in a deep breath.

This is it.

The moment he'd never dared to dream of was here. It was almost surreal. She was walking on the arm of her father to *him*, and he'd never seen her look more beautiful. Layers of champagne chiffon, off the shoulders and cut low in the front. She carried her flowers out in front of her belly. Her aqua eyes on him. His on her. She was crying. He was too. Brendan couldn't imagine loving her any more than he did right then, but he knew he'd love her even more tomorrow.

Her father kissed her and took his seat. Kelly took her flowers and Brendan took her hands. "I love you," he whispered, squeezing them.

"I love you too."

They recited their vows and exchanged rings. He slid the matching custom diamond band on her finger. She slipped a black zirconium band onto his. And then he kissed his wife.

He lifted her into his arms, baby belly and all, just as he had that night, and he kissed her. He probably would have kept on kissing her too if Dillon hadn't tapped him on the shoulder. Brendan shrugged, unembarrassed, and eased her down to the ground.

They posed as Monica's wife, Danielle, instructed for countless pictures. Dillon had his arm around Kelly for a shot and Brendan overheard him try to hit her up. "You wore that for me, didn't you? You know I like slinky, babe."

She rolled her eyes.

"Gonna let me help you get out of it later?"

"Do you still own a penis?"

"Uh, yeah."

"Then the answer is still no."

Poor Dillon.

Brendan turned to his cousin and winked as they walked the trail back to Park Place. "Be mindful, Dillon. The fair folk are about tonight."

It worked for him, didn't it?

Their backyard looked like a faerie garden. Twinkling white lights everywhere. Surrounded by the love of their family. It was all he could see. Venery had a little platform off to the side, acoustic equipment set up on it. They took their places and Monica escorted him and Katelyn to the center of a makeshift dance floor.

Taylor spoke into the mic. "The boys and I wrote a song for you two. We'd like to play it for you now."

Sloan pulled Chloe from her chair to stand with him at the mic, much to everyone's surprise. The song started off slow and folksy. It sounded like the song Katelyn made her entrance to, but there were words to go with the melody now. Brendan took her in his arms and they swayed to the music.

Their first dance was to a song written by his best friends just for them.

Halfway through the song everyone was clapping to the beat and Chloe was belting out background vocals to Sloan's lead. He glanced at all the faces there. Love lit up every one of them.

The future was bright.

It was all he could see.

…A promise is a promise.

It's not like this tattoo hurt worse than any other one he'd gotten, but it was in a delicate area where men do not want to feel any pain. Rubbing the excess ink off was bothering him more than anything. The gauze chafed and irritated him.

Katelyn couldn't watch. She held his hand, patting the baby swaddled to her chest. A tuft of ginger curls peeked out of the blanket. Their son, Declan James, who they named after his grandfather Byrne and his father, definitely favored his Irish lineage. Jesse was still going on about how he got two presents on his thirtieth birthday. The news that Chloe was expecting a daughter and the arrival of his nephew all on the same day.

"Gah," he groaned.

"Are you sure you want me to do the butterfly? If you don't we can stop now. The other part is done." Sweat was beading on the tattoo artist's forehead. He probably wanted this over with as much as Brendan did.

Katelyn glanced over to him. "Really, baby. You don't have to. I didn't expect you to do this."

He was her butterfly man, goddammit. "Do it."

Brendan turned his head and concentrated on his beautiful wife and their precious son sleeping peacefully at her breast. "I love you and I promised. Besides, I figured now was a good time since your pussy is on hiatus."

The tattoo artist put the gun down. "Now my dick's on hiatus too."

There, inked down his shaft in gothic script, with the K resembling a butterfly's wing, was his wife's name. Just as he'd promised.

"I love you, Katelyn."

"I love you too."

"Let's go home, baby."

His home, his heart, his bed were no longer empty.

They were incredibly full.

All because he kissed an angel in the park.

And finally dared to dream.

Epilogue

Fourth of July, the following summer…

Brendan stood at the wedding wall. He and Katelyn's portrait hung to the far left, just below his parents. The space where Dillon's photo would one day go stood glaringly empty. Linnea kept wanting to put a photo of him in the spot, but everyone warned her against it—bad luck and all that.

He still didn't believe in any of that shit, but why chance it?

How many years had it been since that first Fourth of July here with the girls? Three? He remembered it fondly. Linnea and her patriotic fruit. That was the beginning. They just didn't know it then.

Dillon sat on the back deck with Kodiak and the Venery boys. "Where's Kelsey?" he teased.

"Fuck off, Brendan." He was laughing, though. "We've only been out twice. Wouldn't want to scare her off so soon."

He flipped his cousin the bird and went down the stairs to the lawn, kissing Katelyn on the cheek and relieving her of the redheaded ten-month-old she balanced on her hip. "I'll take him, sweetheart."

She skipped off to join the girls who were chasing toddlers on the grass. Brendan sat down with Jesse, who held his four-month-old daughter, Ireland, in his arms, and Kyan, who relaxed under the shade of a tree by the lake.

Kyan peered into his son's eyes. "He's got the Byrne baby-blues, brother."

Brendan chuckled. "Yeah, so far. Katelyn says they can change, though, so we'll see."

Jesse kissed his baby daughter's strawberry-blonde head. "I think Ireland's gonna have them too, aren't you, princess?"

Kyan grinned. Actually, he was beaming. "A new generation, man." They watched the girls with the older babies for a minute. "Hard to imagine all our kids growing up here together like we did."

Yeah. Life was fucking good.

He gazed out across the tranquil lake. Dark clouds were starting to roll in from the other side. Purple, black, and churning in the distance. They reminded him of the dark dreams he used to have. He didn't have them anymore.

A flash of lightning prompted Jesse to lift his head.

The low rumble of thunder followed.

"We better take the kids inside."

"Yeah," he agreed, kissing his son's red curls. "A storm is coming."

Epilogue

Robert "Bo" Robertson, Jr.

The woman on the bed no longer resembled the vibrant young girl he met three years ago. Hell, she didn't look anything like the woman she was just three weeks ago.

She was a ghastly color, if you could call gray a color. Skeletal. Her lips were bluish. Her once-pretty hair stringy and lackluster.

Bo held her cold, dry hand. He waited for her next breath. It took longer and longer for them to come. They rattled in her chest. It pained him to watch her suffer, but he couldn't leave her. No one deserved to die alone. She was only twenty-two.

The nurse came in and took a set of vitals. She smiled at him. "You okay?"

"Um, I'm not sure." He anxiously wet his lips. He could use some water, but he didn't say anything. "Are you sure she's comfortable? It doesn't sound like it to me."

"I can give her some morphine."

An hour later, as tears poured down his face, he watched her take her final breath.

He kissed her forehead.

And he didn't have the slightest clue what the fuck he was supposed to do now.

The End

...until *The Other Brother*

Acknowledgments

Whew! If you're reading this, then I guess it means you survived the storm along with Brendan, Katie, and the crew. I just typed "the end" to *Maelstrom* a few days ago. At the moment, I'm still in bed recuperating from COVID, and there's a motorcycle parade going by my window for a little neighborhood boy who's dying from cancer. Count all your blessings, hug your babies, say I love you. **#TeamDavid**

This book was not an easy one for me to write. I wanted to hold back and Brendan wanted to push the envelope even further. I think we came to an agreeable compromise, though. Maybe. I'm pretty sure he's taken up a permanent residence on my shoulder to push me along because he's bossy like that. The Pinterest board and the playlist for *Maelstrom* on Spotify and YouTube are open. Dillon's story, *The Other Brother*, is next in the *Red Door Series*. As always, I've included a sneak peek into his story, following these acknowledgments. While I'm also working on a standalone titled *Don't Speak*, I hope to have his book finished before the end of 2021. It's up to the muse, though.

It's still just as surreal, writing these acknowledgments after book three, as it was writing them after *Serenity*. When I get toward the end of each book, I start bawling like a baby because their story is over, and while they'll still be around, and we'll get glimpses into how life is working out for them, we won't be inside their heads quite the same ever again.

Without a doubt, I absolutely, positively, could not write these twisted stories if it weren't for the incredible humans who help me, support me, and encourage me every step of the way. I've said it before, but it bears repeating, they are my tribe, my family, and this book is as much theirs as it is mine. I told myself not to get so wordy and keep it short, but I know me and probably won't.

I'm always going to thank my children first and foremost—**Michael** and **Raj**, **Charlie**, **Christian**, **Josie Lynn** and **Josh**, **Zach** and **Sam**, **Jaide**, and **Julian**. They will probably never read a word of any of these books, and that's okay (it's probably better that they don't), because they know the love I have for them is at the heart and soul of every word I write.

My **TL/DR** healthcare family. Never did I think that more than a year later, we'd still be dealing with COVID-19. Well, maybe I did, I just hoped we wouldn't be. Thank you for being the amazing humans that you are every single day. I'm honored to work among you.

Editing is still one of my favorite parts of the writing process, and I don't even want to imagine doing it with anyone except my editor extraordinaire, **Michelle Morgan**. I wish I could have seen her face the first time she read a few of these chapters—I'm sure you know which ones I mean. Can you imagine the gif wars we had with those? I love her to death for not only putting up with my brand of crazy, but liking it, and I couldn't write a book without knowing she was going to be waiting at the end of it. I love you, Michelle! xoxo

Linda Russell and her phenomenal team at **Foreword PR**. When I say Linda is so much more than a publicist to me, I'm not even kidding. She's so much more than a friend and my alpha reader, too. This is a woman who checks on you every week just to see how you're doing, who calls you just because, who offers wise counsel and encourages you. She's a woman of honesty, integrity, loyalty, and trustworthiness—qualities that just seem so rare today, especially in Romancelandia. Linda is truly a sparking gem and she truly cares about her authors—as writers and as people. I wouldn't be here at all if it weren't for her, and I couldn't love her any harder than I do, so trust me when I say, she's my family. *Forever* a Foreword girl! I love you, woman! xoxo

My heartfelt thanks to the beautiful and talented **Michelle Lancaster**, my cover queen of hearts, for shooting this breathtaking image especially for *Maelstrom*, and to **David Tomasic**, for portraying Brendan's character so perfectly. A simple thank you isn't enough for such a stunning and beautiful work of art. Much love to both of you!!! xoxo

You know, **Lori Jackson** is one of the best cover designers in the business. I'm so thrilled I get to work with her. It's not an exaggeration when I tell you how lucky I am to have her. I am wayyyyy more than lucky, and I'm out of kidneys, but she's still here making her magic and creating these drop-dead gorgeous covers for me. She's a beautiful, amazing woman, and I love her to pieces! xoxo

Every graphic, teaser, and those holy-crap fantastic and amazing book trailers were created and designed by **Ashlee O'Brien**, the design goddess behind *Ashes and Vellichor*. I don't remember how I found her now, but she's been with me from the beginning, and I simply cannot imagine doing this without her. She helps me in ways I cannot even begin to list here. She alpha reads, chooses quotes and images, and brings my words to life so artistically— way beyond what I could have ever imagined. My jaw drops every time she sends me a file. To say we've become friends is an understatement of epic proportions. We're family, right, *book daughter*? I love you, girlie! xoxo

I've said it before, and you can bet I'm going to say it every time— **Stacey Blake** of *Champagne Book Design* is the formatting queen!

I can remember reading books she'd formatted and saying to myself that when the day came for me to publish, I wanted her for my books. She makes the pages inside look so beautiful, even when I change fonts on her mid-series. If you follow Stacey on Facebook, then you know, she makes a helluva cocktail too! I'm so thirsty! Love ya, Stacey! xoxo

As always, a special thank-you to the lovely **Siobhan Davis**.

My beta team—**Jessica Biggs, Jennifer Bishop, Kim DePeiro, Heather Hahn, Charbee Lightfield, Marjorie Lord, Melinda Parker, Sabrena Simpson, Rebecca Vasquez,** and **Lindsey Ward**, along with my **ARC team**—a huge thank-you for dropping everything to read *Maelstrom*, for your input and being so excited for Brendan's story. I truly love and appreciate you all, and yes, Salena is really gone. I promise!

Bloggers and Bookstagrammers—I wouldn't be here without you and your dedication to indie authors and their books. I wish I could name each and every one of you, but the list would be a helluva long one. I know who all of you are, you've become a friend, and I try to respond to every like, tag, comment, and share—please know how much I appreciate your beautiful edits and all of your time and effort to spread the word about the *Red Door Series* to readers.
I have an amazing group of beautiful humans in my Facebook readers' group, *Behind the Red Door*. A special thank-you goes to each and every **Redling**—you kept me going. Seriously.

And, of course, my **readers**—thank you for being here and for loving the often-twisted *Red Door* world. I hope you came through the storm unscathed, but I can't promise there won't be another. I guess by now you know to expect a rumble of thunder or two, yeah? I love hearing from you, and I thank you kindly for all your messages, emails, and reviews—they mean everything!

And thank you for wanting more Kyan and Linnea, Chloe, Jesse, and Taylor, Brendan and Katie, Dillon, Bo, Kodiak, Matt, Kit, and Sloan. They're coming.

Thank you for being my family. Until *The Other Brother*...

Much love,
Dyan xoxo

Books by

DYAN LAYNE

The Red Door Series

Serenity

Affinity

Maelstrom

The Other Brother (coming soon)

Standalones

Don't Speak (coming soon)

About the Author

Dyan Layne is a nurse boss by day and the writer of edgy sensual tales by night—and on weekends. She's never without her Kindle, and can usually be found tapping away at her keyboard with a hot latte *and* a cold Dasani Lime—and sometimes champagne. She can't sing a note, but often answers in song because isn't there a song for just about everything? Born and raised a Chicago girl, she currently lives in Tampa, Florida, and is the mother of four handsome sons and a beautiful daughter, who are all grown up now, but can still make her crazy—and she loves it that way! Because normal is just so boring.

Follow me links:

Website: dyanlayne.com
Facebook: www.facebook.com/Dyan.Layne.Author
Behind the Red Door: www.facebook.com/groups/DyanLayne
Instagram: /bit.ly/2GrIwID
Twitter: bit.ly/315hujC
Goodreads: shorturl.at/ciLR5
Amazon: amazon.com/author/dyanlayne
BookBub: Dyan Layne Books—BookBub
Newsletter sign-up: eepurl.com/gS-MAT
Pinterest boards:www.pinterest.com/DyanLayneAuthor
TikTok: www.tiktok.com/@dyan.layne.author

Sneak Peek of *The Other Brother* (Red Door Series #4)

Kyan, where the fuck are you, man?

How many more of these never-ending interviews did they have on the schedule today anyway? He was hungover from partying at the club opening last night. The pounding hammers and buzzing saws pummeled into his already-throbbing brain. The smell of paint and varnish was making him gag. Dillon reached for some ibuprofen and a bottle of water to wash it down.

He glanced around the restaurant, still under construction, that would bear his father's name and took a seat at a table made from two sawhorses and a sheet of plywood. It was hard to believe this place would be ready to open in just a few short weeks. His brother said everything was right on schedule, though.

She tentatively pulled the door open and stuck her head inside, looking right and then left, as if she wasn't sure she was at the right place. Mostly straight dark-blonde hair fell past her breasts, the ends curled into waves. Young. Fresh-faced. No makeup. She wasn't short, but she wasn't tall either, maybe five-four, and slender. Black pants, white shirt, black flats.

This girl was a natural beauty.

Fucking gorgeous.

Dillon glanced at the schedule of interviews in front of him and pulled her application off the top of the stack, quickly scanning it before she reached the table. There wasn't much on it. Recent high school grad enrolled at the university. One previous job at the Dairy Queen in Crossfield. He'd never heard of it.

The girl carefully maneuvered her way into the bar area. Dillon stood and extended his hand. "Linnea? I hope I'm pronouncing that right." He shook her hand. It was so tiny compared to his. Soft and warm. "Dillon Byrne."

She tucked her hair behind her ear and shyly smiled. Her eyes were a stunning shade of light green. "Hi, and yes, you said it right."

They sat across from each other. Dillon loosened his tie. It was hot in here and he felt like he was choking with the damn thing. "So, Linnea, did you move to the city for school?"

"No, but I'm starting online classes in the fall." Her eyes flicked up to his. "I bought a little place over on Oak Street. Near Eighth. By the park. So, this is home now."

He was impressed. How does an eighteen-year-old have the wherewithal, not to mention the smarts, to purchase real estate in an up-and-coming neighborhood in the city? This girl intrigued him.

"Family?"

"Uh, no. My grandmother passed away, so it's just me."

That explained the how. The neighborhood she lived in, while just eight blocks away, leaned toward the seedier side. Gentrification was creeping in her direction, though, so she'd actually made a very wise investment. It worried him that she was on her own in a big city with no one to look out for her. Dillon decided right then and there he was giving her a job here at Charley's, and he'd keep an eye on her. Be her friend—like an older brother.

Maybe one day he could be more. But she was only eighteen and he was twenty-six. So, maybe one day was far away. She screamed virginal innocence and purity. He was anything but. Besides, it probably wasn't a good idea to get involved with the staff and he had no intention of settling down with one girl anytime in the near future—not before he was thirty anyway.

The door opened and Kyan walked in.

She took one look at him from beneath her lashes, and blushing, she smiled.

Of course she did. That's how every female on the planet reacted to his brother. He had a way with the ladies.

Kyan smiled back.

Dillon shook his head with a chuckle.

He blinked his eyes open. Dillon looked across the bed to long brown hair splayed out on the pillow beside him, wondering why his subconscious chose to replay that day six years ago. He loved Linnea then. God, he'd been so in love with her he didn't think he'd survive it when she chose his brother.

It was his own fault. He made her a friend when he really wanted to make her more. Thinking he had time, he'd waited too long.

Admittedly, Dillon went a bit off the deep end after they got engaged. He must have fucked every available pussy from here to Milwaukee in an effort to forget her, which considering they lived next door wasn't exactly easy. They'd been married a couple years now, and were finally expecting their first baby in January. Took fertility treatments to make that happen too. He was genuinely happy for them.

Dillon would always love her, though. He just tucked those feelings away and locked them deep inside his heart, because Linnea was Kyan's, and he was hers.

He ran his fingers through the long brown hair beside him on the pillow. Kelsey was a good girl. They'd been seeing each other a couple months now. Longest he'd dated anybody. Dillon liked her a helluva lot, so maybe he could love her too. He wanted to fall in love with her, and get married and start a family of his own one day. He was thirty-two years old, for fuck's sake, with a big house that he lived in all alone.

New Year's.

Dillon told himself he'd give it until his birthday. If he and Kelsey were still together and happy then, he'd marry her. Besides, she wasn't bad in bed and gave a halfway decent blowjob. He could do worse, right?

He yanked on the long brown hair and nuzzled into her neck, kissing up the column of her throat. She rolled over toward him and smiled.

"Mm, good morning, handsome."

He took her mouth and pulled her warm naked body into his.

Yeah, he could do a helluva lot worse.

Sneak Peek of *Don't Speak*

"Aidan, baby."

His mother took him by the hand and pulled him along behind her as she hurried out of the kitchen. He'd only eaten half of his grilled cheese sandwich and some grapes when the banging started. It startled him and he knocked over his juice. By the time she went to the front door to see who it was, the banging noise was coming from the other side of the house.

"You can't keep me out, bitch."

It was a man. He was yelling. He sounded angry. Aidan didn't recognize his voice.

His mother seemed to, though. Her eyes got real big and she covered her mouth with her hand. It was shaking.

There was a hutch in the living room that the television sat on. It had doors on the bottom. He hid in there sometimes. His mother opened one of the doors, and tossing the toys that were inside it to the floor, she kissed him on his head and urged him to crawl inside.

"We're going to play a game of hide and seek from the loud man outside, okay, baby?" his mother whispered.

Aidan nodded.

The banging got louder.

"You have to be very, very quiet so he doesn't know you're here." It sounded like she was choking and tears leaked out of her eyes, but she smiled at him.

"Like at story time?"

Aidan's mother took him to story time at the library every Saturday, and afterward if he'd been a good boy, she would let him get an ice cream.

"Yes, baby. Just like that." She nodded with tears running down her face. "Now stay very still and don't speak a word until I tell you to—no matter what, okay?"

He nodded again. "Okay, Mommy."

"I love you, Aidan."

"I love you, Mommy."

* * *

Everyone said the place was haunted. The kids at school. The people in town. It didn't look scary, but nobody ever went anywhere near the two-story white clapboard house that was set off by itself on the cove.

It was to be her home now.

Molly stood at the wrought-iron gate with her mother, holding onto her hand. She clutched her *Bear in the Big Blue House* backpack, that she'd had since she was four, with the other. A boy with sandy-blond hair sat on the porch steps. Aidan Fischer. He didn't pay them, or his father unloading their belongings from the U-Haul, any mind. He had a notebook in his lap and a pencil between his fingers. It looked like he was drawing.

The boy chewed on his lip as he moved the pencil over the paper. Even though he was in the fifth grade, and three years older than her, Molly knew who he was. Everybody did. He was the boy who didn't talk. And six days from today, when her mother married his father, that boy was going to be her brother.

Preview of *Serenity* (Red Door Series #1)

'm going to fuck you. You may not know it yet, but I do. It's only a matter of time. I've been watching you. I swear that you've been watching me too, but maybe it's all in my head. No matter. Because I've seen you, I've talked to you and I've come to a conclusion: You are fucking beautiful. And I will make you lust me.

The words danced on crisp white paper. Her fingers trembled and her feet became unsteady, so she leaned against the wall of exposed brick to right herself, clutching the typewritten note in her hand. She read it again. A powerful longing surged through her body and her thighs clenched.

Who could have written it? She couldn't fathom a single soul who might be inspired to write such things to her. Maybe those words weren't meant for her? Maybe whoever had written the note slid it beneath the wrong doormat in his haste to deliver it undetected?

Linnea Martin, beautiful? Someone had to be pulling a prank. *Yeah. That's more likely.*

She sighed as she turned and closed the solid wood front door. She glanced up at the mirror that hung in the entry hall and eyes the color of moss blinked back at her. Long straight hair, the color of which she had never been able to put into a category—a dirty-blonde maybe—hung past her shoulders, resting close to where her nipples protruded against the fitted cotton shirt she wore. Her skin was fair, but not overly pale. She supposed some people might describe her as pretty, in an average sort of way, but not beautiful.

Not anything but ordinary.

Linnea slowly crumpled up the note in her hand. She clenched it tight and held it to her breast before tossing it into the wastebasket.

Deflated, she threw her tote bag on the coffee table and plopped down on the pale-turquoise-colored sofa that she'd purchased at that quaint secondhand store on First Avenue. She often stopped in there on her way home from the restaurant, carefully eyeing the eclectic array of items artfully displayed throughout the shop. Sometimes, on a good day when tips had been plentiful, she bought herself something nice. Something pretty. Like the pale-turquoise sofa.

Linnea grabbed the current novel she was engrossed in from the coffee table and adjusted herself into a comfortable position, attempting to read. But after she read the same page three times she knew she couldn't concentrate, one sentence blurred into the next, so she set it back down. She clicked on the television and scrolled through the channels, but there was nothing on that could hold her interest. The words replayed in her head.

I'm going to fuck you.

Damn him! Damn that fucker to hell for being so cruel to leave that note at her door, for making her feel…things. The words had thrilled her for a fleeting moment, but then the excitement quickly faded, replaced by a loneliness deep in her chest. Love may never be in the cards for her, or lust for that matter, as much as she might want it to be.

Once upon a time she had believed in fairy tales and dreamt of knights on white stallions and handsome princes, of castle turrets shrouded in mist, of strong yet gentle hands weaving wildflowers in her long honeyed locks—just like the alpha heroes in the tattered paperbacks she had kept hidden under her bed as a teenager. She thought if she was patient long enough, her happily-ever-after would come. She thought that one day, when she was all grown up, that a brave knight, a handsome prince, would rescue her from her grandmother's prison and make all her dreams come true.

Stupid girl.

Her dreams turned into nightmares, and 'one day' never came. She doubted it ever would now. It was her own fault anyway. She closed her eyelids tight, trying to stop the tears that threatened to escape, to keep the memories from flooding back. Linnea had spent years pushing them into an unused corner, a vacant place where they could be hidden away and never be thought of again.

It was dark. She must have been sitting there for quite a while, transfixed in her thoughts. The small living room was void of illumination, except for the blue luminescence that radiated from the unwatched television. Linnea dragged herself over to it and clicked it off. She stood there for a moment waiting for her eyes to adjust to the absence of light and went upstairs.

Steaming water flowed in a torrent from the brushed-nickel faucet, filling the old clawfoot tub. She poured a splash of almond oil into the swirling liquid. As the fragrance released, she bent over the tub to breathe in the sweet vapor that rose from the water and wafted through the room. Slipping the sleeves from her shoulders, the silky robe gave way and fell to a puddle on the floor.

Timorously, she tested the water with her toes, and finding it comfortably hot, she eased her body all the way in. For a time serenity could be found in the soothing water that enveloped her.

You may not know it yet, but I do. It's only a matter of time.

At once her pulse quickened, and without conscious thought her slick fingertips skimmed across her rosy nipples. They hardened at her touch. And a yearning flourished between the folds of flesh down below. Linnea clenched her thighs together, trying to make it go away, but with her attempt to squelch the pulsing there, she only exacerbated her budding desire. And she ached.

Ever so slowly, her hands eased across her flat belly to rest at the junction between her quivering thighs. She wanted so badly to touch herself there and alleviate the agony she found herself in. But as badly as she wanted to, needed to, Linnea would not allow herself the pleasure of her own touch. She sat up instead, the now-tepid water sloshing forward with the sudden movement, and reaching out in front of her she turned the water back on.

She knew it was wicked. Lying there with her legs spread wide and her feet propped on the edge of the tub, she allowed the violent stream of water to pound upon her swollen bud. It throbbed under the assault and her muscles quaked. She'd be tempted to pull on her nipples if she wasn't forced to brace her hands against the porcelain walls of the clawfoot tub for leverage.

Any second now. She was so close.

I'm going to fuck you.

And he did. With just his words, he did.

Her head tipped back as the sensations jolted through her body. The sounds of her own keening cries were muffled by the downpour from the faucet. Spent, she let the water drain from the tub and rested her cheek upon the cold porcelain.

Serenity is available now!

Preview of *Affinity* (Red Door Series #2)

Chloe looked around the frilly pink bedroom.

Where to start?

What do you take with you and what parts of your girlhood do you leave behind? She wasn't sure. She didn't feel any different today than she did yesterday, but today was different.

Today her life as a real adult began. She had her acceptance letter into the marketing and graphic design program at the college she wanted. In the city. She had a little apartment just waiting for her to move into. She only had to pack up her life and go.

Armed with empty boxes and tape, Chloe sifted through drawers and emptied her closet. She was surprised at the lack of nostalgia as she sorted her things. She had expected to feel some. She didn't. Her fingertips rubbed at a spot on the bright-pink satin comforter where she sat upon the white canopy bed, memorizing the familiar feel of it, as she scanned the posters and pictures that adorned the walls.

She smiled.

Taylor Kerrigan smiled back at her. Well, sort of. It was more like a smirk. A smoldering bad-boy smirk. He had long lustrous black hair with caramel highlights that flowed over broad shoulders. His bare chest was chiseled and a myriad of tattoos accentuated his perfect olive skin. How could any man be that beautiful?

Photoshop, that's how.

The lead guitarist of Venery had been her fantasy man, her celebrity crush, ever since their first album came out. He was there when she cried her eyes out over that douchebag Danny Damiani when he broke up with her just a week before junior prom last year. She'd wiped the tears from her eyes and there was Taylor with that sexy grin. If that asshole quarterback thought she was going to miss her prom because of him, he'd best think again. Danny took Brittany McCall instead, who apparently drank one too many glasses of spiked punch and yakked up the contents of her stomach in front of the entire junior class in the middle of the dancefloor. Chloe had gone stag with her friends, had a blast and giggled at the sight of Mr. Popular futilely attempting to clean off the vomit that dripped down his tux.

Karma's such a bitch, isn't she?

Chloe carefully removed the poster from the wall and thought of the many nights she'd lain beneath the canopy and touched herself fantasizing it was him, imagining what his guitar-callused fingers would feel like on her petal-soft skin. She thought of all the times he'd watched over her while her father was away on business yet again. He traveled and left her alone a lot. She was used to it.

It was time to throw away her schoolgirl fantasies. Chloe was all grown up now and real life adventures awaited her in the city. Secretly, she still wished that one day she would meet her rock-star crush. He'd fall hopelessly in love with her and she'd be the envy of every girl at school when they saw her face gracing the covers of magazines in the grocery store check-out line on the arm of Taylor Kerrigan.

She scoffed to herself. *Yeah, right. Like that could ever really happen.*

The sound of the squeaky hinges on the front door brought her back to her ordinary reality. "Chloe, are you about finished up there?"

"Yeah, Dad. Five minutes."

He sounded impatient. He was probably in a hurry to get her to the city so he could take off again and not feel so guilty about it.

Hmm. Keep him or toss him?

"Chloe, honey." Michael Bennett stepped inside his only child's bedroom. "I'm going to start taking these boxes down. I've got the U-Haul in the driveway."

She decided to keep him. What was the harm in wishing? Chloe rolled up the poster of the smoldering bad boy and snatched the bright-pink satin blanket from her bed. "I've got everything I need. I'm ready."

And she was. She was ready for whatever awaited her in the

big beautiful city—for the people she'd meet, the new friends she'd make. For her real life to start.

They do say be careful what you wish for because you just might get it.

If only she had known.

Affinity is available now!

Cast of Characters

In alphabetical order by first name

Aggie—owner of gift shop on Maple Street

Angelica—vamp (blood fetish) girl at masquerade ball

Axel—head of security for the Red Door

Becky Brinderman—Taylor's date to senior prom

Bethany—former high school sweetheart to Jesse

Elizabeth "Betsy" Bennett—mother to Michael, grandmother to Chloe

Billings—Kyan's friend from high school, now with the state attorney's office

Robert "Bo" Robertson Jr.—drummer of Venery

Brendan James Murray—eldest of the Byrne cousins, runs the Red Door, husband to Katie

Brigitta Thurner—wife to Hans, hostess at the Red Door

Brittany McCall—high school classmate of Chloe, former fiancée to Danny

Cameron Mayhew—Katie's college classmate/former boyfriend

Catherine Lucille Martin—grandmother to Linnea (deceased)

Chandan William Arthur Kerrigan Nolan—eldest child and son of Chloe, Jesse, and Taylor

Charles Dillon Byrne—brother to Kyan, cousin to Brendan and Jesse

Charles Patrick Byrne—father to Dillon and Kyan, uncle to Brendan and Jesse (deceased)

Chloe Elizabeth Kerrigan Nolan—wife to Jesse and Taylor

Colleen Byrne Nolan O'Malley—mother to Jesse, sister to Charley and Mo, aunt to Brendan, Dillon, and Kyan

Curtis "CJ" James—Venery's manager

Danielle Peters—photographer, wife to Monica

Danny Damiani—high school classmate and former boyfriend to Chloe

Declan Byrne—father to Charley, Mo, and Colleen, grandfather to Brendan, Dillon, Jesse, and Kyan (deceased)

Declan James Murray—son of Brendan and Katie

Andrew "Drew" Copeland—Katie's father

Elliott Peters—son of Danielle and Monica

Eric Brantley—son to Hugh Brantley

Gillian—former bartender at the Red Door (resigned)

Grace Martin—mother to Linnea (deceased)

Hans Thurner—husband to Brigitta, host at the Red Door

Hazel—Tommy's mother, waitress at diner in Crossfield

Hugh Brantley—real estate investor

Ireland Aislinn Kerrigan Nolan—second-eldest child and daughter of Chloe, Jesse, and Taylor

James Murray—father to Brendan, uncle to Dillon, Jesse, and Kyan (deceased)

Pastor Jarrid Black—father to Seth and Linnea

Jason—kitchen boy at Charley's

Jesse Thomas Nolan—cousin to Brendan, Dillon, and Kyan, husband to Chloe and Taylor

Jonathan Reynolds—childhood best friend to Seth (deceased)

Kara Matthews—aunt to Katie and Kevin

Katelyn "Katie" Copeland Murray—barista at Beanie's/college student, wife to Brendan

Kelly Matthews—aunt to Katie and Kevin, owns Beanie's

Kelsey Miller—girlfriend to Dillon

Kevin Copeland—younger brother to Katie

Kim Matthews—aunt to Katie and Kevin

Christopher "Kit" King—bassist of Venery

Seth "Kodiak" Black—half-brother to Linnea

Kristie Matthews Copeland—Katie's mother

Kyan Patrick Byrne—brother to Dillon, husband to Linnea, cousin to Brendan and Jesse

Leena Patel Kerrigan—mother to Taylor

Leonardo "Leo" Hill—baker/Kelly's assistant at Beanie's

Linnea Grace Martin Byrne—wife to Kyan, half-sister to Kodiak Black

Marcus—manager at Charley's

Matthew "Matt" McCready—rhythm guitarist of Venery

Michael Bennett—father to Chloe

Milo—Angelica's partner

Mitch Rollins—state senator, member of the Red Door

Monica Peters—clinical psychologist, wife to Danielle

Margaret "Peggy" Byrne—mother to Dillon and Kyan, aunt to Brendan and Jesse (deceased)

Maureen "Mo" Byrne Murray—mother to Brendan, sister to Charley and Colleen, aunt to Dillon, Jesse, and Kyan (deceased)

Murphy—Brendan's childhood friend, detective with the police department

Payton Brantley—son to Eric and grandson to Hugh Brantley

Phil Beecham—Brendan's attorney

Roberta Torres—obstetrician

Roman—Jesse's Bernese mountain dog

Rourke—alias of arrested priest and former Red Door member

Roy Francis Martin—grandfather to Linnea (deceased)

Salena Dara—former hostess at the Red Door

Shelley Tompkins—groupie who instigated "baby mama drama"

Sloan Michaels—lead vocalist/lyricist of Venery

Stacy—former girlfriend to Kelly Matthews

Taylor Chandan Kerrigan—husband to Chloe and Jesse, lead guitarist of Venery

Thomas Nolan—father to Jesse (deceased)

Timo—Roman's son and Chloe's puppy

Tommy—classmate of Linnea's, cook at diner in Crossfield

William Arthur Kerrigan—father to Taylor

Made in the USA
Monee, IL
21 April 2023